The Last C

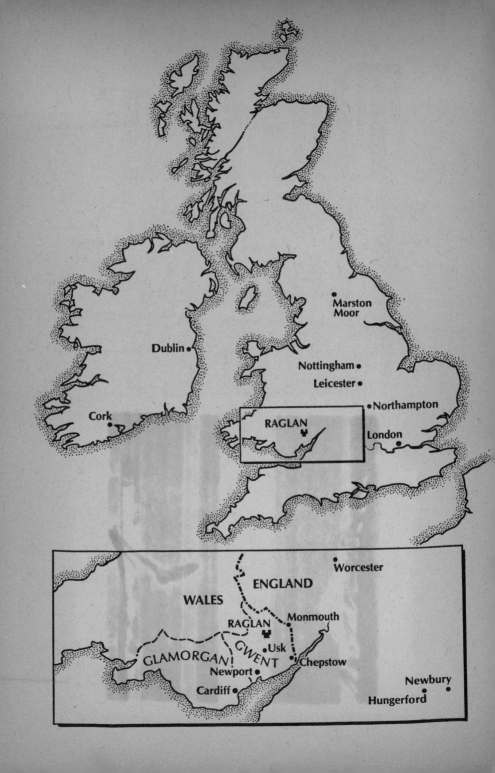

The Last Castle

GEORGE MacDONALD

VICTOR
BOOKS a division of SP Publications, Inc.
WHEATON. ILLINOIS 60187

Offices also in
Whitby, Ontario, Canada
Amersham-on-the-Hill, Bucks, England

The Last Castle was first published in 1875 in England, under the title of *Saint George and Saint Michael.*

Library of Congress Catalog Card Number: 85-62708
ISBN: 0-89693-267-2

VICTOR BOOKS
A division of SP Publications, Inc.
Wheaton, Illinois 60187

Contents

5

Introduction

George MacDonald (1824-1905), a Scottish preacher, poet, novelist, fantasist, expositor, and public figure, is most well known today for his children's books—*At the Back of the North Wind, The Princess and the Goblin, The Princess and Curdie,* and his fantasies *Lilith* and *Phantastes.*

But his fame is based on far more than his fantasies. His lifetime output of more than fifty popular books placed him in the same literary realm as Charles Dickens, Wilkie Collins, William Thackeray, and Thomas Carlyle. He numbered among his friends and acquaintances Lewis Carroll, Mark Tawin, Lady Byron, and John Ruskin.

Among his later admirers were G.K. Chesterton, W.H. Auden, and C.S. Lewis. MacDonald's fantasy *Phantastes* was a turning point in Lewis' conversion; Lewis acknowledged MacDonald as his spiritual master, and declared that he had never written a book without quoting from MacDonald.

Other Victor Books by George MacDonald

A Quiet Neighborhood
The Seaboard Parish
The Vicar's Daughter
The Shopkeeper's Daughter
The Prodigal Apprentice

Editor's Foreword

George MacDonald's *The Last Castle* was originally published as *Saint George and Saint Michael*, appearing as a serial in *Graphic* magazine between April and October of 1875. The significance of Saint George and Saint Michael may not be familiar to many readers. Saint George is the dragon-slaying patron saint of England; he is her champion against all enemies, and his red cross appears in the Union Jack. Saint Michael is Michael the Archangel, who stands for truth and fights against the enemies of the true Church. Saint George's Day is April 23, and the Feast of Saint Michael (Michaelmas) is September 29. Until the eighteenth century, Michaelmas was a national festival as well as a holy day of obligation.

Most of MacDonald's novels were contemporary stories, with characters and episodes taken from life but disguised. *The Last Castle* is different, for it is an historical novel, set in the English Civil War of the 1640s. The events and most of the characters are real, and the major incidents in the story have been taken from the memoirs of Dr. Bayly and other contemporary accounts.

Simplified maps of the Raglan area and Raglan Castle have been provided. The castle map corresponds to the story and not necessarily to the castle as it is presently preserved; MacDonald visited the castle before it was partially repaired, and had to restore the ruins in his imagination. I also recommend reading with a good map of England and Wales at hand.

* * *

In 1640, England was primed for civil war. The line between faith and politics was vague and blurred as King Charles I and Parliament maneuvered and sparred openly for the power to rule England without being overruled. The Church of England was divided into three parties: the Anglicans, the core of the Church of England, who preferred to leave things as they were; the Catholics,

8

who hoped for reconciliation with Rome and a return to the realm of the Pope; and the Puritans, who felt that the British break from Rome's authority had not gone far enough to establish true freedom of conscience and religion.

The Anglicans, backing the King against Parliament, were the foundation of the Royalist group. The Puritans took up arms for Parliament against the King, and earned the nickname Roundheads for the type of armor and headgear they wore. The Catholics, though still remembering the cruel persecutions they had recently suffered under the Crown, yet felt that they would be better off beneath a monarch than Parliament, and so threw their reluctant support behind the King.

Southern Wales stood largely for the King. Monmouthshire contained several strongholds, including Raglan Castle—held by Henry Somerset, Earl of Worcester, a strong Catholic and yet an equally strong Royalist.

Thomas Wentworth, Earl of Strafford, was one of the King's own men—an advisor to the throne, a zealous worker for the causes of Charles—but Charles could not (or would not) save him when Parliament arrested him, accused him of treason, and sentenced him to death; Charles signed his friend's death warrant for political expediency. Lord Strafford was brought to the chopping block on the twelfth of May, 1641. It is here, where Strafford's story ends, that *The Last Castle* begins.

Dan Hamilton
Indianapolis, Indiana
January 1986

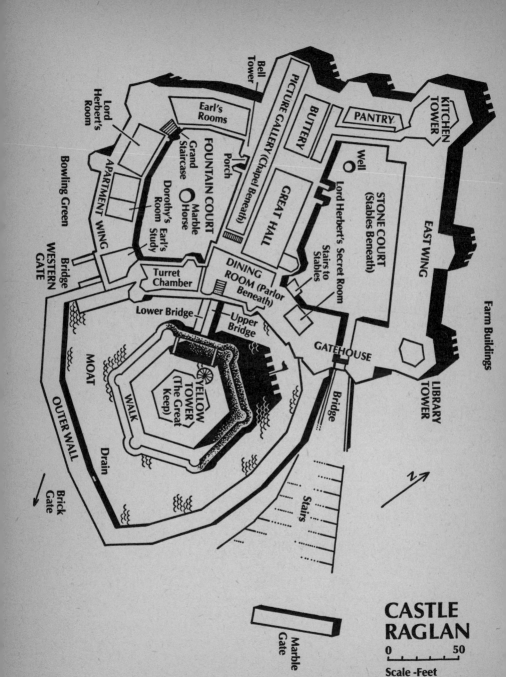

Bell Tower

Lord Herbert's Room

Earl's Rooms

PICTURE GALLERY (Chapel Beneath)

BUTTERY

PANTRY

KITCHEN TOWER

Bowling Green

APARTMENT WING

Grand Staircase

Porch

FOUNTAIN COURT

Dorothy's Room

Marble Horse

Earl's Study

Well

Lord Herbert's Secret Room

Stairs to Stables

STONE COURT (Stables Beneath)

EAST WING

WESTERN GATE

Bridge

Turret Chamber

DINING ROOM (Parlor Beneath)

Lower Bridge

Upper Bridge

GATEHOUSE

Farm Buildings

LIBRARY TOWER

MOAT

WALK

YELLOW TOWER (The Great Keep)

Bridge

OUTER WALL

Drain

Stairs

Brick Gate

Marble Gate

CASTLE RAGLAN

0   50

Scale -Feet

1.
Dorothy and Richard
1641

It was the middle of autumn and the rain had presided all day. Through the panes of the wide oriel window, the world appeared dismal in the dusk that surrounded the Wyfern estate. Dripping hollyhocks and sodden sunflowers bordered the little lawn, and honeysuckle covered the wide porch from which slow rain dropped onto the pebble paving below. In the distance were sloping hedged fields, some green and dotted with red cattle, others crowded with shocks of bedraggled and drooping corn.

The room behind the oriel window was large and low, with a dark oaken floor. A log fire blazed on the hearth, where an old man sat gazing sadly into the flames, which shone rosy through his outspread hands. He was plainly a clergyman, and had a small, pale, thin face, with endurance on his sad brow and a good conscience in his gray eyes.

At the opposite corner of the great low-arched chimney sat a lady—past the prime of life, but still beautiful, though the beauty was all but merged in the loveliness that rises from the heart. She was plainly yet richly dressed in old-fashioned and well-preserved garments. Her hair was cut short above her forehead and frizzed out in bunches of little curls on each side. On her head was a covering of dark stuff like a nun's veil, which fell down behind and onto her shoulders. Close round her neck was a string of amber beads that gave a soft light to her complexion. Her dark eyes rested quietly on the face of the old clergyman.

They had been talking of the fast-gathering tide of opinion

11

which had already begun to beat so furiously against the ramparts of Church and Kingdom. The execution of the Earl of Strafford was still the news of the moment.

"An evil time," said the old man. "The world has seldom seen its like."

"But tell me, Master Herbert," said the lady, "why comes it in our day? For our sins or the sins of our fathers?"

"Be it far from me to presume to set forth the ways of Providence!" returned her guest. "I meddle not, like some that should be wiser, with the calling of the prophet. Ever and again the pride of man will gather to a mighty and fearful head, and like a rain-swollen millpond burst the banks that confine it. Alas! If the beginning of strife be as the letting out of water, what shall be the end of that strife whose beginning is the letting out of blood?"

"Has not it always been thus? That fierce ungodly tempest must ever follow upon peace and comfort."

"Truly, it seems so," he answered. "But I thank God the days of my pilgrimage are nearly numbered. To judge by the tokens, the mourners are already going about my streets; at least the almond tree flourisheth." He smiled as he spoke, and laid his hand on his gray head.

"But those left behind us—how will they fare?" asked the lady in a troubled tone, glancing toward the window.

In the window sat a girl, no longer a child but not yet a woman, gazing out with the look of a child who had uttered all her incantations, and could imagine no abatement in the steady downpour. In the roundness and freshness of girlhood, her face was handsome rather than beautiful, and bore clear indication of a nature to be trusted. If her gray eyes were a little cold, they were honest, with a rare look of steadfastness; and if her lips were a little too closely pressed, it was from any cause other than bad temper.

"We shall leave behind us strong hearts and sound heads," replied Mr. Herbert. "And none stronger or sounder than those of your young cousins, my late pupils, of whom I hear brave things from Oxford."

"You will be glad to hear such good news of your relatives, Dorothy," said the lady, addressing her daughter.

Just then the setting sun broke through the mass of gray cloud and poured over the earth a flood of radiance. The red wheat glowed, and the drops that hung on every ear flashed like diamonds. Dorothy's hair caught it as she turned her face to answer her mother, and an aureole of brown-tinted gold gleamed for a moment about her head.

"I am glad that you are pleased, Madam, but you know that I have never seen or heard of them, except from Master Herbert, who speaks rare things of them."

During the weariness of the long morning of dismal rain, Dorothy had listened to Mr. Herbert dwell feelingly on the arrogance of Puritan encroachment, and the grossness of presbyterian insolence both to kingly prerogative and episcopal authority. He had drawn a touching picture of the irritant thwartings and pitiful insults to which the gentle monarch was exposed in his attempts to support the dignity of his divine office and to cast its protecting skirt over the defenseless Church. He had expressed his hope that Archbishop Laud's devotion to the beauty of holiness might not result in the dignity of martyrdom, as might well be feared by those who were assured that the whole guilt of Strafford lay in his return to duty, and his subsequent devotion to the interest of his royal master. To all this Dorothy had listened, and her uncertain knowledge of the affairs of the nation blossomed in a vague sense of partisanship.

But now she rose, turned to the window, and stood for a moment, rapt in the transfiguration of the world. The vault of gray was utterly shattered, and was hurrying away in rosy masses. The ordered shocks upon the twenty fields sent their long purple shadows across the flush, and the evening wind, like the sighing that follows departed tears, was shaking the jewels from their feathery tops. Then something moving outside caught Dorothy's eye, and another rosy hue than that of sunset gradually blushed her face. She turned suddenly from the window and left the room, shaking a shower of diamonds from the honeysuckle as she passed through the porch to the gravel walk.

Dorothy entered an ancient garden in front of a portion of the house which indicated a far statelier past, closed and done with, like the rooms behind those shuttered windows. For generations the family had been slowly descending in the scale of worldly account, and the small wing of the house now occupied by the widow and daughter of Sir Ringwood Vaughan was still larger than their means could match.

Although Lady Vaughan mingled little with the great families in the neighborhood, she was much respected and would have been a welcome guest. Her own visitor was the Reverend Matthew Herbert, a clergyman from the Welsh border, a man of note and influence who had been the personal friend both of his late relative, George Herbert, and of the famous Dr. Donne. Though strongly attached to the English Church, and recoiling from the practices of the Puritans, he had never yet fallen into such a passion for episcopacy as to feel any cordiality toward the schemes of the Archbishop. To those who knew him, his silence was a louder protest than the fiercest denunciations of the Puritans.

He had been a great friend of the late Sir Ringwood, and although the distance from his parish was great, he seldom let a year pass without visiting his friend's widow and daughter.

Outside, Dorothy dived into a long pleached alley, careless of the drip from overhead. Hurrying through, she came to a circular patch of thin grass rounded by a lofty hedge of yew trees. What had once been a sundial stood in the midst, but the hedge had grown so high that only for a brief hour in summer could the sundial have measured time's march. Indeed, the spot had a time-forsaken look, as if it lay buried in the bosom of the past. She slackened her pace, threw a birdlike glance around the open space, and then looked up to the little disc of sky. The clouds, their roses already withered, sailed dim and gray once more, and behind them the stars were beginning to recall their half-forgotten message from regions unknown to men. She went up to the dial, stood there for another moment, and turned to leave the spot. But with one great bound, a youth stood between her and the entrance to the alley.

"Aha, Mistress Dorothy! You do not escape me so!" he cried, spreading out his arms and catching her hand.

"I do not like such behavior, Richard," she said. "It ill suits the time. Why did you hide behind the hedge and then leap forth so rudely?"

"I thought you saw me there," he answered. "Pardon my heedlessness, Dorothy. I hope I have not startled you too much."

He stooped over her hand and would have carried it to his lips, but she snatched it away and said, with a strange mixture of dignity, sadness, and annoyance in her voice, "There has been something too much of this, Richard, and I begin to be ashamed of it."

"Ashamed! There is nothing but me to be ashamed of, and what can I have done since yesterday?"

"I am not ashamed of you, but of this way of meeting."

"Surely that is strange, when we can no more remember the day in which we have not met than that in which we met first!"

"It is not our meeting, Richard. It is this foolish way we have of late—kissing hands and meeting by the old sundial, or in some other quiet spot. Why do you not come to the house? My mother would give you the same welcome as any time these last—how many years, Richard?"

"Are you quite sure of that, Dorothy?"

"Well, I did fancy she spoke with some ceremony the last time you met. She has seen so much less of you of late, but she has all a mother's love in her heart toward you, for your mother was as dear to her as her own soul."

"I would it were so, Dorothy! Then she would not shrink from being my mother too. When we are married—"

"Married!" She turned sideways from him. "Richard, it has been very wrong to meet you after this fashion. See what such things lead to!"

"Dearest Dorothy!" he exclaimed, taking her hand again, though she seemed hardly aware. "Did you not know from the very vanished first that I have loved you with all my heart, and that to tell you so would have been to tell the sun that he shines warm at midsummer noon? And I did think you held a little *something* for me, your old playmate, that you did not give to every other acquaintance. Think of the houses we have built and the caves we have dug together—of our rabbits and urchins and pigeons and peacocks!"

"We are children no longer, and to behave as if we were would be to keep our eyes shut after we are awake. I *like* you, Richard, but why this new sort of thing? Come up to the house, where Master Herbert is talking to my mother in the parlor. The good man will be glad to see you."

"I doubt it. He and my father, as I am given to understand, think so differently regarding the Parliament and the King—"

"It were more becoming, Richard, if the door of your lips opened to the King first, and let the Parliament follow."

"Well said!" he returned, smiling. "But I speak as I hear."

Her hand had lain quiet in his, but now started like a scared

15

bird. She stepped back and drew herself up, before asking, "And you, Richard? Do you serve God or Satan? Are you of those who set at naught the laws of the land—"

"—insisting on their fulfillment by King as well as people?" interrupted Richard."

"They would tear their mother the Church into pieces."

"No, they would cast out of her the wolves in sheep's clothing that devour the lambs."

She was silent, but anger glowed from her forehead and flashed from her gray eyes. Half turning, she said scornfully, "I must go at once to my mother! I knew not I had left her with such a wolf as Master Herbert!"

"Master Herbert is no bishop!"

"Then the bishops are the wolves?"

"I am but repeating what I hear. I know little of these matters. And what are they to us if we love one another?"

"I tell you I am a child no longer!" flamed Dorothy.

"You were seventeen last Saint George's Day, and I shall be nineteen next Saint Michael's."

"Saint George for merry England!"

"Saint Michael for the Truth!"

"So be it. Good-bye," said Dorothy.

"Dorothy!" said Richard. She stood with her back toward him, hovering midway in a pace, as he continued. "Did not Saint Michael also slay his dragon? Why should the knights part company? I care more for a smile from you than for all the bishops in the Church or all the presbyters out of it."

"You take needless pains to prove yourself a foolish boy, and if I do not go at once, I fear I shall learn to despise you—which I would not do willingly."

"Despise me! Do you take me for a coward then?"

"For the matter of swords and pistols, you are much like other male creatures, but I could never love a man who preferred my company to the service of his King."

Dorothy glided into the alley and sped along its vaulted twilight, her white dress gleaming and clouding by flashes as she went. Richard stood petrified, a still dusky figure under the trees, his rich but somber suit of brown velvet merging with the edge of the night.

She reached the house, but did not run up to her room that she

16

might weep unseen, for she was still too annoyed with Richard to regret taking such leave of him. She only swallowed down a little balloonful of sobs, and went straight into the parlor to her seat in the bay window. Her heightened color and an occasional backward toss of her head were the only signs of her discomposure.

She hardly needed to have treated Richard's political indifference with so much severity, seeing that her own such interest dated from that same afternoon. But her words had touched him, and his first emotion partook of anger. As soon as she was out of sight, a spell seemed broken, and words came to him.

"A boy indeed, Mistress Dorothy! If ever it comes to what certain persons prophesy, you may wish me in, truth, the boy you call me now. But you are right, though I would it had been another who told me so! *Boy* I have been, without a thought in my head but of you. I shall take the side that seems to me the right one, were all the fair Dorothys of the universe on the other. And I should be sorry to find the King and bishops in the right, lest you should think that I had chosen after your showing!"

For the first time in his life, he was experiencing the difficulty of making up his mind—not yet, however, on any of the important questions of state, but merely whether he should seek Dorothy again in the company of her mother and Master Herbert, or return home.

Then he turned his back on the alley, passed through a small opening in the yew hedge, crossed a neglected corner of woodland, and came out upon the main road leading to the gates of his father's park.

2.
Richard and His Father

Richard Heywood was a tall and powerful youth, with square shoulders and well-developed limbs and chest. His clear brown complexion spoke of plentiful sunshine and air. His hazel eyes sparkled merrily with a suggestion of character which had not yet asserted itself. His lips had a boyish fullness and a curve which manly resolve had not yet compressed and straightened out.

Roger Heywood and his son, Richard, were the only male descendants of an old Monmouthshire family, neither Welsh nor Norman but pure Saxon. Roger had been heard to boast humorously that although a simple squire, he could count a longer descent than any of the titled families in the county, not excluding the Earl of Worcester himself. And his character went far to support such an assertion. What his friends called firmness and his enemies called obstinacy was a notable immobility of nature, a seeming disregard of what others thought of him, and a certain remote sternness of manner. These peculiarities produced awe in his inferiors and dislike in his equals. Contact with his superiors came seldom, and to them his behavior was still more distant and unbending.

Though he was far from a favorite in the county, there was nobody who would not have trusted Roger Heywood to the uttermost—at least until the events of late. Even now, foes as well as friends acknowledged that he was to be depended on, and his own son looked up to him with a reverence that somewhat overshadowed his affection. Roger's character had necessarily been slow information, and his opinions had been deliberately and unalterably adopted. Affairs had approached a crisis between King and Parliament before one of his friends knew his opinions thereon, so reserved had been his conversation. But at last it became clear, to the annoyance of many neighbors, that his leanings were toward the Parliament. However, he had never sought to influence his son in regard to the issue.

The Heywood house, Redware, was one of those ancient dwellings which had grown to fit the wants of successive generations, and looked as if it had never been other than old—two-storied and many-gabled. And there Roger had his small study, with a library more notable for quality and selection than size.

The morning after his meeting with Dorothy, Richard sought his father in the study and found him reading a small folio.

"Father," said Richard, "when men differ, is a man bound to take a side?"

"A man is bound not to take a side, save upon reasons well-considered and found good."

"It might be, Father, if you had seen fit to send me to Oxford, I should be better able to judge now."

"I had my reasons. Readier perhaps you might have been, but fitter, no. What points have you in question?"

"There are points at issue betwixt King and Parliament which men consider of mightiest consequence. Why have you never instructed me in these affairs? I trust it is not because you count me unworthy of your confidence."

"Far from it, My Son. My silence has respect to your hearing and to the judgment yet unawakened in you. Who would lay in the arms of a child that which must crush him to the earth? Years did I meditate before I resolved, and I know not yet if you have the power of meditation."

"I could try to understand, Father, if you would unfold your mind."

"When you know what the issues are—that is, when you are able to ask me questions worthy of answer—I shall be ready to answer."

"I thank you. But in the meantime, I am as one who knocks and the door is not opened unto him."

"Rather, you are as one who loiters upon the doorstep, and lifts up neither ring nor voice."

"Surely, Sir, I must first know the news."

"You have ears—keep them open. But know that on the twelfth day of May last, my lord the Earl of Strafford lost his head."

"Who took it from him, Sir? King or Parliament?"

"Even that might be made a question—but I answer the High Court of Parliament."

"Was the judgment right or wrong, Sir? Did he deserve the doom?"

"Ah, there you put a question indeed! Many men say *right* and many men say *wrong*. I might be more ready to speak my mind were it not that I greatly doubt some of those who cry loudest for liberty. I fear that once they had the power, they would be the first to trample her underfoot. Liberty with some men means *my* liberty to do, and *your* liberty to suffer. But all in good time, My Son!"

"Will you tell me, at least, what is the bone of contention?"

"Where there is contention, a bone shall not fail. It is but a legbone now, a rib tomorrow, and by and by, doubtless, the skull itself."

"If you care for none of these things, will not our Master Flowerdew have a hard name for you? I know not what it means, but it sounds of the gallows," said Richard doubtfully.

"Possibly I care more for the contention than for the bone; for while thieves quarrel, honest men go their own ways. But what ignorance I have kept you in, and yet left you to bear the reproach of a Puritan!" said Roger, smiling grimly. "You mean a *Gallio,* and take the Roman proconsul for a gallows bird! Verily you are not destined to prolong the renown of your race for letters. I marvel what your Cousin Thomas would say to the darkness of your ignorance."

"See what comes of not sending me to Oxford, Sir? I know not who is my Cousin Thomas."

"A man both of learning and of wisdom, though his diet is too strong for the stomach of this degenerate age, while the dressing of his dishes is too cunningly devised for its liking. It is no marvel you should be ignorant of him, being as yet no reader of books. Nor is he a close kinsman, being of the Lincolnshire Heywoods."

"Now I know who you mean, Sir. But I thought he was a writer of stage plays, and such things as on all sides I hear called foolish and mummery."

"Among those who call themselves godly, there be those who will endure no mummery but that of their own inventing. Cousin Thomas has written a multitude of plays; but that he studied at Cambridge to good purpose, this book in my hands bears good witness. The greater part is of learning rather than wisdom—the gathered opinions of the wise and good concerning things both high and strange. But I will read you some verses bearing his own mind, which is indeed worthy to be set down with theirs."

He then read that wonderful poem ending Thomas Heywood's second book of the *Hierarchie of the Blessed Angels,* and looked at his son.

"I do not understand it, Sir," said Richard.

"I did not expect that you would. Take the book and read it. If light should dawn upon the page as you read, perhaps you will understand how I care but little for the bones concerning which King and Parliament contend, but how I do care that men—you and I, My Son—should be free to walk in any path whereon it may please God to draw us. But read no further, save with caution, for it deals with many things wherein old Thomas is too readily satisfied with hearsay for testimony."

Richard took the small folio back to his chamber, where he read— but only partly understood—the poem, for he was not ripe enough either in philosophy or religion for such meditations. Having executed his task, he turned through the strange mixture of wisdom and credulity composing the volume. One tale after another of witch and demon and magician, firmly believed and honestly recorded by his worthy relative, drew him on until he sat forgetful of everything but the marvels before him.

Then he was roused by the noise of a quarrel in the farmyard beneath his window, and hastened out to learn the cause.

3.
The Witch

Before Richard reached the yard he saw the first cartload of wheat sheaves from the harvest field standing at the door of the barn. On top of the cart was one of the men—Faithful Stopchase, a well-known Puritan—freely holding forth against someone below. The object of his wrath was a Welshwoman named Goody Rees, by her neighbors considered a witch. Her dress was old-fashioned but not antiquated; common in Queen Elizabeth's time, it lingered still in remote country places—a gown of dark stuff, made with a long waist and short skirt over a huge farthingale, with a ruff sticking up and out from her throat, and a conical Welsh hat invading the heavens.

Stopchase had seen her in the yard and had broken out upon her in language as far removed from conventional politeness as his puritanical principles would permit. Doubtless he considered it a rebuking of Satan, but forgot that he could hardly lay claim to greater privilege in the use of bad language than the Archangel Michael. The old woman, though too prudent to reply, scorned to flee and stood regarding him fixedly. Richard sought to interfere and check the torrent of abuse, but the man seemed unaware of his attempt.

Presently, however, Stopchase began to quail in his storming. The fixed green eyes of the old woman seemed to be slowly fascinating him. At length, in the very midst of a volley of scriptural epithets, he fell suddenly silent, turned from her, and began to pitchfork the sheaves into the barn.

The moment he turned his back, Goody Rees turned hers and walked away—just as a cowboy loosed the fierce watchdog after her. The animal did not heed Richard's recall, and the poor woman had already felt its teeth before Richard could restrain it. She looked pale and frightened, but kept her composure. Richard, who was prejudiced in her favor from having heard Dorothy speak in a friendly fashion to her, expressed his great annoyance that she should have been so insulted on his father's premises, and she received his apologies with dignity and good faith.

He dragged the dog back, rechained it, and was in the act of administering sound and righteous chastisement to the cowboy, when Stopchase fell from the cart onto his head and lay motionless. Richard hurried to him, found his neck twisted and his head bent to one side, and concluded he was dead. A woman who had been working nearby stood for a moment uttering loud cries, then suddenly sped after the witch. Presently she came running back, followed at a more leisurely pace by Goody, whose countenance was grave and inscrutable. She walked up to Stopchase, looked at him for a moment or two, and sat down on the ground beside him. Then she laid hold of his head with a hand on each ear, and pulled at his neck while turning his head. There came a snap, and the neck straightened. She called for a wisp of hay, shaped it a little, slipped it under his head, then rose without a word and walked from the yard.

Stopchase lay for a while, then scrambled all at once to his feet and staggered to his fallen pitchfork. "It is the mercy of the Lord that I fell not upon the prongs of the pitchfork," he said. He had no notion that he had lain for more than a few seconds, and of the return of Goody Rees he knew nothing. Neither the woman nor the cowboy alluded to her, and even Richard, influenced perhaps by his recent reading, was more inclined to think than to speak about her. The man himself, not knowing how close death had come to him, firmly believed that he had had a narrow escape from the net of the great fowler, whose decoy the old woman was.

In reality, Goody Rees, though firmly believing in all kinds of magic and witchcraft, was as innocent of conscious dealings with the powers of ill as the whitest-winged angel. She owed her evil repute to a rare therapeutic faculty, accompanied by a keen sympathetic interest which greatly sharpened her powers of observation. Her touch was so delicate that sprained muscles, dislocated joints, and broken bones seemed to yield to its soft approach. And she understood more of the virtues of some herbs than any doctor in the parish—which, considering the condition of general practice at the time, says little. She firmly believed in the might of certain charms, and occasionally used them.

She had a leaning to the Puritans, chiefly from admiration and respect to the memory of her good-hearted, weak, but intellectually gifted husband. However, the ridicule heaped upon her yet more gifted son Thomas had a good deal shaken this predilection. She now spent her powers solely upon persons, heedless of their principles. Hence she was indifferent as to which party was in the right, or which should lose or win, provided no personal evil befell the men or women for whom she cherished a preference. Like many another, she was hardly aware of the jurisdiction of conscience, save in respect of immediate personal relations.

4.
A Parade of Fools

Later that same afternoon a little company of rustics issued from the low door of the inn in the village near Raglan Castle. They stood for a moment under the sign of the Crown and Mitre, which swung huskily creaking from the bough of an ancient thorn tree, then passed on along the road together.

"Hope you then," said one, "that we shall escape unhurt this parlous business? Not as one of us is afeard, as I knows on, but the old Earl do have a most unregenerate temper."

"I tell you, Master Upstill, it's not the old Earl as I'm afeard on, but the young lord. It be not without cause that men do call him a wizard of the worst sort."

"We shall be out again afore sundown, shan't we?" asked another.

"Up to which hour the High Court of Parliament assembled will have power to protect its own—eh, Master Croning?"

"Nay, that I cannot tell. Whether for love to the truth, or hatred to the scarlet Antichrist with her seven tails—"

"Tush, tush, John! Seven heads, Man, and ten horns, as Master Flowerdew read."

"Did not the scarlet woman sit upon seven hills—eh? Have you there, Master Sycamore!"

"Well, the argument I grant you. But we ha' got to do with no heads nor no tails, neither, save as the sting is in the tail, and then it's not seven times seven will serve to count the stings."

"True," said another, "it be the stings and not the tails we want. Think you his lordship will yield them up to us?"

"I do count it a sorrowful thing," said John Croning, "that the Earl should be such a vile recusant. He never fails with a friendly word or a foolish jest—foolish but honest. What do you think he says to me one day, as I was a-mowin' of the grass in his court, close by the white horse that spouts up the water high as a house from his nose-drills? He comes down the grand staircase, and spies me with my old scythe. 'Why,' says he, 'you look like old Time himself a-mowin' us all down.' 'For sure, My Lord,' says I, 'for all flesh is grass, and all the glory of man is as the flower of the field.' He looks humble at that, for, great and sizable man as he be, he do know his earthly tabernacle is but a frail one. And says he, 'Where did you read that?' 'I am not a larned man, please your lordship,' says I, 'and I read it nowhere, but heerd the words from a book they do call the Holy Bible. But they tell me that they of your lordship's persuasion like it not.' 'You are very much mistaken there,' says he. 'I read my Bible most days—only not the English Bible, which is full of errors, but the Latin, which is all as God gave it.' And I had not the answer to him."

"I fear you proved a poor champion of the truth, Master Croning."

"Confess now, Castdown Upstill, did he not have me on his own hearthstone? Had it not been so, I could have called hard names with the best of you, though that is by rights the gift of preachers of the truth. The good Master Flowerdew so excelleth, sprinkling them abroad from the watering pot of the Gospel. Verily, when my mind is too feeble to grasp his argument, my memory lays fast hold upon the hard names, and while I hold by them, I have it all in a nutshell."

Fortified by ale, and keeping their spirits stirred by talk, they had been occupied all day in searching the Catholic houses of the neighborhood for arms. What authority they had was never clearly understood, though plainly they believed themselves possessed of all that was needful, or they would never have dared it. As it was, they prosecuted with such a bold front, that not until they were gone did it occur to some, who had yielded what arms they possessed, to question whether they had done so wisely.

The day's gleaning of swords and pikes, guns and pistols, had been left in charge of the innkeeper, and the men were now bent on crowning their day's triumph with a supreme act of daring—the renown of which they enlarged in their own imaginations, while they undermined the courage needful for its performance by enhancing the terrors as they advanced. Their quest was daring, for strange things were said of Castle Raglan and the family within. Many were far from satisfied that the occupations of Lord Herbert, the eldest son and heir to the earldom, were not principally ostensible and had nothing to do with the black arts. And all the world knew that ever since King James had set the fashion by taking pleasure in the lions at the Tower of London, strange beasts had also been kept within Raglan Castle.

Then the hexagonal towers of the castle appeared before them, and their hearts fluttered, though they gave no outward sign save silence. Indeed, they were still too full of the importance of unaccustomed authority to fear any contempt for it on the part of others.

At this moment Raglan Castle was full of merrymaking over a wedding, and in these festivities the Earl of Worcester and all his guests were taking a part. Among the members of the household was Goody Rees' son, Thomas, who had risen from turnspit to the position of Earl's fool, chiefly for his immovably lugubrious countenance.

And now the wedding festivities broke out in a mock marriage between Thomas Rees and a young girl serving under the cook. Half the jest lay in the contrast between the long face of the bridegroom, both congenitally and willfully miserable, and that of the bride, rose-purple and as broad as a harvest moon. The bridegroom never smiled, and spoke with his jaws rather than his lips, while the bride seldom uttered a syllable without grinning from ear to ear and displaying a marvelous appointment of huge and brilliant teeth. Tom expressed himself willing to marry the girl, but presented that he had no clothes for the occasion. The Earl directed the fool to go and take what he liked from his wardrobe—even though the Earl was a man of large circumference, and the fool as lank in person as long in countenance.

When Thomas reentered the great hall, the roar of laughter made the glass of its great cupola ring. For not merely was Tom dressed in the Earl's beaver hat and satin cloak, splendid with plush gold and silver lace, but in a suit of his clothes as well, even to his stockings, roses, and garters. And with the help of many pillows he had filled the slack garments and now resembled the Earl himself.

Meanwhile the scullery maid had been attired in a splendid brocade with all suitable belongings of ruff, high collar, and lace wings. Upon her appearance a few minutes after Tom's, the laughter broke out afresh. Then the warder entered and whispered in the Earl's ear that some bumpkins had arrived, and had announced their mission with all the importance and dignity they knew how to assume. The Earl burst into a fresh laugh, which presently quavered a little and ceased—for who could tell what tempest such a mere whirling of straws might forerun?

Tom had been standing a little to one side of the Earl, his solemn countenance radiating disapproval of the tumultuous folly around him. Now he took three strides toward the Earl. "Wherein lieth the new jest?" he asked with dignity.

"A set of country louts," answered the Earl, "are at the gates affirming the right of search in this your lordship's house of Raglan."

"For what?"

"For arms, on the ground that your lordship is a vile recusant—a papist, and therefore a traitor, no doubt, although they use not the word," said the Earl.

"I shall be round with them," said Tom, embracing the assumed proportions in front of him and turning to the door.

Although the Earl was a trifle concerned about the affair, he was of too mirth-loving a nature to interfere with Tom's intended joke. He instantly called for silence in the hall, explained to the assembly what he believed to be Tom's intent, and dispersed the company to upper windows having a view of the courts below.

Then, in the plain garb of rough brownish cloth which he always wore except on state occasions, he followed Tom to the gate, and found him talking through the wicket-grating to the rustics. As the Earl stood in the shadows and listened, Tom proceeded to imitate his master's voice and peculiarities of speech to perfection, addressing the men with perfect courtesy, as if he took them for gentlemen of no ordinary consideration. To the dismay of the Earl, Tom boasted of the enormous quantity of weapons in the castle—sufficient at least to arm ten thousand horsemen! (At the uttermost, there were not more than the tenth part of that amount.) The pseudo-earl went on to say that the armory consisted of one strong room only, with a door so cunningly concealed and secured that no one but himself knew where it was or could open it. But such, he said, was his respect to the will of the most august Parliament, that he would himself conduct them to the said armory and deliver into their safe custody the whole mass of weapons.

And thereupon he opened the gate, behind which the real Earl stood, and received them with the word that he had sent all his people safely out of the way, to avoid the least dangers of a brawl. Bowing to them with utmost politeness, he requested them to step into the court while he closed the wicket. Then he whispered some quiet words to the sergeant of the guard just inside the door of the guardhouse, and led the rustics away.

When they had gone, the sergeant approached the concealed Earl and told him what Tom had said. "What can the rascal mean?" the Earl said to himself. But he told the guard to carry the message exactly as received, and then turned to follow after Tom. Some of the rustics, conceiving fresh importance from the over-strained politeness of their reception, were now attempting to transform their usual loundering gait into a martial stride—with the result of a foolish strut, very unlike the dignified progress of the sham Earl, who had taken good care they should not see his face.

Across the paved court and through the hall to the fountain court they all went. The twilight was falling, and the hall was apparently empty of life in the somber dusk, echoing to every passing step. The men did not see the flash of eyes and glimmer of smiles from the minstrel's gallery, and the whole gloomy castle seemed deserted as they followed the false earl across the second court—with the true one stealing after them like a knave.

To the northwest corner of the court Tom led them, and through a sculptured doorway up the straight wide ascent of the grand staircase. At the top he turned right along a dim corridor, and passed through a suite of bedrooms and dressing rooms. He climbed the stair in the belltower, and brought them into a narrow dark passage ending again in a downward stair, and at the foot they found themselves in the long picture gallery. At the other end of the gallery he crossed into the dining room, then through an antechamber and the drawing room on their way to the arched main entrance, and so through the library to the regions of house-hold economy and cookery.

The Earl, dogging them like a Fate, ever emerging on their track but never beheld, had already begun to pay his part of the penalty of the joke in fatigue. He was not only unwieldy in person but far from robust, and subject to gout. He owed his good spirits to a noble nature, and not to animal well-being. So, when the party crossed from the picture gallery to the dining room, he went down the stair between and into the oak parlor adjoining the great hall. There he threw himself into an easy chair in the great bay window, which looked over the moat to the huge keep of the castle and commanded the stone bridge which crossed it. There he lay back at his ease and waited the result.

His double stalked on before his victims, never turning to show his face; he knew they would follow, were it only for the fear of being left alone. Close behind him they kept, scarce daring to whisper from awe of the vast place. The courage of the beer had by this time evaporated, and the heavy obscurity around them only enhanced their apprehensions. On and on the fool led them, up and down, going and returning, but ever in new tracks. The marvelous old place was interminably burrowed with connecting passages and communications of every sort—some of them the merest ducts which had to be all but crept through. No one understood its crenkles so well as Tom, and for the greater part of an hour he led them on, until they were thoroughly wearied as well as awestruck.

At length, in a gloomy chamber where one could not see the face of another, the false earl turned full upon them, and said in his most solemn tones, "My masters, I should have acquainted you with the fact that at times I am myself unable to find the place. I fear that we are at this moment the sport of a certain member of my family—of whom perhaps your worships have heard things not more strange than true. Against his machinations I am powerless. All that is left us is to go to him and entreat him to unsay his spells."

A confused murmur of objections arose.

"Then your worships will remain here while I go to the Yellow Tower, and come to you again?" asked the mock earl, making as if he would leave them.

But they crowded round him with earnest refusals to be abandoned, for they were upon enchanted ground—and in the dark.

"Then follow me," he said, and conducted them into the open

air of the inner court, almost opposite the archway leading to the stone bridge over the moat of the keep.

The keep of Raglan Castle was surrounded by a moat of its own, separating it from the rest of the castle, so that save by bridge no one could reach it.

Onto the bridge Tom led the way, followed by his dupes, now full in view of the Earl where he sat in his parlor window. When the men reached the center of the bridge and glanced up at the awful bulk of stone towering above them, its walls strangely dented and furrowed, they stood stock still, and refused to go a step further. Their spokesman, Upstill, emboldened by anger, fear, and the meek behavior of the supposed earl, broke out in a torrent of arrogance, wherein his intention was to brandish the terrors of the High Parliament over the heads of the Earl of Worcester and all recusants.

But then a shrill whistle pierced the air, and the next instant arose a chaos of horrible, appalling, and harrowing noises—such a roaring as if the mouth of hell had been wide opened, and all the devils conjured up, doubtless by the arts of the wizard who dwelt in that tower of fearful fame. The men stared at each other with ghastly countenances like images of horror. And then across the tumult of sounds, like a fiercer flash through the flames of a furnace, shot a hideous, long-drawn yell, and a man came running at full speed through the archway from the court, casting terror-stricken glances behind him and shouting, "Look to yourselves, my masters—the lions are loose!"

The new terror broke the spell of the old, and the Parliamentary commissioners fled. But which way from the castle? And which path to the lions' den? In dread agony they rushed hither and thither about the fountain court. The white marble horse seemed to be prancing wildly about the great basin from whose charmed circle he could not break—foaming at the mouth and casting huge waterjets from his nostrils into the perturbed air. From the surface of the moat a great column of water shot up nearly as high as the citadel, and its return into the moat was like a tempest. And with all the elemental tumult was mingled the howling of wild beasts.

All but one of the doors to the hall were shut, and the poor wretches could not find their way out of the court, but ran from door to door like madmen. From every window around the court eager and merry eyes looked down on the spot, themselves unseen and unsuspected. The bumpkins might have been in a place deserted of men, and possessed only by evil tormenting spirits.

At last Upstill managed to open one door to the hall, and shot across and through its eastern door into the outer court. He made for the gate, followed at varied distances by the rest of the routed commissioners of search. With trembling hands Upstill raised the latch of the wicket and darted beneath the twin portcullises. He thundered over the drawbridge, which trembled under his heavy steps and seemed on the point of rising to heave him back into the jaws of the lions—or, worse still, the clutches of the enchanter.

They all passed through the white stone gate (purposely left open for their escape) and rattled down the multitude of steps that told how deep was the moat they had just crossed. Not one looked behind him until they reached the outermost brick gate and so left the awful region of enchantment and feline fury. They eventually reached the Crown and Miter in sad plight, where, however, they found compensation in setting forth their adventures—stressing the heroic manner in which, although vanquished by the irresistible force of enchantment, they had yet brought off their forces without the loss of a single man.

Their story spread over the country, enlarged and embellished at every stage. The tale filled Goody Rees with fresh awe of the great magician, the renowned Lord Herbert; she little thought the whole affair was a jest of her own son.

5.
Preparations

Great was the merriment in Raglan Castle over the discomfiture of the bumpkins, and many were the compliments Tom received in parlor, nursery, kitchen, guardroom—everywhere. The household had looked for a merry time, but had not expected such a full cup of delight as had been pressed out for them betwixt the self-importance of the yokels and the inventive faculties of Tom.

Yet the Earl was solemn that night, for he knew that in some shape or other, and certainly not the true one, the affair would be spread over the country, where prejudice against the Catholics was strong and dangerous in proportion to the unreason of those who cherished it.

It was plain that except the King yielded every prerogative, and became the puppet of the Parliament, their differences must be referred to the arbitration of the sword, in which case the Earl would take the part befitting a peer of the realm. The King was a Protestant, but no less the King; not he but his parents had sinned in forsaking the Church, and now their offspring had to bear the penalty, reaping the whirlwind sprung from the stormy seeds. For what were the Puritans but the lawfully begotten children of the so-called Reformation? In the midst of such reflections, the enchanting hope dawned slowly in the mind of the devout old man that perhaps *he* might be made the messenger of God to lead the wandering feet of his King back to the true fold. In any result, so long as his castle held together, it should stand for the King.

33

Faithful Catholic though he was, the brave old man was English to the backbone.

And there was no time to lose. This attempted search, though ludicrous and despicable, showed clearly how strongly the current of popular feeling was setting against all social distinction, and not kingly prerogative alone. Preparations were needful, but must be prudent.

That same night, then, long after the rest of the household had retired, the Earl led his son, Lord Herbert, and Caspar, his son's man, on a circuit of the castle, taking advantage of a fine half-moon. The three went first along the moat, and next along all the walls and battlements. They halted often, held earnest talk together, sometimes contended, but more often suggested and agreed. At length Caspar retired, and the Earl was left alone with Lord Herbert.

They entered the long picture gallery, faintly lighted from its large court windows and the northern oriel, and sat down. Behind them was a long dim line of portraits, broken only by the great chimneypiece supported by human figures of carved stone; and before them, nearly as dim, was the moon-massed landscape—a lovely view of the woodland, pasture, and red tilth to the north.

They sat silent for a while before the younger said, "You are fatigued, My Lord. It is late, and nature is mortal."

"But therein lieth the comfort: it cannot last. It were hard to say which of the two houses standeth the more in need."

"Were it not for villainous gunpowder, the castle would hold out well enough."

"And were it not for villainous gout, which is a traitor within, this other shouldst hold out as long. Be sure, Herbert, I shall not render the keep for the taking of the outworks."

"I fear," said the son, wishing to change the subject, "that this part where we stand is most liable to the artillery."

"But the ground in front is not such as they would readiest plant it upon. Do not let us forecast evil—only prepare for it."

"We shall do our best, with your lordship's good counsel to guide us."

"Thou shalt lack neither counsel nor purse of mine."

"I thank you, for much depends upon both. And so will His Majesty find—if it comes to the worst."

A brief pause followed.

"Thinkest thou not, Herbert," said the Earl, slowly and thoughtfully, "it ill suits that a subject should have and to spare, and his King go begging? While my King is poor, I must be rich for him. Thou wilt not accuse me, Herbert, after I am gone, that I wasted my substance, Lad?"

"So long as you keep wherewithal to give, I shall be content, My Lord."

"Well, time will show. I but tell thee what runneth in my mind, for thou and I have bosomed no secrets. I will to bed now, but we must go the round again tomorrow—with the sun to hold us a candle."

The next day the same party made a similar circuit three times—in the morning, at noon, and in the evening—that the full light might uncover what the shadows had hidden, and that the shadows might show what a perpendicular light could not reveal.

They reviewed the outer fortifications—if, indeed, they were worthy of the name—enclosing the gardens, the old tilting yard now used as a bowling green, the home farmyard, and other outlying portions. It was here that the most work was wanted, and the next few days were chiefly spent in surveying these works and drawing plans for their extension, strengthening, and connection.

A thorough examination of the various portcullises and drawbridges followed, and next an overhaul of the bolts, chains, and other defenses of the gates. Then came inspection of the ordnance, from the cannons down to the drakes. To conclude the inspection, Lord Herbert, with the master of the armory and the head armorer, passed the mighty accumulation of weapons under the most rigid scrutiny. Many were sent to the forge for repair, and others carried to the keep.

In a quiet way, things began to look busy about the place. Men were blasting the rocks in a quarry not far off, whence laden carts went creeping to the castle in the night. The dry larder was by degrees filled with gammons and flitches of bacon, well dried and smoked. Wheat, barley, oats, and peas were stored in the granary, and potatoes in a pit dug in the orchard.

Strange faces in the guardroom caused wonderings and questions among the women, and the stables began to fill with horses.

6.
Animadversions

Their recent conversations had in some measure dispelled the fog between Roger and Richard Heywood. The father had been but waiting until his son should begin to ask questions; for watchfulness of himself and others had taught him how useless information is to those who have not first desired it— and how poor in influence and soon forgotten. Now that the fitting condition had presented itself, he began to pour his very soul into his son.

Roger's influence went with that party which held that the natural flow of the reformation of the Church from Romanism had stagnated in episcopacy. They consisted chiefly of those who, in demanding the overthrow of that form of church government, sought to substitute for it what they called presbyterianism. But Mr. Heywood belonged to a division which held that to stop with presbyterianism was merely to change the name of the swamp. His was a party whose distinctive and animating spirit was the love of freedom, which broke out upon occasion in the wildest vagaries of speech and doctrine. Yet it justified itself in its leaders, including Milton and Cromwell, who accorded to the consciences of others the freedom they demanded for their own—the love of liberty meaning not merely the love of enjoying freedom, but that respect for the thing itself which renders a man incapable of violating it in another. Milton's anonymous pamphlet, *Reformation Touching Church Discipline*, had already reached Roger, and opened in him the way for Milton's later works.

36

Richard proved an apt pupil, and was soon possessed with such a passion for justice and liberty, as embodied in the political doctrines now presented for his acceptance, that it was impossible for him to understand how any honest man could be of a different mind. No youth of such simple and noble nature could fail to catch fire from the enthusiasm of such a father. Richard's heart swelled within him at his father's words, and swelled yet higher at the passages from the favored pamphlets. It seemed to him, as to most young people under mental excitement, that he had but to tell the facts of the case to draw all men to his side and enlist them in the army destined to sweep every form of tyranny—and especially spiritual usurpation and arrogance—from the face of the earth.

Richard took everyone at their spoken word, and so had not thought of seeking Dorothy again at their former place of meeting. Nor, in the first burst of his new enthusiasm, did he think of her so often as to cause any keen sense of their separation. Yet she returned to his thoughts unbidden. He was a little angry with Dorothy for showing a foolish preference for the Church party, so plainly in the wrong! And what could *she* know about the question to which he had been indifferent—but indifferent only until rightly informed! If he had ever given her just cause to think him childish, certainly she should never apply the word to him again! If he could but see her, he would soon convince her, for the truth was not his to keep, but to share! It was his duty to acquaint her with the fact that the Parliament was the army of God fighting the great red dragon—one of whose seven heads was prelacy, the horn upon it the King, and Archbishop Laud its crown.

A fortnight after he had last seen Dorothy, he took the path through the woods to the old sundial. She would not be there, of course, but he would walk up the pleached alley and call at the house.

As he approached the wood, Dorothy's great mastiff came leaping out to welcome him, and he was prepared to find her not far off. He entered the yew-circle, and there she stood leaning on the dial as if dreaming ancient dreams. She did not move at his approach, but as he stood silent by her side, she lifted her head. He saw the traces of tears on her cheeks, and his heart smote him.

"Weeping, Dorothy? I trust I am not the cause of your trouble."

"You!" returned the girl, quickly, and the color rushed to her pale cheeks. "No, indeed. How should you trouble me? My mother is ill."

She looked so sweet and sad that the old love (which new interests had placed in abeyance) returned in full tide. He had scarcely ever seen her in tears, and her weeping was to him a new aspect of her being.

"Dear Dorothy!" he said. "Your beautiful mother!"

"She *is* beautiful," she responded, and her voice was softer than he had ever heard it before. "But she will die, and I shall be left alone. I left Master Herbert comforting her with the assurance that she was taken away from the evil to come. 'And I trust, Madam,' the dear old man said, 'that my own departure will not be long delayed, for darkness will cover the earth, and gross darkness the people.' Those were his very words."

"Nay, nay!" said Richard hastily. "The good man is deceived. The people that sit in darkness shall see a great light! As for the realm of England, the sun of righteousness will speedily rise thereon, for the dawn draws nigh. And Master Herbert may be just as far deceived concerning your mother's condition; she has been sickly for a long time, and yet has survived many winters."

Dorothy spoke, slowly and with weight. "And what prophet's mantle has fallen upon Richard Heywood, that the word in his mouth should outweigh that of an aged servant of the Church? Can the great light of which he speaks be Richard Heywood himself?"

"As Master Herbert is a good man and servant of God," said Richard coldly, stung by her sarcasm but not choosing to reply to it, "his word weighs mightily; but as a servant of the Church his word is no weightier than my father's, who is also a minister of the true tabernacle, wherein all who are kings over themselves are priests unto God."

Dorothy saw that a wonderful change had passed upon her old playmate; he was in truth a boy no longer, and their relative position was no more what she had considered it. But with the change, a gulf had come to yawn between them.

"Alas, Richard!" she said. "Those who arrogate the gift of the Holy Ghost, while their sole inspiration is the presumption of their own hearts and an overweening contempt of authority, may well mistake signs of their own causing for signs from heaven. I but repeat the very words of Master Herbert."

"Such swelling words hardly sound like your own, Dorothy. But why should the persuasion of man or woman hang upon the words of a mere mortal? Is not the gift of the Spirit free to each who asks it? And are we not told that each must be fully persuaded in his own mind?"

"Nay, Richard! Hang you not by the word of your father, who is one, and despise the authority of the true Church, which is many?"

"The true Church were indeed an authority, but where shall we find it? And the true Church is one thing, and prelatical episcopacy another. And I have yet to learn what authority even the true Church could have over a man's conscience."

"You need to be reminded, Richard, that the Lord of the Church gave power to His apostles to bind or loose."

"I do not need to be so reminded; but I do need to be shown that the power was over men's consciences, and that it was transmitted to others by the apostles—waiving for the moment the question as to the doubtful ordination of English prelates."

Fire flashed from her eyes. "Richard Heywood—the demon of spiritual pride has entered you, and blown you up with a self-sufficiency which I never saw in you before, or I would never have companied with you, as I am now ashamed to think I have done, even to the danger of my soul's health."

"Then I may comfort myself that you no longer count me a boy! But do you then no longer desire that I should take one part or the other and show myself a man? Am I man enough yet for the woman you are?"

In anger, she turned to leave him.

"Dorothy," he added, with a sudden change of tone, "I love you dearly, and am truly sorry if I have offended you. I came hither to share with you the great things I have learned since you left me with just contempt a fortnight ago."

"Then *my* foolish words have cast you into the scorner's seat! Alas, my poor Richard! Never more while you rebel against authority and revile sacred things will I hold counsel with you."

And again she turned to go.

"Dorothy! Will you never speak to me more, though I love you as the daylight?"

"Never more until you repent and turn. I will give you one piece of counsel, and then leave you—if forever, that rests with you. There has lately appeared, like the frog out of the mouth of the dragon, a certain tract—small in bulk, but large with the wind of evil doctrine. Doubtless it will soon reach your father's house, if it be not already there. It is the vile work of one they call a Puritan, though where even the writer can vainly imagine the purity of such work to lie, let the pamphlet itself raise the question. I will not say to *read* the evil thing, but to glance your eye over it. Its title is *Animadversions Upon*— ... I cannot recall the longdrawn title. It is filled—as a toad with poison—so full of evil and scurrilous sayings against good men, abusing them as the very offscouring of the earth, that you cannot yet be so far gone in evil as not to be reclaimed by seeing whither such men and their inspiration would lead you. Farewell, Richard."

Then Dorothy swept away up the pleached alley, her step so stately and her head so high that Richard dared not follow her. He gave a great sigh and turned away, and the old dial was again forsaken.

Richard recognized the *Animadversions* pamphlet as one which his father had received only a few days before, over which they had laughed unrestrainedly. As he walked home he sought in vain to recall anything in it deserving Dorothy's reprobation. Had it been written from the other side, no search would have been necessary, for party spirit blinds the eyes in one direction, yet makes them doubly keen in another. As it was, the abuse in the pamphlet appeared to him to be only warrantable indignation.

And he scorned as presumptuous the exercise of Dorothy's judgment which had led to their separation, and bitterly resented the change in her. Now an angry woman, she had denied him the commonest privileges of friendship until he should abjure his convictions, become a renegade to the truth, and abandon the hope of freedom resulting from strife. There raised such a swelling in his throat as he had only felt once before, when a favorite foal staked herself in trying to clear a fence.

He had neither friend nor sister to turn to, yet how could he confide at all, for to confide would be to blame Dorothy. Even now, on the point of losing her forever, his love threatened to overmaster him. So he wandered home to the stables, now empty of men and nearly so of horses, and sought the stall of Lady, the mare his father had given him. He laid his head on the neck bent round to greet him, and sighed a sore response to her soft, low, tremulous whinny.

As he stood there, overcome by the bitter sense of wrong from the one he loved best in the world, something darkened the stable door. Goody Rees, at first mistaking Richard for one of the servants, called aloud to know if he wanted a charm for the toothache.

Richard looked up and asked, "And what might your charm be, Mistress Rees?"

"Ah! Is it thou, Young Master? Thou wilt marvel to see me about the place so soon again, but verily I desired to know how that godly man, Faithful Stopchase, found himself after his fall."

"Nay, Mistress Rees, make no apology for coming among your friends. I warrant you against further rudeness of man or beast. I have taken them to task, and truly I will break his head who wags tongue against you. As for Stopchase, he does well enough in all except owing you the thanks which he declines to pay. But for your charm, Mistress Rees—what is it?"

She took a step inside the door, peered into every corner, and then asked, "Are we alone—we two, Master Richard?"

"There's a cat in the next stall—if she can hear, she can't speak."

"Don't be too sure, Master Richard. Be there no one else?"

"Not a body—soul there may be. Who knows?"

"I know, and I will tell thee my charm, for he is a true gentleman who will help a woman because she is a woman, be she as old and ugly as Goody Rees herself. Hearken—the tooth of a corpse, drawn after he hath lain a se'en-night in the mold—wilt buy my charm for the toothache? But did I not see thee asking comfort from thy horse for the—"

She paused, peered at him narrowly from under lowered eyebrows, and went on, "for the heartache, eh, Master Richard? Old eyes can see through velvet doublets."

"All the world knows yours can see further than other people's," returned Richard. "But suppose it were a heartache now. Have you a charm to cure that?"

"The best of all charms is a kiss from the maiden. What would thou give me for the spell that should set her by thy side at the old dial under a warm harvest moon, all the long hours 'twixt midnight and crowing?"

"Not a brass farthing, if she came not of her own good will," murmured Richard, turning toward his mare. "But come, Mistress

41

Rees, you could not do it, even if you were the black witch the neighbors would have you."

"Tell me, Young Master—did Goody Rees ever say and not do?"

"You said you would cure my poor old dog, and set him upon his legs again, and you did. Though, to be sure, he will die one of these days, and that no one can help."

"And I say now that, if thou wilt, I will set thee and her together by the old dial tomorrow night."

"All to no good purpose, for we parted this day—and that forever, I fear," said Richard with a deep sigh, but getting some little comfort even from a witch's sympathy.

"Tut, tut! Lovers' quarrels! Crying and kissing! What didst thou and she quarrel about?" The old woman's greenish eyes peered with a half-coaxing, yet sharp and probing gaze into those of the youth.

But how could he confide in one like her? What could she understand of such questions? Unwilling to offend her, he hesitated to refuse her plainly, and so turned away in silence.

"I see!" she said grimly, but not ill-naturedly, and nodded her head so that her hat described great arcs across the sky. "Thou art ashamed to confess that thou lovest thy father's whims more than thy lady's favors. Well, well! Such lovers are hardly for my trouble!"

But then Mr. Heywood came calling his groom. Goody glanced around her as if seeking a covert, peered from the door, and glided noiselessly out.

7.
Reflections

Left alone with Lady, Richard could not help brooding over what Goody Rees had said. Not for a moment did he contemplate accepting her offer; that was in repulsiveness second only to the idea of subjecting Dorothy to her influence. To occupy his hands, that his mind might be restless at will, he gave Lady a careful currying, an extra feed of oats, and a gallop, then went back to the house.

After a long talk with his father in the study, he was left to himself the remainder of the day. As the night drew on, the offer of the witch grew upon his imagination, as did his longing to see Dorothy. Now he sat alone in his chamber in the upper part of a gable, where its one projecting lozenge-paned window looked toward Dorothy's home. He had long been able to see her window from his, through a gap in the trees, and they had once communicated with colored flags. From that window he now sent his soul through the darkness, milky with the clouded light of half an old moon. Never before had he felt enmity in space; it had always been a bridge to bear him to Dorothy, rather than a gulf to divide him from her presence. But now their alienation had affected all around him as well as within him. Space appeared as a solid enemy, and darkness as an unfriendly enchantress, each doing what it could to separate him and the girl to whom his soul was drawn.

Richard was now convinced that he had no power of persuasion to make Dorothy see things as he saw them. The dividing influence of imperfect opposing goods is as potent as that of warring good and evil—with this important difference, that the former is but for a season, and will one day bind as strongly as it parted, while the latter is essential, absolute, impassable, and eternal.

And to Dorothy, Richard seemed guilty of overweening arrogance and its attendant presumption, for she could not see the form ethereal to which he bowed. To Richard, Dorothy appeared the dupe of superstition, for he could not see the God that dwelt within the idol. To Dorothy, Richard seemed to give the holy name of truth to nothing but the offspring of his own vain fancy. To Richard, Dorothy appeared to love the truth so little that she was ready to accept as such anything presented to her, especially by those who loved the word more than the spirit, and the chrysalis of safety better than the wings of power.

But only for a time can good appear evil to the good, and the heart of Dorothy, despite her initiative in the separation, was leaning lovingly and sadly after Richard. However, had they met now, their renewed dissension would have caused a thorough separation in heart, with no heavenly twilights of loneliness giving time for their love to recover from the scorching heat of intellectual jar and friction.

The waning moon peered warily from behind a bank of cloud, and her dim light filled the night with a dream of the day. Richard was no more a poet or dreamer of dreams than any honest youth. But Nature has decreed that all youths and maidens shall, for a period, become aware that they too are of the race of the singers, and at least pass through the zone of song. Through this lyric zone Richard was now passing, and the moon wore to him a sorrowful face—for was she not herself troubled, with half the light of her lord's countenance withdrawn?

Richard had gazed at her for hardly a minute when he found the tears running down his face. Starting up, ashamed of his unmanly weakness, he hardly knew what he was doing before he found himself in the open air. He closed the door behind him, and the hall clock struck twelve—the hour at which Mother Rees had offered him a meeting with Dorothy. However, it was assuredly with no expectation of seeing her that he turned his steps toward her dwelling.

8.
Adventure

Richard passed through the gap in the hedge and needled his way through the unpathed wood, seeking the yew-circle. There he stood for some moments near the mouth of the pleached alley, at the end of which was Dorothy's window.

He entered the alley and walked softly toward the house. Suddenly, Dorothy's mastiff came rushing down the dark tunnel, growling as if his throat were full of teeth—which changed to a boisterous welcome when he discovered who the stranger was. Fearful of disturbing the household, Richard soon quieted the dog, and then approached the house. To gain sight of her window he had to pass both the parlor and the porch. As the dog bounded from him into the porch, Richard saw two figures standing in the deep shadow there. Richard drew nearer, and saw the two to be Dorothy and a young man.

"The gates will be shut," Dorothy was saying.

"Old Eccles will open to me at any hour," came the answer.

"Still it were better you went without delay," said Dorothy— and her voice trembled a little, for she had just seen Richard.

Anger and stupidity are near of kin, and when a man whose mental movements are naturally deliberate is suddenly spurred, he is in great danger of acting the fool.

Richard strode to the porch and said, "Do you not hear the lady, Sir? She tells you to go."

"I am much in the wrong, Sir," replied a cool and self-possessed voice, "if the lady does not turn the command upon yourself."

Richard stepped into the porch, but Dorothy glided between them and gently pushed him out, saying, "Richard Heywood!"

"Whew!" interjected the stranger, softly.

"You can claim no right," she went on, "to be here at this hour. Pray go—you will disturb my mother."

"Will you tell me who this man is, then, whose right seems acknowledged?" asked Richard in ill-suppressed fury.

"When you address me like a gentleman, Richard, such as I used to believe you."

"And when did you cease to regard me as a gentleman?"

"When you learned to despise law and religion. Such a one will hardly succeed in acting the part of a gentleman, even had he the Somerset blood in his veins."

"I thank you, Mistress Dorothy," said the stranger, "and will profit by the plain hint. Once more tell me to go, and I will obey."

"*He* must go first," answered Dorothy.

Richard, stunned, recovered himself with an effort. "I will wait for you," he said, and turned away.

"For whom, Sir?" asked Dorothy, indignant.

"You have refused me the gentleman's name," answered Richard. "Perhaps I may persuade him to be more obliging."

"I shall not keep you waiting long," said the young man as Richard walked away.

Such had been the intimacy between Richard and Dorothy that he might well imagine himself acquainted with all the friends of her house. But the intimacy had been confined to the children; the heads of the two houses, although good neighbors in mutual respect, had not been drawn together into friendship. Hence many of the family and social relations of each were unknown to the other. Lady Scudamore, the mother of the stranger, was a first cousin to Lady Vaughan. Hearing of her cousin's illness, she had come to visit from Raglan Castle under the escort of her son. But the son had lingered and lingered and Dorothy had been unable to get rid of him before an hour strange for leave-taking.

Richard took his stand on the road opposite the gate. When Scudamore came a minute after, a cloud crept over the moon. He did not catch sight of Richard, and turned to walk along the road. Richard thought he had avoided him and so made a great stride or two after him and called aloud, "Stop, Sir! You forget your appointments rather easily."

46

"*There* you are!" said the other, turning. "You want to quarrel with me? It takes two to fight as well as to kiss, and I will not make one tonight. I know who you are, and have no quarrel with you, except that Dorothy tells me you have turned Roundhead as well as your father."

"What right have you to speak so familiarly of Mistress Dorothy?"

"By what right," the other asked airily, "do you haunt her house at midnight? But I would not willingly cross you in cold blood. I wish you a good-night, and better luck next time you go courting."

The moon swam from behind the cloud, and Richard now saw his adversary clearly. The youth had on a doublet of some reddish color, trimmed with silver lace. His rapier hilt, inlaid with silver, shone keenly in the moonlight. A short cloak also trimmed with silver lace hung from his left shoulder, and a little cataract of silver fringe fell from the edges of his short trousers into the wide tops of his ruffled boots. He wore a large collar of lace, and cuffs of the same were folded back from his bare hands. A broad-brimmed beaver hat, its silver band fastened with a jewel holding a plume of willowy feathers, completed his attire. It was hardly the dress for a walk at midnight, but the Cavalier had come in his mother's carriage, and had to go home without it.

Richard stepped close in front of the stranger and said, "Whatever rights Mistress Dorothy may have given you, she had none to transfer in respect of my father. What do you mean by calling him a Roundhead?"

"Why, is he not one?" asked the youth simply, keeping his ground despite the unpleasant proximity. "I mistook him for a ringleader of the same name."

"You did not mistake."

"Then I did him no wrong," rejoined the youth, and started on his way.

Richard, angrier than ever at giving such an easy advantage, kept rudely in front of him.

"By heaven!" said the youth. "If Dorothy had not begged me not to fight with you—" He slipped suddenly past Richard and walked swiftly away. Richard plunged after him and seized him roughly by the shoulder. Instantly the other wheeled around, and as he turned, his rapier gleamed in the moonlight.

Richard seized the blade, wrenched the hilt from the other's grasp, and flung the weapon across the hedge. Then Richard closed with the Cavalier and threw him down upon the turf that bordered the road.

"Take *that* for drawing on an unarmed man," he said.

No reply came, for the youth lay stunned on the ground. Then compassion woke in the heart of the angry Richard, and he hastened to help. The other made an attempt to rise, but only staggered and fell again.

"Curse you for a Roundhead!" he cried. "I can't stand, for you've twisted some of my tackle!"

"I'm sorry for that—but why did you bare steel on an unarmed man? A right malignant you are!"

"Did I? You laid hands on me so suddenly! I ask your pardon."

With Richard's aid he rose, but he could not walk a step on his right knee without great pain. Richard lifted him in his arms and seated him on a low wall of earth, then broke through the hedge, returned with the rapier, and handed it to his opponent. He accepted it courteously, and replaced it in its sheath with difficulty. He once more attempted to walk but gave a groan, and would have fallen had not Richard caught him.

"The devil is in it!" he cried, with more annoyance than anger. "There will be questioning if I am not in my place at my lord's breakfast tomorrow."

"Come home with me," said Richard. "My father will do his best to atone for the wrong done by his son."

"Set foot across the threshold of a Roundhead fanatic?" cried the Cavalier.

"Then let me carry you back to Lady Vaughan's," said Richard, with a torturing pang of jealousy.

"I dare not. I should terrify my mother and my cousin."

"Your mother! Your cousin!" cried Richard.

"Yes," the other said. "My mother is visiting her cousin, Lady Vaughan."

"Alas, I am more to blame than I knew!" said Richard.

"I must crawl back to Raglan," said Scudamore. "If I get there before the morning, I shall be able to show reason why I should not wait upon my lord at his breakfast."

"You belong to the Earl's household, then?"

"Yes, and I fear I shall be gray-headed before I belong to

48

anything else. He makes much of the ancient customs of the country; I would he would follow them. In the good old times I should have been at least a squire by now, but my lordship will never be content without me to hand him his buttered egg at breakfast, and fill his cup at dinner with his favorite claret. Though the Earl has a will of his own, he is a master worth serving. And there is Lady Elizabeth, and Lady Mary, not to mention Lord Herbert! But why do I prate of them to a Roundhead?"

"Why indeed?" returned Richard. "Are they not all traitors, and that of the worst? Are they not enemies of the truth—worshipers of idols, bowing the knee to a woman, and kissing the very toes of an old man so in love with ignorance that he tortures the philosopher who tells him the truth?"

"Go on! You know I cannot chastise you now. And I am no papist, for I speak only as one of the Earl's household—true men all. For them I cast the word in your teeth, you Roundhead traitor! I myself am of the English Church."

"It is but the wolf and the wolf's cub," said Richard. "Prelatical episcopacy is but the harlot veiled—her bloody scarlet blackened in the sulphur fumes of her coming desolation."

"Curse on, Roundhead," sighed Scudamore. "I must crawl home." And once more he made a vain effort to walk. "I must wait until the morning, when some Christian wagoner may pass. Leave me in peace."

"Nay, I am no such boor," said Richard. "If you can ride, I will bring you the best mare in Gwent to bear you home. But tell me your name, that I may know with whom I have the honor of a feud."

"My name is Rowland Scudamore. Yours I know already and, Roundhead as you are, you have some bit of honor in you." He held out his hand, and Richard did not refuse.

Richard hurried home to the stable, where he saddled Lady. His father heard the sound of her hooves in the paved yard, and came out to meet them. He inquired as to Richard's destination at such an hour, and Richard told him of the quarrel.

"Was your quarrel a just one, My Son?"

"No, Sir. I was in the wrong."

"Then you are so far in the right now. You have confessed yourself in the wrong? And you are going to help him home?"

"Yes, Sir."

"Then go—but beware of private quarrels in such a season of strife. You two may meet some day in mortal conflict on the battlefield. For my part, I would rather slay my friend than my enemy."

Roger walked beside his son as he led Lady to the spot of the argument. They found Scudamore stretched on the roadside, plucking handfuls of grass and digging up the turf with his fingers—thus, and thus alone, betraying that he suffered. Although a slight groan escaped him as they lifted him to the saddle, he gathered up the reins at once and sat erect. Lady seemed to know what was required of her, and stood as still as a vaulting horse until Richard took the bridle to lead her away.

"I see!" said Scudamore. "You can't trust me with your horse!"

"Not so," answered Mr. Heywood. "We cannot trust the horse with you. If you will go, you must submit to the attendance of my son, on which I am sorry to think you have so good a claim. But will you not be our guest for the night? We will send a messenger to the castle at first light."

Scudamore declined, but with perfect courtesy, for there was that about Roger Heywood which rendered it impossible for any man who was himself a gentleman to show him disrespect. And the moment Lady began to move, Scudamore felt no further inclination to object to Richard's company. Should Lady prove troublesome, it would be impossible for Scudamore to keep his seat.

He did not suffer so much, however, as to lose all his good spirits, or fail in his part of a light conversation. Both of them avoided disputed topics—the one from a sense of wrong already done, the other from a vague feeling that he was under the protection of his recent injury.

"Have you known my Cousin Dorothy long?" asked Scudamore.

"Longer than I can remember," answered Richard.

"Then you must be more like brother and sister than lovers."

"That, I fear, is her feeling," replied Richard honestly.

"You need not think of me as a rival," said Scudamore. "I never saw the young woman before yesterday, and although anything of a Roundhead's is fair game—though I admire her, as I do any young woman, if she be tolerable—"

"The ape! Coxcomb!" thought Richard to himself.

—"I am not dying for her love. And I give you warning that I *may* be a more dangerous rival for your mare than for any lady."

"What do you mean?" asked Richard gruffly.

"I mean that the King has resolved to be more of a monarch and less of a saint—"

"A saint!" echoed Richard, but the echo was rather a loud one, for it startled Lady and shook her rider.

"Don't shout like that!" cried the Cavalier with an oath. "Saint or sinner—I care not. He is my King and I am his soldier. But with this knee you have given me, I shall be fitter for garrison than field duty."

"Has His Majesty declared open war against Parliament?"

"Faithless Puritan! His Majesty has—with reluctance, I am sorry to say—taken up arms against his rebellious subjects."

"Many such rumors have reached us," said Richard quietly. "The King spares no threats—but for blows!"

"Insolent fanatic!" shouted Scudamore. "I tell you His Majesty is on his way from Scotland with an army of savages—and London has declared for the King!"

Richard quickened their pace. "Then it is time you were in bed, Mr. Scudamore, for Lady and I will be wanted. God be praised! I thank you for the good news. It makes me young again to hear it."

"What the devil do you mean by jerking my knee so?" shouted Scudamore. "Faith, you were young enough in all conscience already! You want to send me to bed and keep me there out of the way! But I give you honest warning to look after your mare. All things being lawful in love and war, not to mention hate and rebellion, this mare, if I am blessed with a chance, shall be—translated."

"From Redware to Raglan?"

"Where she shall be entertained in a manner worthy of her."

"If all they say be true," said Richard quietly, "Raglan stables are no place for a mare of her breeding. Folk say your stables are, like some other Raglan matters, of the infernal sort."

"Whether the stables be under the pavement or over the leads," returned Scudamore after a moment, "there are not a few in them as good as she—of which I hope to satisfy my Lady some day," he added, patting her neck.

"Were you not hurt already, I would pitch you out of the saddle," said Richard.

"Were I not hurt in the knee, you could not."

"I need not lay hand on you. Were you as sound in limb as you

are in wind, you would find yourself on the road ere you knew you
had left the saddle—did I but give Lady the sign she knows."

"By God's grace," said the Cavalier, "she shall be mine, and
teach me the trick of it."

Richard answered only with a grim laugh and again increased
their pace, though more gently this time. Little more passed between them before the towers of Raglan rose in their view.

Richard had never yet been within the castle walls—even
though at any time, almost up to the present hour, he might have
entered without question. The gates had seldom been closed and
never locked, the portcullises had all hung moveless in their rusty
chains, and the drawbridges had spanned the moat like solid ma-
sonry. And now still, during the day, there was little sign of
change, beyond an indefinable presence of busier life. But at night
the drawbridges rose and the portcullises descended, each with its
own peculiar creak and jar and scrape, setting the young rooks
cawing in reply from every pinnacle and treetop. And this was
done never later than the last moment when the warder could see
anything larger than a cat on the brow of the road this side of the
village. For who could tell when, or with what force, the Parliament might claim possession? And now that the King had resorted
to arms, it was altogether necessary to keep watch and ward.

Richard and his burden were admitted at the great brick gate—
the outermost of all—and sought the western gate, sheltered under
the great bulk of the Yellow Tower. Eccles the warder, waked by
the sound of the horse's hooves, began to open the portcullis.

"What, wounded already, Master Scudamore!" cried the warder
as they passed under the archway.

"Yes, Eccles," answered Scudamore. "Wounded and taken pris-
oner and brought home for ransom!" His leg twinged fiercely as
Richard sought to help him out of the saddle. "Curse you for a
Roundhead!" he added.

But Eccles caught the word, and stepped between them and the
wicket. "No damned Roundhead shall set foot across this doorsill,
so long as I hold the gate!"

"Tut, tut, Eccles," returned Scudamore impatiently. "This is
young Mr. Heywood of Redware. Good words are worth much,
and cost little."

"If the old dog bark, he gives counsel," rejoined Eccles.

Richard was amused and stood silent, waiting the result. He had no particular wish to enter, but wanted to see what could be seen, for he had a notion that some present knowledge of the place would be of future service.

"Where the doorkeeper is a churl, what will folk say of the master of the house?" asked Scudamore.

"They may say as they wish. It will hurt neither him nor me," replied Eccles.

"Make haste, my good fellow, and let us through! My kneecap must be broken, in which case I shall not trouble you for a week of months." Scudamore leaned on Richard's arm, and behind them stood Lady as still as a horse of bronze.

"I will but drop the portcullis," said the warder, "and then I will carry thee to thy room in my arms. But no Roundhead shall enter here."

"Let us through at once," ordered Scudamore.

"Not if the Earl himself gave the order."

"Ho, ho! What's that? Let the gentleman through!" cried a voice from somewhere.

Scudamore whispered to Richard, "It is the Earl himself."

The Earl's study was over the gate, and he frequently sought nightwatch refuge from ill sleep and gout with his friends Chaucer, Gower, and Shakespeare.

The warder opened the wicket immediately, stepped aside, and held it open while they entered. But as soon as Richard had helped Scudamore past the threshold, Eccles stepped quietly out again, closed the wicket behind him, took Lady by the bridle, and led her back over the bridge to the bowling green. His design was to secure the mare and pretend she had run away, for a good horse was now more precious than ever.

The Earl spoke again. "What! Wounded, Rowland? How is this? And who hast thou there?"

But just then Richard heard Lady's hooves on the bridge. He bounded back through the wicket, and called her name. Instantly she stood stock still, notwithstanding a vicious kick in the ribs from Eccles. Richard, enraged, dealt him a sudden blow that stretched him at the mare's feet. He vaulted into the saddle and reached the outer gate before Eccles recovered himself. The sleepy porter let Richard through before the warder's cry reached him.

"When next you catch a Roundhead," Richard laughed, "keep him!" He gave Lady the rein and galloped off.

9.
Love and War
1641—1642

W hen Richard reached home and recounted his escape, his father uttered an imprecation, the first Richard had ever heard from his father's lips. With the indiscrimination of party spirit, he looked upon the warder's insolence and attempted robbery as the spirit and behavior of his master, though the Earl was as little capable of such conduct as Mr. Heywood himself.

The next morning Mr. Heywood led his son to a chamber in the roof, where he had been quietly collecting a good store of arms against the time when strength would have to decide the antagonism of opposed claims. It was also in view of this time that he had paid thorough attention to Richard's bodily as well as mental accomplishment, encouraging him in all manly sports such as wrestling, boxing, and riding to hounds, with the more martial training of sword exercises, and shooting with the carbine and the new-fashioned flintlock pistols.

Richard chose a headpiece and mailplates for himself, and next set the village tailor at work upon a coat of buff, thick strong leather dressed soft and pliant, to wear under his armor. After that came the proper equipment of Lady, and that of the twenty men whom his father expected to provide from among his own tenants. The men had to be fitted one by one so as to avoid drawing attention to the proceeding. Hence, both Roger and Richard had much to do and the weeks passed into months.

Richard called again and again on Dorothy, ostensibly to inquire after her mother. Only once did Dorothy appear, to make him understand she was so fully occupied that he must not expect to see her again.

"But I will be honest, Richard," she added, "and let you know plainly that you and I have parted company, and are already so far asunder on different roads that I must bid you farewell at once while we can yet hear each other speak."

There was no anger, only cold sadness in her tone and manner, while her bearing was stately, as toward one with whom she had never had intimacy.

"I trust, Mistress Dorothy," he said with some bitterness, "that you at least will grant me the justice that what I do, I do with a good conscience. An eye at once keener and kinder than yours may see conscience at the very root of the actions which you will doubtless most condemn."

Was this the boy she had despised for indifference?

"Was it conscience that drove you to sprain my cousin Rowland's knee?" she asked.

"No," replied Richard, stung. "It was not conscience but jealousy that drove me to that wrong."

"Did you see the action as such at the time?"

"No, else I would not have been guilty of that for which I am sorry now."

"Then perhaps you will one day look back on what you do now and regard it with like disapprobation. God grant you may!" she added with a deep sigh.

"That can hardly be, Mistress Dorothy. I am in present matters under the influence of no passion, no jealousy, no self-seeking, no—"

"Perhaps a deeper search might discover in you each and all of the bosom-sins you so stoutly abjure," interrupted Dorothy. "But it is needless for you to defend yourself to me—I am not your judge."

"So much the better for me!" returned Richard. "Else my judge should be unjust as well as severe. I, on my part, hope the day may come when you will find something to repent of in such harshness toward an old friend whom you choose to think in the wrong."

"Richard Heywood, God is my witness that I have no choice. What else is there to think? I would I were able to believe you honorably right in your own eyes—not in mine, God forbid! That can never be, not until fair is foul and foul is fair."

She held out her hand to him. Richard took it in his and said solemnly, "God be between me and thee, Dorothy!" Until now he had never realized the idea of a final separation between them and could hardly believe she was in earnest. Even so, he never considered retaining her love by ceasing to act on his convictions. To act upon her convictions instead of his own would have widened a measurable gulf to one infinite and impassable.

Dorothy withdrew her hand and left the room. For a moment he stood gazing after her, forcibly repressing the misery that rose from his heart to his throat. Then he left the house, hurried to the old sundial, threw himself on the grass under the yews, and wept and longed for war.

But war was not to be just yet. Autumn withered and sank into winter. The frost came and swelled and hardened the earth; the snow fell and lay, vanished and came again. Rumor continued to beat the alarm of war, and men were growing harder and more determined on both sides, for reasons to be honored or despised. But he who was most earnest on the one side was least aware that he who was most earnest on the other was as honest as himself. To confess uprightness in one of the opposite party seemed to most men to involve treachery to their own.

The hearts of Richard and Dorothy fared very much as the earth under the altered skies of winter, and behaved much as the divided nation. A sense of wrong endured kept both from feeling at first the full sorrow of their separation; and by the time memory had covered the offense, they had grown a little used to the dullness of a day with its brightest hour blotted out.

Dorothy learned to think of Richard as a prodigal brother beyond the seas, and when they met, which was seldom, he was to her as a sad ghost in a dream. To Richard, Dorothy seemed a lovely celestial, unworthy of worship, but with might enough to hold his swollen heart in her hand and squeeze it very hard.

Dorothy longed for peace and for the return of the wandering chickens of the Church to the shelter of their mother's wings. Richard longed for the trumpet blast of Liberty to call her sons together to a war whose battles should never cease until men were free to worship God after the light He had lighted within them.

Dorothy was under few influences except her mother and,

through his letters, Matthew Herbert. A spiritual repose had descended upon her mother; her anxieties were only for her daughter, her hopes only for the world beyond the grave. Master Herbert had found in the ordinances of his Church everything to aid and nothing to retard his spiritual development, and so had no conception of the Puritanical opposition to its government and rites. Through neither of them could Dorothy come to any true idea of the questions which agitated both church and state. To her the King was a kind of demigod, and every priest a fountain of truth. Her religion was the sedate and dutiful acceptance of obedient innocence—a thing of small account where rooted only in sentiment and customary preference, but of inestimable value in such cases as hers, where action followed upon acceptance.

Richard was under the quickening masterdom of a well-stored and active mind, a strong will, a balanced judgment, and an enlightened conscience—all in his own father. The customary sternness of the Puritan parent had blossomed into confidence, to Richard even more enchanting than tenderness; for to be trusted by such a father is comfort for any youthful sorrow.

Neither Dorothy nor Richard knew how much their hearts were confident of the other's integrity. Such a faith may lie in the heart like a seed buried beyond the reach of the sun, thoroughly alive but giving no sign; for to grow too soon might be to die.

Once, in the cold noon of a lovely day of frost, they met on a lonely country road. Richard walked along the rough lane reading a copy of a poem still only in manuscript, the *Lycidas* of Milton. He understood and enjoyed the thought on which the poem was built, and was borne aloft on its sad yet hopeful melodies. He fiercely desired to share with Dorothy its tenderness and magic music, and then to whisper to her that the marvelous spell came from the heart of the same wonderful man who had issued *Animadversions Upon the Remonstrants Defence Against Smectymnus*, the pamphlet which had so roused her abhorrence. Then he lifted his head and saw her but a few paces from him.

Dorothy caught a glimpse of his countenance—radiant with feeling, and his eyes flashing through a watery film of delight. Her own eyes fell; she said, "Good morning, Richard!" and passed him without deflecting an inch. His delight shattered, he folded the paper, laid it in the breast of his doublet, and walked home through the glittering meadows with a fresh hurt in his heart.

In November the Parliament set a guard upon Worcester House in London, and searched it for persons suspected of high treason— including Lord Herbert whose political drift and religious persuasion could no longer be doubtful. The terrible insurrection of the Catholics in Ireland followed.

Richard kept his armor bright, Lady in good fettle; he talked with his father and waited, sometimes with patience, sometimes without.

In the early spring the King withdrew to York, where a bodyguard of the gentlemen of that neighborhood gathered around him.

Richard renewed the flints of his carbine and pistols.

In April, the King—refused entrance into the town of Hull— proclaimed the governor a traitor. The Parliament declared the proclamation a breach of its own privileges.

Richard got new girths for his saddle.

Summer drew on, and the governor of Portsmouth declined a commission to organize the new levies of Parliament, and administered instead an oath of allegiance to the garrison. Thereupon the place was besieged by Essex; the King proclaimed Essex a traitor, and Parliament retorted by declaring the royal proclamation a libel.

Richard had Lady newly shod.

In August, the royal standard, with the motto, "Give to Caesar his due," was set up at Nottingham.

Richard mounted Lady, and led Stopchase and nineteen other mounted men to offer his services to Parliament, as represented by the Earl of Essex.

10.
Refuge
1642—1643

With the decay of summer, Lady Vaughan began again to sink. The departure of Richard Heywood to join the rebels affected her deeply. The utter rout of the Parliamentary forces at Edgehill lit up her face for the last time with a glimmer of earthly gladness, which the very different news that followed rapidly extinguished. After that she declined even more rapidly, and Mrs. Rees told Dorothy that she would yield to the first frost. But she lingered on many weeks, until one morning she beckoned her daughter near.

"Dorothy," she whispered, "I wish to see good Master Herbert—please send for him. I know it is an evil time for him to travel, being an old man and feeble, but he will come, if only for my husband's sake, whom he loved like a brother. I cannot die in peace without providing for the safety of my little lamb. Alas! I did look to Richard Heywood. . . ."

"Do not take thought about the morrow for me any more than you would for yourself, Madam," said Dorothy. "You know Master Herbert says the one is as the other." She kissed her mother's hand as she spoke, then hastened from the room and dispatched a messenger.

But before the worthy man could arrive, Lady Vaughan was speechless. By signs and looks more eloquent than words, she committed Dorothy to his protection, and died.

Dorothy behaved calmly, for she would not, in her mother's absence, act so as would have grieved her presence. Little passed between her and Master Herbert until the funeral was over, and only then they talked of the future. Her guardian wished to leave everything in charge of the old bailiff, and take her home with him to Llangattock; but he hesitated a little because of the bad state of the roads in winter, much because of the troubled condition of affairs, and most of all because of the uncertain, indeed perilous, position of the episcopalian clergy, who might soon find themselves without a roof to shelter them. Fearing nothing for himself, for Dorothy he contemplated the worst—for matters must grow far worse before they could even begin to mend.

But they had more time for deliberation than they would willingly have taken. Master Herbert caught cold while reading the funeral service, and was compelled to delay his return. The cold settled into a low fever, and for many weeks he lay helpless. The sudden affair at Brentford took place, after which the King, having lost far more than he had gained, withdrew to Oxford, anxious to reopen the treaty which the battle had closed.

The country was now in a sad state. Whichever party was uppermost in any district sought to ruin all of the opposite faction, and violent bands of marauders plundered houses and robbed travelers. It became as perilous to stay in an unfortified house as to travel, and many were the terrors which tried the courage of the girl and checked the recovery of the old man.

One morning after a midnight alarm, Master Herbert spoke to Dorothy at breakfast. "My dear Dorothy, the time will be long ere any but fortified places will be safe abodes, and it is in my mind to seek a refuge for you. You are distantly related to the Somersets, are you not? And is the relationship recognized by them?"

"I cannot tell, Sir, though the Lady Scudamore came herself from Raglan to see my mother. But you do not mean that I should seek safety in a household of papists!"

Dorothy had been educated in fear of the Catholics, and with profound disapproval of those doctrines rejected by the reformers of the Church of England. Indeed, her fear was only surpassed in intensity by her absolute abhorrence of the assumptions and negations of the Puritans.

But Master Herbert, although his prejudices were nearly as strong as hers, had yet reaped this advantage of a longer life; he was better able to balance his dislike of certain opinions with a personal regard for those who held them, and therefore did not automatically recoil from the idea of obligation to one of a different creed—provided that creed was Catholicism and not Puritanism.

He believed that the honorable feelings of Lord Worcester and his family would be hostile to any attempt to proselytize his ward, and he trusted the strength of her prejudices (more than the rectitude of her convictions) to prevent her from being overly influenced by the spiritual atmosphere.

But there was a better fact to convince him. An old friend named Bayly, a true man, a priest of the English Church and a doctor in divinity, had recently taken up his abode in Raglan Castle as one of the household chaplains, perhaps for the sake of Protestants within the walls. There was a true shepherd to care for his lamb, and Master Herbert proposed that Dorothy seek shelter in Raglan Castle, at least until the storm should blow over and permit her to go to Llangattock or return to her own home.

Notwithstanding her natural repugnance to the scheme, such was Dorothy's confidence in her friend that she was easily persuaded of its wisdom. And one more thing inclined her to yield: Roger Heywood wrote her a kindly letter, offering her the shelter and hospitality of Redware, "until better days."

"Better days!" exclaimed Dorothy with contempt. "If such days as he would count better should ever arrive, his house is the last place where I would have them find me!"

She wrote a polite but cold refusal, and rejoiced in the hope that he would soon hear of her refuge in Raglan with the friends of the King.

Meanwhile Master Herbert had solicited Dr. Bayly's mediation toward the receiving of Mistress Dorothy Vaughan into the Raglan Castle family. (The Earl had now been raised to the dignity of the title of Marquis of Worcester—though Parliament, to be sure, declined to acknowledge the patent conferred by His Majesty.) Bayly had promised to do his best in representing the matter to the Marquis, his daughter-in-law, Lady Margaret (the wife of Lord Herbert), and his daughter, Lady Anne who, although the most rigid Catholic in the house, was already the doctor's special friend.

It would have been greatly unlike the Marquis or any of his family to refuse such a petition, and within two days Dorothy received an invitation to enter the family of the Marquis, as one of Lady Margaret's gentlewomen.

Master Herbert and Dorothy set out for Raglan on a lovely

61

spring morning. The bare trees had a kind of glory about them, like old men waiting for their youth, which might come suddenly. A few slow clouds drifted across the pale sky. A gentle wind blew over the wet fields, but when a cloud swept before the sun, the wind blew cold. The winter might yet return for a season, but this day was of the spring and its promises.

Yet the heart of England was troubled with passions both good and evil, with righteous indignation and unholy scorn, with the love of liberty and the joy of license, with ambition and aspiration. No honest heart could yield long to the comforting of the fair world, knowing that her fairest fields would soon be crimson with the blood of her children. But Dorothy's sadness was not all for her country in general; even the loss of her mother had less to do with a certain heaviness than the thought that the playmate of her childhood—and offered lover of her youth—had thrown himself into the quarrel of the lawless and self-glorifying. Nor was she altogether free from a sense of blame in the matter. Had she been less imperative in her mood and bearing, more ready to give than to require sympathy. . . . but she could not change the past, and now the present was calling her.

The towers of Raglan appeared before her, and a pang of apprehension shot through her bosom at this approach to the unknown. Brought up in a retirement that some counted loneliness, she could not help awe at the prospect of entering the household of the Marquis, who lived like a prince in expenditure, attendance, and ceremony. She was used to all gentle and refined ways, but knew little of the fashions of the day; like many modest young people, she was afraid she might be guilty of some mistake which would make her appear ill-bred, or at least awkward.

They reached the brick gate, were admitted within the outer wall, skirted the moat enringing the huge blind keep, and arrived at the western gate. The portcullis rose to admit them, and they rode into the echoes of the vaulted gateway. Turning to congratulate Dorothy on their safe arrival, Master Herbert saw her pale and agitated.

"What ails my child?" he asked in a low voice.

"I feel as if I am entering a prison," she replied with a shiver.

"Is your God the God of the grange and not of the castle?" returned the old man.

11.
Raglan Castle
1643

The side of the fortress which faced the world was frowning and defiant, although the grim, suspicious, altogether repellent look of the old castle had been gradually vanishing in the additions and alterations of more civilized times. But now Dorothy and Master Herbert came into the fountain court, the heart of the building, and saw the face which the house showed its own people.

Spring sunshine filled half the court, and over the rest lay the shadow of the huge towering keep. Many bright windows looked down into the court—the smiling faces of children and ladies peeping out to see the visitors. Here passed a lady in rich attire, there a gentleman half in armor, and here again a serving man or maid. Nearly in the center of the quadrangle stood the giant white marble horse, whose nostrils spouted great jets of water.

Opposite the gate by which they had entered was the little chapel with its triple lancet windows, and over that the picture gallery with its large oriel lights. Far above their roof was the roof of the great hall. From each of the many doors opening into the fountain court, a path of colored tiles led straight to the marble fountain in the center. The falling water caught the sunlight and carried it captive into the shadowed basin, making music as it fell.

The two visitors noted all these things in a moment, for two warder's men already held their horses, and two others came running from the hall to help them dismount. Then a manservant led them to the left toward a porch of carved stone, where the open door revealed a steep, wide, and stately set of stairs going right up between two straight walls. At the top stood Lady Margaret's gentleman usher, Mr. Harcourt, who received them with much courtesy, conducted them to a small room on the left of the landing, and went to announce their arrival to Lady Margaret.

Lady Margaret received them with a frank, though stately, demeanor. "Welcome, Cousin!" she said, holding out her hand. "And you also, Reverend Sir. I am told we are indebted to you for this welcome addition to our family—how welcome none can tell but ladies shut up like ourselves."

Dorothy was already almost at ease, and the old clergyman found Lady Margaret sensible as well as courteous. He was prejudiced, perhaps, by her pleasant pretense of claiming cousinship on the ground of her husband's name. Ere he left the castle, Master Herbert was astonished to find how much friendship had so quickly blossomed with a Catholic lady he had never seen before.

Such a thing, once unthinkable, could now come to pass. Almost forty years had elapsed since the Gunpowder Plot. King Charles' queen was Catholic, and the Catholics were friendly to the government of the King, under which their position was one of comfort if not influence, while under Parliament they would have every reason to anticipate a revival of persecution. And the King was only too glad to receive aid from the loyal families of the old religion; yet he saw that much caution was necessary lest he should alienate the most earnest of his Protestant friends. Hence it was possible that Episcopalian Dr. Bayly should be an inmate of Raglan Castle, and that Protestant Matthew Herbert should seek refuge for his ward with the Catholic Lady Margaret.

Eager to return to the duties of his parish, through his illness so long neglected, Master Herbert declined Lady Margaret's invitation to dinner and took his leave.

As soon as he was gone, Lady Margaret touched a silver bell on a table stand. "Conduct Mistress Dorothy Vaughan to her room, and attend her," she said to the maid who answered it.

And to Dorothy she said, "I request a little haste, Cousin, for My Lord the Marquis is very precise in all matters of household order, and likes ill to see anyone enter the dining room after he is seated. It is his desire that you should dine at his table today, but after this I must place you with the rest of my ladies, who dine in the housekeeper's room."

"As you think proper, Madam," returned Dorothy, a little disappointed, but a little relieved as well.

"The bell will ring presently, and a quarter of an hour thereafter we shall all be seated." Lady Margaret was already dressed in a pale blue satin skirt and bodice with ruby clasps. Her shoulders and forearms were bare, and her sleeves had been looped up with diamond-set studs. Round her neck was a short string of pearls.

Dorothy left, only to return very promptly.

"You take no long time to attire yourself," said Lady Margaret kindly.

"Little time was needed, for I have but the one color. I fear I shall show but a dull bird amidst the gay plumage of Raglan. But perhaps I could have better adorned myself had I not heard the bell, and so feared to make my first appearance before my lord as a transgressor of his household laws."

"You did well, Cousin, for everything goes by law and order and rhyme and reason in this house. The Marquis will be king in his own kingdom. When I first came to the house, I gave the Marquis no little annoyance; more than once or twice I walked into his dining room not only after grace had been said, but after the first course. He took his revenge in calling me the wild Irishwoman." She laughed very sweetly. "The only one who does here as he will is my husband—"

Just then the bell rang a second time. Lady Margaret led Dorothy from the room through a long dim corridor and into a second passage. After several curves and sharp turns, they came to a large room in which were two tables covered for about thirty. In the room were a good many gentlemen, plainly dressed or in simple attire, and among them Dorothy recognized her cousin, Scudamore. Then, crossing a small antechamber, they entered the drawing room, where a number of ladies and gentlemen stood talking. "Ladies," Lady Margaret said, "I will lead the way to the dining room." Those who dined with the Marquis followed her. She had scarcely reached the upper end of the table when the Marquis entered, followed by all his gentlemen. Lady Margaret stepped forward to meet him, leading Dorothy by the hand.

"Ah," he said cheerily, "who is this sober young damsel under my wild Irishwoman's wing? Our young Cousin Vaughan, doubtless, whose praises my worthy Dr. Bayly hast been sounding in my ears." He held out his hand to Dorothy, and bade her welcome to

Raglan Castle.

The Marquis was a man of noble countenance, of the type imagined peculiar to great men of Queen Elizabeth's time. His unwieldy person was dressed in that long-haired coarse woolen stuff called frieze, probably worn by no other nobleman in the country, and fitter for a yeoman. Though he was yet but sixty-five, his eyes were already hazy, and his voice was husky and a little broken, but he carried it all with a grace livelier than his age might seem to afford him.

Lady Margaret made Dorothy sit in one of the two empty places by her.

"Where is this truant husband of thine, My Lady?" asked the Marquis, as soon as Dr. Bayly had said grace. "Knowest whether he eats at all, or when, or where? It is now three days since he has filled his place at thy side, yet he is in the castle. Knowest thou what occupies him today?"

"I do not, My Lord," answered Lady Margaret. "I have had one glimpse of him since the morning, and if he looks now as he looked then, I fear your lordship would drive him from the table rather than welcome him to a seat beside you." She glimpsed a peculiar expression on Scudamore's face, where he stood behind his master's chair. "Your page, My Lord," she continued, "seems to know something of him."

"Scudamore!" said the Marquis, without turning his head. "What hast thou seen of my Lord Herbert?"

"As much as could be seen of him, My Lord," answered Scudamore. "He was new from the powder mill, and his face and hands were as he had been blown up the hall chimney."

"I wouldst thou didst pay more heed to what is fitting, thou monkey, and knewest either place or time for thy foolish jests! It will be long ere thou soil one of thy white fingers for King or country," said the Marquis, neither angrily nor merrily. "Get another flask of claret, and keep thy wits for thy mates, Boy."

Dorothy glanced at her cousin. His face was red as fire, but more with suppressed amusement than shame. Dorothy could not rid herself of the suspicion that he was laughing in his sleeve at his master.

66

12.
One Marquis Too Many

Dinner over, Lady Margaret led Dorothy back to her parlor, and there proceeded to discover what accomplishments and capabilities she might possess. Finding that Dorothy could embroider, sing, and play a little on the spinet, and read aloud both intelligently and pleasantly, she came to the conclusion that the girl was an acquisition destined to grow greatly in value, should they ever suffer the monotony of a protracted siege.

Remarking that Dorothy looked weary, Lady Margaret sent her away to be mistress of her time until supper at half-past five. Dorothy sought her chamber, weary from her journey, but still more weary from the multitude and variety of objects, the talk, and the constant demand of the general strangeness upon her attention. She knew her chamber lay a floor higher, and easily found the stair that rose from the main landing. And she could hardly go wrong as to the passage at the top, leading back over the room she had just left below; but she could not remember or tell which was her own door. Fearing to open the wrong one, she passed on to the end of the dim corridor. There she came to an open door and entered a small chamber evidently not meant for habitation. A little light came in through a crossed loophole, sufficient to show her the bare walls, with the plaster sticking out between the stones, and the huge beams above. In the middle of the floor, opposite the loophole, there was a great arbalest or crossbow. She had never seen one before, but knew enough to guess what it was. Through the loophole came a sweet breath of spring air, and she saw trees bending in the wind, heard their faint far-off rustle, and saw the green fields shining in the sun.

Her only playmate, Richard, had been of an ingenious and practical turn, and Dorothy had developed an interest in mechanical forms. She gazed at this strange engine for a few moments with eyes full of unuttered questions, and then ventured to lay gentle hold upon what looked like a handle. To her dismay a wheezy bang followed, shaking the chamber. Whether she had discharged an arrow, an iron bolt, or a stone—or anything at all—she could not tell.

She started back—not merely terrified, but ashamed also that she should initiate her life in the castle with meddling and mischief. Then a low gentle laugh behind her startled her yet more. Looking around with her heart in her throat, she perceived in the half-light a man watching her from the wall behind the arbalest. There was not enough light to show her a feature of his face. Her first impulse was to run, but she thought she owed an apology ere she retreated.

"I ask your pardon," she said. "I fear I have done mischief."

"Not the least," returned the man, in a gentle, amused voice.

"I had never seen a great crossbow," Dorothy went on, anxious to excuse her meddling. "I thought this must be one, but I was so stupid as not to perceive it was bent, and that this was the handle—do you call it the tricker?—to let it go."

The man, who had at first taken her for one of the maids, had by this time discovered from her speech that she was a lady.

"It is a clumsy, old-fashioned thing," he returned, "but I shall not remove it until I can put something better in its place. It would be a troublesome affair to get even a demiculverin up here, not to mention the bad neighbor it would be to the ladies' chambers. I was just making a small experiment with it on the force of springs. Much may be done with springs—more perhaps, and certainly at less expense, than with gunpowder, which costs greatly, is very troublesome to make, occupies much space, and is an unstable, half-treacherous friend within the gates. Shall I show you how the thing works?"

He spoke in a gentle, even, rapid voice, as if he were thinking to himself rather than addressing another. Neither his tone nor his manner was that of an underling.

Dorothy replied, "No, Sir, I thank you. I must go." She hurried away.

Daring now a little more for fear of worse, she tried the first door and proved it her own room. With a considerable sense of relief, as well as weariness and tremor, she nestled herself into the high window seat and looked out into the quadrangle.

Below her were playing little Molly Somerset—Lady Margaret's only child, a merry but delicate child not yet three years old, two older girls, and Molly's cousin Henry Somerset, a fine-looking boy of thirteen. Suddenly a white rabbit escaped from little Molly's arms and darted like a flash of snow across the shadowy green, followed by the children. Dorothy watched the pursuit, accompanied with sweet outcry and frolic laughter, but then their merriment turned to shrieks of terror as a huge mastiff bounded out of nowhere and rushed straight at the rabbit. The little creature stopped dead with terror and cowered on the grass. Henry reached it before the dog and caught it up in his arms. The dog's rush threw him down, and they rolled over and over, Henry holding fast to the poor rabbit.

By this time Dorothy was halfway down the stair and flying to the rescue. When she issued from the porch below, Henry was up again and running for the house with the rabbit safe in his arms and the mastiff pursuing. Then she saw—to her joy and dismay both at once—that it was her own dog.

"Marquis! Marquis!" she cried. He abandoned the pursuit at once and came bounding to her. She took him by the back of the neck, and her displeasure made him cower at her feet and wince before her open hand.

The same instant a lattice window over the gateway was flung open, and a voice said, "Here I am. Who called me?"

Dorothy looked up. The children had vanished with their rescued darling, but there was the Marquis, leaning half out of the window and looking about.

"Who called me?" he repeated—angrily, Dorothy thought.

But she was not one to hesitate when a thing *had* to be done. Keeping hold of the dog's neck—for his collar was gone—she dragged him toward the gate, and turned her face up to the Marquis like a peony, replying, "I am the culprit, My Lord."

"By St. George! Thou art a brave damsel, and there is no guilt that I know of, except on the part of that intruding cur."

"And the cur's mistress, My Lord."

"Is the animal thy property, Fair Cousin? He is more than I bargained for."

"He is mine, My Lord, but I left him chained when I set out from Wyfern this morning. That he got loose and tracked me here I am not astonished, but it amazes me to find him in the castle."

"That must be inquired into."

"I am very sorry he has carried himself so ill, My Lord. He misbehaved himself on purpose to be taken to me, for at home no one ever dares punish him but myself."

The Marquis laughed. "If thou art so completely his mistress, then why didst thou call on me for help?"

"Alas, My Lord! I was calling him, for I named him Marquis when he was a pup!"

The animal cocked his ears and started each time his name was uttered.

"Aha!" said the Marquis, with a twinkle in his eye. "That begets complications. Two Marquises in Raglan? Two Kings in England! The thing cannot be—but what is to be done?"

"I must take him back, My Lord. I cannot send him, for he would not go. And if they cannot hold him chained I shall have to go, and take the perils of the time as they come."

"But what if thou changest his name?"

"He has been Marquis all his life."

"And I have been Marquis only six months! Clearly he hath the better right. But there would be constant mistakes between us, for I cannot lay aside the honor His Majesty hath conferred upon me. No—one of us two must die."

"Then I must go," said Dorothy, her voice trembling. Although the words of the Marquis were merry, she yet feared for her friend.

"Let the older Marquis die—he has enjoyed the title, and I have not! He shall be buried with honor, under his rival's favorite apple tree in the orchard. What more could dog desire?"

"No, My Lord," answered Dorothy. "Will you allow me to take my leave? I must only find my horse."

Wouldst thou saddle him thyself, Cousin Vaughan?

"As well as e'er a knave in your lordship's stables. I am very sorry to displease you, but to my dog's death I cannot and will not consent. Pardon me, My Lord." The last words brought with them a stifled sob, for she scarcely doubted any more that he was in earnest.

"It is assuredly not gratifying to a Marquis of the King's making that one of a damsel's dubbing should take precedence. Well, it cannot be helped. But thou wouldst ride home alone? Evil men are swarming—this sultry weather brings them out like flies."

"I shall not be alone, My Lord. Marquis will take good care of me."

"I can pledge myself to nothing outside my own walls."

"I meant the dog, My Lord."

"Thou seest how awkward it is. However, as thou wilt not choose between us—and to tell the truth, I am not quite prepared to die—I will send one of the keepers to take him to the smithy, and get him a proper collar and chain—one he can't slip."

"I must go with him myself. They will never manage him else."

"What a demon thou hast brought into my peaceable house! Go with him, and mind thou choosest him a kennel thyself. Thou dost not desire him in thy chamber, Mistress?"

Dorothy secretly thought it would be the best place for him, but she was only too glad to have his life spared. "No, My Lord. I thank your lordship with all my heart."

The Marquis disappeared from the window. Presently young Scudamore came into the court, crossed to the hall, and in a few minutes returned with the keeper. The man would have taken the dog by the neck to lead him away but a soft deep canine curse and a warning from Dorothy made him withdraw his hand.

"Take care," she said, "he is dangerous. I will go with him myself."

"As it please you," answered the keeper, and led the way across the court.

"Have you not a word to throw at a poor cousin, Mistress Dorothy?" asked Rowland, when the man was a pace or two in advance.

"No, Mr. Scudamore," answered Dorothy. "Not until we have first spoken in the presence of My Lord the Marquis or My Lady Margaret."

Scudamore fell behind, followed her a little way, and then vanished.

Dorothy followed the keeper across the hall and the next court to the library tower. Here a stair led down through the wall to a lower level outside, where were the workshops, forges, stables, and farmyard buildings.

71

Dorothy entered the stable to find her own little horse being shod. Marquis and he interchanged a whine and a whinny of salutation, while the men stared at the bright apparition of a young lady in their dingy regions. Having heard her business, the head smith abandoned everything else to alter an old iron collar to fit the mastiff. Dorothy's presence proved entirely necessary, and she had to put the collar on him with her own hands. When the chain had been made fast with a staple driven into a strong post, and Dorothy proceeded to leave, his growling changed to the most piteous whining and from that into a rage of indignant affection. After three or four furious bounds left him sprawling on his back at the end of his chain, he yielded to the inevitable and sullenly crept into his kennel.

Dorothy walked back to the room which had already begun to seem to her a cell.

13.
The Magician's Vault

Dorothy went straight to Lady Margaret and made her apology for the trouble and alarm Marquis had caused. Lady Margaret assured her that the children were nothing the worse, for the dog had not gone a hairbreadth beyond rough play. Poor bunny did not seem hurt, but he would not eat the lovely clover under his nose where he lay in Molly's crib.

Dorothy begged to be taken to the nursery, for she knew all sorts of tame animals well. There she stood with the little creature in her arms, gently stroking its soft whiteness. The children were gathered around her, and she bent herself to initiate a friendship with them, knowing that success with their companion would be the best way to reach them. Under the sweet galvanism of her stroking hand the rabbit presently improved; when she offered him a blade of the neglected clover, the trefoil vanished, and he went on with his meal as if nothing had happened. The children were ecstatic, and Cousin Dorothy was from that moment popular and on the way to being something better.

When suppertime came, Lady Margaret again took her to the dining room, where there was much laughter over the story of the two Marquises. The Marquis himself drove the joke in twenty different but kind directions, and Dorothy found herself emboldened to take a share in the merriment.

Afterward, Lady Margaret once more led Dorothy to her own room, where she worked at her embroidery frame and chatted pleasantly with the girl. Dorothy would have been glad to be set to work also, for she could ill brook doing nothing, and it was hard for her to sit with her hands in her lap.

Lady Margaret at length perceived her discomfort. "I am wearying you, My Child."

"It is only that I want something to do, Madam," she returned.

"I have nothing at hand for you tonight, so suppose we go and find my own Lord Herbert. I have not seen him since we broke fast together, and you have not seen him at all. He must think of leaving home again soon—he seems so anxious to get something or other finished."

Lady Margaret put aside her frame, told Dorothy to fetch herself a cloak, and wrapped herself in a hooded mantle. Dorothy returned, and they passed along the corridor to a small lobby whence a stair descended to the court close by the gate.

"I shall never learn my way about," said Dorothy. "The staircases alone are more than my memory will hold."

Lady Margaret gave a merry little laugh. "Harry set himself to count them the other day—he said there were at least thirty stone ones."

Dorothy's answer was an exclamation; she had forgotten Lady Margaret's presence, and stood gazing up and about her. The twilight had deepened halfway into night. There was no moon, and in the dusk the huge masses of buildings rose full of mystery and awe. Above the rest, the mighty towers on all sides soared into the regions of the air. The castle told the story of an ancient race, and was a solid witness to the past.

Dorothy came to herself with a start. Lady Margaret stood quietly, waiting. Dorothy apologized, but the lady only smiled and said, "I am in no haste, Child. I like to see another impressed as I was when first I stood here. Come, and I will show you something different."

She led the way along the southern side of the court to the end of the chapel. Opposite them an archway pierced the line of building, revealing the mighty bulk of the moated citadel, impregnable to assault by gunpowder—for gunpowder was nearly powerless against walls more than ten feet thick. A stone bridge led across the thirty-foot moat to a narrow walk which ringed the tower. The walk was itself encompassed and divided from the moat by a wall with six turrets at equal distances, surmounted by battlements. At one time the sole entrance to the tower had been by a drawbridge dropping across the walk to the end of the stone bridge, from an arched door in the wall, whose threshold was ten or twelve feet from the ground. Another entrance had since been made on the level of the walk, and by it they now entered.

Passing the foot of a great stone staircase, they came to the door of what had been a vaulted cellar—probably at one time a dungeon, later a storeroom, and now put to a very different use. When Dorothy entered, she found herself in a large place, dully lit from the chinks about the closed doors of a huge furnace. The air was filled with gurglings and strange low groanings as of some creature in dire pain. As her eyes grew used to the ruddy dusk, she could see inexplicable shapes everywhere—forms that suggested instruments of torture, though too strange, contorted, and fantastical for such. She remembered certain woodcuts in *Fox's Book of Martyrs*— and were they not papists into whose hands she had fallen? She could not help some fright as she stood by the door. One thing especially caught her attention—a huge wheel standing near the wall, supported between two strong uprights. It was some twelve or fifteen feet in diameter, and from each of fifty spokes hung a large weight. Its substance mingled with the shadows on the wall behind it, and so intent was Dorothy upon it that she started when Lady Margaret spoke.

"Why, Mistress Dorothy!" she said. "You look as if you had wandered into a magician's cave! But here is my Lord Herbert."

Beside her stood a man rather under the middle stature. As his back was to the furnace, Dorothy could discover little of him, save that he was garbed like a workman, with bare head and arms, and that he held in his hand a long hooked iron rod.

"Welcome indeed, Cousin Vaughan!" he said heartily, in a voice that seemed familiar to Dorothy. He did not offer his hand, which was at the present moment far from fit for a lady's touch. "Are you come for another lesson on the crossbow?"

"I did not know it was you, My Lord, or I might by this time have been capable of discharging bolt or arrow in defense of the castle."

"I confess I was disappointed to find that your curiosity went no further," he replied. "I hoped I had at last found a lady capable of some interest in my pursuits. Lady Margaret cares not a straw for anything I do, and would rather have me keep my hands clean than discover the mechanism of the primum mobile."

75

"In truth," said his wife, "I would rather have you with fair hands in my sweet parlor, than toiling and moiling in this dirty dungeon, with no companion but that horrible fire engine, grunting and roaring all night long."

"No companion? What do you make of Caspar Kaltoff?"

"I make not much of him. He always has secrets with you, and I like it not."

"That they are secrets is your own fault, Peggy. How can I teach you my secrets if you will not open your ears to hear them?"

"I would your lordship would teach me!" said Dorothy. "I might not be an apt pupil, but I should be both an eager and a humble one."

"By Saint Patrick!" said Lady Margaret. "Mistress Dorothy, you go straight to steal my husband's heart from me! If I have no part in his brain, I can the less yield his heart!"

"What would be gladly learned will be gladly taught, Cousin, said Lord Herbert.

"There!" exclaimed Lady Margaret. "I knew you would discharge your poor dull apprentice the moment you found a clever one!"

"And why not? I never was able to teach you anything."

"Ah, husband, there you are unkind indeed!" she said, with something in her voice that suggested the watersprings were swelling.

"My Shamrock of Four!" said her husband in the tenderest tone. "I but jested. How should you be my pupil in anything I can teach? I am yours in all that is noble and good. I did not mean to vex you, Sweetheart."

"Mistress Dorothy," said Lady Margaret, "take the counsel of a forsaken wife, and lay it to heart: never marry a man who loves lathes and pipes and wheels and water and fire."

"But do come in ere bedtime, Herbert," she went on, "and I will sing you the sweetest of English ditties, and make you such a posset as never could be made out of old Ireland any more than the song."

But that moment her husband sprang from her side, shouted, "Caspar! Caspar!" bounded to the furnace, reached up with his iron rod into the darkness over his head, caught something with the hook and pulled hard. Caspar, responding from somewhere in the gloomy place, did the like on the other side. Instantly there followed a fierce, sustained hiss, and in a moment the place was filled with a white cloud. As the hiss changed to a roar, Lady Margaret turned in terror, ran out of the keep, and fled across the bridge and through the archway. Dorothy followed, but more composedly, led by duty and not driven by terror. Indeed, she was reluctant to forsake a spot where there was so much she did not understand. She did not know that they fled from the infant roar of the first father of steam engines, whose cradle was that ancient feudal keep.

That night Dorothy lay down weary. Her own bed at Wyfern had been so still, but here the darkness heaved and rippled with noises of the night. The stamping of horses and the ringing of their halter chains seemed very near. She heard Marquis howl from afar, and said to herself, "The poor fellow! I must get my lord to let me have him in my chamber." Then she listened a while to the sweet flow of the water from the mouth of the white horse. Suddenly there came an awful sound, torturing the dark with dismal fear. It was like a howl, but such as never left the throat of a dog. Dorothy had never heard the cry of a wild beast, but she had heard such beasts were in Raglan Castle, and so guessed it to be.

Worse noises than these could hardly have kept her awake, but not even weariness could prevent them from following her into her dreams.

14.
Ladies and Gentlemen

Lord Worcester had taken a liking to Dorothy, and he was disappointed when he found her place to be not at his table but at the housekeeper's. But he did not meddle with women's affairs, and it would not do for Lady Margaret to favor Dorothy above her other three women, for all were relatives as well as Dorothy.

One, Mrs. Doughty, was a rather elderly, rather plain, rather pious lady. The second, Lady Broughton, was a short, plump, roundfaced, good-natured smiling woman of sixty, excelling in fasts and mortifications, which somehow seemed to agree with her body as well as her soul. The third, Mistress Amanda Serafina, was only two or three years older than Dorothy, and was pretty except when she began to speak. She took an instant dislike to Dorothy, saying to herself that she could not bear the prim, set face of that country-bred heifer who evidently thought herself superior to everyone in the castle. She was persuaded the minx was a sly one, and would carry tales.

Dorothy did not much relish their society. She had little of it except at meals, when they always treated her as an interloper. If Dorothy had shown any marked acknowledgment of their rights, the ladies might have been more friendly. However, while she was capable of endless love and veneration, there was little of the conciliatory in Dorothy's nature. Hence Mrs. Doughty looked upon her with a rather stately indifference, Lady Broughton with a mild wish to save her poor, proud, Protestant soul; and Mistress

Serafina said she hated her. Mrs. Doughty neglected Dorothy, who did not know it; Lady Broughton said solemn things to her, of which she never saw the point; but when Amanda half closed her eyes and looked at her in snake fashion, Dorothy met her with a full, wide-orbed, questioning gaze. Amanda's eyes dropped, and she sank full fathom toward the abyss of real hatred.

During the dinner hour, the three generally talked together—not that they were bosom friends, for two of them had never been united in anything except despising good, soft Lady Broughton. When they were all together in Lady Margaret's presence, they behaved to Dorothy and each other with studious politeness.

Lady Elizabeth and Lady Anne had their own gentlewomen who also ate at the housekeeper's table. They kept somewhat apart from the rest, yet were in a distant way friendly to Dorothy.

But Dorothy was far more apt to attach herself to a few than to please many, and her heart went out to Lady Margaret. She found in her such sweetness (if not quite evenness) of temper, as well as gaiety of disposition, that she learned to admire as well as love her. She would soon have regarded Lady Margaret as a mother, had not the lady behaved more to Dorothy like an elder sister.

Lady Margaret's own genuine behavior had little of the matronly in it; when her husband came into the room, she seemed to grow instantly younger, and her manner changed almost to that of a playful girl. The dignity which belonged to her position never appeared in the society of those she loved, and was assumed like a veil in the presence of those whom she knew or trusted less. Before her ladies, she never appeared without some restraint—a certain measured movement, slowness of speech, and choice of phrase; but before a month was over, Dorothy was delighted to find that the reserve instantly vanished when they happened to be left alone.

Sometimes Dorothy read to Lady Margaret, sometimes worked with her, and every day she practiced a little on the harpsichord. She improved rapidly in performance and grew capable of receiving more and more delight from music. In the chapel was a fine little organ on which blind Delaware (the son of the Marquis' horsemaster) played delightfully. Dorothy never entered the place, but would stand outside listening to his music for an hour at a time.

Dorothy took an early opportunity to inform Lady Margaret of the relationship between herself and Scudamore, stating that she knew little of him, having met him only once before she came to the castle. Scudamore took the first fitting opportunity of addressing her in Lady Margaret's presence, and soon they were known all over the castle to be cousins.

With Lady Margaret's help, Dorothy came to a tolerable understanding of Scudamore. "He is not a bad fellow," said her lady, "but I cannot fully understand how he comes in such grace with the Marquis, who knows well enough that seldom are two things more unlike than men and their words. Yet I do not mean to say of your cousin that he is a hypocrite—he does not mean to be false, but he has no rule of right in him. He is pleasant company—his quips, ready retorts, and courtesy make him a favorite. He is quick yet indolent, good-natured but selfish, generous but counting enjoyment the first thing. I have never known him to act dishonorably, but the star of duty has not yet appeared above his horizon."

Pleased with Scudamore's address and behavior to her, Dorothy yet felt a lingering mistrust of him; the impression of his presence always gave her a sense of not coming near the real man in him. Dorothy did not herself suspect with whome she compared him— the real, sturdy, honest, straightforward, simple man, the youth of fiery temper whom she had chastised.

Visitors to the castle came and went, more now upon state business than matters of friendship or ceremony, and occasional solemn conferences were held in the Marquis' private room. Whoever else was or was not present, Lord Herbert when at home was always there, sometimes alone with his father and the commissioners from the King. His absences had grown more frequent now that His Majesty had appointed him General of South Wales. He had considerable forces under his command, mostly raised by himself and maintained at his father's expense.

It was some time before Dorothy saw Lord Herbert in the light. He had come home from a journey, changed clothes, and taken some food, and now appeared in his wife's parlor, to sun himself a little, he said. When he entered, Dorothy rose to leave the room. But he prayed her to be seated, saying gaily, "I would have you see, Cousin, that I am no beast of prey that loves the darkness. I can endure the daylight. Come, My Lady, have you nothing to amuse your soldier with? No good news? How is my little Molly?"

During the talk that followed, Dorothy had good opportunity to observe. She saw his fair, well-proportioned forehead, with eyes

80

that might owe their remarkable clearness to the mingling of manly confidence with feminine trustfulness. They were dark, not very large, but rather prominent, and full of light. His nose was a little aquiline, and fully formed. A soft mustache revealed generous lips, ever ready to break into a smile. Like Milton's Adam, he wore his wavy hair down to his shoulders. Once thick and curly, now it was thinner and straighter, yet curled where it lay. His hard, discolored hands were small, with the tapered fingers of the artist and the artisan's square thumb.

After husband and wife had conferred for a while, he looked up and seemed newly aware of Dorothy's presence.

"Well, Cousin," he said, "how have you fared since we half saw each other a fortnight ago?"

"Well indeed, My Lord, I thank you, as your lordship may judge, knowing whom I serve. In two short weeks my lady loads me with kindness enough to requite the loyalty of a life."

"Should I believe such laudation of any less than an angel?" said his lordship with mock gravity.

"No, My Lord," answered Dorothy.

Lord Herbert paused, then laughed aloud. "Excellent, Mistress Dorothy! Thank your cousin, My Lady, for a compliment worthy of an Irishwoman."

"I thank you, Dorothy," said Lady Margaret, "although Irishwoman as I am, my lord hath put me out of love with compliments."

"When they are true and come unbidden?" asked Dorothy.

"What! Are there such compliments, Cousin?" said Lord Herbert.

"There are birds of paradise, though rarely encountered."

"Birds of paradise indeed! They alight not in this world, for they have no legs."

"They need them not, My Lord. Once alighted they fly no more. They alight so seldom because men shoo them away."

The supper bell rang, and Dorothy looked up for her dismissal.

"Go to supper, My Lady," said Lord Herbert. "I have but just dined, and will see what Caspar is about."

"I want no supper but my Herbert," returned Lady Margaret. "You will go to that hateful workshop?"

"I have so little time at home now—"

"—that you must spend it from your lady? Go to supper, Dorothy."

15.
Husband and Wife

W hat an old-fashioned damsel!" said Lord Herbert, when Dorothy had left the room.

"She has led a lonely life," said Lady Margaret, "and has read many old-fashioned books."

"She seems a right companion for you, Peggy, and I am glad of it, for I shall be much from you—more till this bitter weather be gone by."

"Alas, Ned! Have you not been more than much from me already? You will certainly be killed, though you have not yet a scratch on your blessed body. I would it were over and all well!"

"So would I—I love fighting as little as you, but it is my duty. Hence it doubtless comes that no luck attends me. God knows I fear nothing a man has to fear; but what service of arms have I yet rendered my King? See how my rascally Welsh yielded before Gloucester, when the rogue Waller stole a march upon them! Had I been there instead of at Oxford, would they have laid down their arms nor struck a single blow? And at Monmouth the harehearts garrisoning the place fled at the bare advent of that same Parliament beagle, Waller! It were easier to make an engine that should mow down a thousand brave men than to put courage into the heart of one runaway rascal. Your husband is a poor soldier, Peggy, for he cannot make soldiers."

"Then leave the field to others, and labor at your engines, Love. I will help you, Sweet, with bare arms like your own."

"No, Wife. The King shall not find me wanting, for in serving my King I serve my God. If the King had but a dozen more such friends as My Lord the Marquis, who pours out his wealth like water on behalf of the King, and has already spent well toward a hundred and fifty thousand pounds! And the good man gives generously, though not carelessly, but has respect to what he spends."

"Surely the saints in heaven will never let such devotion fail of its end."

"My father is but one, and the King's foes are many. Would to God I had not lost those seven great troop horses that the pudding-fisted clothiers of Gloucester did rob me of! I need them sorely now. I bought them with my own money, or rather with yours, Sweetheart. I had been saving the money for a carcanet for your fair neck."

"Just so my neck be fair in your eyes, My Lord, it may go bare and be well clad. I should be jealous of the pretty stones did you give my neck one look the more for their presence. Here! You may sell these the next time in London."

"She put up her hand to unclasp her necklace of large pearls, but he laid his upon it, saying, "Nay, Margaret, there is no need. My father is like the father in the parable—he hath enough and to spare. I did mean to have the money of him again; only as the vaunted horses never came, I could not bring my tongue to ask him—and so your neck is bare of emeralds, My Dove."

"You are in doleful dumps."

"Then sing me a song, Sweetheart."

"I will, My Love." Rising, she went to the harpsichord and sang one of the songs of her native country, a merry ditty, with a breathing of sadness in the refrain, like a twilight wind in a bed of bulrushes.

"Thank you, My Love," said Lord Herbert when she had finished. "But I would I could tell its hidden purport, for I am one of those who think music none the worse for carrying sounds that speak to the brain as well as to the heart."

Lady Margaret gave a playful sigh. "You have one fault—you are a stranger to the tongue in which I learned the language of love. Why, when you are from me, I am loving you in Irish all day, and you never know what my heart says to you! But your Cousin Dorothy did sing a fair song in your own tongue the other day, which I will learn for your sake, though truly it is Greek to me. I will send for her."

She rose and rang the bell on the table, and sent a little page to desire Dorothy's attendance.

"Come, Child," said Lady Margaret when Dorothy entered, "I would have you sing to my lord the love song that you sang for me."

"Excuse me, Madam, but why should I sing that which you care not to hear?"

"I would have my lord hear it, for I would fain prove to him that there are songs in 'plain English' that have as little import to an English ear as the plain truth-speaking Irish ditties which he will not understand. I say *will not* because Irish was the language of Adam and Eve while yet in paradise, and therefore he could by instinct understand it if he would."

"I will sing at your desire, Madam, but the fault will lie in the singing." She seated herself at the harpsichord, and sang some of Sir Philip Sidney's verses set to music.

"There!" cried Lady Margaret, with a merry laugh when it was over. "What says the English song to my English husband?"

"It says much, Margaret," returned Lord Herbert, who had been listening intently. "It tells me to love you forever."

"Tell me then, My Lord, why you are so pleased with the song," said Lady Margaret very quietly.

"Come, Mistress Dorothy," said Lord Herbert, "repeat the song to my lady, slowly, line by line, and she will want no exposition."

Dorothy did so, and Lady Margaret put her arm around her husband's neck, laid her cheek to his, and said, "I am a goose, Husband. It is a fair and sweet song. I thank you, Dorothy. You shall sing it to me when my lord is away, and I shall love to think my lord was ill-content with me when I called it a foolish thing. But my Irish was a good song too."

"Your singing of it proves it, Sweetheart. But come, my fair minstrel Cousin, you have earned a good reward—what shall I give you in return for your song?"

"A boon, a boon, My Lord!" cried Dorothy.

"It is yours ere you ask it," returned Lord Herbert, merrily following the old-fashioned phrase with like formality.

"It has been in my mind ever since my lady took me to the keep, and I saw your marvelous array of engines. I would gladly understand them, My Lord, for who can fail to delight in such inventions?"

She uttered a little sigh with the thought of her old companion Richard, and the things they had together contrived. Already a halo had begun to glimmer about his head—and she had called him a Puritan, fanatic, and blasphemer!

Lord Herbert marked the soundless sigh. "You shall not sigh in vain, Mistress Dorothy, for anything I can give you. To one who loves inventions it is easy to explain them. I hoped you had a hankering that way when I saw you look so curiously at my crossbow ere you discharged it, but in truth I was disappointed when I found your curiosity so easily allayed."

"Indeed, My Lord, it was not allayed, and still is unsatisfied. I had no thought who it was who offered me the knowledge I craved. Had I known, I should never have refused such a courteous lesson; but I was a stranger in the castle."

"You did prudently. A young maiden cannot be too chary of unbuckling her enchanted armor so long as the country is unknown to her; but it would be hard if she were to suffer for her modesty. You shall be welcome to my cave. If I am not there, do not fear the worthy Caspar Kaltoff, who is my right hand to do the things my brain devises. He is sprung from a long race of artificers, and the cloak of their gathered skill has fallen on him. He has been in my service now for many years, but you will be the first lady who has ever wished us Godspeed.

"How few know," he continued thoughtfully, after a pause, "what joy lies in making things obey thoughts! Marvels I have to show, and I never lose sight of the wonder even while amusing myself."

"I thank you, My Lord, with all my heart," said Dorothy. "When have I leave to visit these marvels?"

"When you please. If I am not there, Caspar will be. If Caspar is not there, you will find the door open, for not a soul in Raglan would dare enter that chamber without my permission. It is not only outside the castle walls that I am called a magician! The armorer firmly believes that with a word uttered in my den I could make the weakest wall impregnable. If you come tomorrow morning you will almost certainly find me. But if you find neither of us, do not touch anything. Be content with looking, for fear of mischance."

"You may trust me, My Lord," said Dorothy.

Lord Herbert replied with a smile of confidence.

16.
Dorothy's Initiation

There was much about the castle itself that had already interested Dorothy. Her knowledge of the building advanced no more rapidly than her acquaintance with its inmates—for little could be done from the outside alone, and she could not bear to be met in strange places by strange people.

Twice or thrice every day she would visit the stables, and have an interview first with the chained Marquis and then with her little horse. After that she would look in at the armorer's shop and watch him at his work, so that she was soon familiar with the armor favored in the castle. The blacksmith's and carpenter's shops also drew her, and it was not long before she knew all the artisans about the place.

The wild beasts in their dens in the solid basement of the kitchen tower—a panther, two leopards, an ounce, and a toothless old lion—had already begun to know her a little, for she never went near their cages without carrying them something to eat. For all these visits there was plenty of leisure, for Lady Margaret never required much of her time, and found her reports amusing.

Yet she needed more than even these opportunities, and was eager to make the acquaintance of the ancient keep. So, the next morning after Lord Herbert's invitation, Dorothy was up before the sun and waiting at her window for its arrival. The moment it shone upon the gilded cock of the bell tower, she hastened out. Passing through the archway and over the bridge, she found herself at the magician's door. A tumult of hammering came from within, and for a moment she hesitated; it was plainly of no use to knock, and she could not at once bring herself to enter unannounced and uninvited. But confidence in Lord Herbert soon aroused her courage, and she gently opened the door and peeped in. There he stood, in a linen frock that reached from his neck to his knees, already hard at work at a small anvil on a bench. Caspar was still harder at work at a huge anvil on the ground in front of a forge, which with its mighty bellows occupied one of the six sides of the room. Now silent and cold, the great roaring, hissing thing that had so frightened Lady Margaret occupied another side.

Neither man saw Dorothy. She entered, closed the door, and approached Lord Herbert, but he continued unaware of her presence until she spoke. Then he ceased his hammering, turned, and greeted her with his usual smile of absolute sincerity.

"Are you always as true to your appointments, Cousin?" he asked.

"It was hardly an appointment, My Lord, and yet here I am—and I wonder greatly what is made here."

"Had I three tongues, and you three ears," he answered, "I could not tell you all. But look round you, and when you spy the thing that draws most your eye, ask me of that, and I will tell you."

Dorothy looked, and asked first after the giant wheel, and next a huge and elaborate escutcheon chest. Lord Herbert explained to her the ways of his perpetuum mobile, which he had demonstrated to the King himself in the Tower of London, and the secrets of the escutcheon chest, which locked stoutly and invisibly with a delicate key that a woman might easily use.

Then he opened a cabinet, took from it a little thing in form and color like a plum, and told her to eat it. She saw from his smile that there was something at the back of his playful request, hesitated for a moment, and then put it in her mouth.

Her mouth suddenly filled with iron, and she was gagged. She could not open or shut her mouth a hairbreadth, nor cry out or make any noise beyond an ugly one she would not make twice. The tears came into her eyes, for she imagined that Lord Herbert was making game of her, but he hastened to relieve her. He sprung a tiny key from his ring and applied it to the plum in her mouth. The little steel bolts that had been thrown out receded, and he drew the thing easily from her mouth.

"You little fool," he said sweetly, "did you think I would hurt you?"

"No, My Lord, but I did fear you were making game of me."

"You have come to the wrong house if you cannot put up with a little chafing. There!" he added, putting the thing in her hand. "It is an untoothsome plum, but the moment may come when you will find it useful enough to repay you for the annoyance of a smile that had in it ten times more friendship than merriment."

"I ask your pardon, My Lord," said Dorothy, by this time blushing deep with shame of her mistrust and oversensitiveness, and on the point of crying outright. But he smiled so kindly that she took heart and smiled again.

He then showed her how to raise the key hid in the ring, and how to unlock the plum.

"Do not try it on yourself," he said, as he put the ring on her finger. "You might find that awkward. And do not let anyone know you have such a thing, or that there is a key in your ring."

"I will not, My Lord."

The breakfast bell rang.

"If you will come again after supper," he said as he pulled off his linen frock, "I will show you my fire engine at work, and tell you all that is needful for the understanding thereof; only you must not publish it to the world, for I mean to make much gain by my invention."

Dorothy promised, and they parted—Lord Herbert for the Marquis' parlor, Dorothy for the housekeeper's room, and Caspar for the third table in the great hall.

After breakfast Dorothy practiced with her plum until she could readily manage it. She found that the steel bolts it threw out when pressed were so rounded and polished that they could not hurt, and that nothing but the key would retract them again within their former sheath.

17.
The Magician's Tower

A s soon as supper was over, Dorothy sped to the keep and found Caspar at work.

"My lord is not yet come from supper, Mistress," he said. "Will it please you to wait while he comes?"

Dorothy would have waited till midnight, so long as there was a chance of his appearing. Caspar did his best to amuse her, and the time went rapidly as he showed her one curious thing after another. All the while the fire engine was at work on its mysterious task, with occasional attention from Caspar—a billet of wood or a shovel of sea coal on the fire, a pull at a cord, or a hint from the hooked rod.

Twilight was over, Caspar had lighted his lamp, and the moon had risen before Lord Herbert came.

"I am glad you have patience as well as punctuality for a virtue," he said as he entered. "I too am punctual, and am sorry to have failed now, but I had to attend my father. For his sake pardon me. Come now, and I will explain to you my wonderful fire engine."

He took her by the hand and led her toward it. The creature blazed, groaned, and puffed, but there was no motion to be seen about it save that of the flames through the cracks in the door of the furnace. Neither was there any noise of clanking metal, although a great rushing sound somewhere in the distance seemed to belong to it.

"It is a noisy thing," he said as they stood before it, "but when

I make another, it shall do its work so that you will not hear it outside the door. Now, Cousin, should it come to a siege and I am not at Raglan, Caspar will be wanted everywhere. This engine is essential to the health and comfort—even life—of the castle, and no one is capable of managing it save us two. A very little instruction, however, would enable anyone to do so. Will you undertake it, Cousin, in case of need?"

"Make me assured that I can, and I will, My Lord."

"A good and sufficing answer. First I must show you its necessity to the castle."

He led the way from the room and ascended the stair which rose just outside it. Dorothy followed, winding up through the thickness of the wall. She could not hear the engine here, though the rushing sound drew nearer and nearer. When they had surmounted three of the five lofty stories, they could scarcely hear each other for the roar of water falling in jets. At last they came out on the top of the wall, with nothing between them and the moat below but the battlemented parapet. The mighty tower was roofed with water—a little tarn filled all the space within the surrounding walk.

"You see now what yon fire-souled slave below is laboring at," said Lord Herbert. "His task is to fill this cistern, and that he can in a few hours. Yet he is such a slave that a child who understands him can guide him at will."

"But, My Lord," questioned Dorothy, "is there not water enough here to supply the castle for months? And there is the draw well in the pitched court besides."

"Enough for the merest necessities of life, but what would become of its pleasures? Would not the ladies miss the bounty of the marble horse? And how would my lord's tables fare, with armed men besetting every gate, the fish ponds dry, and the fish rotting in the sun? And if this tower becomes the final retreat, with the rest of the castle in the hands of the enemy, where then is your draw well?"

"But this tower, large as it is, could not house all those now within the walls of the castle."

"They will be fewer ere its shelter is needful."

For one moment of sudden sickness Dorothy knew what siege and battle meant, but she recovered herself with a strong effort. "And whence comes all this water?"

"Have you observed a well in my workshop below, not far from the great chest? That is a very deep well with a powerful spring, and large pipes lead from that to my fire engine. The fuller the well, the more rapid the flow into the cistern; and the shallower the water below, the more labor falls to my giant. He finds it hard work now, for the cistern is nearly full."

"Having such a well in your foundations, whence the need of such a cistern on your roof?"

"The enemy would assuredly change the siege into a blockade—that is, he would try to starve instead of fire us out, and might dig deep enough to cut the water veins which supply that well, and, thereafter, all would depend upon the cistern. From the moment, therefore, when the first signs of siege appear, it will be wisdom and duty to keep it constantly full—full as a cup to the health of the King.

"But there is more in it yet—look down through this battlement upon the moat. You see the moon in it? No? It is low, and covered with weeds—so little defense that a boy might wade through."

He left her side and walked a few paces away, but went on speaking. She turned to him—but he had vanished.

She looked down at the moat again, and suddenly there arose a hollow bellowing, a pent-up rumbling. Seized by terror, she clung to the parapet. The great wall trembled under her feet, and then the water in the moat rushed swiftly upward in wild uproar. A multitude of fountain jets rushed high toward their parent cistern, but failed to reach it. The uproar ceased as suddenly as it had commenced, but the moat mirrored a thousand moons in the agitated waters which had overwhelmed its mantle of weeds.

"You see now," said Lord Herbert, rejoining her while still she gazed, "how necessary the cistern is to the keep? Without it, the few poor springs in the moat would not sustain it. From here I can fill it to the brim."

"Would not a simple overflow serve?"

"It would, were there no other advantages. I can also use this water as offense against anyone setting unlawful or hostile foot upon the stone bridge. I can turn that same bridge into a rushing aqueduct and sweep from it a whole company of invaders. As soon as the bridge is clear, the outflow ceases. One sweep, and my waterbroom would stop, and the rubbish lie sprawling under the arch—or halfway across the court. And I *could* make the water boiling."

"But your lordship *would* not?" faltered Dorothy.

"That depends," he answered with a smile. "But all this is child's play. Cousin Dorothy, I will give you the largest possible proof of my confidence, by not only explaining to you the working of my fire engine, but acquainting you with it—only you must not betray me."

"I will give your lordship this proof of my confidence: I promise to keep your secret before knowing what it is."

"Listen then. That engine is a discovery and invention such as has no equal since the first mechanical powers were brought to the light. For this shall animate lever, screw, pulley, wheel and axle—what you will. My fire engine shall uplift England above the richest and most powerful nations. When this rebellion is over, when peace shall again smite this country, and I have time to perfect the work of my hands, I shall present it to the King. It shall forever raise him and his royal progeny above the need of benevolences or taxes, to rule his kingdom as independent of his subjects in reality as he is in right. This water-commanding engine which God hath given me to make shall be the source of such wealth as no accountant can calculate. Marshland may be thoroughly drained, and dry land perfectly watered; great cities kept sweet and wholesome; mines rid of water and drawn of their wealth; houses served plentifully on every stage; dry gardens comforted with fountains."

Dorothy wondered whether such independence might be altogether good—for the King himself or the people thus subjected to his will.

All this time they had been standing on the top of the moonlit keep. In their ears had been the noise of the water flowing from the dungeon well into the sky-roofed cistern, but now it came in diminished flow.

"It is the earth that fails in giving, not my engine in taking," said Lord Herbert as he turned and led the way down the winding stair. As they entered the vault at the bottom, the fire engine gave a failing stroke or two and ceased. A dense white cloud bloomed out to meet them.

"Stopped for the night, Caspar?" asked Lord Herbert.

"Yes, My Lord. The well is nearly out."

"Let it sleep. Like a man's heart it will fill in the night. Thank God for the night and darkness and sleep, in which good things draw nigh like God's thieves and steal themselves in—water into wells, and peace and hope and courage into the minds of men."

Dorothy looked up into his face with reverence and understanding in her eyes. This was one of the idolatrous Catholics! She was beginning to learn that a man may be right, although the creed for which he is ready to die may contain much that is wrong.

"I cannot show you the working of the engine tonight," continued Lord Herbert. "Caspar has decreed otherwise."

"I can soon set her a-going again, My Lord," said Caspar.

"No, no. We must be away to the powder mill, Caspar. Mistress Dorothy will come again tomorrow, and you must yourself explain to her the working and management of it. And do not fear to trust her, although she be a softhanded lady. Let her have the brute's halter in her own hold."

Grateful for the trust reposed in her, Dorothy took her leave, and the two workmen abandoned their shop for the night. They left the door wide open behind them to let out the fire engine vapors—confident that no unlicensed foot would dare cross the threshold—and so spent the rest of the night laboring in the powder mill.

Lord Herbert was unfavorable to the storing of powder because of the danger, seeing they could in one week prepare enough to keep the castle's ordnance busy for two. And he believed that spring-projection engines could be built that might throw a hundred-weight stone into a city from a quarter-mile's distance, with no noise audible to those within. It was such a device he was brooding over when Dorothy came upon him by the arbalest.

One who happened to see Lord Herbert within his father's walls—busy yet unhasting, earnest yet cheerful, rapid in movement yet composed—would hardly have imagined that a day or two at a time was all he was now able to spend there. For not merely was he enlisting large numbers of men, but also commanding both horse and foot, and meeting all expense from his own pocket, or with the assistance of his father. Only a few months before, he had in eight days raised six regiments, fortified Monmouth and Chepstow, and garrisoned half-a-dozen smaller but yet important places. And he had enrolled, and furnished with horses and arms, about a hundred noblemen and gentlemen. So prominent indeed were his services on behalf of the King that his father was uneasy for the jealousy and hate it would certainly rouse in the minds of some of His Majesty's well-wishers.

18.
Moonlight and Apple Blossoms

The next morning after breakfast, Lord Herbert set out for Chepstow and Monmouth and the business of war. That same hour Dorothy went to Caspar, and was by him instructed in the mysteries of the fire engine. On the third day after, so entirely was he satisfied with her understanding and management that he gave over to her the whole water business.

Yet, among the tides of war and rumor of battle, all was peaceful within the defenses of Raglan, and its towers looked abroad over a quiet country. A smoke might sometimes be seen from the watchtower, and across the air would come the dull boom of a great gun from one of the fortresses, and Lady Margaret's cheek would then turn pale. Every day something was being done to strengthen the castle: masons were at work about the walls, and Caspar was busy in all directions, repairing crossbows and peculiar old-fashioned engines of war; yet there was no hurry and no confusion, and little outward appearance of unusual activity.

All around them buds were creeping out, unfolding, and breathing the air of heaven. Apple blossoms appeared, and the orchard was lovely with a storm of roseate snow. Ladies passed through the gates and walked in the gardens, where the fountains had begun to play and the swans and ducks on the lakes felt the return of spring.

And Dorothy sat at the springhead of the waters, for, through her dominion over the fire engine, she had become the naiad of Raglan. The horse of marble spouted and ceased at her will, though in general she let the stream flow from his mouth all day long. From the urn of her pleasure the cistern was daily filled, and from the summit of defense her flood poured into the moat and mantled it to the brim. She understood all the secrets of the aqueous catapult—only hinted at by Lord Herbert—and believed she could arrange it for action without assistance.

Her new responsibilities required but a portion of her leisure, and Lady Margaret was pleased that her husband considered the wiseheaded girl fit to be put in charge of his darling invention. But Dorothy kept silence concerning the trust to all but her mistress. And Lady Margaret was prudent enough to avoid any allusion which might raise yet higher the jealousy of her gentlewomen, who already regarded Dorothy as supplanting them in the favor of their mistress.

One lovely evening in May, the moon was at the full, the air was warm yet fresh, the apple blossoms were at their largest, and the nightingales were singing from their very bones. The season invaded every chamber in the castle, seized the heart of both man and beast, and turned all into one congregation of which the nightingales were the priests. All the inhabitants came out-of-doors, the ladies and gentlemen strolling in groups here and there about the gardens and lawns and islands, and the domestics wandering hither and thither where they pleased.

The Ladies Margaret and Elizabeth and Anne, with their companies, were walking on the lawn beneath the picture gallery. The Marquis himself, notwithstanding a slight attack of the gout, had hobbled on his stick to a chair set for him on the same lawn. Beside him sat Lady Mary, who was specially devoted to her father.

Rowland Scudamore joined Lady Margaret's people, and in a moment Lady Broughton was laughing merrily. Behind them was Amanda Serafina, with her eyes on her feet and the corners of her pretty mouth drawn down in contempt. Now and then Scudamore, satisfied with his own wit, would throw a glance behind him, knowing that Amanda heard him. This group sauntered on into the orchard.

After them came Dorothy with Dr. Bayly, talking of their common friend, Matthew Herbert. The elder ladies soon floated away together under the canopies of blossoms; Rowland fell behind and joined the waiting Amanda, and the two flitted about like moths in the moonshine. Dorothy and Dr. Bayly halted in an open spot, the divine talking eagerly, and the maiden looking up at the moon and heeding the nightingales more than the divine.

"*Can* these be English nightingales?" she asked thoughtfully.

The doctor was bewildered, for he had been talking about himself; but he recovered like a gentleman.

"Assuredly, Mistress Dorothy," he replied. "This is the land of their birth, and hither they come again when the winter is over."

"Yes, but they take no part of our troubles. They will not sing to comfort our hearts in the cold, but give them warmth enough; and they sing as careless of battlefields and dead men as if they were but moonlight and apple blossoms."

"Is it not better so?" returned the divine after a moment's thought. "How would it be if everything in nature but reechoed our moan? These may serve to remind us that these evil times will go by, the King shall have his own again, the fanatics will be scourged as they deserve, and the Church will rise like the phoenix from the ashes of her purification."

"But how many will lie out in the fields all the year long, yet never see blossoms or hear nightingales more!"

"Such will have died martyrs," rejoined Dr. Bayly.

"On both sides?" suggested Dorothy.

The good man stood for a moment checked, for he had not even thought of the dead on the other side. "That cannot be," he said finally.

Dorothy looked up again at the moon, but she listened no more to the nightingales, and they left the orchard together in silence.

Amanda saw them go, and said, "Come, Rowland, we must not be found here alone. But tell me one thing—is Mistress Dorothy Vaughan indeed your cousin?"

"Her mother and mine were sisters' children."

"I thought it could not be a near cousinship, for you are not alike at all. Hear me, Rowland, but let it die in your ear—I love not Mistress Dorothy."

"And the reason, lovely hater? She is not fair as some are fair, but she will pass, and offends not."

"She is fair enough—not beautiful, not even pleasing—but the demure look she puts on may bear the fault of that. Rowland, I would not speak evil of anyone, but your cousin is a hypocrite. She is false at heart, and hates me. Trust me, she but bides her time to let me know it—and you too, my Rowland."

"I am sure you mistake her, Amanda. Her looks are but modest, and her words but shy, for she came here from a lonely house. I believe she is honest and good."

"Do you not see how she makes friends with none but her betters? Already she hath wound herself around my lady's heart! And now she pays her court to the puffing chaplain! And how oft she crosses the bridge to the Yellow Tower! She thinks to curry favor with my lord by pretending to love locks and screws and pistons and such like. And if she pleases my lord well, who knows but that he may give her a pair of watches to hang at her ears, or a box that cannot be opened without a secret as well as the key? They say my lord hath twenty cartloads of such wonderful things.

"Once I was sent to carry young Lady Raven thither, to see my lord earn his bread. And what should my lord give her but a ball of silver which, thrown into a vessel of water, would plainly show the very hour and minute of the day or night! Tell me not, Rowland, that the damsel hath no design. Her looks betoken a better wisdom. Doth she not honestly far more resemble a pinch-nosed Puritan than a loyal maiden?"

"Be not too severe with my cousin," pleaded Scudamore. "She is much too sober to please my fancy, but why for that should I hate her? And she may bear the look of a long-faced fanatic, for she hath but now, as it were, lost her mother."

"But now! And I never knew! Ah, Rowland, how lonely is the world!"

"Lovely Amanda!" said Rowland.

So they passed from the orchard and parted, fearful of being missed. And what should such a pair do, but after its kind? Life was dull without romance, so they created their own. And the more they had, the more they wanted, until casual encounters would no longer serve their turn.

19.
The Enchanted Chair

A cloud was slowly deepening upon the brow of the Marquis. In his judgment the King was losing ground, not only in England but in the deeper England of its men.

Lady Margaret also showed a more continuous anxiety than was to be accounted for by Lord Herbert's absences and dangers—little Molly, the treasure of her heart next to her lord, had always been delicate but now was sickly. Lady Margaret continued unchangingly kind to Dorothy, and the girl's tireless efforts to amuse and please little Molly awoke the deep gratitude of a mother. She began to take an interest in Dorothy's new charge, the engine, and would even listen with patience to her expositions of its wonderful construction and abilities.

One evening, after playing with little Molly until she fell asleep, Dorothy ran to see her other baby. The cistern had fallen rather low, and she intended to fill it. She found Caspar had lighted the furnace as requested, so she set the engine going, and it warmed to its work.

The place was hot, and Dorothy was tired. But where in that wide and not overclean place should she find anything fit to sit on? Looking about, she soon found an apparently forgotten chair hidden in a corner of a recess behind the furnace. She dragged it out, dusted it, set it as far from the furnace as practicable, and sat down.

Instantly, iron bands shot out from the chair and pinned her fast by both arms and legs. She screamed from mingled indignation and terror, fancying herself seized by human arms; but she quieted when she found herself only in the power of one of her cousin's curiosities, knowing that Caspar would pay a visit to the workshop before going to bed. The pressure of the trap did not hurt her, but when she made the least attempt to stir, the thing showed itself immovably locked. She had too much confidence in the workmanship of her cousin and Caspar to dream of opening it without their aid. Her worst fear was that the engine might require attention, and she did not know what the consequences would be.

However, something in the powder mill detained Caspar far beyond his usual time for retiring; he knew that Dorothy was tending the engine and would know where to find him. Because of the hour, he went to bed without paying his customary visit to the keep.

So Dorothy sat and waited in vain. The last drops of day trickled down the side of the world, the night covered the globe, and the red glow of the furnace was all that lighted the place. She waited, but Caspar did not come. The rush of the water grew slower and slower, and soon ceased. The fire sank lower and lower, and its red eye dimmed, darkened, and went out, but still Caspar did not come.

Faint fears began to gather about Dorothy's heart. It was clear at last that she must stay there all night, and who knows how far into the morning? Firm of heart as she was, she discovered that she too was assailable by the terror of the night. The misery grew quickly, and she felt almost as if she were buried alive. But Dorothy knew that the unavoidable must be encountered with whatever courage could be found, so she summoned all her energy and braced herself to endure.

She knew that any attempt to make herself heard would be fruitless; and to spend the night confined was a far lesser evil than to be discovered by staring domestics, and exposed to the open merriment of her friends and the mockery of her enemies. She was certain of Caspar's silence, and so she sat on.

The night passed very slowly, and she grew chilly and cramped. She dozed and woke and dozed again. She woke from a troubled sleep to the sound of whispering voices. The subdued manner of the conversation indicated the awe with which the speakers had ventured within the forbidden precincts.

Her first idea was to utter some frightful cry such as would deliver her and at the same time punish with the pains of terror this foolhardy intrusion. But as always, she reflected before she acted, and she realized that Lord Herbert and the Marquis had a right to know who would secretly meet thus in the middle of the night—and on prohibited ground. Who could tell what conspiracy or treason might be involved? And any alarm would destroy every chance of their discovery. She compelled herself to absolute stillness, but their words were inaudible to her.

Their talk lasted a long time, but with sudden silences and broken renewals; for the genius of the place, though braved, yet had its terrors. At length she heard something like a half-conquered yawn, and soon after the voices ceased.

A weary time passed, and she fell asleep. She woke in the gray of morning, and after two more hours of hopeful waiting, heard Caspar's welcome footsteps. His first look of amazement was followed with an expression of pitiful dismay, and she burst into tears.

He was distressed at the suffering his breach of custom had so cruelly prolonged. "And I haf bin slap in my bed!" he exclaimed.

But relieving her was no easy matter. The key to the chair was in the black cabinet; the black cabinet was secured with one of Lord Herbert's marvelous locks; the key of that lock was in Lord Herbert's pocket; and Lord Herbert was at Chepstow or Monmouth or Usk. But Caspar lost no time moaning the circumstances: he proceeded to light a fire in the forge, and within a few minutes fashioned a picklock. After several trials the bolts yielded, and Dorothy rose at last from the terrible chair. But so benumbed were all her limbs that she escaped being relocked in it only by Caspar's intervening arms. He led her about like a child, until at length she could venture the slow creeping journey to her chamber. Few of the household were yet astir, and she met no one. When she covered herself up in bed, then first she knew how cold she was, and felt as if she should never be warm again.

She slept long and soundly. Her maid could not wake her, left her asleep, and did not return till breakfast was over. Finding her still asleep, she became a little anxious, and told Mistress Amanda that Mistress Dorothy might be ill. But Amanda herself was sleepy and cross, and gave a sharp answer. Lady Broughton, on her way to Sunday Mass, told the maid to let Dorothy have her sleep.

The noise of horses on the stone paving finally roused Dorothy;

she rose confounded and drew back the window curtain. Below, Lord Herbert walked into the fountain court, followed by some forty or fifty officers, and the noise of their armor and feet and voices dispelled at once the dim Sabbath vapor that hung about the place. They gathered around the white horse to wait while their leader entered the staircase nearest his wife's apartment.

Now Dorothy had gone to sleep in perplexity, and all through her dreams she had been trying to decide what course she should take. The Marquis should know of the nocturnal intrusion, but he was just recovering from an attack of the gout, and ought not to be troubled unless it were absolutely necessary. Should she tell Lady Margaret? Caspar? Dr. Bayly? But here was Lord Herbert back, and her doubt vanished. She dressed and hurried to Lady Margaret's room. No one was there or in the nursery, so Dorothy seated herself in the parlor, supposing he and Lady Margaret had gone to the morning service.

Those two had in reality gone to the oak parlor, where the Marquis generally made his first appearance after a gout attack.

"Welcome home, Herbert," said the Marquis kindly, holding out his hand. "And how does my wild Irishwoman this morning? Crying her eyes out because her husband is back? But Herbert, Lad, whence all the noise of spurs and scabbards, clanking and clattering through the hall like a torrent of steel? Here I sit, a deserted old man, with not even a page to bring me word!"

"Being on my way to the Forest of Dean, My Lord, and coming round by Raglan to inquire after you and my lady, I did bring with me some of my officers to dine and drink your lordship's health on the way."

"You shall all be welcome, though I fear I shall not make one," said the Marquis, with a grimace of pain.

"I am sorry to see you suffer, Sir."

"Man is born to trouble as the sparks fly upward," returned the Marquis. Then came a pause, and Lady Margaret departed, leaving the men to affairs of war.

Returning to her own room, Lady Margaret found Dorothy waiting for her. "Well, my little lig-a-bed!" she said sweetly. "What is amiss? You look sober."

"I am well, Madam, and that I look sober you will not soon wonder. But I pray for my lord's presence, that he may know all."

"What is the matter, Child?" cried Lady Margaret. "Do you

mean my own Herbert, or my Lord Worcester?"

"My Lord Herbert, My Lady. I dread lest he should go ere I have time to tell him."

"He rides again after dinner," said Lady Margaret.

"Then, Dear Lady, if you would keep me from great doubt and disquiet, let me have the ear of my lord for a few moments."

Lady Margaret sent for Lord Herbert. Within five minutes he was with them, and within five more Dorothy had told her tale of the night, uninterrupted save by Lady Margaret's exclamations of sympathy.

"And now, My Lord, what am I to do?" Dorothy asked.

Lord Herbert made no answer for a few moments, but walked up and down the room. Dorothy thought he looked angry as well as troubled. Then he burst into a laugh and said merrily, "I have it! We may save my father annoyance without concealment. Instead of trouble, my father shall have laughter; and instead of annoyance, such a jest as may make good amends for the wrong done him by the breach of his household laws. Cousin Dorothy, Caspar has explained to you all concerning the waterworks?"

"All, My Lord."

"Then so soon as it is dark this evening, you and he will set the springs which lie under the paving of the bridge. Thereafter the first foot set upon it will drop the drawbridge to the stone bridge, and convert the two into an aqueduct, and loose a rushing torrent to sweep the intruders away. Before they can gather their wits or raise their prostrate bones, my father will be out upon them—nor shall they find shelter for their shame ere every soul in the castle has witnessed their disgrace. But you must take heed, Dorothy, not to forget what you have done. Should you go onto the bridge after setting your vermin-trap, you must place your feet precisely where Caspar shows you, else you will ride a watery horse halfway to the marble one.

"Our trusty and well-beloved Cousin Dorothy, I herewith, in presence of our lady, appoint you my deputy during my absence. No one but you and Caspar have a right to cross that bridge after dark. I shall inform and warn my father what is to be done, and shall contrive a bell in his chamber that shall ring if the drawbridge falls."

He left to make the appropriate arrangements with Caspar and the Marquis. And after dinner, while the horses were being brought out, Lord Herbert returned to Lady Margaret's room. Little Molly was waiting to kiss him good-bye, and she sat on his knee until it was time for him to go. The child's looks saddened his heart, and his wife could not restrain her tears when she saw his mournful gaze. At the moment of departure he rose with a heavy heart, gave Molly into her mother's arms, clasped them both in one embrace, and hurried from the room.

He ought to be a noble King for whom such sacrifices are made. Such devotion on the part of her admired lord and lady raised Dorothy's prejudice to a degree of worship which greatly narrowed what she took for one of the widest gulfs separating her from the creed of her friends.

Immediately upon nightfall she and Caspar speedily arranged Lord Herbert's watery counterplot, and waited. But night after night passed, and the bell in the Marquis' room remained voiceless.

20.
Molly and the White Horse

Meantime Lord Herbert came and went. There was fighting here and there, a castle taken and defended and retaken, here a little success or a worse loss, now on this side or on that. But the King's affairs made little progress, and little Molly's body and soul progressed in opposite directions.

Dorothy's cares were divided between the duties of naiad and nursemaid, for the child clung to her as to no one else except Lady Margaret. The thing that pleased Molly best was to see the two whalelike spouts rise suddenly from the nostrils of the great white horse, curve apart in the air, and fall back into the basin on either side. "See horse spout," she would say. Dorothy would be notified, and Molly would be carried forth to the verge of the marble basin. Gazing up at the rearing animal, she would call, in a tone daintily wavering between entreaty and command, "Spout, horse, spout." Dorothy, looking down from the summit of the tower, would turn her hand and send the captive water shooting down its dark channel to reascend in sunny freedom.

On a bright day this would happen repeatedly. The instant Molly turned from it, satisfied for a moment, the fountain ceased to play. For the sake of renewing Molly's delight, the horse remained spoutless, awaiting the revival of the darling's desire—for she was not content to see him spouting, but must see him spout.

One day, by some accident, Dorothy had not reached her post before Molly arrived at the horse. Her usual application was in vain, and she waited about three seconds in perfect patience. She turned her head slowly round, and gazed in her nurse's countenance with questioning eyes. Then she turned again to the horse, and a smile broke over her face.

She cried, in the tone of one who has made a great discovery, "Horse has ears of stone—he cannot hear Molly." Then she turned her face up to the sky, saying, "Dear holy Mary, tell horse to spout."

That moment the two jets shot into the sun. Molly clapped her little hands in delight and cried, "Thanks, dear holy Mary! I knowed you would do it for Molly!"

The nurse told the story to Lady Margaret, and she to Dorothy. It set the first two feeling, and Dorothy to thinking. "It must be," she thought, "that a child's prayer will reach its goal, even should she turn her face to the west or the north instead of up to the heavens! A prayer differs from a bolt or a bullet."

Later, Lady Margaret said to Dorothy, "How *can* you Protestants live without a woman to pray to?"

"Her Son Jesus never refused to hear a woman, and I see not wherefore I should go to His mother, Madam," answered Dorothy bravely.

"You and I will not quarrel, Dorothy," returned Lady Margaret sweetly, "for sure I am that would please neither one nor the other of them."

Dorothy kissed her hand, and the subject was dropped.

After that Molly never asked the horse to spout, but turned her request to the Mother Mary. Nor did the horse ever fail to spout, notwithstanding an evil thought which arose in the Protestant part of Dorothy's mind—the temptation to try Molly with a second failure. But the rest of her being protested so violently that no parley was possible, and the conscience of her intellect cowered before the conscience of her heart.

It was from this indulgence of Molly's fancy that the castle at large came to know Dorothy as ruler of the Raglan waters. No one save Dorothy and Lord Herbert and Caspar and the Marquis, however, knew of the watershoot or the artificial cataract, the mechanism of which Dorothy and Caspar set every night and detached every morning.

21.
The Damsel Who Fell Sick

Within the great fortress, a lovely child-soul was gently rising as from the tomb. The bonds of earthly life were giving way, and little white-faced, big-eyed Molly was leaving father and mother and grandfather and spouting horse and all, to find what she wanted.

One sultry evening in the second week of June, the weather again engulfed the inhabitants of the castle. Clouds had slowly steamed up all day from several sides of the horizon, and as the sun went down they met in the zenith. The air was hot and heavy to breathe: it was weather that made *some* dogs bite their masters, made the maids quarrelsome, the men more or less sullen, and the hearts of lovers throb for the comfort of each other's lonely society. It made Dorothy sad, Molly long after she knew not what, Lady Margaret weep, and the Marquis feel himself growing old. The fish lay still in the ponds, the pigeons sat motionless on the roof-ridges, and the fountains did not play, for Dorothy's heart was so heavy that she had forgotten them.

The Marquis, fond of all his grandchildren, had never taken special notice of Molly beyond what she naturally claimed as the youngest. But when it appeared that one of the spring flowers of the human family was withdrawing, she began to pull at his heart with the dearness caused by the growing shadow of death. Every morning he paid her a visit, and every morning little Molly was waiting for him, for the young and the old recognize that they belong to each other, despite the unwelcome intervention of wrin-

kles and baldness and toothlessness. Her arms would be stretched
out to him, and she would ask, "Prithee, tell me a tale, Sir."

"Which tale wouldst thou have, my Molly?"

The little one would answer, "Of the good Jesu," and generally
add, "and of the damsel who fell sick and died."

Torn as the country was, all good grandparents told their children the same tales about the same Man. And in order to keep his
treasure supplied with things new as well as old, the Marquis went
often to his Latin Bible to refresh his memory for Molly's use, and
was both in receiving and giving a gainer. When the old man came
to pour out his wealth to the child, Lady Margaret became aware
of the depth of religious knowledge and feeling in her father-in-law.
Neither Sir Toby Matthews nor Dr. Bayly ever lighted the lamps
behind Molly's great eyes; but her grandfather's voice, the moment he began to speak to her of the good Jesu, brought her soul
to its windows.

This sultry evening Molly was restless. "Madam! Madam!" she
kept calling to her mother.

"What wouldst you, my heart's treasure?"

"Madam, I know not," the child would answer.

Twenty times in an hour the same words would pass between
them. At length, however, Molly answered, "Madam, I would see
the white horse spout."

Dorothy rose and crept from the room, crossed the court and the
moat, and dragged her heavy heart to the top of the keep. There
she looked down upon Molly's open window, where Lady Margaret stood with Molly in her arms. Lady Margaret fluttered a handkerchief where only Dorothy could see, and said, with such well-
simulated cheerfulness as only mothers can put on whose hearts
are ready to break, "Now, Molly, tell the horse to spout."

"Mother Mary, tell the horse to spout," said Molly—and up
went the watery parabolas. The old flame of delight flushed the
child's cheek like the flush in the heart of a white rose, but it died
almost instantly. Murmuring, "Thanks, Good Madam!"—whether
to Mother Mary or Lady Margaret it little mattered—Molly
turned toward the bed, and her mother knew that the child sought
her last sleep, as we call it. God forgive us our little faith!

"Madam!" panted the child, as Lady Margaret laid her down.
"I would see my Lord Marquis." He was sent for instantly, as the
child continued, "Molly is going—going—where is Molly going?"

"Going to Mother Mary, Child," answered Lady Margaret, choking back the sobs that would have kept the tears company.

"And the good Jesu?"

"Yes."

"And the good God over all?"

"Yes, yes."

Dorothy returned, and then the Marquis entered, pale and panting. He knew the end was near. Molly stretched out to him one hand instead of two, as if her hold upon earth were half-yielded. He sat down by the bedside and wiped his forehead with a sigh.

"Thee tired too, Marquis?" asked the odd little lovebird.

"Yes, I am tired, my Molly. Thou seest I am so fat."

"Shall I ask the Good Mother, when I go to her, to make thee spare like Molly?"

"No, Molly, thou need'st not trouble her about that. Ask her to make me good."

"Would it be easier to make thee good than spare?"

"No, Child, but it is so much more worth doing. If she makes me good, she will have another in heaven to be good to."

"Then I know she will. But I will ask her. Mother Mary has so many to mind, she might be forgetting." After this she lay very quiet, with her hand in his. All the windows of the room were open, and from the chapel came the mellow sounds of the organ. Young Delaware had captured Tom Fool to blow the bellows, and through the heavy air the music surged in.

Molly was dozing a little, and she spoke as one that speaks in a dream. "The white horse is spouting music," she said. "See, Marquis, see! Spout, horse, spout!"

She lay silent again for a long time. The old man sat holding her hand, while her mother sat on the far side of the bed, leaning against one of the footposts and watching the white face of her darling with eyes in which love ruled distraction. Dorothy sat in one of the windowseats and listened to the music surging in, mingled with the plash of the twin fountain spouting from the horse.

"What is it?" said Molly, waking up. "My head doth not ache, and I am not affrighted. He cometh! He is here! Marquis, the good Jesu wants Molly's hand. Let Him have it, Marquis. He is lifting me up. I am quite well—quite—"

The sentence remained broken. The hand which the Marquis had yielded—with the awe of one in bodily presence of the Holy, and which he saw raised as if in the grasp of one invisible—fell back on the bed, and little Molly was quite well.

But she left sick hearts behind. Lady Margaret threw herself on the bed and wailed aloud. The Marquis burst into tears, left the room, and sought his study. There he mechanically took a book and sat down, but never opened it; rose again and took his Shakespeare, opened it, but could not read; rose once more, took his Vulgate, and read: *Quid turbamini, et ploratis? Puella non est mortua, sed dormit.*—"Why do you make a tumult and weep? The child is not dead, but sleeping." He laid down that book also, fell on his knees, and prayed for her who was not dead but sleeping.

Dorothy, feeling that Lady Margaret would rather be alone with her dead, also left the room and sought her chamber, where she threw herself on the bed. The chapel music ceased, and all was still save the plashing from the fountain. Then the storm burst in a glare and a peal. The rain fell in straight lines and huge drops, drowning the noise of the fountain, and setting every gutterspout gurgling musically. The one court was filled with a clashing on its pavement, and the other with a soft singing upon its grass.

At the first thunderclap, Lady Margaret fell on her knees and prayed in agony for the little soul that had gone forth into the midst of the storm. Like many women she had a horror of lightning and thunder, and it never came into her mind that Molly was far more likely to be reveling in the elemental tumult, with all the added ecstacy of newborn freedom and health, than to be trembling like her mortal mother below.

Dorothy was not afraid, but she was weary and heavy; the thunder stunned her, and the lightning took the power of motion from the shut eyelids through which it shone. She lay without moving, and at length fell fast asleep.

Of the mourners, the storm brought relief to the Marquis alone. He had again opened his New Testament and tried to read, but in vain. When the thunder burst he closed the Book and opened the window wide. Like a tide from the plains of innocent heaven came the coolness to his brow and heart. So is the wind of the living God to the bodies of men, His Spirit to their spirits, His breath to their hearts. One must have already ceased to believe in God ere he could believe that the wind that blows where it will is free because God has forgotten it, and that it bears from Him no message.

109

22.
The Cataract

The chapel music ended as young Delaware suddenly found the keys dumb beneath his helpless fingers. He called aloud, and his voice echoed through the empty chapel, but no living response came back. Tom Fool had grown weary and forsaken him. Disappointed and baffled, he rose and left the chapel.

Although Tom had deserted his post, young Delaware was mistaken as to the reason. Oppressed with the sultriness of the night, Tom had fallen fast asleep leaning against the organ. At the thunder of the breaking storm, he slipped from the stool and stretched full length upon the floor. The pouring rain made his sleep sweeter and deeper, and he lay and snored until midnight.

The rain ended and the night was still. Although the moon was clouded, there was light enough to recognize a figure in any part of the court.

A bell rang in the Marquis' chamber, and a great clang echoed loudly through the court, followed by a roar of water, as if a captive river had broken loose and grown suddenly frantic with freedom. The Marquis, already a good deal shaken, started violently. A torrent, visible by the light of its foam, shot from the archway, hurled itself against the chapel door, and vanished. Though sad and startled, the Marquis required no explanation—he laughed aloud and hurried from the room. When he came into the court, there was Tom Fool flying across the turf in mortal terror, his face white as another moon and his hair standing on end.

The first call of his master was insufficient to stop him. At the second, however, he halted and stood speechless. The Marquis, laying his hand on Tom's arm to satisfy himself that he was really as dry as he seemed, brought him to himself. He was soon able to tell how he had fallen asleep in the chapel, had waked and departed but a minute ago, and was crossing the court to his room when a hellish explosion—followed by the most frightful roaring, mingled with shrieks and demonic laughter—arrested him. The same instant he saw a torrent rush from the archway, full of dim figures wallowing and shouting. Then they all vanished, and the flood poured into the hall, wetting him to the knees and almost carrying him off his legs.

"Who were they whom thou sawest in the water, Tom?" asked the Marquis.

Tom shook his head with awful significance, looked behind him, and said nothing.

Seeing there was no more to be had from him, the Marquis sent him to bed. Then the Marquis walked up to the archway, seeing nothing save the grim wall of the impassive keep. Never doubting he had lost his chance by taking Tom for the culprit, the Marquis contented himself with the reflection that whoever the nightwalkers were, they had received both a fright and a ducking. He betook himself to bed, where in his dreams he saw little Molly in the arms of Mother Mary—who presently became his own beloved Lady Anne, and held out a hand to help him up beside them. Just then the bubble of sleep—unable to hold the swelling of his gladness—burst, and he woke as the first rays of the sun smote the gilded cock on the belltower.

The noise of the falling drawbridge and rushing water had roused Dorothy, along with most of the lighter sleepers in the castle, but they saw nothing save Tom's flight across the turf, its arrest by the Marquis, and their conference.

Meanwhile, Amanda and Rowland stood dripping inside the chapel door, where the sudden flood had cast them into a safe harbor. Amanda was crying even as the half-stunned Scudamore secured the door to the court.

All the time that the Marquis was drawing his story from Tom, the two stood trembling in great bewilderment and sensible misery, bruised, drenched, and horribly frightened, more even at what might be than by what had been. What were they to do next?

111

Amanda contributed nothing, for tears and reproaches resolve no enigmas. There were many ways of issue, but their watery trail, if soon enough followed, would be their ruin. Scudamore, the slave of perplexity, did nothing.

Presently they heard the approaching step of the Marquis, who stopped within a few feet of them. Through the thick door they could hear his asthmatic breathing. They kept as still as their trembling and the mad beating of their hearts would permit. But the Marquis never thought of the chapel, having concluded that the intruders had fled through the open hall. Had he not, however, been so weary and sad and listless, he would probably have found them, for he would have crossed the hall to look into the next court, and the absence of all wet footprints on the floor would have surely indicated the direction of their refuge.

The acme of terror happily endured but a moment. The sound of the Marquis' departing footsteps took the ghoul from their hearts; they began to breathe and to hope that the danger was gone. But, like wild animals overtaken by the daylight, they waited long ere they ventured to creep out of their shelter back to their quarters.

In the morning the Marquis was in no mood to begin any inquiry. His little lamb Molly had vanished from his fold, and he was sad and lonely. Had it been otherwise, the shabby doublet which Scudamore wore might have set him thinking.

Amanda did not show herself for several days; a bad cold luckily afforded sufficient pretext for the concealment of a bad bruise on her cheek.

Ere long, the lovers began to feel themselves safe, though for a whole fortnight they never dared exchange a word.

23.
The Aftermath

Rowland was inclined to attribute the mishap to the displeasure of Lord Herbert, whose supernatural powers had enabled him to both discover and punish their intrusion.

Amanda, on the other hand, felt certain that Dorothy had laid the watery snare with the hope of catching them, and she read in her, therefore, jealousy and cruelty as well as coldness and treachery. Dorothy's odd ways, lawless movements, and vulgar tastes had for some time been the subject of gossip, and it seemed to Amanda that in watching and discovering what she was about lay her best chance for revenge.

The charge of low tastes was founded upon the fact that Dorothy knew, and addressed by name, every artisan about the castle. Her detractors never found significance in the fact that she also knew and addressed by name every animal about the place. She would wander about the farmyard and stables for an hour at a time, visiting all that were there, and especially her little horse.

The charge of lawlessness was founded on another fact: she was often seen in the court after dusk, not only running to the keep—as she did at all hours—but loitering about in full view of the windows. This took place only when the organ was playing—but then who played the organ? Was not the poor afflicted boy, barring the blankness of his eyes, as beautiful as an angel? And so the tattling streams flowed on, and the ears of Mistress Amanda willingly listened to their music, nor did she disdain to contribute to the reservoir of fact and fiction, conjecture and falsehood.

Lord Herbert came home to bury his little one. All that was left of her was borne to the parish church of Raglan, and there laid beside the Marquis' father and mother. He remained a fortnight, and his presence was much needed to lighten the heavy gloom that settled over both his wife and his father.

As if it were not enough to bury the departed, there were those (including the Marquis and Lady Margaret) who sought to lay the stone of silence over the memory of the dead, never speaking of her but when compelled, and then almost as if to utter her name were an act of impiety. Radiant as she was by nature, Lady Margaret in sorrow could do little toward her own support. The Marquis said to himself, "I am growing old, and cannot smile at grief so well as I ought." Little Molly was never mentioned between them, but sudden floods of tears were the signs of the mother's remembrance, and the outbreak of ambushed sighs (hastily attributed to the gout) were the signs from the grandfather.

Dorothy too belonged to the unspeaking, but her spirit's day was evenly, softly lucent, like one of those clouded calm gray mornings of summer which seem more likely to end in rain than sunshine.

Lord Herbert was of a very different temperament. He had hope enough in his one single nature to serve the whole castle, if only he could have shared it. The veil between him and the future glowed with radiant fire. It was not that he, anymore than the rest, imagined he could see through it; for him it was enough that beyond it lay the luminous.

Such as he are misjudged as shallow by those who love them not. Depth to some is indicated by gloom, and affection by persistent brooding, as if there were no homage to the past of love save sighs and tears. When they meet a man whose eyes shine, whose step is light, and on whose lips hovers a smile, they shake their heads and say, "There goes one who has never loved, and therefore knows no sorrow." But that man is one over whom death has no power, whom neither time nor space can part from those he loves, and who lives in the future more than the past!

But even Lord Herbert had his moments of sad longing after his dainty Molly. Such moments came to him, however, not when he was at home with his wife, but when he rode by his troops on a night march, or when he sought sleep that he might fight better on the morrow.

24.
Marquis and the Mogul
1643

One evening Tom Fool and his groom friend Shafto were taking their selfish pastime of teasing the wild beasts, whose cages were in the basement of the kitchen tower, with a little semicircular yard before them. They were solid stone vaults, with open fronts grated with huge iron bars.

One panther, the Great Mogul, had a special dislike for grimaces, and therefore a special capacity for being teased. And so betwixt two bars of the cage, Tom was busy presenting the panther with one hideous face after another. But to his disappointment, Mogul on this occasion had resolved upon a dignified resistance to temptation, and had withdrawn in sultry displeasure to the back of his cage, where he lay sideways, deigning to turn neither his back nor his face toward Tom. One such glance would ruin his grand oriental sulk, and he would fly at the hideous ape-visage insulting him in his prison.

Tom grew more daring and threw little stones at him, but the panther seemed only to grow the more imperturbable, and to heed Tom's missiles as little as his grimaces. And at length Tom took stronger measures—he procured a pole to poke at the beast, but found the pole too thick at the base to pass through the bars far enough to reach the Mogul. Thereupon, in utter foolhardiness backed by Shafto, he undid the door a little way and pushed the pole right in the creature's face. One hideous yell—and though Shafto was holding the door, neither of them knew what was happening until they saw the tail of the panther disappearing over the six-foot wall that separated the cages from the stableyard.

Tom fled at once for the stair to the stone court, while Shafto ran to warn the stablemen and to get help to recapture the animal.

The panther, clearing the wall, no doubt hoped to find himself in the savage forest; instead, he came down in a hurricane of canine hate. An uproarious tumult of mad barking arose from the chained dogs and entered the ears of all in the castle, penetrating even those of the rather deaf host of the White Horse Inn in Raglan Village. Dorothy heard it while sitting in her room, and hurried to see what was the matter. Halfway across the stone court, Dorothy met Tom running, saw his face, and knew that something serious had happened.

"Get indoors, Mistress!" he cried. "The Great Mogul is out!"

Dorothy ran too, though not after Tom, but rather for the stableyard. Her first terror was the possible danger to her horse, and the first comfort that followed was the thought of her dog.

The panther, frightened by the maddened dogs, crept like a snake under what covert seemed readiest—a cart—and disappeared just as Shafto entered to look for him in a style wherein caution predominated. Seeing no trace of the beast, and concluding that it had been driven further by the clamor of the dogs, he went on across the yard before he became suddenly aware that his arm, not hurting until now, was both broken and torn. The sight of blood completed the mischief, and he fell down in a swoon.

Then Dorothy entered, and saw nothing but the dogs raging at their chains as if they would drag the earth itself after them to reach the enemy. When she specially noticed the fury of Marquis, she perceived the danger to him and all the dogs if the panther should attack them one by one on the chain, not one of them would have a chance. She sped across to Marquis, who fortunately was not far from the door. Feeling him a little safer now that she stood by his side, she looked about for the panther.

All the dogs were straining their chains in one direction, and all their lines converged upon the little cart. Under the cart, between the lowered shafts, she spied a doubtful luminosity, and there saw the two huge cat eyes. She checked the spot where her mastiff's chain was attached to his collar, for she would have kept the latter to defend his neck and throat—but the one was riveted to the other, and the two must go together.

And now she saw Shafto lying on the ground within a few yards of the shed. She first thought that the panther had killed him, but then she saw the terrible animal creeping out from under the cart with his great cat chin on the ground, making for the man.

With resolute though trembling hands, she undid Marquis' collar. Freed, the fine animal went at the panther like a bolt from a crossbow. But Dorothy loved him too well to lose a moment in even glancing after him. Leaving him to his work, she flew to hers, which lay at the next kennel, that of O'Brien, the Irish wolfhound, whose curling lip showed his long teeth to the very root and whose straining fury had redoubled at the sight of his rival shooting past him free for the fight. Then O'Brien too was loosed and on the panther, and the sounds of battle swelled.

But now she heard the welcome cries of men and a clatter of weapons. Some came rushing down the stair, and others were approaching from the opposite side, armed with scythes and pitchforks—the former more dangerous to man than to beast. Dorothy was now thoroughly excited by the conflict she ruled, although she had wasted not a moment in watching it. She had just freed the fourth dog, and was flying to let go the fifth when the crowd swept in; the beast was captured and the dogs taken off him, ere Dorothy had a glimpse of the battle. The men dragged the torn panther away with cartropes, and Tom Fool followed them with his hands in his pockets, sheepish because of the share he had in letting it loose, and of the share he had not had in securing him again.

Dorothy was looking for Marquis when he bounded up to her and, exultant in the sense of accomplished duty, leaped up against her, at once turning her bloody and frightful to behold. His wounds were bad, although none were serious except one in his throat which was so severe that to replace his collar was out of the question. In the confidence that she might now ask for him what she would, she led him out of the yard, up the stair, and across the stone court—making a red track all the way.

The Marquis had heard the first noises and warnings from his study, but had been in no such haste as Dorothy; only after a little, when the noise increased and other sounds mingled with it, did he rise in some anxiety. When he came out of the hall, he saw Dorothy and her mastiff, and looked pale and frightened himself before he perceived that she was bloody but unhurt.

He cast a glance at her disreputable attendant, and said, "Now I understand! It is that precious mastiff of yours, and no panther of mine, that has been making this uproar in my quiet house! Prithee keep him off me!"

He drew back, for the dog, not liking the tone in which he addressed his mistress, had taken a step nearer to him.

Dorothy, for the first and only time in her life angry with her benefactor, laid hold of the animal and said, "My Lord, you do my poor Marquis wrong. At the risk of his own life, he has just saved your lordship's groom Shafto from being torn in pieces by the Great Mogul."

While she spoke, some of the men who had secured the animal came up into the court. Their approach, in the relaxation of discipline following excitement, was rather tumultuous. At their head was Lord Charles, who had led them to the capture. As they saw Dorothy with her mastiff beside her, even in their lord's presence they could not resist the impulse to cheer her. Annoyed at their breach of manners, the Marquis had not however committed himself to displeasure ere he spied a joke.

"I told you so, Mistress Dorothy!" said the Marquis. "That rival of mine has, as I feared, already made a party against me. My own knaves, before my very face, cheer my enemy! I presume, My Lord," he went on, removing his hat to Marquis, "it will be my wisdom to resign castle and title at once, and so forestall deposition."

Marquis growled, and amidst subdued yet merry laughter Lord Charles hastened to enlighten his father. "My Lord, the dog has done nobly and deserves reward, not mockery—which it is plain he understands and likes not. But it was his fair mistress I and my men presumed to salute in your lordship's presence."

"Prithee, now, take me with thee," said the Marquis. "Was or was not the Great Mogul forth of his cage?"

"Indeed he was, My Lord, and might now be in the fields but for Cousin Vaughan. When we got into the yard, there was the Great Mogul with three dogs upon him, and Mistress Dorothy uncollaring another, and Shafto lying on the stones about three yards off the combat. It was the finest thing I ever saw, My Lord."

The Marquis turned to Dorothy. "Mean you . . . mean you—" he stammered, addressing Lord Charles, though staring at Dorothy.

"I mean, My Lord," answered his son, "that Mistress Dorothy, with rare courage and equal judgment, came to the rescue, stood her ground, and loosed dog after dog—her own first—upon the animal. And by heaven! It is owing to her that he is already secured and carried back to his cage, without any harm done save to Shafto and the dogs, of which poor Strafford hath a hind leg crushed by the jaws of the beast, and must be killed."

"He shall live!" cried the Marquis. "As long as he hath legs enough to eat and sleep with! Mistress Dorothy," he went on, "what is thy request?"

"Your Lordship sees my poor dog can endure no collar; let him therefore be my chamber-fellow until his throat be healed, when I shall again submit to your lordship's mandate."

"What thou wilt, Cousin. He is a noble fellow, and hath a right noble mistress," granted the Marquis.

"Will you, then, My Lord Charles," asked Dorothy, "order a bucket of water drawn for me, that I may wash his wounds ere I take him to my chamber?"

Ten men flew to the draw well, but Lord Charles ordered them all back to the guardroom. With his own hands he then drew three bucketfuls of water, which he poured into a tub, that Dorothy might wash her four-legged hero in the paved court. The Marquis looked on, smiling to see how the sullen animal allowed his mistress to handle his wounds without a whine, not to say even a growl at the pain she must have caused him.

"I see!" he said at length. "I have no chance with a rival like that." He walked slowly away up to the oak parlor, and sat there in his great chair, thinking of the courage and patience of the mastiff. "God made us both," he said, "and He can grant me patience as well as him."

His washing over, the exhausted dog followed his mistress up the grand staircase and the second spiral one that led yet higher to her chamber. There presently came Lady Elizabeth, carrying a cushion and deerskin for him to lie upon. The wounded and wearied Marquis followed his tail but one turn and, with apparent satisfaction, dropped like a log on his well-earned couch.

The night was hot, and Dorothy fell asleep with her door wide open. In the morning, Marquis was nowhere to be found, though Dorothy searched for him.

"It is because you mocked him," said Lord Charles to his father at breakfast. "I doubt not he said to himself, 'If I *am* a dog, my lord need not have mocked me, for I could not help it, and only

119

did my duty.' "

"I would make him an apology," returned the Marquis, "an' I had but the opportunity. But, Charles, didst thou ever learn how he got into the castle? It was assuredly thy part to discover that secret."

"No, My Lord, it has never been found out so far as I know."

"That is an unworthy answer, Lord Charles. As governor of the castle, thou shouldst to have had the matter thoroughly searched into."

"I will see to it now, My Lord," said the governor, rising.

And Lord Charles did inquire, but not a ray of light did he succeed in letting in upon the mystery. The inquiry might, however, have lasted longer and been more successful, had not Lord Herbert just then come home with the welcome news of the death of Lord John Hampden, from a wound received in attacking Prince Rupert at Chalgrove. He brought news also of Prince Maurice's brave fight at Bath, and Lord Henry Wilmot's victory over Sir William Waller at Devizes. The Queen had reached Oxford, bringing large reinforcement to her husband, and Prince Rupert had taken Bristol, castle and all.

Lord Herbert was radiant, and Lady Margaret, for the first time since Molly's death, was merry. The castle was enlivened, and the missing Marquis forgotten by all but Dorothy.

25.
Richard's Woes

Things looked ill for the Puritans in general, and Richard Heywood had his full portion of the allotted evils. Following Lord Thomas Fairfax, he had shared his defeat by the Marquis of Newcastle on Atherton Moor. Of his score of men he had lost five, and was, along with his mare, severely wounded. Hence, it had become absolutely necessary for both of them, if they were to render good service at any near future, to have rest and tending.

Toward the middle of July, therefore, Richard, Stopchase, and several others in need of nursing rode up to Roger Heywood's door. Lady was taken off to her own stall, and Richard was led into the house by his father—without a word of tenderness, but with eyes and hands that waited and tended like those of a mother.

Roger was troubled. There was now a strong peace party in Parliament, and to him peace and ruin seemed the same thing. If Parliament should listen to overtures of accommodation, everything for which he and his kind had striven was in the greatest peril. He was comforted in his anxiety that his son had showed himself worthy—not merely in the matter of personal courage, which he took for granted in a Heywood—but in his understanding of and spiritual relation to the questions really at issue, and not those only which filled the mouths of men. For the best men and the weightiest questions are never seen in their time, save by the few.

But now a doubt had come to Richard's mind—from his wounds, as he thought, and the depression belonging to the haunt-

121

ing sense of defeat. Because it was born *in* weakness, he very pardonably saw it as born *of* weakness, and therefore regarded it as weak and cowardly. What was all this fighting for? It was well indeed that no king nor bishop should interfere with a man's rights, either in matters of taxation or worship; but the war could set nothing right either betwixt him and his neighbor, or betwixt him and his God.

"Am I not free now?" he said to himself as he lay on his bed in his own gable. "Am I not free to worship God as I please? Who will interfere with me or prevent me? What are form and ceremony to worship? Shall I be better when all this is over, even if the best of our party carry the day? Will Cromwell rend for me the heavy curtain which threatens to come rolling down between me and Him whom I call my God? If I can pass within that curtain, what are Charles or Newcastle or the mighty Cromwell himself and all his Ironsides to me? Am I not on the wrong road for the high peak?"

But then he thought of other things—of the oppressed and superstitious, of injustice done and not endured, of priests who knew not God but substituted ceremonies for prayer and led the seeking heart afar from its goal—and he knew that his arm could at least fight for the truth in others, if only his heart could fight for the truth in himself. No, he would go on, but his business now was plainly to gain strength of body, that the fumes of weakness might no longer cloud his brain. If he had to die for the truth, he must die in power like the blast of an exploding mine, and not like the flame of an expiring lamp. And as his body grew stronger, his doubts grew weaker, and he became more and more satisfied that he was on the right path.

After a few days of oats and barley in profusion, Lady outstripped her master in the race for health. At least twice every day Richard went to see her, and envied the rapidity of her recovery from the weakness which scanty rations, loss of blood, and the inflammation of her wounds had caused.

But there was no immediate call for their services. The struggle was not now occurring in the fields of battle but in the house of words. Waller and Essex were almost without an army between them, and were at bitter strife with each other, while the peace party seemed likely to carry everything before them.

But at length, chiefly through the exertions of the presbyterian preachers and the Common Council of London, the peace party was defeated. A vigorous levying and pressing of troops began anew, and the hour had come for Richard to mount. His men were all in health and spirits, and their vacancies had been filled up. Lady was frolicsome, and Richard was perfectly well.

The day before they were to start, he took Lady out for a gallop across the fields. Never had he known her so full of life; she rushed at hedge and ditch as if they were squares of Royalist infantry. Her madness woke the fervor of battle in Richard's own veins, and that night he scarcely slept for eagerness to be gone.

Waking early, he dressed and armed himself and ran to the stables, where already his men were bustling about. Lady had a loose box for herself, and there Richard went, wondering as he opened its door that he did not hear her usual morning welcome. The box was empty.

He called Stopchase. "Where is my mare?" he asked. "Surely no one has been fool enough to take her to the water just as we are going to start."

Stopchase stood and stared without reply, then turned and left the stable, but came back immediately, looking horribly scared. Lady was nowhere to be seen or heard. Richard rushed about, storming, but not a man could enlighten him. All knew she was in the box the night before; none knew when she left it or where she was now.

He ran to his father, but Roger could say no more than was plain to everyone—the mare had been carried off in the night, and that with a skill worthy of a professional horsethief.

Richard wept, feeling half a soldier without his mare. His country called him, oppressed humanity cried aloud for his sword and arm, and his men waited for him, but Lady was gone. What was he to do?

"Never heed, Dick, my boy," said his father. Not once since his son had put on men's attire had he called him Dick. "You shall have my Oliver—a horse of good courage, as you know, and twice the weight of your little mare."

"Ah, Father! You do not know Lady so well as I. Not Cromwell's best horse could comfort me for her. I *must* find her. Go I will, if it be on a broomstick, but this morning I ride not. Let the men put up their horses, Stopchase, and break their fast."

"It is a wile of the enemy," said Stopchase.

"How much of her hay has she eaten?" asked Roger.

"About a bottle, Sir," answered Stopchase rather indefinitely. The conclusion was drawn that she had been taken very soon after the house was quiet.

Ever since the return of the soldiers, poor watch had been kept by the people of Redware. Increase of confidence had led to carelessness. Roger made inquiry, and had small reason to be satisfied with what he discovered.

"The thief must have known the place," said Stopchase. "How else swooped he so quietly upon the best animal?"

"She was in the place of honor," answered Mr. Heywood.

"Scudamore!" said Richard. "Sir," he said, turning to his father, "I would I had a plan of Raglan stables, for I believe Lady is at this moment in one of those vaults they tell us of."

"It may be. The Earl hath of late been generous in giving of horses. The King will find them poor soldiers that fight for horses—or for titles either. Such will never stand before them that fight for the truth. When the end cometh, we shall see how it hath all gone. When, then, will you ride?"

"Tomorrow, if it please you, Sir. I should fight but ill with the knowledge that I had left my best battlefriend in the hands of the Philistines, nor sent even a cry after her."

"What boots it, Richard? If she be within Raglan walls, they yield her not again. Bide your time, and when you meet your foe on your friend's back, woe betide him!"

"Amen, Sir! But with your leave I will not go today. I give you my promise I will go tomorrow."

"Be it so, then. Stopchase, let the men be ready at this hour on the morrow. The rest of the day is their own." So saying, Roger turned away, in no small distress both at the loss of the mare and his son's grief over it.

The moment he was gone, Richard saddled Oliver, rode slowly out of the yard, and struck across the fields. After a half-hour's ride he stopped at a lonely cottage at the foot of a rock on the banks of the River Usk. There he dismounted, fastened his horse to the little gate in front, and entered a small garden full of sweet-smelling herbs mingled with a few flowers. He knocked at the cottage door, and then lifted the latch.

26.
The Witch's Cottage

Goody Rees met Richard at the threshold and welcomed him with the kindness of an old nurse. She led the way across the tidy cottage to the one chair in the room, beside the hearth where the peat fire was smoldering. From the smoky rafters hung many bunches of dried herbs, which she used partly for medicines and partly for charms.

"I am in trouble, Mistress Rees," said Richard as he seated himself.

"Most men do be in trouble most times, Master Heywood. Dost thou find thou hast taken the wrong part, eh? 'Tis a bit easier to cast off a maiden than to forget her—eh?"

"No, Mistress Rees, I came not to trouble you concerning what is past and gone," said Richard with a sigh. "It is a taste of your knowledge I want rather than your skill. Tell me, have you not been within the gates of Raglan Castle?"

"Yes, My Son—oftener than I can tell thee, for my lad, who was turnspit there once upon a time, is now a great man with my lord and all the household."

"They tell strange things of the stables there—that they are underground. Do you think horses can fare well underground? You know a horse as well as a dog, Mother."

The old woman caught up a three-legged stool, set it down by Richard, seated herself at his knee, and assumed the look of mystery wherewith she garnished every bit of knowledge, real or fancied.

"Hear me, and hold thy peace, Master Heywood. Good horses go down into Raglan vaults—but yet when they lift their heads they look out to the ends of the world. In the pitched court, betwixt the antechamber to my lord's parlor and the great bay window of the hall, there goeth a descent—of stairs only, as it seemeth. But to him that knoweth how to pull a certain tricker, the whole thing turneth around, and straightway from a stair passeth into an easy sloping way by which the horses go up and down. The sloping way leadeth to vaults which pass under the Marquis' oak parlor, and under all the breadth of the court. Then there is a great iron door in the foundations of one of the towers, behind which is a stair by which they climb round and round, and ever the rounder the higher, as a fly might crawl up a corkscrew. And there is also a stair in the same screw by which the people of the house do go up and down, and know nothing of the way for horses within, neither of the stalls at the top of the tower where they stand and see the country. Yet they do often marvel at the sounds of hooves and harness and cries and the champing of corn. And that is how Raglan can send forth so many horsemen for the King.

"But alack! Master Heywood, thou art of the other part, and these are secrets of state within the castle! And what will become of me now that I have told them to a Heywood, myself being known as no more a Royalist than another?"

"What should it signify, Mother," said Richard, "so long as neither you nor I believe a word of it?"

"In good sooth, Master Heywood, I tell the tale as t'was told to me. I avouch it not for certain, knowing that my son Thomas hath a seething brain and loveth a joke passing well. But the stair for horses have I seen with mine own eyes, though for the horses to come and go, that truly I have not seen."

"I would I might see the place!" murmured Richard.

"But it boots not talking, Master Heywood. Thou art too well known for a Puritan—Roundhead they call thee. And thou hast given them and theirs too many hard knocks to let thee gaze on the wonders of their great house."

"Have you art enough, Mother, to set me within Raglan walls for an hour or two after midnight?"

"An' I had, I dared not use it," answered the old woman, "for is not my Lord Herbert there? His art is stronger than mine, and from his knowledge I could hide nothing. And I dare not for thy sake, either. Once inside those walls of stone, those gates of oak, and those portcullises of iron, thou comest not out alive again, I warrant thee."

"I would I knew what part of the wall a man might scramble over in the dark."

"Thinkest thou that My Lord Marquis has been fortifying his castle for two years that a young Heywood should make a vaulting horse of it? I know but one who knows the way over Raglan walls, and thou wilt hardly persuade him to tell thee," said Mother Rees.

She rose and went toward her sleeping chamber, where Heywood could now hear a scratching and whining. When she opened the door, out ran a wretched looking dog, huge and gaunt, with the red marks of recent wounds all over his body, and his neck swathed in a discolored bandage. He went straight to Richard, and began fawning upon him and licking his hands.

"My poor Marquis!" said Richard. "What evil has befallen you? What would your mistress say to see you thus?"

Marquis whined and wagged his tail as if he understood every word. Richard was stung to the heart, and could have taken Marquis in his arms.

"Has your mistress then forsaken you too?"

"I think not so," said Goody. "He hath been with her in the castle ever since she went there."

"Poor fellow, how you are torn!" said Richard. "What animal could have brought you into such a plight? But that you have beaten him I am well assured."

Marquis wagged an affirmative.

"Fangs of the biggest dog in Gwent never tore him like that, Master Heywood. Heark'ee now—he cannot tell his tale, so I must tell thee all I know of the matter. I was over to Raglan Village three nights agone, to get me a bottle of strong waters from mine host of the White Horse, when he told me that about an hour before there had come from the way of the castle the most terrible noise that ever pierced human ears, as if every devil in hell of dog or cat kind had broken loose, and fierce battle was waging between them in the Yellow Tower. I said little, but had my fears for Lord Herbert, and came home sad and slow and went to bed. Now what should wake me the next morning, just as daylight broke the neck of the darkness, but a pitiful whining and obstinate scratching at my door! And who should it be but that little lap dog now standing by thy knee! But had thou seen him then, Master Richard! It was the devil's hackles he had been through! Whether he had the better or the worse of the fight, like the wise dog he always was, he came off to old Mother Rees to be plaistered and physicked. But what perplexes my old brain is how, at that hour of the night, and him hardly able to stand when I let him in, he got out of that prison, watched as it is both night and day."

"He couldn't have come over the wall?"

"Had thou seen him thou would not so question."

"Then he must have come through it or under it—there are but three ways," said Richard to himself. "He's a *big* dog," he added aloud, regarding him thoughtfully and patting his head.

The dog whined and moved all his feet, one after the other, but without taking his chin off Richard's knee.

"Have you seen your mistress' little Dick, Marquis?" asked Richard.

Again the dog whined, moved his feet, and turned his head toward the door.

"Will you take me to Dick, Marquis?"

The dog turned and walked to the door, then stood and looked back, as if waiting for Richard to open it and follow him.

"No, Marquis, we must not go before night."

The dog returned slowly to his knee, and laid his chin on it.

"What will the dog do next, Mother? When he finds himself well again, I mean? Will he run from you?"

"He would be like neither dog nor man I ever knew, did he not," returned the old woman. "He will go back where he got his hurts, to revenge them if he may."

"Could you make sure of him that he runs not away till I come again? Do so as you love me, and I will be here with the darkness."

"An' I love thee, Master Richard? Nay, but I do love thy good face an' thy true words, be thou Puritan or Roundhead or whatever evil name the wicked fashion of the times granteth to men to call thee."

"Harken to me, Mother. I will call no names, but they of Raglan have, as I truly believe, stolen from me my Lady."

"Nay, nay, Master Richard! Did I not tell thee with my own mouth that she went of her own free will? And with Master Herbert?"

"Alas! I meant not Mistress Dorothy. She is lost to me—but so is my poor mare, Lady, which was stolen last night from Redware."

"But what dreamest thou of doing? Not surely, before all the saints in heaven, wilt thou adventure thy body within Raglan."

"This good dog," said Richard, stroking Marquis, "must have some way of leaving Raglan without the knowledge or will of its warders. And where dog can go, man may endeavor to follow."

"For the love of God, Master Heywood, what wouldst thou do inside that stone cage? Thy mare cannot overleap stone walls— and thinkest thou they will raise portcullis and open gate and drop drawbridge to let thee and her ride forth in peace?"

"What I shall do within the walls, I cannot tell, Mother, nor have I ever yet known much good in forecasting. It will be given me to meet what comes."

"I know better than to bar the path to a Heywood. And thou hast been vilely used, Young Master. I will do what I can to help thee gain thine own—and no more than thine own. Swear to me by the holy cross, Puritan as thou art, that thou wilt make no other use of what I tell thee but to free thy stolen mare."

"I will not swear by the cross, which was never holy, for thereby was the Holy slain. I will not swear at all, but will pledge the word of a man who fears God, that I will in no way dishonorable make use of that which you tell me. If that suffice not, I will go without your help, trusting in God who never made that mare to carry the enemy of the truth into battle."

"But what an' thou take the staff of strife to measure thy doings? That may seem honorable, done to an enemy, which thou would scorn to do to one of thine own part even if he wronged thee."

"Nay, Mother, but I will do nothing *you* would think dishonorable—that I promise you. I will use what you tell me for no manner of hurt to my Lord of Worcester or aught that is his. But Lady is *not* his, and her I will carry, if I may, from Raglan stables back to Redware."

"I am content. Hearken then. Raglan watchword for the rest of the month is 'Saint George and Saint Patrick.' May it stand thee in good stead."

"I thank you, Mother, with all my heart," said Richard, rising jubilant. "One day it may lie in my power to requite you."

"Thou hast requited me beforehand, Master Heywood, and old Mother Rees never forgets. However, the day of my need may yet come. Go now, and return with the last of the twilight."

129

27.
The Secret of the Keep

Richard left the cottage and mounted Oliver. To pass the time and indulge a painful memory, he rode round by Wyfern.

When he reached home, he found that his father had gone to pay a visit some miles off. He went to his own room, cast himself on his bed, and tried to think. But the birds of his thoughts would not come at his call, or, coming, would but perch for a moment, and again fly. Then his eyes fell upon his cousin Thomas Heywood's little folio, lying on the window seat where he had left it two years ago, and straightway his fluttering thoughts alighted there. He thought how the book had been lying there unopened all the months, while he had been passing through so many changes and commotions. How still the room had been around it, how silent the sunshine and the snow, while he had inhabited tumult— tumult in his heart, tumult of sorrows and vain longings, tumult of tongues and of swords! Where was his gain? Was he nearer to that center of peace which the book seemed to typify? The maiden loved from childhood had left him for a foolish king and a phantom church, but had he himself been pursuing anything better? He had been fighting for the truth—but how, of all loves, was he to grasp the thing his soul thirsted after?

To many a sermon had he listened since he left that volume there—in church, in barn, in open field—but the religion which seemed to fill all the horizons of the preachers' visions was to him little better than another tumult of words. But far beyond all the

130

tumults hung still that shapeless something bearing a name around which hovered a vague light of the dimly understood—after which, in every moment of unbreaking silence, his soul straightway began to thirst.

His thoughts went wandering away, and vision after vision arose and passed before him, now of war and now of love, now of earthly victory and now of unattainable felicity. And at length he decided to glance again into his cousin's book. He had but to stretch out his hand to take it, for his bed was close by the window. He turned over the volume, half thinking, half brooding.

"I will look again," he thought, "at the verses which that day my father gave me to read. Truly I did not well understand them."

Once more he read the poem through, and this time felt he had gained something—that he at least partly understood, and from the lines took courage to go on with his flight.

But to go on, he must first recover Lady. He rose, descended the little creaking stair of black oak to his father's study, and wrote a letter informing him of the intended attempt. The rest of his time after dinner he spent in making overshoes for Lady from an old buff jerkin. As soon as the twilight began to fall, he set out on foot for the witch's cottage.

She was expecting him, but with no hearty welcome.

"I had liefer by much thou had not come so pat upon thy promise, Master Heywood. Then I might have looked to move thee from thy purpose, for truly I like it not. But thou wilt never bring an old woman into trouble, Master Richard?"

"Or a young one either, if I can help it, Mother Rees," answered Richard. "But you must trust me, and tell me all I want to know."

He drew paper and pencil from his pocket, and began to question her as to the castle. With every answer he added to his roughly drawn plan.

"And at what hour does the moon rise, Mistress Rees?"

"She will be halfway to the top of her hill by midnight."

"Then it is time Marquis and I were going."

"Here, take some fern seed in thy pouch, that thou may walk invisible—or may eat if thou be hungered." She transferred something from her pocket to his.

She opened her chamber door and out came Marquis, who

walked to Richard and stood looking up in his face as if he knew perfectly well his business was to accompany him. Richard bade the old woman good-night and stepped from the cottage.

Fearing he might lose sight of the dog in the dark, Richard tied his handkerchief around Marquis' neck, and fastened to it the thong of his riding whip—the sole weapon he had brought with him. And so they walked together, Marquis pulling Richard on. Ere long, the moon rose, and the country dawned into the dim creation of the light.

On and on they trudged, Marquis pulling at his leash like a blind man's dog; and on and on beside them crept their shadows, flattened and distorted on the road. But when they had come within about two miles of Raglan, Marquis began to grow restless, and to snuffle about on one side of the way. When by a narrow bridge they had crossed a brook, the dog insisted on leaving the road and going down into the meadow to the left. Across field after field his guide led him until, but for the great keep towering dimly up into the moonlit sky, Richard could hardly have conjectured where he was. But ever as they came out of copse or hollow, there was the huge thing in the sky, nearer than before.

At last he descried a short stretch of the castle rampart beside them, and found they were on a rough carttrack to the quarry. Straight into the quarry Marquis went, pulling eagerly; but Richard was compelled to follow with caution, for the ground was rough and broken, and the moon cast black misleading shadows. Toward the blackest of these the dog led, and entered a hollow way. Richard went straight after him, guarding his head with his arm against a sudden descent of the roof. It was a very rough tunnel, forming part of one of Lord Herbert's later contrivances for the safety of the castle.

Richard could not even hazard a conjecture as to the distance they advanced before he heard the noise of a small runnel of water making an abrupt descent from some little height. Then the handle of the whip pulled upward and was left loose in his grasp; the dog was away, leaving the handkerchief at the end of the thong. So now he had to guide himself, and began to feel about him. He could touch both sides of the passage by stretching out his arms, and in front a tiny stream of water came down the face of the rough rock. But what had become of Marquis? The water must come from somewhere, and doubtless its channel had spare room enough for the dog to pass. He felt up the rock, and found that at about the height of his head the water came over an obtuse angle. Climbing a foot or two, he discovered that the opening was large enough for him to enter. Lengthened creeping was necessary, with water under him, pitch-darkness all about him, and the rock within an inch or two of his body all round. By and by the slope became steeper and the ascent more difficult. Then came a hot breath, and a pair of eyes gleamed before his face. Had he followed into the den of that animal which had so frightfully torn Marquis? No, it was Marquis himself, waiting.

"Go on, Marquis," he said, with a sigh of relief.

The dog obeyed, and in another moment a waft of cool air came in. Presently a glimmer of light appeared, through an alarmingly narrow opening a little higher than his head. But as he crept nearer it grew wider, and when he came under it he found it large enough to let him through. When cautiously he poked up his head, there was the huge mass of the keep towering above him! On a level with his eyes, the lilied waters of the moat lay betwixt him and the citadel.

Marquis had brought him to the one neglected spot of the whole building. Before the well was sunk in the keep, the supply of water to the moat had been far more bountiful, and provision for free overflow was necessary. For facility in construction, the passage had been made larger than needful at the end next to the moat. About midway to its outlet—a mere drain-mouth in a swampy hollow—it had narrowed to a third of its compass. But the quarriers had cut across it above the point of contraction. No danger of access had occurred to Lord Herbert or the quarry surveyor, and since they found a certain service in the tiny waterfall, they had left it as it was.

28.
Raglan Stables

The overflow passage was under the sunken walk which enclosed the keep and its moat, and the only way out was into the moat. As quietly as Richard could, he got through the opening and into the water, among the lilies, where he swam gently along. As he looked up from the water, however, to the huge craglike tower over his head, the soft moonlight smoothing the rigor but bringing out all the wasteness of the grim blank, it seemed a hopeless attempt he had undertaken. But he kept his eye on the tower side of the moat, and had not swum far before he caught sight of the little stair enclosed in one of the six small round bastions, which led up from the moat to the walk immediately around the citadel. The foot of this stair was one of the only two points in the defenses of the moat not absolutely commanded from either gate of the castle. The top of the stair, however, was visible from one extreme point over the western gate, and the moment Richard put his head out of the bastion, he caught sight of a warder far away against the moonlit sky. He drew back and sat down on the top of the stair, to think and let the water run from his clothes. When he issued, it was on all fours.

He had to go round the tower in search of some way to reach the courts beyond, and no sooner had he passed the next angle than he found himself within sight of one of the towers of the main entrance. He crept slowly along, as close as he could squeeze to the root of the wall; when he rounded the next angle, he was in the shadow of the keep, and he had but to cross the walk to be covered by the parapet on the edge of the moat. This he did, and having crept round the curve of the next bastion, he was just beginning to fear lest he should find only a lifted drawbridge and have to take to the water again, when he came to the stone bridge.

It was well for him that Dorothy and Caspar had now omitted the setting of their watertrap; otherwise he would have entered the fountain court in a manner unfavorable to his project. As it was, he crossed in safety, never ceasing his slow crawl until he found himself in the archway. Here he stood up, straightened his limbs, and went through a few silent, energetic gymnastics to send the blood through his chilled veins.

Peering from the mouth of the archway, he saw to his left the fountain court with the gleaming head of the great horse rising from the sea of shadow into the moonlight. Close to his right was an open door into the great hall, and opposite the door glimmered the large bay window of which Mrs. Rees had spoken.

The stables opened on the pitched court, and in that court was the main entrance with its double portcullis and drawbridge. But in front of it was a great flight of steps the whole depth of the ditch, with the marble gate at the foot of them. Not knowing the carriageway, he feared both suspicion and loss of time where a single moment might be all that divided failure from success. Speed was essential, seeing that at any moment sleeping suspicion might awake, and find enough to keep her so. But at the other gate was but one portcullis and no drawbridge, while from it he knew perfectly the way to the brick gate. And he thought he could turn to account his knowledge of the fact that the Marquis' room was over it. Clearly this was the preferable path for his attempt.

He pulled off his shoes and stepped softly into the hall. A little moonlight fell on the northern gable wall, and in the shadow under the minstrel's gallery he found the door he sought, standing open but dark.

Gliding along by the side of the hall and round the great bay window, he came to the stair indicated by Goody Rees, and descending a little way, stood and listened. Plainly enough to his practiced ear, the underground passage to the airiest of stables was itself full of horses. To go down among these in the dark, and in ignorance of the construction of the stable, was somewhat perilous, but he had not come there to avoid risk. Step by step he stole softly down and seated himself on the last stair, to wait until his eyes should grow accustomed to the darkness.

Then Richard began to whistle, very softly, a certain tune well known to Lady, one he always whistled when he fed or curried her himself. A low, drowsy whinny replied from the depths of the darkness before him, and Richard's heart leaped in his bosom for joy. He ceased for a moment, then whistled again. Again came the response, but this time, although still soft and low, free from all wooliness of sleep. He dropped on his hands and knees, and crawled carefully along for a few yards, then stopped, whistled again, listened, and soon found himself at Lady's restless heels.

He crept into the stall beside her, spoke to her in a whisper, got up on his feet, caressed her, and told her to be quiet. Pulling the buff shoes from his pockets, he drew them over her hooves and tied them securely about her pasterns. Then with one stroke of his knife he cut her halter, hitched the end round her neck, and led her softly through the stable and up the stair. She followed like a cat, though not without some noise, to whose echoes Richard's bosom seemed the beaten drum. The moment her back was level, he flung himself upon it, and rode straight through the porch and into the hall.

But here he was overtaken by an ally unequal to the emergency. Marquis, who had been occupied with his friends in the stableyard, came bounding up into the court just as Richard threw himself on the back of his mare. At the sight of Lady with her master on her back—a vision of older and happier times—Marquis rushed through the hall like a whirlwind, and burst into a tempest of barking in the middle of the fountain court. There was not a moment to lose. Richard rode out of the hall and made for the gate.

29.
The Apparition

The voice of her lost Marquis roused Dorothy at once. She sprang from her bed, flew to the window, and flung it wide. That same moment, from the shadows about the hall door, came forth a man on horseback, riding along the tiled path to the fountain where never horse had trod. The tramp sounded far away, and woke no echo in the echo-haunted place. A phantom surely—horse and man! As they drew nearer the head of the rider rose out of the shadow into the moonlight, and she recognized Richard and Lady. Dorothy trembled from head to foot. Were they both dead, slain in battle, and Richard here to pay her a last visit ere he left the world? On they came. Her heart swelled up into her throat, and the effort to control herself and neither shriek or drop on the floor was like struggling to support a falling wall. When the specter reached the marble fountain, it drew bridle, looked keenly around, and turned in the direction of the gate, heedless of her presence. A pang of disappointment shot through her bosom, and for the moment quenched her sense of relief from terror. She noted how draggled and soiled his garments were, how his hair clung about his temples, and that his mare had only a halter. Yet Richard sat erect and proud, and Lady stepped like a mare full of life and vigor. And there was Marquis, not cowering or howling as dogs do in spectral presence, but jubilantly bounding and barking!

The acme of her bewilderment was reached when the phantom came under the Marquis' study window and called aloud, "Ho, Master Eccles! Must my lord's business cool while you rub your sleepy eyes awake? What? Yes, My Lord, I will punctually attend to your lordship's orders. Expect me back within the hour."

The last words were uttered in a much lower tone, with respect, but quite loud enough to be distinctly heard by Eccles or anyone else in the court.

Dorothy leaned from her window and looked sideways to the gate, expecting to see the Marquis bending over his windowsill and talking to Richard. But his window was closed shut, nor was there any light behind it.

A minute or two passed, during which she heard the combined discords of the rising portcullis. Then out came Eccles, slow and sleepy.

"By St. George and St. Patrick!" cried Richard. "Why keep six legs standing idle? Is your master's business nothing to you?"

Eccles looked up at him. He was coming to his senses.

"Thou ridest in strange graith on my lord's business," he said, as he put the key in the lock.

"What is it to you? Open the gate, and make haste. If it please my lord that I ride thus to escape eyes that else might see further than mine, keen as they are, Master Eccles, it is nothing to you."

The lock clanged, the gate swung open, and Richard rode through.

By this time Dorothy was convinced that something was wrong. By what authority was Richard riding from Raglan with muffled hoofs between midnight and morning? His speech to the Marquis was plainly a pretense, and doubtless that to Eccles was equally false. To allow him to pass unchallenged would be treason against both her host and her King.

"Eccles! Eccles!" she cried, her voice ringing clear through the court. "Let not that man pass."

"He gave the word, Mistress," said Eccles, in dull response.

"Stop him, I say," cried Dorothy again, with frantic energy, as she heard the gate swing to heavily. "You shall be held to account."

"He gave the word. He's a true man, Mistress," returned Eccles in a tone of self-justification. "Heard you not My Lord Marquis give him his last orders from his window?"

"There was no Marquis at the window. Stop him, I say."

"He's gone," said Eccles quietly, but with awaking uneasiness.

"Run after him!" Dorothy screamed. "Stop him at the gate! It is

138

young Heywood of Redware, one of the busiest of the Round-heads."

Eccles was already running and shouting and whistling, and she heard his feet resounding from the bridge. With trembling hands she flung a cloak about her, and sped barefoot down the grand staircase and along the north side of the court to the belltower, where she seized the rope of the alarm and pulled with all her strength. A piercing clangor tore the stillness of the night, echoed by the response from the buildings around. Window after window flew open, head after head popped out—among the first that of the Marquis, shouting to know what was amiss. But the question found no answer. The courts began to fill. Some said the castle was on fire; others, that the wild beasts were all out; others, that Waller and Cromwell had scaled the rampart, and were now storming the gates; others, that Eccles had turned traitor and admitted the enemy. In a few minutes all was outcry and confusion.

The moment Richard was clear of the portcullis, he set off at a sharp trot for the brick gate, and had almost reached it when he became aware that he was pursued. He knew to whom he owed it—he had heard the voice of Dorothy as he rode out. But yet there was a chance. Rousing the porter with such a noisy reveille as drowned in his sleepy ears the cries of the warder and those that followed him, he gave the watchword, and the huge key was just turning in the wards when the clang of the alarm bell suddenly filled the air. The porter stayed his hand, and stood listening.

"Open the gate," said Richard in authoritative tone.

"I will know first, Master—" began the man.

"Do you not hear the bell?" cried Richard. "How long will you endanger the castle with your dullness?"

"I shall know first," repeated the man deliberately, "what the bell—"

Ere he could finish the sentence, the butt of Richard's whip laid him along the threshold of the gate. Richard flung himself from his horse and turned the key, but his enemies were now close at hand. If the porter had but fallen the other way! Ere he could open the gate, they were on him with blows and curses. But the Puritan's blood was up, and with the heavy handle of his whip he felled one and wounded another ere he himself was stretched on the ground with a sword cut in the head.

30.
Richard and the Marquis

Dorothy flew back to her chamber, hurried on her clothes, and descended again to the court, which was now in full commotion. The western gate stood open, with the portcullis beyond it high in the wall, and there she took her stand, waiting the return of Eccles and his men.

Presently Lord Charles came through the hall from the stone court, and seeing the gate open, called aloud in anger to know what it meant. Receiving no reply, he ran to drop the portcullis.

"Is there a mutiny amongst the rascals?" he cried.

"There is no cause for dread, My Lord," said Dorothy from the shadow of the gateway.

"How know you that, Fair Mistress?" returned Lord Charles. "You must not inspire us with too much of your spare courage. That would be to make us foolhardy."

"Indeed, there is nothing to fear, My Lord," persisted Dorothy. "The warder and his men have but this moment rushed out after one on horseback, whom they had let pass with too little question. They are ten to one," added Dorothy with a shudder, as the sounds of the fray came up from below.

"If there is no cause for fear, Cousin, why look you so pale?" asked Lord Charles, for the gleam of a torch had fallen on Dorothy's face.

"I think I hear them returning, doubtless with a prisoner," said Dorothy, and stood with her face turned aside, looking anxiously through the gateway and along the bridge. She had obeyed her conscience, and had now to fight her heart, which would insist on hoping that her efforts had been foiled. But in a minute more came Eccles leading Lady in grim silence; next came Richard, pale and bleeding, betwixt two men, each holding him by an arm; the rest of the guard crowded behind. As they entered the court, Richard caught sight of Dorothy, and his face shone into a wan smile.

"Bring the prisoner to the hall," Lord Charles cried.

Eccles led the mare away, and the rest took Richard to the hall, which was soon lighted in a blaze of candles about the dais. When Dorothy entered, it was crowded with household and garrison; she placed herself near the door where she could see Richard.

"What meaneth all this tumult?" the Marquis began. "Who rang the alarm bell?"

"I did, My Lord," answered Dorothy in a trembling voice.

"Thou, Mistress Dorothy!" exclaimed the Marquis. "Then I doubt not thou hadst good reason for doing so. Prithee what was the reason? Verily it seems thou wast sent hither to be the guardian of my house! But come now, instruct me. Who is this prisoner, and how comes he here?"

"He be young Mr. Heywood of Redware, My Lord, and a pestilent Roundhead," answered one of his captors.

"Who knowest him?"

A moment's silence followed before Dorothy's voice came again, "I do, My Lord."

"Tell me then all thou knowest from the beginning, Cousin," said the Marquis.

"I was roused by the barking of my dog," Dorothy began.

"How came *he* hither again?"

"My Lord, I know not. But I heard him bark in the court, and looking from my window I saw Mr. Heywood riding through on horseback. Ere I could recover from my astonishment, he had passed the gate, and then I rang the alarm bell," said Dorothy.

"Who opened the gate for him?"

"I did, My Lord," said Eccles. "He made me believe he was talking to your lordship at the study window."

"Ha! A cunning fox!" said the Marquis. "And then?"

"And then Mistress Dorothy fell out upon me—"

"Let thy tongue wag civilly, Eccles."

"He speaks true, My Lord," said Dorothy. "I did fall out upon him, for he was but half awake, and I knew not what mischief

141

might be at hand."

"Eccles is obliged to thee, Cousin. And so the lady brought thee to thy senses in time to catch him?"

"Yes, My Lord."

"How comes he wounded? He was but one to a score."

"My Lord, he would else have killed us all."

"He was armed then?"

Eccles was silent.

"Was he armed?" repeated the Marquis.

"He had a heavy whip, My Lord."

"Hm!" said the Marquis, and turned to the prisoner. "Is thy name Heywood, Sirrah?" he asked.

"My Lord, if you treat me as a clown, you shall have but a clown's manners of me."

" 'Fore heaven! Our squires would rule the roost."

"He that doth right, marquis or squire, will one day rule, My Lord," said Richard.

" 'Tis well said," returned the Marquis. "I ask thy pardon, Mr. Heywood. In times like these a man must be excused for occasionally dropping his manners."

"Assuredly, My Lord, when he stoops to recover them as gracefully as doth the Marquis of Worcester."

"What then would'st thou in my house at midnight, Mr. Heywood?" asked the Marquis courteously.

"Nothing save mine own, My Lord. I came but to look for a stolen mare."

"What! Thou takest Raglan for a den of thieves?"

"I found the mare in your lordship's stable."

"How then came the mare in my stable?"

"That is not a question for me to answer, My Lord."

"Doubtless thou didst lose her in battle against thy sovereign."

"She was in Redware stable last night, My Lord."

"Which of you knaves stole the gentleman's mare?" cried the Marquis. "But Mr. Heywood," he continued, "there can be no theft upon a rebel. He is by nature an outlaw, and his life and goods forfeit to the King."

"He will hardly yield the point, My Lord. So long as Might, the sword, is in the hand of Right, the—"

"By Right, I suppose you mean, the Roundhead," interrupted the Marquis. "Who carried off Mr. Heywood's mare?"

"Tom Fool," answered a voice from the obscure distance.

A buzz of suppressed laughter followed, which instantly ceased as the Marquis looked angrily around.

"Stand forth, Tom Fool," he said.

Through the crowd came Tom, and stood before the dais, looking frightened and sheepish.

"Sure I am, Tom, thou didst never go to steal a mare of thine own notion; who went with thee?" said the Marquis.

"Mr. Scudamore, My Lord," answered Tom.

"Ha, Rowland! Art thou there?" cried his lordship.

"I gave him fair warning two years ago, My Lord, and the King wants horses," said Scudamore cunningly.

"Rowland, I like not such warfare. Yet can the Roundheads say naught against it, who would filch kingdom from King and Church from bishops," said the Marquis, turning to Heywood.

"As they from the Pope, My Lord," rejoined Richard.

"True," answered the Marquis, "but the bishops are the fairer thieves, and may one day be brought to reason and restitution."

"As I trust your lordship will in respect of my mare."

"Nay, that can hardly be. She shall go to Gloucester to the King. I would not have sent to Redware to fetch her, but finding thee and her in my house at midnight, it would be plain treason to set such enemies at liberty. What! Hast thou fought against His Majesty? Thou art scored like an old buckler!"

Richard had started on his adventure very thinly clad, for he had expected to find all possible freedom of muscle necessary. In the scuffle at the gate, his garment had been torn open, and the eye of the Marquis had fallen on the scar of a great wound on his chest, barely healed.

"What age art thou?"

"One and twenty, My Lord—almost."

"And what wilt thou be by the time thou art one and thirty, an' I let thee go?" said the Marquis thoughtfully.

"Dust and ashes, My Lord, most likely. Faith, I care not." As he spoke, he glanced at Dorothy, but she was looking on the ground.

"Nay, nay!" said the Marquis feelingly. "These are but wild and hurling words for a fine young fellow like thee. Long ere thou be a man, the King will have his own again, and all will be well. Come, promise me thou wilt never more bear arms against His

Majesty, and I will set thee and thy mare at liberty the moment thou shalt have eaten thy breakfast."

"Not to save ten lives, My Lord, would I give such a promise."

"Roundhead hypocrite!" cried the Marquis, frowning to hide the gleam of satisfaction he felt breaking from his eyes. "What wilt thy father say when he hears thou liest deep in Raglan dungeon?"

"He will thank heaven that I lie there a free man instead of walking abroad a slave," answered Richard.

" 'Fore heaven!" said the Marquis, and was silent for a moment. "Owest thou then thy King *nothing*, Boy?" he resumed.

"I owe the truth everything," answered Richard.

"The truth!" echoed the Marquis.

"Now speaks my Lord Worcester like Pilate," said Richard.

"Hold thy peace, Boy," returned the Marquis sternly. "Thy godly parents have ill taught thee thy manners. How knowest thou what was in my thought when I did but repeat after thee the sacred word thou didst misuse?"

"My Lord, I was wrong and I beg your lordship's pardon. But an' your lordship were standing here with your head half beaten in, and your clothes-"

Here Richard bethought himself, and was silent.

"Tell me how thou gat'st in, and thou shalt straight to bed."

"My Lord," returned Richard, "you have taken my mare, and taken my liberty, but the devil is in it if you take my secret."

"I would thy mare had been poisoned ere she drew thee hither on such a fool's errand! I want neither thee nor thy mare, and yet I may not let you go!"

"A moment more, and it had been an exploit, and no fool's errand, My Lord."

"Then the fool's cap would have been thine, Eccles. How camest thou to let him out? Thou a warder, and open the gate and up portcullis 'twixt waking and sleeping!"

"Had he wanted in, My Lord, it would have been different," said Eccles. "But he only wanted out, and gave the watchword."

"Where got'st thou the watchword, Mr. Heywood?"

"I will tell you what I gave for it, My Lord. More I will not."

"What gavest thou then?"

"My word that I would work neither you nor yours any hurt."

"Then there are traitors within my gates!" cried the Marquis.

"Truly, that I know not, My Lord," answered Richard.

"Prithee tell me how thou gat thee into my house, Mr. Heywood. It were but neighborly."

"It were but neighborly, My Lord, to hang young Scudamore and Tom Fool for thieves."

"Tell me how thou gat hold of the watchword, and I will set thee free, and give thee thy mare again."

"I will not, My Lord."

"Then the devil take thee!" said the Marquis, rising.

Richard reeled, and but for the men about him, would have fallen heavily. Dorothy darted forward, but could not come near him for the crowd.

"My Lord Charles," cried the Marquis, "see that the poor fellow is taken care of. Let him sleep, and perchance on the morrow he will listen to reason. Mistress Watson will see to his hurts. I would to God he were on our side! I like him well."

The men took him up and followed Lord Charles to the housekeeper's apartment, where they laid him on a bed on a little turret and left him, still insensible, to her care, with injunction to turn the key in the lock if she went from the chamber but for a moment. "For who can tell," thought Lord Charles, greatly perplexed, "but as he came he may go?"

Some of the household had followed them, and several of the women would gladly have stayed, but Mrs. Watson sent all away. Gradually the crowd dispersed, the castle grew still, and most of its inhabitants fell asleep again.

"A hot-livered Roundhead coxcomb!" said the Marquis to himself, pacing his room. "I doubt not the boy would tell everything rather than see his mare whipped. He's a fine fellow, and it were a thousand pities he turned coward and gave in. But the affair is not mine—it is the King's. Would to God the rascal were on our side! He's the right old English breed. How could he ever dream of carrying off a horse from the courts of Raglan Castle? And yet, by Saint George, he would have done it too, but for that brave Vaughan wench! What a couple the two would make! They'd give us a race of Arthurs and Orlandos between them. God be praised there are such left in England! Those coward rascals need never have mauled him like that. Yet, had the blow gone a little deeper, it had been a mighty gain to our side. Out he shall not go till the war be over, else it would be downright treason."

So ran the thoughts of the Marquis as he paced his chamber. But at length he lay down once more, and sought refuge in sleep.

31.
The Sleepless

Amanda Serafina Fuller lay awake thinking. She was a twig
or leaf upon one of many decaying branches which yet
drew what life they had from an ancient genealogical tree.
Property gone, but the sense of high birth swollen to a vice, the
one thought in her mother's mind had been how, with stinted
resources, to make the false impression of plentiful ease. For one of
the most disappointing things in high descent is that the descent is
occasionally into depths of meanness.

Hence Amanda had been brought up with the ingrained idea
that she and her widowed mother had been wronged, spoiled indeed of their lawful rights, by a combination of their rich relatives.
In truth they had been the objects of very considerable generosity,
which they resented the more that it had been chiefly exercised by
such of the family as could least easily afford it.

The evil tendencies which she had inherited had been nourished
in her from birth—chief of these envy and a strong tendency to
dislike. Mean herself, she suspected others, and found much pleasure in penetrating what she took to be disguise, and laying bare
the despicable motives which her own character enabled her either
to discover or imagine.

One redeeming element in Amanda was her love to her mother,
but it partook of the nature of a cultivated selfishness, and had lost
much of its primal grace. The remaining chance for such a woman
was that she should either fall in love with a worthy man or, by
her own conduct, be brought into dismal disgrace.

She had stood in the hall within a few yards of Dorothy, and had intently watched her face all the time Richard was before the Marquis. But Amanda was not able to read the heart, for without love there can be no understanding. Hate will sharpen observation, affording opportunity for many a shrewd guess, and the construction of clever and false theories, but will leave the observer blind to the whole.

Amanda came quickly enough to the conclusion that the sly puritanical minx was in love with the handsome young Roundhead. What else could explain the deathly pallor of her countenance while she fixed her eyes wide and unmoving upon his face, and the flush that ever and anon swept its red shadow over the pallor as she cast them on the ground at some brave word from his lips? But how, in that case, was her share in his capture to be explained? But here Amanda constructed a very clever theory, taking for granted that Dorothy's nature corresponded to her own. This was her theory: Dorothy had expected Richard, and had contrived his admission. His presence betrayed by the mastiff, and his departure challenged by the warder, she had flown instantly to the alarm bell, to screen herself in any case, and to secure the chance, if he should be taken, of liberating him later without suspicion. The theory was a bold one, but then it accounted for all the points—among the rest, how he had gotten the password and why he would not tell.

Of all times since she had learned to mistrust her, this night must Dorothy be watched; and it was with a gush of exultation over her own acuteness that she saw her follow the men who bore Richard from the hall.

If Dorothy knew more of her own feelings than she who watched her, she was far less confident that she understood them. Indeed, she had found them strangely complicated and difficult to control, while she stood gazing on the youth who through her found himself helpless and wounded in the hands of his enemies. He was all in the wrong, no doubt—a rebel against his King, and an apostate from the Church of his country; but he was the same Richard with whom she had played all her childhood, whom her mother had loved, and between whom and herself had never fallen shadow before that cast by the sudden outblaze of the star of childish preference into the sun of youthful love. And was it not when the shadows swept between them, and separated them forever, that first she knew how much she had loved him? Love of child or love of maiden, Dorothy never asked herself which it had been, or how it was now. But now all was over, for Richard had taken the path of presumption, rebellion, and violence. Yet how then came her heart to beat with such a strange delight at every answer he made to the Marquis? How was it that his approval of the intruder made her heart swell with pride and satisfaction, causing her to forget the youth's rude rebellion?

For the moment, her heart had the better of her conscience. In the delight which the manliness of the young fanatic awoke in her, she even forgot the dull pain which had been gnawing at her heart ever since first she saw the blood streaming down his face as he passed her in the gateway. But when at length he fell fainting in the arms of his captors, and the fear that she had slain him writhed through her heart, it was with a grim struggle indeed that she kept silent. The voice of the Marquis, committing him to the care of Mrs. Watson instead of the rough ministrations of the guard, came with the power of a welcome restorative, and she hastened after his bearers to satisfy herself that the housekeeper understood that he was carried to her at the Marquis' behest. She then retired to her own chamber, in the corridor passing Amanda, whose room was in the same quarter.

The moment her head was on her pillow the great fight began. She had done her duty, but what a remorseless thing that duty was! She did not, she could not, repent that she had done it, but her heart *would* complain that she had had it to do. She had not yet learned the mystery of her relation to the Eternal, whose nature in His children first shows itself in the feeling of duty. Dorothy was not yet capable of knowing that, however like it may look to a hardship, no duty can be other than a privilege. Nor did she perceive that she was already rewarded for the doing of the painful task, at the memory of which her heart ached and rebelled. Had it fallen to someone else to defeat Richard's intent and secure his person, she would have both suffered and loved less. The love was the reward of the duty done.

Even as her wearied brain was sinking under the waves of sleep, up rose the face of Richard from its depths, deathlike, with matted curls and bloodstained brow, and drove her again ashore on the rocks of wakefulness. And then instead of the face of Richard it was his voice, ever calling aloud for help in a tone of mingled entreaty and reproach, until at last she could no longer resist the impression that she was warned to go and save him from some impending evil. She rose, threw on a dressing gown, and set out in the dim light to find again the room into which she had seen him carried.

There was yet another in the house who could not sleep—Tom Fool. He had a strong suspicion that Richard had learned the watchword from his mother who, like most people desirous of a reputation for superior knowledge, was always looking out for scraps and orts of peculiar information. When Mother Rees had succeeded, without much difficulty on her own, or sense of risk on her son's part, in drawing from him the watchword of the week, she was aware in herself of a huge accession of importance. She felt as if she had been entrusted with the keys of the main entrance, and she trod her clay floor as if the fate of Raglan were hid in her bosom, and the great pile rested in safety under the shadow of her wings. But her imagined gain was likely to prove her son's loss, for, as Tom reasoned with himself, would Mr. Heywood, now that he knew him for the thief of his mare, persist in refusing to betray his mother? If not, then the fault would at once be traced to him, with the least result of disgraceful expulsion from the Marquis' service. Almost any other risk would be preferable.

But he had yet another ground for uneasiness. He knew well his mother's attachment to young Mr. Heywood, and had taken care she should have no suspicion of the way he was going after leaving her the night he told her the watchword. Such was his belief in her possession of supernatural powers, that he feared the punishment she would certainly inflict for the wrong done to Richard, should it come to her knowledge, even more than the wrath of the Marquis. For both of these reasons he must try to strengthen Richard in his silence, and was prepared with an offer, or promise of assistance in his escape.

As soon as the house was once more quiet, he got up, and made his way through dusk and dark, through narrow passage and wide chamber, until at last he stood, breathless with anxiety and terror, at the door of the turret chamber.

32.

The Turret Chamber

Mrs. Watson had gently bound up Richard's wounded head and given him a composing draught, before sitting down by his bedside. As soon as she saw it begin to take effect, she withdrew, in the certainty that he would not move for some hours at least. Although he did fall asleep, Richard's mind was too restless and anxious to yield itself to the natural influence of the potion. He had given his word to his father that he would ride on the morrow; the morrow had come, and here he was!

The key was in the lock, and Tom Fool softly turned it, then lifted the latch, peeped in, and entered. Richard started to his elbow and stared wildly about him. Tom made him an anxious sign; Richard, fevered but half-awake, kept silence, while Tom approached the bed and began to talk rapidly in a low, trembling voice. Richard gathered that his visitor was running no small risk in coming to him, and was in mortal dread of discovery. He needed but the disclosure of who Tom was, which presently followed, to spring upon him and seize him by the throat.

"Master, Master!" Tom gurgled, "let me go. I will swear any oath you please—"

"And break it any moment you please," returned Richard through his set teeth. He caught with his other hand the coverlid, dragged it from the bed, and twisting it first round Tom's face, flung the remainder about his body. Then, threatening to knock his brains out if he made the least noise, he proceeded to tie him up in it. No sound escaped poor Tom beyond a continuous mumbled entreaty through its folds. Richard laid him on the floor, pulled all the bedding upon the top of him, glided out, and closed the door. To Tom's unspeakable relief, Richard did not lock it behind him.

Tom's sole anxiety was now to get back to his garret unseen, and nothing was further from his thoughts than giving the alarm. The moment Richard was out of sight and hearing, Tom devoted his energies to getting clear of his entanglement, which he did not find very difficult. Then stepping softly from the chamber, he crept with a heavy heart back as he had come through a labyrinth of byways.

About half an hour after, Dorothy came gliding through a long circuit of corridors. Gladly would she have avoided passing Amanda's door, and involuntarily she held her breath as she approached it, stepping as lightly as a thief. But the moment she had passed, Amanda peeped out and crept after her barefooted, and to her joy, saw Dorothy enter the chamber and close the door behind her. Then Amanda made one noiseless tiger bound, turned the key, and sped back to her own chamber.

Dorothy was startled by the slight click, but concluded at once it was nothing but a further fall of the latch, and was glad it was no louder. The same moment she saw, by the dim rushlight, the signs of struggle which the room presented, and discovered that Richard was gone. Her first emotion was an undefined agony—they had murdered him, or carried him off to a dungeon! There were the bedclothes in a tumbled heap upon the floor! And, yes, it was blood with which they were marked! Sickened at the thought, and forgetting all about her own situation, she sank on the chair by the bedside.

Knowing the castle as she did, she was convinced that if he had met with violence it must have been in attempting to escape. And if he had made the attempt, might he not have succeeded? There had certainly been no fresh alarm given. But upon this consoling supposition followed instantly the pang of question—what was now required of her? The same hard thing as before? Ought she not again to give the alarm, that the poor wounded boy might be recaptured? Alas! Had not evil enough befallen him at her hand? And if she did, what account could she give this time of her discovery? What indeed but the truth? And to what vile comments and suspicion would not the confession of her secret visit to the chamber of the prisoner expose her? And if he had escaped, the alarm would serve no good end, and her shame could be spared. But he might be hiding somewhere about the castle, and she must choose between treachery to the Marquis on the one hand, and renewed hurt, and wrong, perhaps, to Richard, coupled with the bitterest disgrace to herself, on the other. To weigh such a question impartially was impossible; for in the one alternative no hurt would befall the Marquis, while from the other her very soul recoiled. Thus tortured, she sat motionless, the one moment vainly endeavoring to rouse up her courage and look her duty in the face that she might know with certainty what it was; the next, feeling her whole nature rise rebellious against the fate that demanded such a sacrifice. Ought she to be punished for an intent of the purest humanity?

There came a new sense of her position in the very jaws of slander. Any moment Mrs. Watson or another might enter and find her there, and what then more natural or irrefutable than the accusation of having liberated him? She sprang to her feet and darted to the door. It was locked!

Her first thought was relief—she no longer had to decide. Her second, that she was a prisoner till, horror of horrors, the soldiers of the guard came to seek Richard and found her, or Mrs. Watson appeared, grim as one of the Fates. Or, if Richard had been carried away, until she was compelled by hunger and misery to call aloud for release. But no, she would rather die.

The hours passed, and the gray heartless dawn began to peer through the dull green glass that closed the one loophole. It grew and grew, and its growth was the approach of the grinning demon of shame. The cruel light seemed gathering its strength to publish her shame to the universe. Blameless as she was, she would have gladly accepted death in escape from the misery that every moment grew nearer. Now and then a faint glimmer of comfort reached her in the thought that at least the escape of Richard, if he had escaped, was thus ensured, and that without any blame to her. And perhaps Mrs. Watson would be merciful—only she too had her obligations, and as housekeeper was severely responsible. And even if she should prove pitiful, there was the locking of the door! It followed her so quickly that someone must have seen her enter and wittingly snared her, most likely believing that she was not alone in the chamber.

The terrible bolt at length slid back in the lock. Mrs. Watson entered, stood, and stared. Before her sat Dorothy in her dressing gown, her hair about her neck, her face like the moon at sunrise, and her eyelids red and swollen with weeping. She stood speechless, staring first at the disconsolate maiden and then at the disorder of the room. The prisoner was nowhere.

The moment Dorothy found herself face to face with her doom, her presence of mind returned. The blood rushed from her heart to her brain, and she rose.

"Where is the young rebel?" asked the astounded matron sternly.

"I know not," answered Dorothy. "When first I entered the chamber, he had already gone."

"And what then hadst thou to do entering it?" asked the housekeeper, in a tone that did Dorothy good by angering her.

Mrs. Watson was a kind soul in reality, but few natures can resist the debasing influence of a sudden sense of superiority. Besides, was not the young gentlewoman in great wrong? And therefore before her must she not personify an awful Purity?

"That I will tell to none but My Lord Marquis," answered Dorothy, with sudden resolve.

"Oh, by all means, Mistress! But an' thou think to lead him by the nose while I be in Raglan—"

"Shall I inform his lordship in what high opinion his housekeeper holds him?" said Dorothy. "It seems to me he will hardly savor it."

"It would be an ill turn to do me, but My Lord did never heed a talebearer."

"Then will he not heed the tale you would yield him concerning me."

"What tale should I yield him but that I find thee here—and the prisoner gone?"

"The tale I read in your face and voice. You look and talk as if I were a false woman."

"Verily to my eyes the thing looketh ill."

"It would look ill to any eyes, and therefore I need kind eyes to read, and just ears to hear my tale. This is a matter for My Lord, and if you spread any report in the castle ere his lordship hear it, whatever evil springs from it will lie at your door."

"My life! What dost thou take me for, Mistress Dorothy? Am I

153

THE LAST CASTLE

one to go tattling about the courts forsooth?"

"Pardon me, Madam, but a maiden's good name may be as precious to Dorothy Vaughan as a matron's respectability to Mistress Watson. If you had left me with that look on your face, and had but spoken my name to it, someone would have guessed ten times more than you know—or I, either."

"I must tell the truth," said Mrs. Watson, relenting a little.

"You must, or I will tell it for you—but to the Marquis. You shall be there to hear, and if, after that, you tell it to another, then you have no mother's heart in you."

Dorothy gave way at last, and burst into tears. Mrs. Watson was touched.

"Nay, Child, I would do thee no wrong," she rejoined. "Get thee to bed. I must rouse the guard to go look for the prisoner, but I will say nothing of thee to any but My Lord Marquis. When he is dressed and in his study, I will come for thee myself."

Dorothy thanked her warmly, and betook herself to her chamber, considerably relieved.

33.
Judge Gout

Dorothy had hardly reached her room when the castle was once more astir. The rush of the guard across the stone court, the clang of opening lattices, and the voices that called from outshot heads, again filled her ears, but she never once peeped from her window. A moment, and the news was all over the castle that the prisoner had escaped.

Lord Charles went at once to his father's room. The old man was ill-pleased to be already (and for a second time) startled back to conscious weariness. When he heard the bad tidings, he was silent for a few moments.

"I would Herbert were at home, Charles, to stop this rathole for me," he said at length. "Let the Roundhead go—I care not. I had but half a right to hold him, and he deserves his freedom. But what a governor art thou, My Lord! Prithee, dost know the rents in thine own clothing, who knowest not when thy gingerbread bulwarks gape? Find this rathole, I say, or I will depose thee and send for thy brother, whom the King can ill spare."

"Have patience with me, Father," said Lord Charles gently, "I am more ashamed than you are angry."

"Thou know'st I did but jest, My Son. But in truth, an' thou find it not, I will send for Lord Herbert. If he find what thou canst not, that will be no disgrace to thee. But find it we must."

"Think you not, My Lord, it were best to set Mistress Dorothy on the search? She hath a wondrous gift of discovery."

"A good thought, Charles! But search the castle first that we

155

may be assured the Roundhead hath indeed vanished."

The sun rose higher, the day's talk began, and nothing was in anybody's mouth but the escape of the prisoner. His capture and trial were already of the past, forgotten in the nearer astonishment. Lord Charles went searching, questioning, peering about everywhere, but could find neither the prisoner nor the traitorous hole.

Meantime Mrs. Watson was not a little anxious until she should have revealed what she knew to the Marquis, for the prisoner was in her charge when he disappeared. In the course of the morning Lord Charles came to her apartment to question her, but she begged to be excused, because of a certain disclosure she was not at liberty to make to any but his father. Lord Charles yielded, and Mrs. Watson soon came to the Marquis in his study. He was looking pale from the trouble of the night, which had resulted in unmistakable symptoms of the gout. He listened to all she had to tell him without comment, looked grave, and told her to fetch Mistress Dorothy. As soon as she was gone he called Scudamore from the antechamber, and sent him to request Lord Charles' presence. He came at once, and was there when Dorothy entered.

She was very white and worn, and her eyes were heavily downcast. Her face wore that expression so much resembling guilt, which indicates the misery the innocent feel under the consciousness of suspicion. At the sight of Lord Charles, she crimsoned; it was one thing to confess to the Marquis, and quite another to do so in the presence of his son.

The Marquis sat with one leg on a stool, already in the gradually contracting grip of his ghoulish enemy. Before Dorothy could recover from the annoyance of finding Lord Charles present, or open her mouth to beg for a more private interview, he addressed her abruptly.

"Our young rebel friend hath escaped, it seems, Mistress Dorothy!" he said, gently but coldly, looking her full in the eyes, with searching gaze, and hard expression.

"I am glad to hear it, My Lord," returned Dorothy, with a sudden influx of courage.

"Ha!" said the Marquis, quickly. "Then it is news to thee, Mistress Dorothy!"

"Indeed it is, My Lord. I hoped it might be so, I confess, but I knew not that it was so."

"What, Mistress Dorothy! Knewest thou not that the young

thief was gone?"

"I knew that Richard Heywood was gone from his chamber—
whether from the castle I knew not. He was no thief, My Lord.
Your lordship's page and fool were the thieves."

"Cousin, I hardly know myself in the marvelous change I find
in thee! In the dark night thou takest a Roundhead prisoner. In
the gray morning thou settest him free again! Hath one visit to his
chamber so wrought upon thee? To an old man it seemeth less
than maidenly."

Again a burning blush overspread poor Dorothy's countenance.
But she governed herself, and spoke bravely, although she could
not keep her voice from trembling.

"My Lord," she said, "Richard Heywood was my playmate. We
were as brother and sister, for our fathers' lands bordered each
other."

"Thou didst say nothing of these things last night!"

"My Lord! Before the whole hall? Besides, what mattered it? All
was over long ago, and I had done my part against him."

"Fell you out together then?"

"What need is there for your lordship to ask? Thou seest him of
the one part, and me of the other."

"And from loving thou didst fall to hating?"

"God forbid, My Lord! I but did my part against him, though I
would to God it had not fallen to me."

"Thinking better of it, therefore, and repenting of thy harshness,
thou didst seek his chamber in the night to tell him so? I would
fain know how a maiden reasoneth with herself when she doth
such things."

"Not so, My Lord. I will tell you all. I could not sleep for
thinking of my wounded playmate. And as to what he had done,
after it became clear that he sought but his own, and meant no
hairbreadth of harm to your lordship, I confess the matter looked
not the same."

"Therefore you would make him amends and undo what you
had done? You had caught the bird, and had therefore a right to
free the bird when you would? All well, Mistress Dorothy, had he
been indeed a bird! But being a man, and in thy friend's house, I
doubt thy logic. The thing had passed from thy hands into mine,"
said the Marquis, into the ball of whose foot the gout that moment
ran its unicorn horn.

157

"I did not set him free, My Lord. When I entered the prison chamber, he was already gone."

"Thou had the will and did it not! Is there yet another in my house who had the will and did it?" cried the Marquis, who, although more annoyed that she should have so committed herself, yet was willing to give such scope to a lover, that if she had but confessed she had liberated him, he would have pardoned her heartily. He did not yet know how incapable Dorothy was of a lie.

"But, My Lord, I had not the will to set him free," she said.

"Wherefore then didst go to him?"

"My Lord, he was sorely wounded, and I had seen him fall fainting," said Dorothy, repressing her tears with much ado.

"And thou didst go to comfort him?"

Dorothy was silent.

"How camest thou locked into his room? Tell me that, Mistress."

"Your lordship knows as much of that as I do. Indeed, I have been sorely punished for a little fault."

"Thou dost confess the fault then?"

"If it *was* a fault to visit him who was sick and in prison, My Lord."

The Marquis was silent for a whole minute.

"And thou canst not tell how he gat him forth of the walls? Must I believe him to be forth of them, My Lord?" he said, turning to his son.

"I cannot imagine him within them, My Lord, after such search as we have made."

"Still," returned the Marquis, the acuteness of whose wits had not been swallowed up by that of the gout, "so long as thou canst not tell how he gat forth, I may doubt whether he be forth. If the manner of his exit be acknowledged hidden, wherefore not the place of his refuge? Mistress Dorothy," he continued, altogether averse to the supposition of treachery amongst his people, "thou art bound by all obligations of loyalty and shelter and truth to tell what thou knowest. An' thou do not, thou art a traitor to the house, yea to thy King; for when the worst comes, and this castle is besieged, much harm may be wrought by that secret passage— yea it may be taken thereby.

"All I ask of thee is to bar the door against his return—except, indeed, thou did from the first contrive so to meet thy Roundhead lover in my loyal house. Then indeed it were too much to require of thee!"

"My Lord, you wrong me much," said Dorothy, and burst into tears. "I did think that I had done enough both for my Lord of Worcester and against Richard Heywood, and I did hope that he had escaped. There lies the worst I can lay to my charge even in thought, My Lord, and I trust it may be found pardonable."

"It sets an ill example to my quiet house if the ladies therein go anight to the gentleman's chambers."

"My Lord, you are cruel," said Dorothy.

"Not a soul in the house knows it but myself, My Lord," said Mrs. Watson.

"Hold there, my good woman! Whose hand was it turned the key upon her? More than thou must know thereof. Hear me, Mistress Dorothy. He is a fine fellow, and I am glad he hath escaped. Do thou but find out the cursed rathole by which he goes and comes, and I will gladly forgive thee all the trouble thou hast brought into my sober house. For truly never hath been in my day such confusions and uproars therein as since thou camest hither, and thy dog and thy lover and thy lover's mare followed thee."

"Alas, My Lord. If I were fortunate enough to find it, what would you say but that I found it where I knew well to look for it?"

"Find it, and I promise thee I will never say word on the matter again. Thou art a good girl, an' thou do venture a hair too far for a lover."

"My Lord! My Lord!" cried Dorothy, but ended not, for his lordship gave a louder cry. His face was contorted with anguish, and he writhed under the tiger fangs of the gout.

"Go away," he shouted, "or I shall disgrace my manhood before women, God help me!"

"I trust thou wilt bear me no malice," said the housekeeper, as they walked in the direction of Dorothy's chamber.

"You did but your duty," said Dorothy quietly.

"I will do all I can for thee," continued Mrs. Watson, "if thou dost confess to me how thou didst contrive the young gentleman's escape, and wherefore he locked the door upon thee."

Dorothy's answer to the impertinence was to walk into her room and shut the door—which entirely satisfied Mrs. Watson of her guilt.

34.
An Evil Time

A nd now began an evil time for Dorothy. She retired to her
chamber more than disheartened by Lord Worcester's
behavior to her, vexed with herself for doing what she
would have been more vexed with herself for having left undone,
feeling wronged, lonely, and disgraced, conscious of honesty, yet
ashamed to show herself—and all for the sake of a presumptuous
boy, whose opinions were a disgust to her and his actions a horror!
Yet not only did she not repent of what she had done, but began,
with mingled pleasure and annoyance, to feel her heart drawn
toward the fanatic as the only one left in the world capable of
doing her justice, of understanding her.

She thus unknowingly made a step toward the discovery that it
is infinitely better to think wrongly and act rightly upon that
wrong thinking, than it is to think rightly and not to do as that
thinking requires us. He who acts rightly will soon think rightly;
he who acts wrongly will soon think wrongly. Any two persons
acting faithfully upon opposite convictions are divided but by a
wall; any two, in belief most harmonious, who do not act upon it,
are divided by infinite gulfs of the blackness of darkness, across
which neither ever beholds the real self of the other.

Dorothy ought to have gone at once to Lady Margaret and told
her all, but she naturally and rightly shrank from what might seem
an appeal to the daughter against the judgment of the father;
neither could she dare hope that, if she did, her judgment would
not be against her also. There was no one to whom she could turn.

Gladly would she have forsaken the castle, and returned to the dangers of her lonely home, but that would be to yield to a lie, to flee from the devil instead of facing him, and with her own hand to fix the imputed smirch on her forehead, exposing herself besides to the suspicion of having fled to join her lover and cast her lot with his among the traitors. Besides, she had been left by Lord Herbert in charge of his fire engine and the water of the castle, which trust she could not abandon. Whatever might be yet to come of it, she must stay and encounter it. She would in the meantime set herself to discover the secret pathway by which dog and man came and went at their pleasure. This she owed her friends, even at the risk of confirming the Marquis' worst suspicions.

She was not altogether wrong in her unconscious judgment of Lady Margaret, whose nature rendered her perfectly capable of understanding either of the two halves of Dorothy's behavior, but was not sufficient to the reception of the two parts together. That is, she could have understood the heroic capture of her former lover, or she could have understood her going to visit him in his trouble, and even what Dorothy was incapable of, his release. But she was not yet equal to understanding how she should set herself so against a man, even to his wounding and capture, whom she loved so much as to dare the loss of her good name by going to his chamber, so placing herself in the power of a man she had injured, as well as running a great risk of discovery on the part of her friends. Hence she was quite prepared to accept the solution of her strange conduct which by and by came to be offered and received all over the castle—that Dorothy first admitted, then captured, and finally released the handsome young Roundhead.

Lady Margaret received her first impressions of the affair from Lord Charles, who was prejudiced against Dorothy, and no doubt jealous of the relation of the fine young rebel to a loyal maiden of Raglan. The unspoken suspicion that she knew and would not reveal the flaw in his castle annoyed him more and more.

For some little time, not perceiving the difficulties in her way, and perhaps not understanding her disinclination to self-defense, Lady Margaret continued to expect a visit from Dorothy, with excuse, at least, if not confession and apology upon her lips; and she was hurt by her silence as much as offended by her behavior. When they first met, she wore an air of reticence, and regarded and addressed her coldly, so that Dorothy was confirmed in her

disinclination to confide in her. Dorothy had nothing to tell but
what she had already told; everything depended on the interpretation accorded to the facts, and the right interpretation was just the
one thing she had found herself unable to convey. If her friends
did not, she could not justify herself.

She tried hard to behave as she ought, for she felt it would be
unjust to allow her affection toward her mistress to be in the least
shaken by her treatment of her; and she was, if possible, more
submissive and eager in her service than before. But in this she
was rudely checked by the fear that Lady Margaret would take it
as the endeavor of guilt to win favor. Do what she would, instead
of getting closer to her, she felt, every time they met, that the
hedge of separation which had sprung up between them had in the
interval grown thicker. By degrees her mistress assumed toward
the poor girl an impervious manner of self-contained dignity.

And there came a change in another member of the household.
While Dorothy had been intent upon Richard as he stood before
the Marquis, not Amanda only, but another as well had been
intent upon her. As Scudamore stood regarding now the face of the
prisoner and now that of Dorothy, he noticed that every phrase of
the prisoner might be read on Dorothy. He found himself attracted
by the rich changefulness of expression on a countenance usually
very still. He surmised little of the conflict that sent it to the
surface, and had to construct no theory to calm the restlessness of
intellectual curiosity. Emotion in the face of a woman was enough
to attract Scudamore; the prettier the face, the stronger the attraction, but the source or character of the emotion mattered nothing
to him. In a word, Dorothy had now become interesting to him.

As soon as she found a safe opportunity, Amanda told him of
Dorothy's being found in the turret chamber, a fact she pretended
to have heard in confidence from Mrs. Watson, concealing her
own part in it. But as Amanda spoke, Dorothy became to Rowland
twice as interesting as ever Amanda had been. There was a real
romance about the girl. And she *looked* so quiet! He never thought
of defending her or playing the true part of a cousin. Amanda
might think of her as she pleased! Rowland was content. How far
Dorothy had been right or wrong in visiting Heywood, he did not
even consider. It was enough that she, who had been to him like
the blank in the center of the African map, was now a region of
vague but interesting marvels and possibilities. As to her loving

the Roundhead fellow, that would not long stand in the way.

In this period of gloom and wretchedness, Dorothy became aware of increased attention on the part of her cousin. This she attributed to kindness generated of pity. But to accept it, and so confess that she needed it, would have been to place herself too much on a level with one she did not respect, and at the same time confirm him in whatever probably mistaken grounds he had for offering it. She therefore met his advances kindly but coldly, a treatment under which his feelings began to ripen into something a little deeper and more genuine.

During the next ten days or so, Dorothy was regarded by almost everyone in the castle as in disgrace. Only one of the servants—a kitchen maid, Tom Fool's bride in the marriage jest—showed her the same respect as formerly. This girl came to her one night in her room, and with tears in her eyes besought permission to carry her meals thither, that she might be spared eating with the rude ladies. But Dorothy saw that to forsake Mrs. Watson's table would be to fly the field; therefore, hateful as it was to meet the looks of those around it, she did so with unveiled lids and an enforced dignity. But the effort was as exhausting as painful, and the reflex of shame (in spite of innocence) was eating into her heart.

But she had still one refuge, the workshop, where Caspar Kaltoff wrought like an artificial god. The worthy German altered his manner to her not a whit, but continued to behave with the mingled kindness of a father and devotion of a servant. His respect and trustful sympathy showed that he, if no other, believed nothing to her disadvantage, but was as much her humble friend as ever. For a long time she never said her prayers by her bedside without thanking God for Caspar.

Ere long her worn look, thin cheek, and weary eye began to work on the heart of Lady Margaret, and she relented in spirit. But to the favor which followed, the poor girl could not throw wide her windows, knowing it arose from no change in Lady Margaret's judgment concerning her. The conviction burned in her heart like cold fire that, but for compassion upon the orphan, she would have been at once dismissed from the castle. Sometimes she ventured to think that if Lord Herbert had been at home, all this would not have happened. But now what could she expect other than that on his return he would regard her and treat her in the same way as his wife and father and brother had already done?

35.
The Deliverer

But she found some relief in applying her mind to the task to which Lord Worcester had set her. Many a night as she tossed sleepless on her bed she would turn from the thoughts that tortured her, to brood upon the castle and invent some new possible way of getting out of it unseen. And many a morning she would hasten (ere the household was astir) to examine some spot which might contain the secret. One time it was a chimney that might have a door and stair concealed within it; another, the stables, where she examined every stall in the hope of finding a trap to an underground way. Had anyone else been in question but Richard, the traitor, the Roundhead, she might have imagined an associate within the walls, in which case further solution would not have been for her. But she could not entertain the idea in connection with Richard. Besides, it had grown plain to her that both Richard and Marquis had that night been through the moat.

Some who caught sight of her in the early dawn, wandering about peering here and there, thought that she was losing her senses; others more ingenious in the thinking of evil imagined she sought to impress the household with her innocence by pretending a search for the concealed flaw in the defenses.

Ever since she had been put in charge of the waterworks, she had been in the habit of lingering a little on the roof of the keep as often as occasion took her thither, for she delighted in the far outlook on the open country. On one of these occasions, in the first the twilight, she was leaning over one of the battlements looking down upon the moat and its white and yellow blossoms and great green leaves, and feeling very desolate. Her young life seemed to have crumbled down upon her and crushed her heart, and all for one gentle imprudence.

"O my Mother!" she murmured. "If you could hear me, you would help me an' you could. Your poor Dorothy is sorely sad and forsaken, and she knows no way of escape. O my Mother, hear me!" As she spoke she looked away from the moat to the sky and spread out her arms in the pain of her petition.

There was a step behind her.

"What! My little Protestant praying to the naughty saints! That will never do!"

Dorothy turned with a great start, and stood speechless and trembling before Lord Herbert.

"My poor Child!" he said, holding out both his hands, and taking those which Dorothy did not offer. "Did I startle you then so much? I am truly sorry. I heard but your last words—be not afraid of your secret. But what has come to you? You are white and thin, there are tears on your face, and it seems that you are not so glad to see me. I hope you are not sick, but plainly you are ill at ease! Go not yet after my Molly, Cousin, for truly we need you here yet a while."

"Would I might go to Molly, My Lord!" said Dorothy. "Molly would believe me."

"You need not go to Molly for that, Cousin. I will believe you. Only tell me what you would have me believe, and I will believe it. Am I not magician enough to know whom to believe and whom not?"

At his kind words the poor girl burst into a passion of weeping, fell on her knees before him, and holding up her clasped hands, cried out in a voice of sob-choked agony—for she was not used to tears, and it was to her a rending of the heart to weep. "Save me, My Lord! I have no friend in the world who can help me but you!"

"No friend! What do you mean, Dorothy?" said Lord Herbert, taking her two clasped hands between his. "There is my Margaret and my father!"

"Alas, My Lord! They mean well by me, but they do not believe me, and if your lordship believe me no more than they, I must go from Raglan. Yet, believing me, I know not how you could any more help me."

"Dorothy, my child, I can do nothing till you take me with you. I cannot even comfort you."

"Your lordship is weary," said Dorothy, rising and wiping her eyes. "You cannot have eaten since you came. Go, My Lord, and hear my tale first from them that believe me not. They will assure you of nothing that is not true, only they understand it not, and wrong me in their conjectures. Let Lady Margaret tell it you, and then if you have yet faith enough in me to send for me, I will come and answer all you ask. If you send not for me, I will ride from Raglan tomorrow."

"It shall be as you say, Dorothy. Fear me not; I trust in God to judge fairly betwixt friend and foe, and I doubt not it will be now to the lightening of your trouble, my poor storm-beaten Dove."

It startled Dorothy with a gladness that stung like pain to hear the word he never used but to his wife thus flit from his lips in the tenderness of his pity, and light like the dove itself upon her head. She thanked him with her whole soul, and was silent.

"I will send here for you, Child, when I require your presence— and when I send, come straight to my lady's parlor."

Dorothy bowed her head, but could not speak, and Lord Herbert walked quickly from her. She heard him run down the stair with a boy's headlong speed.

Half an hour passed slowly, before Lady Margaret's page came lightly up the steps, bearing the request that she would favor his mistress with her presence. She rose from the battlement and followed him with beating heart.

When she entered the parlor she found herself clasped to a bosom heaving with emotion.

"Forgive me, Dorothy," sobbed Lady Margaret. "I have done you wrong. But you will love me yet again—will you not, Dorothy?"

"Madam! Madam!" was all Dorothy could answer, kissing her hands.

Lady Margaret led her to her husband, who kissed her on the forehead, and seated her betwixt himself and his wife, and for a space there was silence. Then at last Dorothy spoke.

"Tell me, Madam, how is it that I find myself once more in the garden of your favor? How know you that I am not all unworthy thereof?"

"My lord tells me so," returned Lady Margaret simply.

"And whence doth my lord know it?" asked Dorothy, turning to Lord Herbert.

"If you be not satisfied of your own innocence, Dorothy, I will ask you a few questions. Listen to your answers, and judge. How came the young Puritan into the castle that night?"

Dorothy laughed—her first laugh since the evil fog had ascended and swathed her.

"My Lord," answered Dorothy, "I look to you to tell me so much, for before God I know not."

"Nay, Child! You need not buttress your words with an oath," said his lordship. "Your fair eyes are worth a thousand oaths. But wherefore did you not let the young man go when first you spied him? Wherefore did you ring the alarm bell? You saw he was upon his own mare, for you knew her, did you not?"

"I did, My Lord, but he had no business there, and I was of my Lord Worcester's household. Here I am not Dorothy Vaughan, but my lady's gentlewoman."

"Then why did you go to his room thereafter? Did you not know it might have proved worse than perilous?"

"No, My Lord. Other danger was none where Richard was," returned Dorothy with vehemence.

"It bears a look as if maybe you do or might one day love the young man!" said Lord Herbert in slow pondering tone.

"My spirit has of late been driven to hold him company, My Lord. It seemed that, save Caspar, I had no friend left but him. God help me! It were a fearful thing to love a fanatic! But I will resist the devil."

"Truly we are in lack of a few such devils on what we count the honest side, Dorothy!" said Lord Herbert, laughing. "Not every man that thinks the other way is a rogue or a fool. But you have not told me why you ran the heavy risk of seeking him on the night."

"I could not rest for thinking of him, My Lord, with that terrible wound in the head I had as good as given him, and from whose effects I had last seen him lie as one dead. He was my playmate, and my mother loved him."

Here poor Dorothy broke down and wept, but recovered herself with an effort, and proceeded.

"I kept starting awake, seeing him thus at one time, and at another hearing him utter my name as if entreating me to go to him, until at last I believed that I was called."

"Called by whom, Dorothy?"

"I thought . . . I thought, My Lord, it might be the same that called Samuel, who had opened my ears to hear Richard's voice. But for that I would not have gone. Yet surely I mistook, for see what has come of it," she added, turning to Lady Margaret.

"We must not judge from one consequence where there are a thousand yet to follow," said his lordship. "And when you entered the room, you found no one there?"

"I say so, My Lord, and it is true. I was filled with fear when I saw the bedclothes all in a heap on the floor, but I hoped that he had had the better in the struggle, and had escaped, for now at least he could do no harm in Raglan, I thought. But when I found the door was locked—"

"Now who locked the door on you?"

"Might it not have been Satan himself, My Lord?"

"I believe he was only acting in his usual fashion, which must be his worst—through the heart and hands of someone in the house who would bring you into trouble."

"I would it were the other way, My Lord."

"So would I heartily. But have you no suspicion of anyone owing you a grudge, who might be glad of such opportunity to pay it with interest?"

"I must confess I have, My Lord, but I beg of your lordship not to question me on the matter further, for it reaches only to suspicion. I know nothing, and might, if I uttered a word, be guilty of grievous wrong."

Lord Herbert looked hard at his wife. Lady Margaret drooped her head.

"You are right, indeed, my good Cousin!" he said, turning again to Dorothy. "For that would be to do by another as you suffer so sorely from others doing by you. I must send my brains about and make a discovery or two for myself. It is well I have a few days to spend at home. And now to the first part of the business in hand. Have you any special way of calling your dog? It is a moonlit night, I believe."

He rose and went to the window, over which hung a heavy curtain of Flemish tapestry.

"It is a three-quarter moon, My Lord," said Dorothy, "and very bright. I did use to call my dog with a whistle my mother gave me when I was a child."

"Do you have it with you in Raglan?"

"I have it in my hand now, My Lord."

"What then with the moon and your whistle, I think we shall not fail."

"Have lost your wits?" said his wife. "Or what fiend would you raise tonight?"

"I would lay one rather," returned Lord Herbert. "But first I would discover this perilous fault in the armor of my house. Is your horse still in your control, Dorothy?"

"I have no reason to think otherwise, My Lord."

"Dare you then ride him alone in the moonlight—outside the walls?"

"I dare anything on Dick's back."

"Does your dog know Caspar—in friendly fashion, I mean?"

"Caspar is the only other in the castle he is quite friendly with, My Lord."

"Then is all as I would have it. And now I would not have a soul in the place but my lady here know that I am searching with you after this dog-and-man-hole. Therefore I will saddle your little horse for you myself, and—"

"No, no, My Lord!" interrupted Dorothy. "That I can do."

"So much the better. Then you shall ride him forth, and Marquis will see you go from the yard. Then I will mount the keep, and from that point of vantage look down upon the two courts, while Caspar stands by your dog. You shall ride slowly along for a minute or two, then blow your whistle and set off at a gallop to round the castle, still ever and anon blowing your whistle. If I should fail to see Marquis leave the castle, you may perchance discover at least from which side of the castle he comes to you."

Dorothy sprang to her feet.

"I am ready, My Lord," she said.

"And so am I," returned Lord Herbert, rising. "Will you come to the top of the keep, Wife, and grant me the light of your eyes in aid of the moonshine?"

"You shall find me there, I promise. Mother Mary speed your quest."

169

36.
The Discovery

All was done as had been arranged. Aided by Dorothy, Lord Herbert saddled Dick, lifted her to his back, and led her to the gate in full vision of Marquis. The dog went wild at the sight, and threatened to pull down his kennel in his endeavors to follow them. Lord Herbert opened the yard gate for Dorothy, then walked by her side down to the brick gate. A moment later she was free and alone, with the wide green fields and the yellow moonlight about her.

She had some difficulty in making Dick go slowly for the first minute or two. He had had but little exercise of late, and moved as if his four legs felt like wings. Dorothy had ridden him very little since she came to the castle, but Lord Charles had used him, and one of the grooms had always taken him to ride messages. Notwithstanding, he had had but little of the pleasure of speed for a long time, and when Dorothy at length gave him the rein, he flew as if every member of his body from tail to ears and eyelids had been an engine of propulsion. But Dorothy had more wings than Dick, for her whole being was full of wings. It was a small thing that she had not had a right gallop since she left Wyfern; as the strength she had been putting forth to bear the Atlas burden lifted from her soul, she seemed to soar aloft.

Three shrill whistles she had blown, about a hundred yards from the gate, had heard the eager bark of her dog in answer, and then Dick went flying over the fields like a water bird over the lake, that scratches its smooth surface with its feet as it flies.

Around the rampart they went. The still night was jubilant about them as they flew. The stars shone as if they knew all her joy, that the shadow of guilt had been lifted from her, and that to her the world again was fair.

At intervals she blew her whistle, and kept her keen eyes and ears awake, in the hope of hearing her dog or seeing him come bounding through the moonlight.

Meantime Lord Herbert and his wife had taken their stand on top of the great tower, and were looking down—the lady into the stone court, and her husband into the grass one. Dorothy's shrill whistle came once, twice, and just as it began to sound a third time, Lady Margaret cried out.

"Here he comes!"

A black shadow went from the foot of the library tower, tearing across the moonlight to the hall door, where it vanished. But in vain Lord Herbert kept his eyes on the fountain court, in the hope of its reappearance there. Presently they heard a heavy plunge in the water on the other side of the keep, and, running round, saw a little black object making his way across the moat through the obstructing floats of water lilies. Marquis scrambled out of the water up against the steep side of the moat and suddenly disappeared.

"I have it!" cried Lord Herbert. "Come down with me, My Dove, and I will show you. Dorothy's Marquis has gone into the drain of the moat! He is a large dog, and beyond a doubt that is where the young Roundhead entered. I had no thought it was such a size."

Dorothy made the circuit, arrived again at the brick gate, and found Lord Herbert waiting there.

"I have seen nothing of him, My Lord," she said. "Shall I ride round once more?"

"Do, prithee, for I see you enjoy it. But we have already learned all we want to know to the security of the castle. There is but one Marquis in Raglan and he is, I believe, in the oak parlor."

"You saw my Marquis make his exit then, My Lord?"

"My lady and I both saw him."

"What then can have become of him? We did go very fast, and I suppose he gave up the chase in despair."

"You will find him the second round. But stay—I will get a horse and go with you."

Dorothy went within the gate as Lord Herbert ran back to the stables. In a few minutes he was by her side again, and together they rode. The moon was glorious, with a few large white clouds around her, like great mirrors hung up to catch and reflect her light. The stars were few, but shone like diamonds in the dark spaces between the clouds. No noise broke the stillness save the dull drumbeat of their horses' hooves on the turf, or the cymbal clatter when they crossed a road, and the occasional shrill call from Dorothy's whistle.

To Dorothy it seemed as if peace itself had taken form in the feathery weight that filled the flaky air. As her horse galloped along, flying like a bird over ditch and mound, her own heart so light that her body seemed to float above the saddle rather than rest upon it, she felt like a soul which, having been dragged to hell by a lurking fiend, a good strong angel was bearing aloft into bliss. Few delights can equal the mere presence of one whom we trust utterly.

No mastiff came to Dorothy's whistle, and having finished their round, they rode back to the stables, put up their horses, and rejoined Lady Margaret where she was pacing the sunk wall around the moat. There Lord Herbert showed Dorothy where her dog had vanished, comforting her with the assurance that nothing should be altered before the faithful animal returned, as doubtless he would the moment he despaired of finding her in the open country.

Lord Herbert said nothing to his father that night lest he should spoil his rest. But finding him a good deal better the next morning, he laid open the whole matter to him according to his conviction concerning Dorothy and her behavior, ending with the words, "That maiden, My Lord, has truth enough in her heart to serve the whole castle. To doubt her is to wrong the very light. I fear there are not many maidens in England with such courage and honesty."

The Marquis listened attentively, and when Lord Herbert had ended, sat a few moments in silence. Then, for an answer, he said, "Go and fetch her, My Lad."

When Dorothy entered, he said from his chair, "Wilt thou kiss an old man who hath wronged thee—for so my son hath taught me?"

Dorothy stooped, and he kissed her on both cheeks, with tears glistening in his eyes.

"Thou shalt dine at my table," he said, "an' thy mistress will permit thee, until thou art weary of our dull company. Thou art a good girl, Dorothy. Now I am sure of thee, and I will no more doubt thee—not if I wake in the night and find thee standing over me with a drawn dagger. An' my worthy Bayly had been at home, perchance this had not happened. Forgive me, Dorothy, for the gout is the sting of the devil's own tail, and driveth men mad. Verily it seemeth now as if I could never have behaved to thee as I have done. Why, one might say the foolish fat old man was jealous of the handsome young Puritan! The wheel will come round, Dorothy. One day thou wilt marry him."

"Never, My Lord!" exclaimed Dorothy with vehemence.

"And when thou dost," the Marquis went on, "all I beg of thee is, that on thy wedding day thou whisper to thy bridegroom, 'My Lord of Worcester told me so,' and therewith thou shalt have my blessing, whether I be down here in Raglan, or up the great stair with little Molly."

Dorothy was silent. The Marquis held out his hand. She kissed it, left the room, and flew to the top of the keep.

37.
The Astrologer

In the middle of the previous night, Marquis had returned, and announced himself by scratching and whining for admittance at the door of Dorothy's room. She let him in, but not until the morning discovered that he had a handkerchief round his neck, and in it a letter addressed to herself. Curious, perhaps something more than curious to open it, she yet carried it straight to Lord Herbert.

"Can you not break the seal, Dorothy, that you bring it to me? I will not read it first," said his lordship.

"Will you open it then, Madam?" she said, turning to Lady Margaret.

"If my lord will not, why should I?" rejoined her mistress.

Dorothy opened the letter without more ado, crimsoned, read it to the end, and handed it to Lord Herbert.

"Pray read, My Lord," she said.

He took it and read.

Mistress Dorothy,
I think, and yet I know not, but I think you will be pleased to learn that my wound has not proved mortal, though it has brought me low, yea, very near death's door. Think not I feared to enter. But it grieves me to the heart to ride another than my own mare to the wars, and it will pleasure you to know that without my

174

Lady, I shall be but half the man I was. But do the like again when you may, for you but did your duty according to your lights, as how else should anyone do? Mistaken as you are, I love you as my own soul.

As to the ring I left for you with a safe messenger, concerning whom I say nothing, for you will con her no thanks for the doing of aught to pleasure me, I restored it not because it was yours, for your mother gave it me—but because if for lack of my mare I should fall in some battle, then would the ring pass to a hand whose heart knew nought of her who gave it me. I am what you know not, yet your old playfellow, Richard. When you hear of me in the wars, then curse me not, but sigh an' you will, and say," He also would in his blindness do the thing that lay at his door."

God be with you, Mistress Dorothy. Beat not your dog for bringing you this.

Richard Heywood

Lord Herbert gave the letter to his wife, and paced up and down the room while she read. Dorothy stood silent with glowing face and downcast eyes. When Lady Margaret had finished it, she handed it to her and turned to her husband with the words, "Is this not a brave epistle?"

"There is matter for thought therein," he answered. "Will you show me the ring whereof he writes, Cousin?"

"I never had it, My Lord."

"Whom then does he call his safe messenger? Not your dog, plainly, for the ring had been sent before."

"My Lord, I cannot even conjecture," answered Dorothy.

"There is matter herein that asketh attention. Not a word of all this until I consider what it may import! Beat not your dog, Dorothy; that were other than he deserves at your hand. But he is a dangerous go-between, so let him be chained up at once."

Ere the next day was over, it was understood throughout the castle that Lord Herbert was constructing a horoscope—not that many in the place understood what a horoscope really was. And no sooner was the sun down than there was Lord Herbert atop the keep, his head in an outlandish Persian hat and his long flowing

175

gown of a golden tint, wrought with hieroglyphics in blue. There he was still when the household retired to rest, and there, in the gray dawn, his wife, waking and peeping from her window, saw him still, against the cold sky, pacing the roof with bent head and thoughtful demeanor, or gazing through various wondrous instruments at the sky. In the morning he was gone, and no one but Lady Margaret saw him during the whole of the following day.

Nor indeed could any but herself or Caspar have found him, for the tale Tom Fool told the rustics of a magically concealed armory had been suggested by a rumor that Lord Herbert had a chamber of which none of the domestics knew door or window, or even the locality. That recourse should have been to spells and incantations for its concealment, however, would have seemed trouble unnecessary to anyone who knew the mechanical means his lordship employed for the purpose. The touch of a pin on a certain spot in one of the bookcases in the library admitted him to a wooden stair constructed in an ancient disused chimney, which led down to a small chamber in the roof of a sort of porch built over the stair from the stone court to the stables. There was no other access to it, nor had it any window but one which they had constructed in the roof so cunningly as to attract no notice. All the household supposed the hidden chamber to be in the great tower, somewhere near the workshop.

Here he kept his books of alchemy and magic, and some of his stranger instruments. It would have been hard for even himself to say what he did or did not believe of such things. In certain moods, especially when under the influence of some fact he had just discovered without being able to account for it, he was ready to believe everything; in others, especially when he had just succeeded in explaining anything to his own satisfaction, he doubted them all considerably. His imagination leaned lovingly toward them, but his intellect required proofs which he had not yet found. In the present case, he trusted for success his knowledge of human nature rather than his questioning of the stars.

Thither then he had retired, and before the second day was over, it was everywhere whispered that he was occupied in discovering the hidden way by which entrance and exit had been found through the defenses of the castle. And the next day it was known that he had been successful—as who could doubt he must, with such powers at his command?

For a time, curiosity got the better of fear, and there was not a soul in the place who did not that day accept Lord Herbert's general invitation, and pass over the Gothic bridge to see the hidden opening from the opposite side of the moat. To seal the conviction that the discovery had indeed been made, permission was given to anyone to test it with his own person—but of this only Shafto availed himself. It was enough, however; he disappeared within the shaft, and while the group which saw him enter the opening was yet anxiously waiting his return by the way he had gone, he reentered by the western gate and came upon them from behind and so settled the matter. As soon as curiosity was satisfied, Lord Herbert rendered the drain as impassable to man or dog as the walls of the keep itself.

The discovery and announcement of the secret entrance having been accomplished, Lord Herbert retired yet again to his secret chamber, and that night was once more seen by many consulting the stars from the top of the tower. The following morning another rumor was abroad, to the effect that his lordship was now occupied in questioning the stars as to who in the castle had aided the young Roundhead in making his escape.

In the evening, soon after supper, there came a gentle tap on the door of Lady Margaret's chamber. At that time she was understood to be disengaged, and willing to see any of the household. Little Henry happened to be with her, and she sent him to the door to see who it was.

"It is Tom Fool," he said, returning. "He begs speech of you, Madam—with a face as long as the baker's shovel and a mouth as wide as his oven door."

Lady Margaret smiled; this was probably the first fruit of her husband's astrological investigations.

"Tell him he may enter, and do leave him alone with me, Henry," she said.

Henry had truly reported Tom's appearance. He was trembling from head to foot and very white.

"What ails you, Tom? You look as if you had seen a hobgoblin," asked Lady Margaret.

"Please you, My Lady," answered Tom, "I am in mortal terror of my Lord Herbert."

"Then have you been doing amiss, Tom, for no welldoer ever yet was afraid of my lord. Do you come because you would confess the truth?"

"Aye, My Lady," faltered Tom.

"Come, then—I will lead you to My Lord."

"No, an't please you, My Lady!" cried Tom, trembling yet more. "I will confess to you, My Lady, and then do you confess to my lord, so that he may forgive me."

"Well, I will venture so far for you, Tom," returned her ladyship, "that is, if you be honest, and tell me all."

Thus encouraged, Tom cleansed his stuffed bosom, telling all the part he had borne in Richard's escape, even to the disclosure of the watchword to his mother. (Is there not this peculiarity about the fear of the supernatural, even let it be of the lowest and most slavish kind, that under it men speak the truth, believing it alone can shelter them?)

Lady Margaret dismissed him with hopes of forgiveness, and going straight to her husband in his secret chamber, amused him with her vivid mimicry of Tom's looks and words as he made his confession.

Here was much gained, but Tom had cast no ray of light upon the matter of Dorothy's imprisonment. The next day Lord Herbert sent for him to his workshop, where he was then alone. Tom appeared in a state of abject terror.

"Now, Tom," said his lordship, "have you made a clean breast of it?"

"Yes, My Lord," answered Tom. "There be but one thing more. As I went back to my chamber, I stopped to recover my breath at the top of the stair leading down from my lord's dining parlor to the hall, and knelt on the seat of the little window that commands the archway to the keep, I saw the prisoner below—"

"How knew you the prisoner ere it was yet daybreak, and that in the darkest corner of all the court?"

"I knew him by the way my bones shook at the white sleeves of his shirt, My Lord," said Tom, who was too far gone in fear to make the joke of pretending courage.

"Hardly evidence, Tom. But go on."

"And with him I saw Mistress Dorothy—"

"Hold there, Tom!" cried Lord Herbert. "Why did you not impart this last night to my lady?"

"Because my lady loveth Mistress Dorothy, and I dreaded she would therefore refuse to believe me."

"What a heap of cunning goes to the making of a downright fool!" said Lord Herbert to himself, but so as Tom could not fail to hear him. "And what passed between them?" he asked.

"Only a whispering with their heads together," answered Tom.

"And what did you hear?"

"Nothing, My Lord."

"And what followed?"

"The Roundhead left her, and went through the archway. She stood a moment and then followed him. But I, fearful of her coming up the stair and finding me, gat me quickly to my own place."

"Tom, Tom! I am ashamed of you! Afraid of a woman? Verily your heart is of wax."

"That can hardly be, My Lord, for I find it still on the wane."

"If your wit were no better than your courage, you would never have enough to play the fool with."

"No, My Lord. I should have had to turn philosopher."

"A fair hit, Tom! But one thing perplexes me—if you saw Mistress Dorothy in the court with the Roundhead, how did she come thereafter, to be locked up in his chamber?"

"It behooves that she went into it again, My Lord."

"How do you know that she had been there before?"

"Nay, I do not, My Lord. I know nothing of the matter."

"Why say it then? Take heed to your words, Tom. Who do you think locked the door on her?"

"I know not, My Lord, and dare hardly say what I think. But let your lordship's wisdom determine whether it might not be one of those demons whereof the house hath been full ever since that night I saw them rise from the water of the moat and rush into the fountain court."

"Meddle not, even in your thoughts, with things that are beyond you," said Lord Herbert. "By what signs did you know Mistress Dorothy in the dark, as she stood talking to the Roundhead?"

"There was light enough to know woman from man, My Lord."

"And there were then that night no women in the castle but Mistress Dorothy?"

"Why, who else could it have been, My Lord?"

"Why not your own mother, Tom, ridden hither on her broomstick to deliver her darling?"

Tom gaped with fresh terror at the awful suggestion.

"Now hear me, Thomas Rees!" his lordship went on. "An' ever it come to my knowledge that you say you saw Mistress Dorothy, when all you saw was a woman who might have been your own mother, talking to the Roundhead, as you call a man who might indeed have been Caspar Kaltoff in his shirt sleeves, I will set every devil at my command upon your back and belly, your sides and soles. Be warned, and not only speak the truth—as you have for a whole half-hour been trying to do—but learn to distinguish between your fancies and God's facts. For verily you are a greater fool than I took you for, and that was no small one. Be gone, and send Mistress Watson here."

Tom crawled away, and presently Mrs. Watson appeared, looking offended, and a little frightened.

"I cannot but think you are somewhat remiss in your ministrations to a sick man, Mistress Watson," he said, "to leave him so long to himself. Had he been a King's officer now, would you not have shown him more favor?"

"That, indeed, may be, My Lord," returned Mrs. Watson with dignity. "But an' the young fellow had been very sick, he wouldst not have made his escape."

"And left the blame thereof with you. Besides, that he did his escape, he may have done it in the strength of the fever that followed such a wound."

"My Lord, I gave him a potion, wherefrom he shouldst have slept until I sought him again."

"Was he or you to blame that he did not feel the obligation? When a man instead of sleeping runs away, the potion was ill-mingled, Mistress Watson."

"She who waked him when he ought to have slept must bear the blame, not I, My Lord."

"You should, I say, have kept better watch. But tell me who you mean by *she*."

"She who was found in his chamber, My Lord," said Mrs. Watson, compressing her lips, as if, come what might, she would stand on the foundation of the truth.

"Ah! By the way, I would gladly understand how it came to be known throughout the castle that you did find her there? I have the assurance of My Lady, My Lord Marquis, and my Lord Charles, that never did one of them utter word so to slander an orphan as you have now done in my hearing."

"You wrong me grievously, My Lord," cried Mrs. Watson.

"You have yourself to thank for it then, for you have this night said in mine own ears that Mistress Dorothy waked your prisoner, importing that she thereafter set him free, when you know that she denies the same, and is therein believed by My Lord Marquis and all his house."

"Therein I believe her not, My Lord—but I swear by all the saints and angels, that to none but your lordship have I ever said the word, neither have I ever opened my lips against her, lest I shouldst take from her the chance of betterment."

"I will be more just to you than you have been to my cousin, Mistress Watson, for I will believe that you did only harbor evil in your heart, not send it from the doors of your lips to enter into other bosoms. Was it you then that locked the door on her?"

"God forbid, My Lord!"

"You think it was the Roundhead?"

"No, surely, My Lord, for where would be the need?"

"Lest she should issue and give the alarm."

Mrs. Watson smiled an acid smile.

"Then the doer of that evil deed," pursued Lord Herbert, "must be now in the castle, and from this moment every power I possess in earth, air, or sea, shall be taxed to the uttermost for the discovery of that evil person. Let this vow of mine be known, Mistress Watson, as a thing you have heard me say—not commissioned you to report."

Mrs. Watson left the workshop in humbled mood. To her spiritual benefit, Lord Herbert had succeeded in punishing her for her cruelty to Dorothy.

And now he, depending more upon his wits than his learning, found himself a good deal in the dark. Confident that neither Richard, Tom Fool, nor Mrs. Watson had locked the door upon Dorothy, he gave one moment's examination to the lock, and was satisfied that an enemy had done it. He then started his thoughts on another track: how was it that the Roundhead had been able in the darkness, and without alarming a single sleeper, to find his way from a part of the house where there were no stairs near, and many rooms, all occupied? Clearly by the help of *her* whom Tom Fool had seen with him by the hall door. She had guided him down my lord's stair, and thus avoided the risk of crossing the paved court to the hall door within sight of the warders of the main entrance. And to her indubitably the young Roundhead had committed the ring for Dorothy.

Perhaps this woman was the same person who turned the key on Dorothy. What did her presence so soon again in the vicinity of the turret chamber indicate? Possibly that her own chamber was near it. He inquired, and found there were two who slept alone in the neighborhood of the turret chamber: Amanda and Mrs. Watson.

From Dorothy, Lord Herbert drew an accurate description of the ring to which Richard's letter had alluded, and immediately set about making one after it. From stage to stage of its progress, he brought it to her for examination and criticism until, before the day was over, he had completed a model sufficiently like to pass for the same.

The greater portion of the next day he spent in getting into perfect condition a certain mechanical toy he had constructed many years before. Next he ordered the alarm bell to be rung, and the herald of the castle to call aloud that on the following day, after dinner, so soon as they should hear the sound of the alarm bell, every soul in the castle, even to the infant in arms, should appear in the great hall, that Lord Herbert might perceive which among them had insulted the lord and the rule of the house by the locking of one of its doors to the imprisonment and wrong of his lordship's cousin, Mistress Dorothy Vaughan. Three strokes of the great bell opened and closed the announcement, and a great hush of fearful expectancy fell upon the place.

38.
The Exorcism

There was little talk in the hall during dinner the next day, and not much in the Marquis' dining room.

In the midst of the meal at the housekeeper's table, Mistress Amanda was taken suddenly ill, and nearly fell from her chair. A spoonful of one of Mrs. Watson's strong waters revived her, but she was compelled to leave the room.

After dinner the room was cleared, and solemn preparations were made in the hall. The dais was covered with crimson cloth, and chairs were arranged on each side for the lords and ladies of the family, while in the wide space between was set the Marquis' chair of state. Immediately below the dais, chairs were placed by the walls for the ladies and officers of the household. The minstrel's gallery was hung with crimson, and all the windows (save the painted one) were hung with thick cloth of the same color, so that a dull red light filled the huge place. The floor was then strewn with fresh rushes, and candles were placed and lighted in sconces on the walls. About one o'clock the alarm bell gave three great tolls, and then silence fell.

Almost noiselessly, and with faces more than grave, the people of the castle in their Sunday clothes began trooping in, among them Tom Fool, the very picture of dismay. In came the garrison also, with clank and clang, and took their places with countenances expressive of neither hardihood nor merriment, but a grave expectancy. The ladies and officers, among them Dorothy, seated themselves below the dais. The two doors were closed, and silence reigned.

A few minutes more and the ladies and gentlemen of the family, in full dress, entered by the door at the back of the dais. Next came the Marquis in full dress, leaning on Lord Charles. He placed himself in the great chair, and sat upright, looking serenely around, while Lord Charles took his station erect at his left hand. Last of all Lord Herbert entered alone, in his garb of astrologer. He bowed profoundly to his father, and taking his place by his right hand, cast a keen eye around the assembly. His look was grave, even troubled.

"Are all present?" he asked, and was answered only by silence. He then waved his right hand three times toward heaven, each time throwing his palm outwards and upwards. At the close of the third gesture, a roar of thunder broke and rolled about the place, making the huge hall tremble, and the windows rattle and shake. It grew darker, and through the dim-stained window many saw a dense black smoke rising from the stone court—and what could it be but the chariot upon which the demon rode up from the infernal lake? Again Lord Herbert waved his right arm three times, and again the thunder broke and rolled vibrating about the place. A third time he gave the sign, and once more, but now close over their heads, the thunder broke, and high in the oak roof appeared a little cloud of smoke. Lord Herbert made one step forward, and held out his hand like a falconer presenting his wrist to a bird.

"Ha! Art thou here?" he said.

And a creature like a bat suddenly perched upon his forefinger, waving its filmy wings up and down. He looked at it for a moment, bent his head to it, seemed to whisper, and then addressed it aloud.

"Go," he said, "alight upon the head of the one who hath wrought this evil in this house. For it was of thine own kind, and would have smirched a fair brow."

He cast the creature aloft. A smothered cry came from some of the women, and Tom Fool gave a great sob and held his breath tight. Once round the wide space the bat flew, midway between floor and roof, and returned to perch on Lord Herbert's hand.

"Ha!" said his lordship, stooping his head over it. What meanest this? Is not the evildoer in presence? Not within the hall?"

He lifted his head, turned to his father, and said, "Your lordship's commands have been disregarded. One of your people is

184

absent from the hall."

"Search and see, and bring me word who is absent," commanded the Marquis.

The ushers went down into the crowd, one from each side of the dais. A minute or two passed, and then one brought the report that Mistress Amanda Fuller was not there.

Lord Herbert turned to his wife. "My Lady," he said, "Mistress Amanda is of your people. Why is she not here?"

"I know not, My Lord," replied Lady Margaret. "Lady Broughton, will you go and inquire why the damsel disregards my lord's commands?"

Lady Broughton came back pale and trembling with the report that she could not find her. A shudder ran through the whole body of the hall, for plainly she had been *fetched*. The thunder and smoke had not been for nothing—the devil had claimed and carried off his own! On the dais the impression was somewhat different, but every eye was fixed on Lord Herbert.

For a whole minute he stood, apparently lost in meditation. The bat rested on his hand, but its wings were still. He had intended to settle it on Amanda's head, but now he must alter his plan. Nor was he sorry to do so, for it had involved no small risk of failure; the toy required most delicate adjustment, and its management occasioned him no little anxiety. If by any chance the mechanical bat should alight upon the head of another—say Mrs. Doughty or Lady Broughton, instead of Amanda—what then? He was not sorry to find himself rescued from this jeopardy and speedily devised a new plan. While he felt bound to bring Amanda to shame should she prove guilty, he was yet willing to remember mercy, so that should she be innocent, no harm would result. He turned and whispered to his father.

"I will back thee, Lad. Do as thou wilt," returned the Marquis, gravely nodding his head.

"Ushers of the hall," cried Lord Herbert, "close and lock all the doors. Make the holy sign upon the lintel and the doorposts. Leave the door to the pitched court until I am gone forth and it is closed behind me, and then do the same, after which let all sit in silence. Move not, neither speak, for any sound of fear or smell of horror. For the gift that is in him from his mother, Thomas Rees shall accompany me. Go to the door, and wait until I come."

Having thus spoken, he raised the bat toward his face and once more talked to it in whispers. Then he bent his ear toward it to listen, and it fluttered its wings. A moment more and he cast the creature from him. It flew aloft and vanished into the farthest corner of the roof, a little dark recess. Then, bowing low to his father, the magician stepped down from the dais, and walked through the awestruck crowd to the door, where Tom stood waiting his approach. The fool's heart fluttered, for the hall seemed now the only place of security, and all outside it given over to goblins or worse.

The moment they crossed the threshold, the door was closed behind them, and the holy sign made over them.

All eyes were turned upon the Marquis, who sat motionless. Motionless too, as if they had been carved in stone like the leopards and wyvern over their heads, sat all the lords and ladies. The ladies beneath the dais were troubled and pale, for Amanda was one of them, and their imaginations were busy with what might now be befalling her. Dorothy sat in much distress, for although she could lay no evil intent to her own charge, she was yet the cause of the whole fearful business. As for Scudamore, though he too was white of face, he said to himself that the devil might fly away with Amanda and welcome, for what he cared. One woman in the crowd fainted and fell, but uttered never a moan. The very children were hushed by the dread that pervaded the air, and the smell of sulphur grew from a suspicion to a plain presence.

After about half an hour of frightened expectation, three great knocks came to the porch door. In walked Lord Herbert with Tom Fool, in whom the importance had now at length banished almost every sign of dread. Lord Herbert reascended the dais, bowed once more to his father, spoke a few words to him in a tone too low to be overheard, and then turning to the assembly, said with solemn voice and stern countenance, "The air is clear. The sin of Raglan is purged. Everyone to his place."

Had not Tom Fool led the way from the hall, perhaps no one would have ventured to stir. But with many a deep-drawn breath and sigh of relief, they trooped slowly out after him, while in their hearts keen curiosity and vague terror contended like fire and water.

From that hour the face of Amanda Serafina was no more seen within the walls of Raglan Castle, though that same midnight shrieks and loud wailings were heard.

186

Lord Herbert led the members of his own family (Dorothy now included) to the oak parlor, and revealed the true story of the strange proceedings.

He had taken Tom Fool both because he knew the castle so well, and because he believed he might depend on his dread for secrecy. They had scarcely left the hall when they were joined by Caspar, who had been waiting on the balcony. After a long search they found Amanda in an empty stall in the subterranean stable, as if, in the agony of her terror at the awful noises and the impending discovery, she had sought refuge in the companionship of the innocent animals. She was crouching, the very image of fear, under the manger. She gave no cry when Lord Herbert entered, and seemed to gather a little courage when she found that the approaching steps were those of a human being.

"Mistress Amanda Fuller," said his lordship with awful severity, "You have in your possession a jewel which is not your own."

"A jewel, My Lord?" faltered Amanda. "I know not what your lordship means. Of what sort is the jewel?"

"One very like this," returned Lord Herbert, producing the false ring.

"Why, there you have it, My Lord!"

"Traitress to your King and your lord, out of your own mouth have I convicted you! This is not the ring. See!" He squeezed it betwixt his finger and thumb to a shapeless mass and threw it from him. "You are the one who showed the rebel his way from the prison into which he was cast!"

"He took me by the throat, My Lord," gasped Amanda, "and put me in mortal terror."

"You slander him," returned Lord Herbert. "The Roundhead is a gentleman, and would not to save his life have harmed you, even had he known what a worthless thing you are. I will grant that he put you in fear. But wherefore did you give no alarm when he was gone?"

"He made me swear that I would not betray him."

"Let it be so. Why did you not reveal the way he took?"

"I knew it not."

"And why did you not deliver the ring he gave you for Mistress Dorothy?"

"I feared she would betray me, that I had held talk with the prisoner."

"Let that too pass as less wicked than cowardly. But wherefore did you lock the door upon her when you saw her go into the Roundhead's prison? You knew that she must bear the blame of having set him free—with other blame worse for a maiden to endure?"

"It was a sudden temptation, My Lord, which I knew not how to resist, and was carried away thereby. Have pity upon me," moaned Amanda.

"I will believe you there also, for I fear you have had so little practice in the art of resisting temptation, that you might well yield. But how was it that, after you had leisure to reflect, you spread abroad the report that she was found there, and that to the hurt not only of her loyal fame, but of her maidenly honor, understanding well that no one was there but herself, and that he alone who could bear testimony to her innocence and your guilt was parted from her by everything that could divide them but hatred? Was the temptation to that also too sudden for your resistance?"

Amanda was speechless, and hung her head, for the first time in her life ashamed of herself.

"Go to your chamber. I will follow."

She rose to obey but could scarcely walk, and he ordered the men to assist her. In her room she delivered up the ring, and at Lord Herbert's command proceeded to gather together her few possessions. Then they led her away to the rude chamber in the watch tower, and left her with the assurance that if she cried out or gave any alarm, it would be to the publishing of her own shame.

In the dead of night Caspar and Tom, with four picked guards, came to lead her away. Worn out by that time, and with nothing to sustain her from within, she fancied they were going to kill her, and giving way utterly, cried and shrieked aloud. Obdurate but gentle, they gave no ear to her petitions, but bore her through the western gate to the brick gate, placed her in a carriage behind six horses, and set out with her for Caerleon, where her mother lived. At her door they put her down, left the carriage at Usk, mounted the horses, and returned to Raglan one by one in the night. The warders who admitted them supposed them to be returned from distinct missions on the King's business.

Many were the speculations in the castle as to the fate of Mistress Amanda Serafina Fuller, but the common belief continued to be that she had been carried off by Satan, body and soul.

39.
Newbury

Early in the morning following Richard's twilight departure
for Raglan Castle, Mrs. Rees was awakened by the sound of
a heavy blow against her door. When with difficulty she
opened it, Richard fell across her threshold. Like poor Marquis, he
had come to her for help and healing.

What with his wound, his loss of blood, his double wetting, his
sleeplessness after Mrs. Watson's potion, want of food, disappointment, and fatigue, he was in a high fever. She administered a drop
or two of one of her restoratives, and prepared her own bed for
him. Finding his wound very tolerably dressed, Mrs. Rees would
not disturb the bandages. She gave him a cooling draught and
watched by him till he fell asleep. He raved a good deal, generally
in the delusion that he was talking to Dorothy—who sought to kill
him, and to whom he kept giving directions, at one time how to
guide the knife to reach his heart, at another how to mingle her
poison so that it should act with speed and certainty.

At length, when the red sun shone level through the window,
and made a red glory on the wall, he came to himself a little.

"Is it blood?" he murmured. "Did Dorothy do it? How foolish I
am! It is but a blot the sun has left behind him! Ah! I see! I am
dead and lying on the top of my tomb. I am only marble, and this
is Redware church. O Mother Rees, is it you? I am very glad.
Cover me a little."

His eyes closed, and for a few hours he lay in a deep sleep, from
which he woke very weak but clearheaded.

"I must get up, Mother Rees. My father will be anxious about me. Besides, I promised to set out for Gloucester today."

She sought to quiet him, but in vain, and was at last compelled to inform him that his father had armed himself, mounted Oliver, and himself led Richard's little company to join the Earl of Essex, who was now on his way to raise the siege of Gloucester.

She had much ado to convince him that the best thing in all respects was to lie still and submit to being nursed, so to get well as soon as possible, and join his father.

"Alas, Mother, I have no horse," said Richard, and hid his face on the pillow.

"The Lord will provide what thee wants, My Son," said the old woman with emotion, neither asking nor caring whether the Lord was on the side of the King or of the Parliament, but as little doubting that He must be on the side of Richard.

After a few days he would be restrained no longer. Go he must, he said, or his soul would tear itself out of his body, and go without it.

The eve of the day of Richard's departure, Marquis paid Mrs. Rees a second visit. He wanted no healing or help this time, seeming to have come only to offer his respects. But the knowledge that here was a messenger, dumb and discreet, ready to go between and make no sign, set Richard longing to use him. Hence was sent the letter Dorothy received.

At Redware Richard found a note from his father, telling him where to find money, and informing him that he was ready to yield him Oliver the moment he should appear to claim him. Richard put on his armor and went to the stable. The weather had been fine, and the harvest was wearing gradually to a close. The few horses that were left were overworked, for the necessities of the war had been severe; Mr. Heywood had scarce left an animal judged at all fit to carry a man and keep up with the troop.

When Richard reached the stable, there were in it but three horses. The first was one ancient in bones, with pits profound above his eyes, and gray hairs all about a face which had once been black.

"You are but fit for old Father Time to lay his scythe across when he is weary," said Richard, and turned to the next—huge-bodied, short-legged, as fat as butter, and with lop-ears and sleepy eyes. Having finished her corn she was churning away at a mangerful of grass. "You would burst your belly at the first charge," said Richard, and was approaching the third, one he did not recognize, when a vicious kick informed him that here was a temper and spirit. Before him stood the ugliest brute that ever ate barley. He was very long-bodied and rather short-legged, with great tufts at his fetlocks, and the general look of a huge rat, in part from having no hair on his long undocked tail. He was biting viciously at his manger, and Richard could see one eye glaring at him askance in the gloom.

"Dunnot go nigh him, Sir," cried Jacob Fortune, who had come up behind. "Thou knowest not his tricks. His name be his nature, and we call him Beelzebub when Master Stopchase be not by. I be right glad to see your honor up again."

Jacob was too old to go to the wars, and too indifferent to regret it, but he was faithful, and had authority over the few men left.

"I thank you, Jacob," said Richard. "What brute is this? I know him not."

"We all knows him too well, Master Richard, though verily Stopchase bought him but the day before he rode, thinking belike he might carry an ear or two of wheat. If he be not very good, he was not parlous dear; he paid for him but an old song. He was warranted to have work in him if a man but knew how to get it out."

"He is ugly."

"Ugly enough to fright death where he doth fail in his endeavor to kill; and he do kick, and he do bite like the living Satan. He wonnot go in no cart, but there he do stand eating his head off, as fast as he can. An' the brute were mine, I would slay him, I would, in good sooth."

"An' I had but time to cure him of his evil kicking! I fear I must ever ride the last in the troop," said Richard.

"Why for sure, Master, thee never will ride such a devil-pig as he to the wars! Will Farrier say he do believe he take his strain from the swine the devils go into in the miracle. All the children would make a mock of thee as thou did ride through the villages. Look at his legs—like stile posts, and do but look at his tail!"

"Lead him out, Jacob, and let me see his head."

"I dare not go nigh him, Sir. I be not nimble enough to get out of the way of his hoof. I be too old, Master."

Richard pulled on his thick buff glove, and went straight into the stall. The brute made a grab at him with his teeth, and was met by a smart blow from Richard's fist. Rearing, he would have struck at him with his near forefoot, but Richard caught it by the pastern, and with his left hand again struck him on the side of the mouth. The brute then submitted to be led out by the halter. And verily he was ugly to behold. His neck stuck straight out, and so did his tail, but the latter went off in a point, and the former in a hideous knob.

"Here is Jack!" cried the old man. "He lets Jack ride him to the water. Here, Jack! Get thee upon the hogback of Beelzebub, and mind the bristles do not flay thee, and let Master Richard see what paces he hath."

The animal tried to take the lad down with his hind foot as he mounted, but scarcely was he seated when he set off at a winging trot, in which he plied his posts in a manner astonishing. Spirit indeed he must have had, and plenty, to wield his legs in such fashion. His joints were so loose that the bones seemed to fly about, yet they always came down right.

"He is guilty of hypocrisy against the devil," said Richard, "for he is better than he looks. Anyhow, if he but carry me thither, he will do as well as a handsomer horse. Have you a saddle for him?"

"An' he had not brought a saddle with him, thou would not find one in Gwent to fit him," said the old man.

Richard found himself compelled to tarry yet another day, which he spent in armoring Beelzebub to the best of his ability, with the result of making him, if possible, still uglier than before.

Richard on Beelzebub was much stared at by the inhabitants of every village he passed through. Apparently, however, there was something about the centaur-compound which prevented their rudeness from going further. Beelzebub bore him well, and though not a comfortable horse to ride, he threw the road behind him at a wonderful rate, as often and as long as Richard was able to bear it.

By the time he began to draw nigh to Gloucester, Richard was in excellent spirits, though one painful thought haunted him—the fear that he might, while mounted on Beelzebub, have to encounter someone on his beloved Lady. He was consoled, however, to think that the brute was less dangerous to one in front than one behind him, heels being worse than teeth.

He soon became aware that either Gloucester had fallen or Essex had raised the siege, for army there was none, though the signs of a lately upbroken encampment were visible on all sides. Presently he learned that on the near approach of Essex, the besieging army had retired, and that the general had turned again in the direction of London. Richard fed Beelzebub, had his own dinner, mounted his hideous charger once more, and pushed on to get up with the army.

Essex had not taken the direct road to London, but kept to the south. Richard followed him as far as Swindon, and the next morning, reached Hungerford which he found in great commotion; at Newbury, only seven miles distant, Essex had found his way stopped by the King, and a battle had been raging ever since the early morning.

Having given his horse a good feed of oats and a draught of ale, Richard mounted again and rode hard for Newbury. Nor had he ridden long before he heard the straggling reports of carbines. He looked to the priming of his pistols and loosened his sword in its sheath.

Under the wall of Craven Park he could distinguish the noise of horses' hooves, and now and then the confused cries and shouts of hand-to-hand conflict. At Spein, he was all but in it, for there he met wounded men, retiring slowly or being carried by their comrades. These were of his own party, but he did not stop to ask any questions. Beelzebub snuffed at the fumes of the gunpowder and seemed to derive fresh vigor.

The lanes and hedges between Spein and Newbury had been the scenes of many bloody tussles that morning, for nowhere had either army found room to deploy. Some places had been fought over more than once or twice. But just before Richard came up, the tide had ebbed from that part of the way, for Essex's men had driven the King's men through the town and over the bridge. As Richard reached Spinhamland, and turned sharp to the right into the main street of Newbury, he was met by a rush of Parliament men retreating from a few of the King's cavalry coming at a sharp trot down the main street. They were now putting the Kennet with its narrow bridge between them and the long-feathered Cavaliers, in the hope of gaining time and fit ground for forming and presenting a bristled front. In the midst of this confused mass Richard found himself, the now maddened Beelzebub every moment lashing out behind him when not rearing or biting.

Before him the bridge rose steep to its crown, contracting as it rose. At its foot, where it widened to the street, stood a single horseman, shouting impatiently to the last of the pikemen, and spurring his horse while holding him. As the last man cleared the bridge, the Roundhead gave him rein, and with a bound and a scramble reached the apex and stood within half a neck of the foremost Cavalier trooper. A fierce combat instantly began between them. The bridge was wide enough for two to have fought side by side, but the Roundhead so worked his antagonist, who was a younger but less capable and less powerful man, that no comrade could get up beside him for the to-and-fro shifting of his horse.

The moment Richard was clear of the crowd, he made a great bolt for the bridge, and then perceived who the brave man was.

"Hold your own, Father!" he shouted. "Here I am!"

He sent Beelzebub up the steep crown of the bridge, and wedged him in between Oliver and the parapet, just as a second Cavalier made a dart for the place. Beelzebub sprang like a fury, rearing, biting, and striking out with his forefeet. He was frightful to see, for with ears laid back and gleaming teeth he looked more like a beast of prey. The Cavalier's horse recoiled in terror, rearing also, but snorting and backing and wavering, so that he would, but for the crowd behind him, have fallen backward down the slope.

A bullet from one of Richard's pistols sent his rider over his tail, the horse fell sideways against that of Mr. Heywood's antagonist, and the path was for a moment barricaded.

"Well done, good Beelzebub!" cried Richard, as he reined him back on to the crest of the bridge.

"Boy!" said his father sternly, at the same instant dealing his encumbered opponent a blow on the headpiece and tumbling him from his horse. "Is the sacred hour of victory a time to sully with profane and foolish jests? I little thought to hear such words at my side—not to say from the mouth of my own son!"

"Pardon me, Father—I only praised my horse," said Richard. "It cannot corrupt him, for he is such an ill-conditioned brute that they named him Beelzebub."

"I am glad your foolish words were so harmless," returned Mr. Heywood, smiling. "In my ears they sounded so evil that I could ill accept their testimony. Verily, the animal is marvelous ill-favored, but he has done well. The first return we make him shall be to give him another name."

"What shall we call him then, Father?" asked Richard.

"He is amazing like a huge rat!" said his father. "Let us henceforth call him Bishop."

The enemy had not been able to get near to attack them, for both horses and their riders were down. But just then a large troop of horsemen appeared at the top of the street. Glancing behind them in some anxiety, Richard and his father saw to their relief that the pikemen had now formed themselves into a hollow square at the foot of the bridge, and were prepared to receive cavalry. They turned therefore, and passing through, rode to find their own regiment.

From that day Bishop, notwithstanding his faults many and grievous, was regarded with respect by both father and son. Richard vowed never to mount another, let him laugh who would, so long as the brute lived and he had not recovered Lady.

But they had to give him room for two on the march, and the place behind him was always left vacant, seeing Bishop kicked out his leg to twice its walking length. Before long, however, they had grown so used to his ways that they almost ceased to regard them as faults, and Bishop began to grow a favorite in the regiment.

40.
Love and Treason

The minds of the Marquis and Lord Charles were now at rest both as regarded the gap in the defenses of the castle and the character of its inmates. The fate of Amanda was allowed gradually to ooze out, but the greater portion both of domestics and garrison continued in the firm belief that she had been carried off by Satan. Young Delaware asserted that he *saw* the devil fly away with her—a testimony which gained as much in one way as it lost in another by the fact that he could not see at all.

To Scudamore her absence was only a relief. She had ceased to interest him, while Dorothy had become to him like an enchanted castle, the spell of which he flattered himself he was the knight born to break. All his endeavors, however, to attract from her a single favorable response were disappointed. She seemed absolutely unsuspicious of what he sought. Had she become an inmate of Raglan immediately after he first made her acquaintance, that might have ripened to something more hopeful; but she came to the castle in sorrow and felt no comfort from him, while he was then beginning to yield to the tightening bonds Amanda had flung around him. Nor had he since afforded her any ground for altering either her first impressions or the word portrait Lady Margaret had presented of him.

Strange to say, however, he soon began to be vaguely wrought upon by the superiority of her nature. The establishment of her innocence in the eyes of the household had threatened at first to destroy something of her attraction; yet he began to respect her,

196

began to feel drawn as if by another spiritual sense than that of which Amanda had laid hold. He found in her an element of authority. His own conscious influences (to whose triumph he had been accustomed) had proved powerless upon her, while those that in her resided unconscious were subduing him.

He began to be aware that this was no light preference, no passing fancy, but something more serious—that, in fact, he was really (though uncomfortably and unsatisfactorily) in love with her. She was not like any other girl he had given his shabby love to. She kept him at a distance, and that he began to find tormenting.

One day, meeting her in the court as she was crossing toward the keep, he asked Dorothy of her work.

"I would you took apprentices, Cousin," he said, "so I might be one, and learn the mysteries of your trade."

"Wherefore, Cousin?"

"That I might spare you something of your labor."

"That were no kindness, for I am not like you. I find labor a thing to be courted rather than spared."

Scudamore gazed into her gray eyes, but found there nothing to contradict, nothing to supplement the indifference of her words. There was no lurking sparkle of humor, no acknowledgment of kindness. He stammered—who had never stammered before— broke the joints of an ill-fitted answer, swept the tiles with the long feather in his hat, and found himself parted from her.

Lord Herbert again left the castle, for more soldiers must be raised for the King. Winter drew nigh, and stayed somewhat the rush of events, brought a little sleep to the world and coolness to men's hearts, and led in another Christmas.

Nor did the many troubles heaped on England yet dull the merriment at Raglan. Customs are like carpets, forever wearing out whether we mark it or not; but Lord Worcester's patriarchal prejudices, cleaving to the old and looking askance on the new, caused them to endure long in Raglan. The old were the things of his fathers which he had loved from his childhood, and the new were the things of his children which he had not proven.

What a fire blazed on the hall hearth under the great chimney! No one could go within yards of it for the fierce heat of the blazing logs and huge lumps of coal. On the evenings of special merrymaking, the candles were lit, the musicians played, and a country dance filled the length of the great floor.

On such an occasion Rowland had attempted a nearer approach to Dorothy, but had gained nothing. She neither repelled nor encouraged him, but smiled at his better jokes, looked grave at his silly ones, and altogether treated him like a boy, young (or old) enough to be troublesome if encouraged. He grew desperate, and so one night summoned up courage as they stood together waiting for the next dance.

"Why will you never talk to me, Cousin Dorothy?" he said.

"Is it so, Mr. Scudamore? I was not aware. If you spoke and I answered not, I am sorry."

"No, I mean not that," returned Scudamore. "But when I speak, you always make me feel as if I ought not to have spoken. When I call you Cousin Dorothy, you reply with Mr. Scudamore."

"The relation is hardly near enough to justify a more familiar observance."

"Our mothers loved each other."

"They found each other worthy."

"And do you not find me such?" sighed Scudamore, with a smile meant to be both humble and bewitching.

"N-n-o. You have not made me desire to hold with you much converse."

"Tell me why, Cousin, that I may reform that which offends you."

"If a man see not his faults with his own eyes, how shall he see them with the eyes of another?"

"Will you never love me, Dorothy, not even a little?"

"Wherefore should I love you, Rowland?"

"We are commanded to love even our enemies."

"Are you then my enemy, Cousin?"

"No, forsooth! I am the most loving friend you have."

"Then I am sorely to be pitied for having none better. But, thank God, it is not so."

"Must I then be your enemy indeed before you will love me?"

"No, Cousin: cease to be your own enemy and I will call you my friend."

"Wherein then am I my own enemy?"

"I know you better than you think, Cousin. I have read your title page, if not your whole book."

"Tell me then how reads my title page, Cousin."

" 'The art of being willfully blind,' or 'The way to see no further than one would.' "

"Fair preacher," began Rowland, but Dorothy interrupted him. "If you betake to your gibes, I have done," she said.

"Be not angry with me—it is but my nature, which for your sake I will control. If you cannot love me, will you not then pity me a little?"

"That I may pity you, answer me what good thing is there in you wherefore I should love you?"

"Would you have a man trumpet his own praises?"

"I fear not that of one who has but the trumpet. I will tell you this much—I have never seen that you loved save for the pastime thereof. I doubt if you love your master for more than your place."

"Cousin!"

"Be honest with yourself, Rowland. If you would have me for your cousin, it must be on the ground of truth."

Rowland possessed at least good nature; few young men would have borne to be so severely handled. But then, while one's good opinion of himself remains untroubled, hostile criticism will not reach to the quick. The thing that hurts is that which sets trembling the ground of self-worship, and lays bare the shrunk cracks and wormholes under the golden plates of the idol.

The dance called them, and their talk ceased. When it was over, Dorothy left the hall and sought her chamber. But by the marble basin in the dim fountain court her cousin overtook her, and had the temerity to resume the conversation. The moth would still at any risk circle the candle. It was a still night, and therefore not very cold, although icicles hung from the mouth of the horse.

"You do me scant justice, Cousin," said Rowland, "maintaining that I love but myself or for my own ends. I know that I love you better than so."

"For your own sake, I would be glad of the assurance, might I but believe it. But—"

Dorothy had recently become aware that there had been an understanding between Amanda and Rowland. The question now rose in her mind—could these two have been the nightly intruders on the forbidden ground of the workshop, and afterward the victims of the watershoot? The suspicion grew to a conviction. And she had found it remarkable that Rowland revealed no concern for Amanda's misfortunes, or anxiety about her fate. Dorothy therefore ventured a bold stroke.

"When I think how you bore yourself with Mistress Amanda—"

"My precious Dorothy!" exclaimed Scudamore, filled with a sudden gush of hope. "You will never be so unjust to yourself as to be jealous of her! She is to me as nothing—as if she had never been, nor care I forsooth if the devil has indeed flown away with her bodily. She had no heart like yours, Dorothy, as I soon discovered. She had indeed a pretty wit of her own, but that was all. And then she was spiteful. She hated you, Dorothy."

He spoke of her as one dead.

"How did you know that? Were you then so far in her confidence? Where is your own heart, Mr. Scudamore?"

"In your bosom, lovely Dorothy."

"You are mistaken. But maybe you imagine I picked it up that night you laid it at Mistress Amanda's feet in My Lord's workshop in the keep?"

Dorothy fixed her eyes on him as she spoke, and kept them fixed when she had ended. He turned visibly pale in the shadowy night, and did not attempt to cover his confusion.

"Or perhaps," she continued, "it was torn from you by the waters that swept you from the bridge, as you ventured with her yet again upon the forbidden ground."

He hung his head, and stood before her like a chidden child.

"Do you think," she went on, "that my lord would easily pardon such things?"

"You knew it and did not betray me! O Dorothy!" murmured Scudamore. "You are a very angel of light." He seized her hand, and but for the possible eyes watching them, would have flung himself at her feet.

Dorothy, however, would not yet lay aside the part she had assumed of moral surgeon. "But notwithstanding all this, Cousin Rowland, when trouble came upon the young lady, what comfort was there for her in you? You never loved her, although I doubt not you did vow and swear thereto a hundred times."

Rowland was silent, and began to fear her.

"What love you had was of such sort that you did encourage in her that which was evil, and then let her go like a haggard hawk. You marvel that I should be so careless of your merits! Tell me, Cousin, what is there in you that I should love? Can there be love for that which is in no wise lovely? I but appeal to your own conscience, Rowland, when I ask you—is this well?"

"Will you not teach me to be good like you, Dorothy?"

"You must teach yourself to be good like the Rowland you know in your better heart, when it is soft and lowly."

"Would you then love me a little, Dorothy, if I vowed to be your scholar, and study to be good?"

"He that is good is good for goodness' sake, Rowland. Yet who can fail to love that which is good, in king or knave?"

"Ah! Do not mock me, Dorothy. Such is not the love I would have of you."

"It is all you ever can have of me, and it is not likely you will ever have it, for truly you are of nature so light that any wind may blow you into the Dead Sea."

"I see!" cried Scudamore. "For all your fine reproof, you too can spurn a heart at your feet. You love the Roundhead, and are but a traitress, for all your goodness."

"I am indeed traitress enough to love any Roundhead gentleman better than a Royalist knave," said Dorothy, and turning from him, she sought the grand staircase.

41.
A New Soldier

Moments had scarcely passed after Dorothy left him at the fountain ere Scudamore grievously repented, and would gladly have offered apology and what amends he might.

But Dorothy, neither easily moved to wrath nor active resentment, was not ready to forget the results of moral difference, or to permit him any nearer approach. She granted him only distant recognition in company, neither seeking nor avoiding him, and as to all opportunity of private speech, entirely shunning him. For some time, in the vanity of his experience, he never doubted that these were only feminine arts, or that when she judged him sufficiently punished, she would relax the severity of her behavior and begin to make amends.

He began to doubt the universality of his experience, and to dread lest the maiden should actually prove what he had never found maiden before—inexorable. In truth, her thoughts rarely turned to him at all. She was simply forgetting him, busy perhaps with some self-offered question that demanded an answer, or perhaps brooding a little over the past, in which the form of Richard often came and went.

So long as Rowland imagined the existence of a quarrel, he imagined therein a bond between them. When he became convinced that no quarrel—only indifference—separated them, he began to despair. Seizing therefore an opportunity, he began a talk upon the old basis.

"Will you then never forgive me, Dorothy, for offending you with rude words?" he said humbly.

"Truly, I have forgotten them."

"Then shall we be friends?"

"Nay, that follows not."

"What quarrel then have you with me?"

"I have no quarrel with you; yet is there one thing I cannot forgive you."

"And what is that, Cousin? Believe me, I know not. I need but to know, and I will humble myself."

"That would serve nothing, for how should I forgive you for being unworthy? For such thing there is no forgiveness. Cease to be unworthy, and then is there nothing to forgive. I were an unfriendly friend, Rowland, did I befriend the man who befriends not himself."

"I understand you not, Cousin."

"And I understand not your not understanding. Therefore there can be no communion between us."

So saying, Dorothy left him. However great had been the freedom with which he had lost and changed many a foolish liking, he found he had not the power to shake himself free from the first worthy passion ever roused in him. It had struck root below the sandy upper stratum of his mind into a clay soil beneath where, at least, it was able to hold, and whence it could draw a little slow, reluctant nourishment.

He fell into a sort of willful despair, and disrelished everything except his food and drink, so much so that the Marquis perceived his altered cheer and one day addressed him to know the cause.

"What aileth thee, Rowland?" he said kindly. "For this se'ennight past, thou lookest like one that oweth the hangman his best suit."

"I rust, My Lord," said Rowland, with a tragic air of discontent. The notion had risen in his foolish head that the way to soften Dorothy's heart would be to ride to the wars and be severely but not mortally wounded. Then he would be brought back to Raglan and, thinking he was going to die, Dorothy would nurse him, and then she would be sure to fall in love with him. Yes, he would ride forth on the fellow Heywood's mare, seek him in the field of battle and slay him, but be himself thus grievously wounded.

"Ha! Thou wouldst to the wars!" replied the Marquis. "I like thee for that, Boy. Truly the King wanteth soldiers, and that more than ever. Thou art a good cupbearer, but I will do my best to savor my claret without thee. Thou shalt to the King, and what poor thing my word may do for thee shall not be wanting."

Scudamore had expected opposition, and was a little non-plussed. He had judged himself essential to his master's comfort, and had even hoped he might set Dorothy to use her influence toward reconciling him to remain at home. But although self-indulgent and lazy, Scudamore was no coward, and had never had any experience to give him pause; he did not know what an ugly thing a battle is after it is over, when the mind has leisure to attend to smarting wounds.

"I thank your lordship with all my heart," he said, putting on an air of greater satisfaction than he felt, "and with your lordship's leave would prefer a further request."

"I owe thee something for long and faithful service. An' I can, I will."

"Give me the Roundhead's mare that I may the better find her master."

"Thou art the last who ought to get any good of her. It were neither law nor justice to hand the stolen goods to the thief. Yet thou shalt have her. Thou shalt not rust at home for the sake of a gouty old man and his claret. Ere thou ride, look well to thy girths, and as thou ridest say thy prayers, for it pleaseth not God that every man on the right side should live, and thou mayest find the presence in which thou standest change suddenly from that of mortal man to living God. And of all things, Lad, remember this, that a weak blow were ever better unstruck. Go now to the armor-er, and to him deliver my will that he fit thee out for His Majesty's service. I can give thee no rank, for I have no regiment in the making at the present; but it may please His Majesty to take care of thee, and give thee a place in my Lord Glamorgan's regiment of bodyguards."

The prospect thus suddenly opened to Scudamore, of a wider life and greater liberty, might have dazzled many a nobler nature than his. Lord Worcester saw the light in his eyes, and as he left the room gazed after him with pitiful countenance.

"Poor lad!" he said to himself. "I hope I see not the last of thee! God forbid! But here thou didst but rust, and it were a vile thing in an old man to infect a youth with the disease of age."

Rowland soon found the master of the armory, and with him crossed to the armor store in the keep above the workshop. At the foot of the stair he talked loudly in the hope that Dorothy might be with the fire engine and hear him. Having filled his arms with such pieces as pleased his fancy, he contrived to drop them all with a huge clatter at the foot of the stair.

The noise brought out Dorothy. "Do I see you arming, Cousin?" she said. "I congratulate you."

She held out her hand to him. He took it and stared. The reception of his news was different from what he had been vain enough to hope. So little had Dorothy's behavior in the capture of Richard enlightened him as to her character!

"You would have me slain then to be rid of me, Dorothy?" he gasped.

"I would have any man slain where men fight," returned Dorothy, "rather than idling within stone walls!"

"You are hard-hearted, Dorothy, and know not what love is, else would you pity me a little."

"What! Are you afraid, Cousin?"

"Afraid! I fear nothing under heaven but your cruelty, Dorothy."

"Then what would you have me pity you for?"

"I would, an' I had dared, have said because I must leave you. But you would mock at that, and therefore I say instead because I shall never return—for I see well that you never have loved me even a little."

Dorothy smiled. "An' I had loved you, Cousin," she rejoined, "I had never let you rest until you had donned your buff coat and buckled on your spurs and departed to be a man among men, and no more a boy among women."

So saying, she returned to her engine, which all the time had been pumping and forcing with fiery inspiration.

Scudamore mounted and rode, followed by one of the grooms. He found the King at Wallingford, presented the Marquis' letter, proffered his services, and was at once placed in attendance on His Majesty's person.

42.
Glamorgan
1644—1645

The winter passed, and still the sounds of war came no nearer to Raglan, which lay like a great lion that the hunter dared not arouse. The whole of Wales, except a castle or two, remained subject to the King; and this he owed in great measure to the influence and devotion of the Somersets, his obligation to whom he seemed more and more bent on acknowledging.

One day in early summer Lady Margaret was sitting in her parlor, busy with her embroidery, and Dorothy was by her side assisting her, when Lord Herbert, who had been absent, walked in.

"How does my Lady Glamorgan?" he said gaily.

"What mean you, my Herbert?" returned his wife, looking in his eyes eagerly.

"Your Herbert am I no more, neither plume I myself any more in the spare feathers of my father. You are, My Dove, as you deserve to be, Countess of Glamorgan, in the right of your own husband, first Earl of same. Such is the will of His Majesty. Come, Dorothy, are you not proud to be cousin to an Earl?"

"I am proud that you should call me cousin, My Lord," answered Dorothy, "but truly to me it is all one whether you be called Herbert or Glamorgan. So you remain my cousin and my friend, the King may call you what he will, and if you are pleased, so am I."

"St. George! You have well spoken, Cousin!" cried the Earl.

206

"Hath she not, Wife?"

"So well that if she often saith as well, I shall have much ado not to hate her," replied Lady Glamorgan. "When did you ever cry 'well spoken' to your mad Irishwoman, Herbert?"

"All you do is well, My Lady. You have all the titles to my praises already in your pocket. Besides, Cousin Dorothy is young and meek, and requires a little encouragement."

"Whereas your wife is old and bold, and cares no more for your good word, my new Lord of Glamorgan?"

Dorothy looked so grave that they both fell laughing.

"I would you could teach her a merry jest or two, Margaret," said the Earl. "We are decent people enough in Raglan, but she is much too sober for us. Cheer up, Dorothy! Good times are at hand; that you may not doubt it, listen—but this is only for your ear, not for your tongue. The King has made me generalissimo of his three armies, and admiral of a fleet, and truly I know not what all, for I have yet but run my eye over the patent. And, Wife, I verily do believe the King bides his time to make my father Duke of Somerset, and then one day you will be Duchess, Margaret! Think on that!"

Lady Glamorgan burst into tears.

"I would I might have a kiss of my Molly!" she cried.

She had never before in Dorothy's hearing uttered the name of her child since her death. New dignity awoke the thought of the darling to whom titles were but words, and the ice was broken. A pause followed.

"Yes, Margaret, you are right," said Glamorgan at length. "It is all but folly; yet, as the marks of a King's favors, such honors are precious."

"It is I who pay for them," said his wife.

"How so, My Dove?"

"Do they not cost me you, Herbert—and cost me very dear? Are not you ever from my sight?"

"Yes, Margaret, it is hard on you, and hard on me too," said the Earl tenderly. "Yet not so hard as upon our King, who selleth his plate and his jewels."

"Pooh! What of that, then, Herbert? If he would leave me you, he might have all mine, and welcome, for you know I but hold them for you to sell when you will."

"I know, and the time may come, though, thank God it is not

yet. What would you say, Countess, if with all your honors you did yet come to poverty? Can you be poor and merry?"

"So you were with me, Herbert—Glamorgan, I would say, but my lips frame not themselves to the word. I like not the title greatly, but when it means you to me, then I shall love it."

"My Lord, if I have leave to speak," said Dorothy, "did you not say the diamond in that ring Richard Heywood sent me was of some worth? Then would I cast it in the King's treasury."

"No, Child. The King robs not orphans."

"Did the King of kings rob the poor widow who cast in her two mites, then?"

"No, but perhaps the priests did. Still, as I say, the hour may come when all our mites may be wanted, and yours be accepted with the rest; but my father and I have yet much to give, and shall have given it before that hour comes. Besides, Dorothy, what would that handsome Roundhead of yours say if, instead of keeping well the ring he gave you, you had turned it to the use he liked the least?

"He will never ask me concerning it," said Dorothy, with a faint smile.

"Be not oversure of it, Child. My lady asks me many things I never thought to tell her before the priest made us one. Dorothy, I have no right and no wish to spy into your future, but when these wars are over, and the King has his own again, there will be few men in his three kingdoms so worthy of the hand and heart of Dorothy Vaughan as that same Roundhead fellow, Richard Heywood. I would to God he were as good a Catholic as he is a mistaken Puritan!"

Parliament had secured the assistance of the Scots. Their forces entered England early in 1644, and the King was now attempting to secure the assistance of the Irish Catholics. But it was a game of terrible danger, for if he lost, he lost everything. The Irish Catholics had, truly or falsely, been charged with such enormities during the rebellion, that they had become absolutely hateful in the eyes of all English Protestants, and any alliance with them must cost him far more in Protestants than he could gain by it in Catholics. It was necessary, therefore, that he should go about it with the utmost caution, but his wariness far exceeded his dignity, and was practiced at the expense of his best friends. The King was such a believer in the divine right of his inheritance, that not only would he himself sacrifice everything to the dim shadow of royalty which usurped the throne of his conscience, but would (although not always without remorse) accept any sacrifice which a subject might have devotion enough to bring.

His slowly maturing intention to employ Lord Herbert in a secret mission to Ireland had led the King to bind him yet more closely by conferring on him the title of Glamorgan. But it was not until 1645, when his affairs seemed on the point of becoming desperate, that King Charles proceeded to carry out his design.

Early in the year, he gave a secret commission for Ireland to the Earl of Glamorgan, with immense powers, among them that of coining money, in order that he might propose certain secret arrangements with the Irish Catholics. Glamorgan, therefore, took a long leave of his wife and family, and in the month of March set out for Dublin. At Caernarvon, his party boarded a small bark laden with corn, and in the rough weather that followed, were cast ashore on the coast of Lancashire. A second attempt failed also, when, pursued by a Parliament vessel, they were again compelled to land on the same coast. It was the middle of summer before they reached Dublin.

Meantime the Scots had invaded England, and the Parliament had largely increased their forces in the hope of a decisive engagement, but the King refused battle and gained time. In the north, Prince Rupert made some progress and brought on the battle of Marston Moor, where victory was gained by Cromwell after all had been regarded as lost by the other Parliamentary generals. On the other hand, the King gained in the west country over Essex and his army.

The trial and execution of Archbishop Laud that year was a terrible sign to the house of Raglan of the capabilities of the presbyterian party. But to Dorothy it would have given a yet keener pain, had she not begun to learn that neither must the excesses of individuals be attributed to their party, nor those of a party taken as embodying the mind of everyone in it. At the same time the old difficulty returned—how could Richard belong to such a party?

43.
Lady and Bishop

A succession of events enhanced the influence of Cromwell in the Parliament, and in his strengthened position he made Roger Heywood colonel of one of his favorite regiments of horse, with his son Richard as major. Richard continued to ride Bishop, now as famous for courage as for ugliness.

It was strange company in which Richard rode. Nearly all were of the independent party, all holding, or imagining they held, the same tenets. The opinions of most of them, however, were merely the opinions of the man to whose influences they had first been subjected. But in Roger Heywood and his son dwelt a pure love of liberty; the ardent attachment to liberty which most of the troopers professed would have prevented few of them from putting a heretic in the stocks, or at least whipping him. In some was the devoutest sense of personal obligation, and the strongest religious feeling; in others was nothing but talk. That they all believed earnestly enough to fight for their convictions did not go very far in proof of their sincerity; to most of them fighting came by nature, and was no doubt a great relief to the much oppressed old Adam not yet by any means dead in them.

At length the King led out his men for another campaign, and was followed by Fairfax and Cromwell into the shires of Leicester and Northampton. Then came the battle at the village of Naseby. Prince Rupert, whose folly so often lost what his courage gained, defeated Ireton and his horse, and followed them from the field. Cromwell with his superior numbers turned Sir Marmaduke

210

Langdale's flank. The King saw that Rupert, returned from the pursuit, was attacking the enemy's artillery, and dispatched Rowland in hot haste to bring him to the aid of Sir Marmaduke.

The straightest line to reach him lay across a large field to the rear of Sir Marmaduke's men. Richard, on the other side, caught sight of the fleeing messenger, struck spurs into Bishop's flanks, and tore at full speed to head him off from the prince.

Rowland rode for some distance without perceiving that he was being followed. If Richard could but get within pistol shot of him, for alas, he seemed to be mounted on the fleeter animal. . . . Could it be? Yes, it was! It was his own lost Lady the Cavalier rode!

Rowland became aware that he was pursued, but at the first glimpse of the long, low, ratlike animal on which the Roundhead came floundering after him, he burst into a laugh of derision, and jumped a young hedge into a clayish fallow, which his mare found heavy. Soon Richard jumped the hedge also, and immediately Bishop had the advantage. But now, they heard the sounds of conflict, from beyond the tall hedge they were approaching. There was no time to lose. Richard uttered a long, wild, peculiar cry. Lady started, raised her head high, wheeled, and despite Rowland's spur and rein, bore him, with short deerlike bounds, back toward his pursuer.

Not until then did Rowland begin to suspect who had followed him. Then a vague recollection of Richard's words that night by Redware crossed his mind, and he grew furious. In vain he struggled with the mare, and all the time Richard kept plowing on toward them.

Rowland took a pistol from his holster, and Richard did the same; when he saw Rowland raise the butt-end to strike Lady on the head, Richard fired and missed, but saved Lady the blow, for the bullet whistled past Rowland's ear. Richard uttered another peculiar but different cry. Lady reared, plunged, threw her heels in the air, emptied her saddle, and came flying to Richard.

But now arose a fresh anxiety—what if Bishop should attack Lady? At her master's word, however, she stood a few yards off, and waited with arched neck and forward-pricked ears, while Bishop, perhaps moved with admiration of the manner in which she had unseated her rider, scanned her with no malign aspect.

By this time Rowland had regained his feet. Mindful of his duty, and hopeful that Richard would be content with his prize, he set off as hard as he could run for a gap in the hedge. But in a moment Richard and Bishop, followed by Lady, headed him off.

"You had better cry quarter," called Richard.

Rowland's reply was a bullet that struck Bishop below the ear, and tumbled Richard over. Rowland ran toward the mare, hoping to catch her and be off ere the Roundhead could recover himself. Richard, unhurt, lay still and watched. Lady seemed bewildered as Rowland seized her bridle and sprung into the saddle. Richard gave his cry a second time, and again up went Rowland in the air. Lady trotted daintily to her master, scared but obedient. Rowland fell on his back, and Richard rose and drew his sword from its sheath. As he perceived who his antagonist was, a pang went to his heart at the remembrance of his father's words.

"Mr. Scudamore," he cried, "I wish you had not stolen my mare, so that I might fight with you in a Christian fashion."

"Roundhead scoundrel!" gasped Scudamore, wild with wrath. "Your unmannerly varlet tricks shall cost you dear. You a soldier? A juggler with a vile hackney which you have taught to caper!"

"A soldier—and seatless?" returned Richard. "A soldier—and rail? A soldier—and steal my mare, then shoot my horse? Bah! An' the rest were like you, we might take the field with dog whips."

Rowland drew a pistol from his belt, and glanced toward the mare.

"An' you lift your arm, I will kill you," cried Richard. "Did I not give you warning while yet I judged you a thief but in jest? Go your way. I shall do my country better service by following braver men than by taking you. An' I killed you, I should do your master less hurt than I would. See yonder how your master's horse do knot and scatter!"

Richard approached Lady to mount and ride away, but Rowland rushed at him with drawn sword. The contest was brief; with one heavy blow, Richard beat down Rowland's guard and wounded him severely in the shoulder, dividing his collarbone.

As Richard feared being surrounded by Sir Marmaduke's retreating men, he leapt into Lady's saddle and flew back to his regiment, just as Cromwell turned them upon the rear of the Royalist infantry.

This decided the battle. Ere Rupert returned, the affair was so hopeless that not even the entreaties of the King could induce his cavalry to form again and charge.

44.
The King

During the period of the Earl of Glamorgan's absence and journey to Dublin, there was great anxiety in Raglan, the chief part of which was Lady Glamorgan's. At times she felt that but for the sympathy of Dorothy, she would quite have broken down under the burden of ignorance and its attendant anxiety.

In the prolonged absence of her husband and the irregularity of tidings, her yearnings after her vanished Molly returned with all their early vehemence, and she began to brood on the meeting beyond the grave of which her religion waked her hope. Her religion itself grew more real, for the love of a little child is very close to the love of a great Father; and the loss that sets any affection aching and longing heaves, as on a wave from the very heart of the human ocean, the laboring spirit up toward the source of life and restoration. The hearts of the two women drew closer to each other, and Protestant Dorothy was able to speak words of comfort to Catholic Lady Glamorgan, which the hearer found would lie on the shelf of her creed none the less quietly that the giver had lifted them from the shelf of hers.

One evening, while yet Lady Glamorgan had had no news of her husband's arrival in Ireland, and the bright June weather continued clouded with uncertainty and fear, Lady Broughton came panting into her parlor with the tidings that a courier had just arrived at the main entrance, himself pale with fatigue and his horse white with foam.

"Alas!" cried Lady Glamorgan, and fell back in her chair, faint with apprehension, for what might not be the message he bore? Ere Dorothy had succeeded in calming her, the Marquis himself came hobbling in, with the news that the King was coming.

"Is that all?" said the Countess, heaving a deep sigh, while the tears rose and ran down her cheeks.

"Is that all!" repeated her father-in-law. "How, My Lady! Is there then nobody in all the world but Glamorgan? Verily, I believe thou wouldst turn thy back on the Angel Gabriel, if he dared appear before thee without thy husband under his arm. Bless thy Irish heart! I never gave thee my son that thou shouldst fall down and worship the fellow!"

"Bear with me, Sir," she answered faintly. "It is but the pain of ignorance here. I cannot tell but that he perchance lies at the bottom of the Irish Sea."

"If he do lie there, then lieth he in Abraham's bosom, where I trust there is room for thee and me also. Come then, my wild Irishwoman—"

"Alas, My Lord! Tame enough now," sighed the Countess.

"Not too tame to understand that she must represent her husband before the King's majesty," said Lord Worcester.

Lady Glamorgan rose, kissed her father-in-law, wiped her eyes, and said, "Where, My Lord, do you purpose lodging His Majesty?"

"In the great north room, over the buttery, and next to the picture gallery. I did think of the great tower, but it is gloomy. The tower chamber makes me think of all the lords and ladies who have died therein—and the north room of all the babies that have been born there."

"Spoken like a man!" murmured Lady Glamorgan. "Have you given directions, My Lord?"

"I have sent for Sir Ralph. Come with me, Margaret; thou and Mary must keep thine old father from blundering. Run, Dorothy, and tell Mr. Delaware and Mr. Andrews that I desire their presence. I miss that rogue Scudamore. They tell me he hath done well and is sorely wounded. He must feel the better for the one already, and I hope he will soon be nothing the worse for the other."

The whole castle was presently alive with preparations for the King's visit. Hope revived in Lady Glamorgan's bosom—she would take the coming of the King as a good omen for the return of her husband.

Dorothy ran to do the Marquis' pleasure. As she ran, it seemed as if some new spring of life had burst forth in her heart. The King actually coming! The God-chosen monarch of England! The head of the Church! The wronged, the saintly, the wise! He who fought with bleeding heart for the rights, that he might fulfill the duties to which he was born! She would see him! Breathe the same air with him! Gaze on his gracious countenance! The thought was too entrancing, and she wept as she ran.

The King and his court of officers arrived on the evening of the third of July. Travel-stained and weary, on foam-flecked horses, but with flowing plumes, flashing armor, and ringing chains, they arrived at the brick gate. Lord Charles himself threw the two leaves open to admit them, and bent the knee before his King. As they entered the marble gate, they saw the Marquis descending the great white stair to meet them, leaning for his lameness on the arm of his brother, Sir Thomas of Troy, and followed by all the ladies and gentlemen and officers in the castle. The Marquis approached the King's horse, bent his knee, kissed the royal hand, and rose with difficulty, for the gout had aged him beyond his years.

The King dismounted, ascended the marble steps with his host, nearly as stiff as he from the long ride, crossed the moat on the undulating drawbridge, passed the echoing gateway, and entered the stone court.

In the court, the garrison was drawn up to receive him, with an open lane leading through to the stair to the King's apartment. At the foot of the stair, on plea of his gout, the Marquis delivered His Majesty to the care of Lord Charles, Sir Ralph Blackstone, and Mr. Delaware, who conducted him to his chamber.

The King supped alone, but after supper, Lady Glamorgan and the other ladies of the family were ushered into his presence. Each of them took with her one of her ladies in attendance, and Dorothy, chosen by her mistress for the great honor—not without the rousing of a strong feeling of injustice in the bosoms of the elder ladies—entered trembling behind her mistress, as if the room were a temple where divinity dwelt.

His Majesty received them courteously, said kind things to several of them, but spoke and behaved at first with a certain long-faced reserve rather than dignity, which, while it jarred a little with Dorothy's ideal of the graciousness that should be mingled with majesty in the perfect monarch, yet operated only to throw her spirit back into that stage of devotion wherein the awe overlays the love.

A little later the Marquis entered, walking slowly and leaning on the arm of Lord Charles, but carrying in his own hands a present of apricots to the King.

Meantime Dorothy's love had begun to rise again from beneath her awe; but when the Marquis came in, old and stately, reverend and slow, with a silver dish in each hand and a basket on his arm, and she saw him bow three times ere he presented his offering— himself serving whom all served, himself humble whom all revered—then again did awe nearly overcome her. The King graciously received the present, and chose for each of the ladies one of the apricots. Coming to Dorothy last, he picked out and offered the one he said was likest the bloom of her own fair cheek. Gratitude again restored the sway of love, and in the greatness of the honor she almost let slip the compliment. She could not reply, but she looked her thanks, and the King doubtless missed nothing.

The next day His Majesty rested, but on following days rode to Monmouth, Chepstow, Usk, and other loyal towns in the neighborhood. After dinner he generally paid the Marquis a visit in the oak parlor, then perhaps had a walk in the grounds, or a game on the bowling green.

The arrival of His Majesty had added to Dorothy's labors, for now again the horse must spout every day, but with no Molly to see it and rejoice. Every fountain rushed heavenward, and the air seemed filled with the pleasant sound of waters. This required the fire engine to be kept pretty constantly at work, and Dorothy had to run up and down the stair of the great tower several times a day. But she lingered on the top as often and as long as she might.

She would gaze down the bowling green, and in the afternoons she could see some of the game. It was like looking at a toy representation of one, for everything below was wondrously dwarfed. It was a pretty sight—the bright garments, the moving figures, the bowls rolling like marbles over the green carpet, while the sun, and the blue sky, and just enough air of wind to turn every leaf into a languidly waved fan, enclosed in its loveliness and filled it with life.

While Dorothy was looking down and watching the game, the

Marquis finished a bowl and approached the King.

"If Your Majesty hath had enough of the game," he said, "and will climb with me to the top of the tower, I will show thee what may give thy mind some ease."

"I should be sorry to set your lordship such an arduous task," replied the King. "But I am very desirous of seeing your great tower, and if you will permit me, I will climb the stair without your attendance."

"Sir, it would pleasure me to think that the last time ever I ascended those stairs, I conducted Your Majesty. For, indeed, it shall be the last time. I grow old."

As the Marquis spoke, he led his guest toward the twin-arched bridge over the castle moat, then through the western gate, and along the side of the court to the gothic bridge, on their way dispatching one of his gentlemen to fetch the keys to the tower.

"What are those pipes let into the wall up there?" the King asked, stopping in the middle of the bridge and looking up at the keep.

"Sire, my son Edward Herbert must tell thee that, for he taketh strange liberties with the mighty old hulk. But I will not injure his good grace with Your Majesty by talking of that which I understand not. I trust that one day, when thou shalt no more require his absence, thou wilt yet again condescend to be my guest, when my son, by Your Majesty's favor now my Lord Glamorgan, will have things to show thee that will delight thine eyes to behold."

The Marquis took the King up the stair, unlocked the entrance to the first floor, and ushered him into a lofty vaulted chamber, old in the midst of antiquity, dark, vast, and stately.

"This is where I did first think to lodge Your Majesty," he said, "but Your Majesty sees it is gloomy, for the windows are narrow, and the walls are ten feet through."

"It maketh me very cold," said the King, shuddering. "Good sooth, but I were loath to be a prisoner!"

He turned and left the room hastily. The Marquis rejoined him on the stair, and led him two stories higher to the armory, now empty compared to its former condition, but still capable of affording some supply. The next space was filled with stores, and the highest was now kept clear for defense, for the reservoir so fully occupied the top that there was no room here for engines of any sort.

Reaching the summit, the King gazed with silent wonder at the little tarn. Then the Marquis conducted him to the western side, and pointed with his finger at various points of interest in the landscape. The King listened politely, but he was looking at Dorothy where she stood at the opposite side of the reservoir, unable to reach the stair without passing the King and the Marquis. The King asked who she was, and the Marquis, telling him a little about her, called her. She came, curtsied low to His Majesty, and stood with beating heart.

"I desire," said the Marquis, "thou shouldst explain to His Majesty that trick of thy Cousin Glamorgan, the watershoot, and let him see it work."

"My Lord," answered Dorothy, trembling betwixt devotion and doubtful duty, "it was the great desire of my Lord Glamorgan that none in the castle should know the trick."

"What, Cousin! Cannot His Majesty keep a secret? And doth not all that Glamorgan hath belong to the King?"

"God forbid I should doubt either, My Lord," answered Dorothy, turning very pale, and ready to sink, "but it cannot well be done in the broad day without someone else seeing. At night, indeed—"

"Tut, tut! It is but a whim of Glamorgan's. Thou wilt not do a jot of ill to show the game before His Majesty in the sunlight."

"My Lord, I promised."

"Here standeth one who will absolve thee, Child! His Majesty is paramount to Glamorgan."

"My Lord! My Lord!" said Dorothy, almost weeping, "I am bewildered and cannot well understand. But I am sure that if it be wrong, no one can give me leave to do it, or absolve me beforehand. God Himself can but pardon after the thing is done, not give permission to do it. Forgive me, Sire, but so Master Herbert hath taught me."

"And very good doctrine, too," said the Marquis emphatically, "let who will propound it. Think you not so, Sir?"

But the King stood with dull, imperturbable gaze fixed on the distant horizon, and made no reply. An awkward silence followed. The King requested his host to conduct him to his apartment.

"I marvel, My Lord," said His Majesty as they went down the stair, seeing how lame his host was, "that, as they tell me, your lordship drinks claret. All physicians say it is naught for the gout."

"Sir," returned the Marquis, "it shall never be said that I forsook my friend to pleasure my enemy."

The King's face grew dark, for he was beginning to see a double meaning of rebuke in what the Marquis said. He made no answer, and avoided his attendants who waited for him in the fountain court, expecting him to go by the bell tower. Passing through the hall and the stone court, he ascended to his room alone, and went into the picture gallery, where he paced up and down till supper time.

The Marquis rejoined the little company of his own friends who had left the bowling green after him, and were now in the oak parlor. Though a little troubled at the King's carriage toward him, he entered with a merrier bearing than usual.

"Well, Gentlemen?" he said gaily.

"We were but now presuming to warrant, My Lord," answered Mr. Pritchard, "that if you would, you might be Duke of Somerset."

"When I was Earl of Worcester," returned the Marquis, "I was well-to-do. Since I am Marquis, I am worse by a hundred thousand pounds. If I should be Duke, I should be an arrant beggar. I would rather go back to my Earldom, than keep this pace to the Dukedom of Somerset."

45.
Gifts of Healing
1645

About a month after the battle of Naseby, and while the King was going and coming to Raglan, the wounded Rowland was brought home to the castle, long before he was fit to be moved from the farmhouse where his servant had found him shelter. Shafto, as faithful as harebrained, had come upon him almost accidentally, after long search, and just in time to save his life. Mrs. Watson received him with tears, and had him carried to the same turret chamber whence Richard had escaped, in order that she might be nigh him. The poor fellow was but a shadow of his former self, and looked more likely to vanish than to die in the ordinary way. Hence he required constant attention, which was so far from lacking that the danger, both physical and spiritual, seemed rather to lie in overservice. Hitherto, of the family, it had been the Marquis chiefly that spoiled him; but now that he was so sorely wounded for the King and lay at death's door, all the ladies of the castle were paying him such attentions as nobody could be trusted to bear uninjured except a doll or a baby. One might have been tempted to say that they sought his physical welfare at the risk of his moral ruin. But there is just that in sickness which leads men back to a kind of babyhood, and while it lasts there is comparatively little danger. It is with returning health that the peril comes.

He had lost much blood, having lain a long time in the field before Shafto found him. Oft-recurring fever, extreme depression, and intermittent and doubtful progress followed. Through all the

commotion of the King's visits, the coming and going, the clang of
hoofs and clanking of armor, the heaving of hearts and clamor of
tongues, he lay lapped in ignorance and ministration, hidden from
the world and deaf to the gnarring of its wheels, imprisoned in a
twilight dungeon to which Richard's sword had been the key.

The Marquis went often to see him, full of pity for the youth
thus brought low; but he would lie pale and listless, now and then
turning upon him eyes worn and large with the wasting of his face,
and looking as if he only half heard him. His master grew sad
about him, and the next time His Majesty came, asked him if he
remembered the youth, telling him how he had lain wounded ever
since the battle at Naseby. The King remembered him well
enough, but had never missed him. The Marquis then told him
how anxious he was about him, as nothing woke him from the
weary heartlessness into which he had fallen.

"I will pay him a visit," said the King.

When Rowland saw the King, his face flushed, the tears rose in
his eyes, and he kissed the hand the King held out to him. "Pardon, Sire," murmured Rowland. "If I had ridden better, the battle
might have been yours. I reached not the prince."

"It is the will of God," said the King, remembering for the first
time that he had sent him to Rupert. "You did your best, and man
can do no more."

"Nay, Sire, but if I had ridden honestly," returned Rowland, "I
mean, had my mare been honestly come by, then had I done Your
Majesty's message."

"Ha!" said the Marquis. "Then it was Heywood met thee, and
would have his own again? Told I not thee so? Ah, that mare,
Rowland! That mare!"

"You did your duty like a brave knight and true, I doubt not,"
said the King, kindly wishing to comfort him. "And that my word
may be a true one," he added, drawing his sword and laying it
across the youth's chest, "although I cannot tell you to rise
and walk, I tell you, when you do arise, to rise up Sir Rowland
Scudamore."

The blood rushed to Rowland's face, but fled again as fast. "I
deserve no such honor, Sire," he murmured.

But the Marquis struck his hands together with pleasure, and
cried, "There, My Boy! There is a King to serve! Sir Rowland
Scudamore!"

Rowland summoned strength to thank His Majesty, but when his visitors left, he sighed sorely. "Honor without desert!" he said to himself. "But for the Roundhead's taunts, I might have run to Rupert and saved the day."

The next morning the Marquis went again to see him. "How fares Sir Rowland?" he said.

"My Lord," returned Rowland, in beseeching tone, "break not my heart with honor unmerited."

"How! Darest thou, Boy, set thy judgment against the King's?" cried the Marquis. "Sir Rowland thou art, and Sir Rowland wilt the archangel cry when he calls thee from thy sleep."

"To my endless disgrace," added Rowland.

"What! Hast not done thy duty?"

"I tried, but I failed, My Lord."

"The best fail as often as the worst," rejoined the Marquis.

"I mean not merely that I failed of the end. That, alas, I did. But I mean that it was by my own fault that I failed," said Rowland.

Then he told the Marquis all the story of his encounter with Richard. He ended with the words, "And now, My Lord, I care no more for life."

"Stuff and nonsense!" exclaimed the Marquis. "Thinkest thou the Roundhead would have let thee run to Rupert? It was not to that end he spared thy life. Thy only chance was to fight him."

"Does your lordship think so indeed?" asked Rowland, with a glimmer of eagerness.

"On my soul I do. Thou art weakheaded from thy sickness and weariness. Comfort thyself that the evil is come and gone, and think not that such chances are left to determine great events. Naseby fight had been lost, in spite of a hundred messages to Rupert. Not care for life, Boy? Leave that to old men like me. Thou must care for it, for thou hast many years before thee."

"But nothing to fill them with, My Lord."

"What meanest thou there, Rowland? The King's cause will yet prosper."

"Pardon me, My Lord. I spoke not of the King's majesty or his affairs. It is a nameless weight, or rather emptiness, that oppresseth me. 'Wherefore is there such a world?' I ask, 'Why are men born there into? Why should I live on and labor therein? Is it not all vanity and vexation of spirit?' I would the Roundhead had but struck a little deeper, and reached my heart."

A pause followed.

"I pray, Sir," Rowland then continued, "can you tell me if Mistress Dorothy knows it was before Heywood I fell?"

"I know not, but had she known, I would have heard the thing myself from her. Who, indeed, should tell her? Shafto knew it not. And why should she conceal it?"

"I cannot tell, My Lord. She is not like the other ladies."

"She is like all good ladies in this, that she speaketh the truth. Why then not ask her?"

"I have had no opportunity, My Lord. I have not seen her since I left to join the army."

"Tut, tut!" said his lordship, and frowned a little. "I thought the damsel might well have favored a wounded knight with a visit."

"She is not to blame. It is my own fault," sighed Rowland.

The Marquis looked at him for a moment pitifully, but made no answer, and presently took his leave. He went straight to Dorothy, and expostulated with her. She answered him no further or otherwise than was simply duteous, but went at once to see Rowland.

He was but the ghost of the jolly, self-satisfied, good-natured Rowland. Pale and thin, with drawn face and great eyes, he held out a wasted hand to Dorothy and looked at her, not pitifully, but despairingly. He was one of those from whom one may take health and animal spirits, and yet who have nothing in themselves.

"My poor Cousin!" said Dorothy, touched with profound compassion at the sight of his lost look. But he only gazed at her, and then burst into tears.

"I know you despise me, Dorothy," he sobbed, "and you are right—I despise myself."

"You have been a good soldier to the King, Rowland," said Dorothy, "and he has acknowledged it fitly."

"I care nothing for King or kingdom, Dorothy. Nothing is worth caring for. I am not going to talk presumptuously. I love you not, Dorothy. I never did love you, and you do right to despise me, for I am unworthy. I would I were dead. Even the King's Majesty has been no whit the better for me, but rather the worse. For another man, not mounted on a stolen mare, would have performed his behest unhindered of foregone fault."

"You did not think you were doing wrong when you stole the

223

mare," said Dorothy, seeking to comfort him. "He that is sorry is already pardoned, I think, Cousin. Then what you have done evil is gone and forgotten."

"Nay, Dorothy. Even if it were forgotten, yet would it exist. If I forgot it myself, yet would I not cease to be the man who had done it. And you know, Dorothy, in how many things I have been false, so false that I counted myself honorable all the time. Tell me wherefore should I not kill myself, and rid the world of me."

"That you are of consequence to Him who made you. For surely He sent you here to do some fitting work for Him."

More talk followed, but Dorothy did not seem to herself to find the right thing to say, and retired to the top of the tower with a sense of failure, and oppressed with helpless compassion for the poor youth.

The available doctors of divinity and of medicine differed concerning the cause of his sad condition. The doctor of medicine said it arose entirely from a check in the circulation of the animal spirits. The doctor of divinity thought, but did not say, only hinted, that it came of a troubled conscience, and that he would have been well long ago but for certain sins, known only to himself, that bore heavy upon his life.

Yet the cure was a deeper and harder matter than Dr. Bayly understood, or than probably Rowland himself would for years attain to, while yet the least glimmer of its approach would be enough to initiate physical recovery.

46.
The King and the Marquis

Though money came from the Marquis like drops of blood, yet was he contented that every drop within his body should be let out if only he might bring His Majesty back to the bosom of the Catholic Church. Therefore, expecting every hour that the King would apply to him for more money, the Marquis had resolved that at such time he would make an attempt to lead the stray sheep back within the fold—for the Marquis was not one of those who regarded a Protestant as necessarily a goat.

But the King shrank from making the request in person. Having learned that the Marquis had been at one point in his history under the deepest obligation to Dr. Bayly, he requested through his own colonel that the doctor should mediate between him and the Marquis.

Dr. Bayly undertook the business, though with reluctance, and sought the Marquis in his study.

"My Lord," he said, "the thing that I feared is now fallen upon me. I am made the unwelcome messenger of bad news—the King wants money."

"Hold, Sir—that's no news," interrupted the Marquis. "Go on."

"My Lord," said the doctor, "there is one comfort yet, that, as the King is brought low, so are his demands, and, like his army, are come down from thousands to hundreds, and from paying the soldiers of his army, to buying bread for himself and his followers. My Lord, the King's desire is but three hundred pounds."

Lord Worcester remained a long time silent, and Dr. Bayly waited.

"My good Doctor," said his lordship at length, "hath the King himself spoken unto thee concerning any such business?"

"The King himself has not, My Lord, but others did, in the King's hearing."

"Might I but speak to him. . . . But I was never thought worthy to be consulted, though in matters merely concerning the affairs of my own country! I would supply his wants, were they never so great, or whatsoever they were."

"If the King knew as much, My Lord, you might quickly speak with him," remarked the doctor.

"The way to have him know so much is to have somebody tell him of it," said the Marquis testily.

"Will your lordship give me leave to be the informer?"

"Truly, I spake to that purpose," answered the Marquis.

Away ran the little doctor, ambling through the picture gallery, half running like some short-winged bird to the King's chamber, his heart trembling lest the Marquis should change his mind and call him back, and so his pride in his successful mediation be mortified. He told His Majesty, with diplomatic reserve, that he had perceived his lordship desired some conference with him, and that he believed, if the King granted such conference, he would find a more generous response to his necessities than perhaps expected. The King readily consented, and the doctor went on to say that his lordship much wished the interview that very night. The King asked how it could be managed, and the doctor told him the Marquis had contrived it before His Majesty came to the castle, having for that reason appointed his bedchamber elsewhere than the great tower.

"I know my lord's drift well enough," said the King, smiling. "Either he means to chide me, or else to convert me to his religion."

"I doubt not, Sire," returned the doctor, "but Your Majesty is temptation-proof as well as correction-free, and will return the same man as you go, having made a profitable exchange of gold and silver for words and sleep."

So it was arranged that the Marquis would be awaiting His Majesty at eleven o'clock in a certain room to which the doctor would conduct him.

Although he had not a better friend in all England than the Marquis, the King feared losing his Protestant friends from their jealousy of Catholic influence, and he had never invited the Marquis of Worcester to sit with him in council. The Marquis, on his part, was afraid both of injuring the cause of the King, and of being himself impeached for treason. Should any of the King's attendant lords discover they two were closeted together, suspicion and accusation of conspiracy might follow. His lordship therefore instructed Dr. Bayly to go, as the time drew nigh, to the drawing room, which was next to the Marquis' chamber and to the dining parlor, through both of which he must pass to reach the appointed place, and clear them of any company which might be in them.

But having thus arranged, the Marquis grew anxious again. It was not unusual to pass to the hall from the north side of the fountain court, and thence through the picture gallery—and through this gallery the doctor must lead His Majesty. The Marquis, therefore, felt that the assistance of a second confidante was more than desirable, and could think of no one whom he could trust so well—and who would be so little liable to the sort of suspicion he dreaded—as Dorothy. He sent for her, told her as much as he thought proper, and directed her to be in the gallery ten minutes before eleven, to lock the door at the top of the stair leading down into the hall, and take her stand in the window at the foot of the stair from the bell tower, where the door was without a lock, and see that no one entered—by order of the Marquis for the King's repose. He enjoined upon her that whatever she saw or heard from any quarter, she must keep perfectly still, and let no one discover that she was there. Considerably relieved, his lordship dismissed her and went to have a nap if he could.

As soon as eleven o'clock drew near, Dr. Bayly proceeded to the Marquis' bedroom. Opening the inner door as softly as he could, he crept in and found the Marquis fast asleep. So slowly, so gently id he wake him, that his lordship insisted he had not slept at all. He took a pipe of tobacco and a little glass of *aqua mirabilis*, and said, "Come now, let us go in the name of God," and crossed himself.

It was indeed a strange tableau—King and Marquis, attended by a doctor of divinity, of the faith of the one but the trusted friend of the other—meeting at midnight to discuss points of finance and theology, with both men ln mortal terror of discovery.

Meantime Dorothy had done as she had been ordered, had felt her way through the darkness to the picture gallery, had locked the door at the top of the stair, and taken her stand in the recess at the foot of the other—in pitch darkness, close to the King's bedchamber.

The door of that same chamber opened silently, and a glimmer of light shone out, revealing a figure entering the gallery. The door closed softly and slowly, and all was darkness again. She heard a deep sigh, as from a sorely burdened heart. Then, in an agonized whisper from the depths of the spirit, came the words: "O Strafford, thou art avenged! I left thee to thy fate, and God hath left me to mine. Thou didst go for me to the scaffold, but thou wilt not out of my chamber. O God, deliver me from bloodguiltiness."

Dorothy stood in dismay, her emotions in tumult. The King reentered his chamber and closed the door. Then a light appeared at the far end of the gallery and Dr. Bayly came gliding toward her. He stopped within a yard or two of the King's door, and stood there with his candle in his hand. His round face was pale instead of its normal red, and his small keen eyes shone in the candlelight with mingled importance and anxiety. He saw Dorothy, and turned from her with his face toward the King's door so that his shadow might shroud the recess where she stood.

A minute or so passed, and the King's door reopened. He came out, said a few words in a whisper to his guide, and walked with him down the gallery, whispering as he went.

Dorothy hastened to her chamber, threw herself on the bed, and wept. The King was cast from the throne of her conscience, but taken into the hospital of her heart.

When, after a long talk, Dr. Bayly had conducted the King back to his chamber and then returned again to the Marquis, he found the old man in the dark upon his knees.

The King left soon after, on the fifteenth of September.

47.
The Poet and Physician

Early in November, Dorothy received a letter from Mr. Herbert informing her that her cousin, Mr. Vaughan, one of his former pupils, would be passing near Raglan and would call upon her. Willing enough to see her relative, she thought little more of the matter, until at length the day was at hand.

He was ushered into Lady Glamorgan's parlor. Her ladyship and Dorothy saw a rather tall young man of twenty-five, with a small head, clear gray eyes, and a sober yet changeful countenance. His carriage was dignified yet graceful, and his self-restraint was evident. A certain sadness brooded like a thin mist above his eyes, but his smile now and then broke out like the sun through a gray cloud. Dorothy did not know that he was getting over the end of a love, or that he had just had a book of verses printed and had already begun to repent of it.

After the usual greetings, and when Dorothy had heard the latest news of Mr. Herbert, Lady Glamorgan (who was not sorry to see her with a young man whose Royalist predilections were plain and strong) proposed that Dorothy should take him over the castle.

As she led him to the top of the tower, their talk revealed to Dorothy that here was a man who was her master in everything toward which she had most aspired, and a great hope arose in her heart for her Cousin Scudamore. Mr. Vaughan had studied medicine, and she promptly entreated him to go and visit Scudamore.

229

He consented, and Dorothy led him straight to the turret chamber where the sick man was sitting by the fire, folded in blankets, listless and sad.

She would have left them, but Rowland turned on her such beseeching eyes that she willingly remained to hear what this wonderful young physician would say.

"Is it very irksome to be thus imprisoned in your chamber, Sir Rowland?" he asked.

"No," answered Scudamore, "or yes, I care not."

"Have you no books with you?" asked Mr. Vaughan, glancing about the room.

"Books!" repeated Scudamore, with a wan, contemptuous smile.

"You do not then love books?"

"Wherefore should I love books? What can books do for me? I love nothing. I long only to die."

"And go——?" suggested Mr. Vaughan.

"I care not whither, anywhere away from here, if indeed I go anywhere. But I care not."

"Have you not the notion that if you were hence, you would leave behind you a certain troublesome attendant who is scarce worth his wages? I know well what ails you, for I am myself but now recovering from a similar sickness, brought upon me by the haunting of the same evil one who torments you."

"You think, then, that I am possessed?" said Rowland, with a faint smile and a glance at Dorothy.

"Truly you are, and grievously tormented. The demon has a name that is known among men, though it frightens few and draws many, alas! His name is Self, and he is the shadow of your own self. First he made you love him, which was evil, and now he has made you hate him, which is evil also. But if he be cast out and never more enter into your heart, but remain as a servant in your hall, then you will recover from this sickness, and be whole and sound, and will find the varlet serviceable."

"Are you an exorciser, then, Mr. Vaughan, as well as a discerner of spirits? I would you could drive the said demon out of me, for truly, I love him not."

"Through all your hate you love him more than you know. You see him vile, but instead of casting him out, you mourn over him with foolish tears. And yet you dream that by dying you would be rid of him. No, it is back to your childhood you must go to be free.

"No man can rid him of himself and live, for that involves an impossibility. But he can rid himself of that haunting shadow of his own self, which he has pampered and fed upon shadowy lies, until it is bloated and black with pride and folly. When that de-mon-king of shades is once cast out, and the man's house is pos-sessed of God instead, then first he finds his true substantial self, which is the servant—nay, the child—of God. To rid you of your-self you must offer it again to Him who made it. Be empty so that He may fill you. Let me impart to you certain verses, for they will tell you better what I mean:

> I carry with me, Lord, a foolish fool,
> That still his cap upon my head would place.
> I dare not slay him, he will not go to school,
> And still he shakes his bauble in my face.
>
> I seize him, Lord, and bring him to Thy door;
> Bound on Thine altar-threshold him I lay.
> He weepeth; did I heed, he would implore;
> And still he cries *alack* and *well-a-day!*
>
> If Thou wouldst take him, Lord, and make him wise,
> I think he might be taught to serve Thee well;
> If not, slay him, nor heed his foolish cries.
> He's but a fool that mocks and rings a bell."

Something in the lines appeared to strike Scudamore. "I thank you, Sir," he said. "Might I put you to the trouble, I would request that you would write out the verses for me, that I may study their meaning at my leisure."

Mr. Vaughan promised, and soon took his leave.

From that visit on, Rowland began to think more and to brood less. He would ask questions of right and wrong, suppose cases, and ask Dorothy what she would do in various circumstances. With many cloudy relapses, there was a suspicion of a sun-filled dawn on his far horizon.

"Do you really believe, Dorothy," he asked one day, "that a man ever did love his enemy? Did you ever know one who did?"

"I cannot say I did," returned Dorothy. "I have, however, seen few that were enemies. But I am sure that had it not been possible, we should never have been commanded thereto."

"The last time Dr. Bayly came to see me, he read those words, and I thought within myself all the time of the only enemy I have, and tried to forgive him, but could not. When I look on you, Dorothy, one moment it seems as if for your sake I could forgive him anything—except that he slew me outright—and the next that never can I forgive him, even that wherein he never did me any wrong."

"What! Do you then hate him who struck you down in fair fight? You are of meaner soil than I judged you. What man in battlefield hates his enemy, or thinks it less than enough to do his endeavor to slay him?"

"Know whom you would have me forgive? He who struck me down was your friend, Richard Heywood."

"Then he has his mare again?" cried Dorothy eagerly.

Rowland's face fell, and she knew that she had spoken heartlessly. She knew also that, for all his protestations, Rowland yet cherished the love she had so plainly refused. But the same moment she knew something more. For, in her mind's eye, by the side of Rowland, stood Henry Vaughan, as wise as Rowland was foolish, as accomplished and learned as Rowland was narrow and ignorant; but between them stood Richard, and her feeling for him was neither tenderness nor reverence, and yet included both. She rose in some confusion, and left the chamber.

From that moment Scudamore was satisfied she loved Heywood, and, with much mortification, tried to accept his position. Slowly his health began to return, and slowly the deeper life unfolding began to inform him. Heartless and poverty-stricken as he had hitherto shown himself, the good in him was not so deeply buried under refuse as in many another man. Sickness had awakened in him a sense of requirement, of need and loneliness and dissatisfaction. He grew ashamed of himself and conscious of defilement, and something new began to rise above and condemn the old.

Mr. Vaughan came to see him again and again and, with the concurrence of Dr. Spott, prescribed for him. As the spring approached, he grew able to leave his room. The ladies of the family had him to their parlors to spoil and feed, but he was not now so easily injured by kindness as when he believed in his own merits.

48.
Honorable Disgrace
1646

January of 1646 brought with it the heaviest cloud that had yet overshadowed Raglan.

Entering Lady Glamorgan's parlor, Dorothy found it deserted. A moan came to her ears from the adjoining chamber, and there she found her mistress on her face on the bed.

"Madam," said Dorothy, "what is it?"

"My lord is in prison," gasped Lady Glamorgan, and bursting into fresh tears, she sobbed and moaned.

"Has my lord been taken in the field, Madam, or by cunning of his enemies?"

"Would to God it were either," sighed Lady Glamorgan. "Then were it a small thing to bear."

"What can it be, Madam? You terrify me," said Dorothy.

Only a fresh outburst of agonized and angry weeping followed.

"Since you will tell me nothing, Madam, I must take comfort that of myself I know one thing."

"Prithee, what do you know?" asked the Countess, but as if careless of being answered, so listless was her tone, so nearly inarticulate her words.

"That it is but what brings him fresh honor, My Lady," answered Dorothy.

The Countess started up, threw her arms about her, kissed her, and held her fast, sobbing worse than ever.

"Madam! Madam!" murmured Dorothy from her bosom.

"I thank you, Dorothy," she sighed out at length, "for your

words and your thoughts have ever been of a piece."

"Surely, My Lady, no one did ever yet dare think otherwise of my lord," returned Dorothy, amazed.

"But many will now, Dorothy. My God! They will have it that he is a traitor. He is a prisoner in the castle of Dublin!"

"But is not Dublin in the hands of the King, My Lady?"

"Ay! There lies the sting of it! What treacherous friends are these heretics! Having denied their Saviour, they malign their better brother! Lord Glamorgan of Ormond says frightful things of my Herbert.

"As long as his wife believes him the true man he is," said Dorothy, "he will laugh to scorn all that false lips may utter against him."

"My lord is grievously abused, Dorothy—I say not by whom."

"By whom but his enemies, Madam?"

"Not certainly by those who are to him friends, but yet by those to whom he is the truest of friends."

"Is my Lord Ormond then false? Is he jealous of my Lord Glamorgan? Has he falsely accused him? I would I understood all, Madam."

"I would I understood all myself, Child. Certain papers have been found bearing upon my lord's business in Ireland, and all ears are filled with rumors of forgery and reason—coupled with the name of my lord—and he is a prisoner in Dublin Castle!"

"Weep not, Madam," said Dorothy, in foolish sympathy.

"What better cause could I have out of hell?" returned the Countess, angrily.

"That it were no lie, Madam."

"It is true, I tell thee."

"That my lord is a traitor, Madam?"

Lady Glamorgan dashed her from her and glared at her like a tigress. An evil word was on her lips, but her better angel spoke, and she listened and understood. "God forbid!" she said, struggling to be calm. "But it is true that he *is* in prison."

"Then give God thanks, Madam, who hath forbidden the one and allowed the other," said Dorothy. Finding her own composure on the point of yielding, she curtsied and left the room. It was a breach of etiquette without leave, but the face of the Countess was again on her pillow, and she did not heed.

For some time things went on as in an evil dream. The Marquis was in angry mood, with no gout to lay it upon, and the gloom spread over the castle.

One evening not long after, Dorothy found her mistress much excited, with a letter in her hand. "Come here, Dorothy. See what I have!" she cried in triumph, weeping and laughing alternately.

"Madam, it must be something precious indeed," said Dorothy, "for I have not heard your ladyship laugh for a weary while. May I not rejoice with you?"

"You shall, my good Dorothy. Hearken, and I will read."

My dear Heart,

I hope this will precede any news of my commitment to the Castle of Dublin lest you be apprehensive. I assure you I went as cheerfully and as willingly as they could wish, and should as unwillingly go forth were the gates both of the castle and town open unto me, until I were cleared. They are willing to make me unserviceable to the King, and lay me aside. I should never desist from doing what in honor I was obliged to do.

I grow confident that in this you will now show your magnanimity, and by it the greatest testimony of affection that you can possibly afford me. I need not tell you how clear I am, and void of fear, the only effect of a good conscience. I am guilty of no disloyalty to His Majesty, or of what may stain the honor of my family, or set a brand upon my future posterity. So let not any of my friends there believe anything, until you have the perfect relation of it from myself.

The pleasure of receiving news from his son did but little, however, to disperse the cloud that hung about the Marquis. He had been advised of the provision made for the King's vindication by his anticipated self-sacrifice of Glamorgan. The Marquis judged that the King's behavior in the matter was that neither of a Christian nor a gentleman. As in the case of Strafford, he had accepted the offered sacrifice; and, in view of possible chances, he had in Glamorgan's commission omitted the usual authoritative formalities, thus keeping it in his power (with Glamorgan's connivance, it must be confessed, but at Glamorgan's expense) to repudiate his agency. This he had now done in a message to the Parliament, and this the Marquis knew.

His Majesty had also written to Lord Ormond, "And albeit I have too just cause, for the clearing of my honor, to prosecute Glamorgan in a legal way, yet I will have you suspend the execution."

At the same time his secretary wrote to Ormond and the council, "And since the warrant is not sealed with the signet, your lordships cannot but judge it to be at least surreptitiously gotten, if not worse; for His Majesty saith he remembers it not. The King hath commanded me to advertise that the patent for making the said Lord Herbert of Raglan Earl of Glamorgan is not passed the great seal here, so he is not peer of this kingdom. Notwithstanding, he so styles himself, and hath treated with the rebels in Ireland, by the name of Earl of Glamorgan, which is as vainly taken upon him as his pretended warrant was surreptitiously gotten." (The title had, meanwhile, been used by the King himself in many communications with the Earl.)

When these letters came to the Marquis' knowledge, it was no wonder that the straightforward old man, walking erect to ruin for his King, should fret and fume, and yield to downright wrath and enforced contempt. Of the King's behavior in the matter, Dorothy knew nothing yet.

In February, a messenger from the King arrived at Raglan, on his way to Ireland to Lord Ormond. He had found the roads so beset that he had been compelled to leave his dispatches in hiding, and reached the castle only with great difficulty and after many adventures. He begged of Lord Charles a convoy to secure his dispatches and protect him on his journey, but Lord Charles received him by no means cordially, for the whole heart of Raglan was sore. He brought him to his father who, although indisposed and confined to his chamber, consented to see him. When the messenger was admitted, Lady Glamorgan was in the chamber behind the bed-curtains, and there remained.

"Hast thou in thy dispatches any letters from His Majesty to my son Glamorgan?" he inquired, frowning unconsciously.

"Not that I know of, My Lord," answered the weary man. He then proceeded to give a friendly message from the King concerning the Earl. But at this the smoldering fire broke out from the bosom of the injured father and subject.

"It is the grief of my heart," cried his lordship, that the King is wavering and fickle. To be the more his friend, it too plainly appeareth, is but to be the more handled as his enemy."

"Say not so, My Lord," returned the messenger. "His Gracious Majesty looketh not for such unfriendly judgment from your lips. Have I not brought your lordship a most gracious and comfortable message from him concerning my Lord Glamorgan, with his royal thanks for your former loyal expressions?"

"Thou knowest naught of the matter. Thou hast brought me a budget of fine words, but deeds alone are certainty of the true faith. Verily, the King setteth his words in the forefront of the battle, but his deeds lag in the rear, and let his words be taken prisoners."

"My Lord! Surely your lordship knoweth better of His Majesty."

"To know better may be to know worse. Was it not enough to suffer my Lord Glamorgan to be unjustly imprisoned by my Lord Ormond for what he had His Majesty's authority for, but that he must in print protest against his proceedings and his own allowance, and not yet recall it? But I will pray for him, and that he may be more constant to his friends, and as soon as my other employment will give you leave, you shall have a convoy to fetch securely your dispatches."

The messenger was dismissed, with Lord Charles accompanying him from the room.

"False as ice!" muttered the Marquis to himself. "My Boy, thou hast built on a quicksand, and thy house goeth down to the deep. I am wroth with myself that ever I dreamed of persuading such a bag of chaff to return to the bosom of his honorable Mother."

"My Lord," said Lady Glamorgan from behind the curtains, "have you forgotten that I and my ears are here?"

"Ha! Art thou indeed there, my mad Irishwoman! I had verily forgotten thee. But is not this King of ours as the Minotaur, dwelling in the labyrinths of deceit, and devouring the noblest in the land? There was his own Strafford, next his foolish Laud, and now comes my son, worth a host of such!"

"In his letter, my Lord Glamorgan complains not of His Majesty's usage," said the Countess.

"My Lord Glamorgan is patient. He would pass through the pains of purgatory with never a grumble, though purgatory is for none such as he. In good sooth, I am made of different stuff. My soul doth loathe deceit, and worse in a King than a clown. What

King is he that will lie for a kingdom?"

Day after day passed, and nothing was done to speed the messenger, who grew more and more anxious to procure his dispatches and be gone. But Lord Worcester had so lost faith in the King himself that he had no heart for his business, and also wished to delay the messenger, in order that a messenger of his own might reach Glamorgan before Ormond should receive the King's dispatches. For a whole fortnight, therefore, no further steps were taken, and the messenger, wearied out, applied to the Countess to use her influence in his behalf. Dorothy was in the room when the messenger waited on her mistress.

"May it please your ladyship," he said, "I have sought speech of you that I might beg your aid for the King's business, remembering you of the hearty affection my master the King bears toward your lord and all his house."

"Indeed, you do well to remember me of that, for it goes so hard with my memory in these troubled times that I had nigh forgotten it," said the Countess dryly.

"I most certainly know, My Lady, that His Majesty has gracious intentions toward your lord."

"Intention is but an addled egg," said the Countess. "Give me deeds."

"Alas! The King has but little in his power, and the less that his business is kept waiting."

"Your haste is more than your matter. Believe me, whatsoever you consider of it, your going so hurriedly is of no great account, for to my knowledge there are others gone already with duplicates of the business."

"Madam, you astonish me."

"I speak not without book. My own cousin, William Winter, is one, and he is my husband's friend, and has no relation to my Lord Ormond," said Lady Glamorgan significantly.

"My lord, Madam, is your lord's very good friend, and I am very much his servant. But if His Majesty's business be done, I care not by whose hand it is. But I thank your honor, for now I know wherefore I am stayed here."

With these words he withdrew. When he was gone, Lady Glamorgan, turning a flushed face, encountered Dorothy's pale one, and gave a hard laugh. "Why, Child! You look like a ghost! Were you afraid of the man in my presence?"

"No, Madam, but it seems to me marvelous that His Majesty's messenger should receive such words from my mistress, and in my Lord of Worcester's house."

"In faith, marvelous it is, Dorothy, that there should be such good cause so to use him!" returned Lady Glamorgan, tears of vexation rising as she spoke. "But if you think I used the man roughly, you should have heard the Marquis speak to him of the King his master."

"Has the King then shown himself unkingly, Madam?" said Dorothy aghast.

Lady Glamorgan told her all she knew, and of what the Marquis had said to the messenger. "Trust me, Child," she added. "My Lord Worcester, no less than I, is cut to the heart by this behavior of the King. That my husband, silly angel, should say nothing, is but like him. He would bear and bear till all was borne."

"But," said Dorothy, "the King is still the King."

"Let him be the King then, and look to his kingdom. Why should I give him my husband to do it for him and be disowned therein? I can do without a King, but I can't do without my Herbert, and there he lies in prison for him who cons him no thanks! Not that I would overmuch heed the prison if the King would but share the blame with him; but for the King to deny him—to say that he did all of his own notion and without authority! Why, Child, I saw the commission with my own eyes, nor count myself under any further obligation to hold my peace concerning it! The King hath little heart and no conscience. My good husband's fair name is gone—blasted by the King, who raises the mist of Glamorgan's dishonor that he may hide himself safe behind it. I tell you, Dorothy, I should not have grudged His Majesty my lord's life, if he had been but a right kingly King. I should have wept enough and complained too much, in womanish fashion, doubtless, but would not have grudged it. But my lord's truth and honor are dear to him, and the good report of them is dear to me. I swear I can ill brook carrying the title he hath given me. It is my husband's and not mine, else would I fling it in his face who thus wrongs my Herbert."

This explosion from the heart of the wild Irishwoman sounded dreadful in the ears of the king-worshiper. Notwithstanding her struggle to keep her heart to its allegiance, such a rapid change took place in her feelings that she began to confess to herself that if the Puritans could have known what the King was, their conduct would not have been so unintelligible—not that she thought they had an atom of right on their side, or in the least feared she might ever be brought to think in the matter as they did. She confessed only that she could then have understood them.

The Marquis was still very gloomy. Lord Charles often frowned and bit his lip. And the flush that so frequently overspread the face of Lady Glamorgan, as she sat silent at her embroidery, showed that she was thinking in anger of the wrong done to her husband. In this feeling all in the castle shared, for the matter had now come to be a little understood, and, as they loved the Earl more than the King, they took the Earl's part.

Meantime, he for whose sake the fortress was troubled was released on large bail, and was away with free heart to Kilkenny, busy as ever on behalf of the King, full of projects and eager in action. Not a trace of resentment did he manifest—only regret that His Majesty's treatment of him, in destroying his credit with the Catholics as the King's commissioner, had put it out of his power to be so useful as he might otherwise have been. His brain was ever contriving how to remedy things, but loyalties were complicated, and none quite trusted him now that he was disowned by his master.

49.
Siege

The lightning and thunder of the war began to stoop over the Yellow Tower of Gwent, for the doings of the Earl of Glamorgan in Ireland had hastened the vengeance of Parliament.

There was no longer any royal army. Most of the King's friends had accepted the terms offered them, and only a few of his garrisons held out, but no longer in such trim for defense as at first. The walls of Raglan were rather stronger than before, the quantity of provisions large, and the garrison sufficient; but their horses were comparatively few, and the fodder in store was scanty, in prospect of a long siege. The worst of all, indeed the only weak and therefore miserable fact, was that the spirit (not the courage) of the castle was gone. Its enthusiasm had withered; its inhabitants no longer loved the King as they had, for even stern-faced General Duty cannot bring his men to hand-to-hand conflict with the same power as Queen Love.

The rumor of approaching troops kept gathering, and at every fresh report Scudamore's eyes shone.

"Sir Rowland," said Lord Charles one day, "have you not had enough of fighting yet, for all your lame shoulder?"

" 'Tis but my left shoulder, My Lord," answered Scudamore.

"You look for the siege as if it were but a tussle and over—a flash and a roar. If you had to answer for the place like me—well!"

"Nay, My Lord, I would fain show the Roundheads what an honest house can do to hold out rogues."

241

"Ay, but there's the rub!" returned Lord Charles. "Will the house hold out the rogues? There is not a spot in it for defense except the keep and the kitchen."

"We can make sallies, My Lord."

"To be driven in again by ten times our number, and kept in while they knock our walls in about our ears! However, we will hold out while we can. Who knows what turn affairs may take?"

Toward the end of April, the news reached Raglan that the desperate King had made his escape from beleaguered Oxford. In the disguise of a servant, he had betaken himself to the headquarters of the Scots army—only to find himself no King, no guest even, but a prisoner who had sought shelter and found captivity.

The Marquis dropped his chin on his chest and murmured, "All is over!" But the pang that shot to his heart awoke wounded loyalty. He had been angry with his monarch, and justly, but he would fight for him still.

"See to the gates, Charles," he cried, springing from his chair, in spite of his unwieldiness. "Tell Caspar to keep the powder mill going night and day. Would to God my boy Herbert were here! His Majesty hath wronged me, but enthroned or imprisoned he is my King still. And that church tower overlooking our walls must come down, Charles. The dead are for the living, and will not cry out."

When the tower which commanded some portions of the castle fell, it was to Dorothy like taking down the standard of the Lord. She went with some of the ladies for a last look at the ancient structure, and saw section after section fall from the top to crash hideously at the foot amidst the broken tombstones. That was sad enough, but the destruction of the cottages around it, so that the enemy might not shelter there, was sadder still. The women wept and wailed; the men growled, and asked what was Raglan to them, that their houses should be pulled from over their heads. The Marquis offered compensation and shelter. All took money, but few accepted the shelter, for the prospect of a siege was only attractive to such as were fond of fighting, and even then some would rather attack than defend.

The next day the castle heard that Sir Trevor Williams was at Usk with a strong body of men, and that Colonel Birch was besieging Gutbridge Castle. Two days passed, and then Colonel Kirk appeared to the north and approached within two miles. The ladies began to look pale as often as they saw two persons talking together, for there might be fresh news. Every soul in the castle fancied that Lord Glamorgan's presence would have made it impregnable.

Dorothy felt as if she and Caspar were the special servants of that absent power. Ceaselessly, therefore, she saw and spoke and reminded and remedied where she could, so noiselessly, so unobtrusively, that none were offended, and all took heed of the things she brought before them. But her chief business was still the fire engine, whose machinery she anxiously watched; for if anything should happen to Caspar and then to the engine, what would become of the defenders when driven into the tower?

The next day Sir Trevor Williams and his men sat down before the castle with a small battery, and the siege was fairly begun. Dorothy, on top of the keep, heard the sudden bellow of one of their cannon. Two of the battlements beside her flew together, and the stones of the parapet between them stormed into the cistern. Had her presence been the attraction to that thunderbolt? Often after this, while she tended the engine below in the workshop, she would hear the dull thud of an iron ball against the body of the tower.

The same night a sally was prepared. Rowland ran to Lord Charles, begging leave to go. But his lordship would not hear of it, telling him to get well, and that he should have enough sallying before the siege was over. The Roundheads were surprised and lost a few men, but soon recovered themselves and drove the Royalists home, following them to the very gates, whence the guns of the castle sent them back in turn.

Many such sallies and skirmishes followed. At first there was great excitement within the walls when a party was out, and eager and anxious eyes followed them from every point of vision. But at length they got used to it, as to all the ordinary occurrences of siege.

By and by, Colonel Morgan appeared with additional forces, and made his headquarters to the south at Llandenny. In two days more the castle was surrounded, and they began to erect a larger battery on the east of it, and to dig trenches and prepare for mining. The chief point of attack was that side of the stone court which lay between the towers of the kitchen and the library. Here came the hottest of the siege, and very soon that range of building gave show of affording an easy passage by the time the outer works should be taken.

After the first mortar ball there came no more for some time, as Sir Trevor awaited the arrival of Captain Hooper, who was to be at the head of the mining operations. Hence, most of the inmates of the castle began to imagine that a siege was not such an unpleasant thing after all. They lacked nothing; the apple trees bloomed, the moon shone, the white horse fed the fountain, the pigeons flew about the courts, and the peacock strutted on the grass. But then the Roundheads began digging their approaches and mounting their guns on the east side, Sir Trevor opened his battery on the west, and the guns of the Tower replied. The inhabitants were nearly deafened, and frequently failed to hear what was said.

The guns of the eastern battery opened fire, and at the first discharge a round shot, bringing with it a barrowful of stones, came down upon the kitchen chimney, knocking the lid through the bottom of the cook's stewpan, and scattering all the fire about the place. Then a spent shot struck the bars of the Great Mogul's cage, and set him furious, making them think what might happen, and wishing they were sure of the politics of the wild beasts. Every now and then a great rumble told of a falling wall, as that side of the court rapidly turned to a heap of ruins. At such times were heard cries and screams, more of terror than of injury, and all began to understand that it was not starvation, but something more peremptory to which they were doomed to succumb. At times there would fall a lull—perhaps a few hours, perhaps a few minutes—to end in a fury of sudden firing on both sides, mingled with shouts, the rattling of bullets, and the falling of stones, when the women would rush to and fro screaming, and all would imagine the castle was breached.

But the gloom of the Marquis seemed to have vanished. True, when a portion of his house would rumble and fall, he would look grave for a moment, but the next moment he would smile and nod his head, as if all were just as he had expected and would have it.

One evening in the drawing room after supper, the Marquis, in good spirits, and for him in good health, was talking more merrily than usual. Lady Glamorgan stood near him in the window. The captain of the garrison was giving a spirited description of a sally they had made the night before upon Colonel Morgan in his quarters at Llandenny, and Sir Rowland was vowing that, leave or no leave, he would ride the next time—when something crashed in the room, the Marquis put his hand to his head, and the Countess fled in terror. A bullet had come through the window, glanced off a marble pillar, and struck the Marquis on the side of the head. The Countess, finding herself unhurt, ran no farther than the door.

"I ask your pardon, My Lord, for my rudeness," she said, with trembling voice, as she slowly came back. "But indeed, Ladies, she added, "I thought the house was coming down."

"Daughter, you had reason to run away when your father was knocked on the head," said the Marquis. He put his finger on the flattened bullet where it had fallen on the table, and turned it round and round. Then, with the pretense that the bullet had been flattened upon his head, he remarked, "Gentlemen, those who had a mind to flatter me would tell me that I had a good head in my younger days; but so I have in my old age, or else it would not have been musket-proof."

But although he took the thing thus quietly, and indeed merrily, it revealed to him that their usual apartments were no longer fit for the ladies. He gave orders, therefore, that the great rooms in the tower should be prepared for them and the children.

In the midst of the roar from the batteries and towers and walls, the ladies betook themselves to the stronger quarters, and the family was lodged where no hostile shot could reach them, although the frequent fall of portions of its battlemented summit rendered even a peep beyond its impenetrable shell hazardous. Dorothy would lie awake at night and listen to the baffled bullets falling from the wall, and to the roar of the artillery, sounding dull and far away through the ten-foot thickness. Ever and again the words of the ancient Psalm would return to her: "Thou hast been a shelter for me, and a strong tower from the enemy."

She tended the fire engine more carefully than ever, kept the cistern full, and the water lapping the edge of the moat, but let no fountain flow except that from the mouth of the white horse.

The Marquis would not leave his own rooms and the supervision they gave him. The domestics were mostly lodged within the thick kitchen tower, but all between that and the library tower was rapidly becoming a chaos of stone and timber.

50.
A Sally

Meantime Mr. Heywood had returned home to look after his affairs, and brought Richard with him. In the hope that peace had come, they had laid down their commissions; but hardly had they reached Redware when they heard the news of the active operations at Raglan. Richard rode off to see how things were going, not a little anxious concerning Dorothy and full of eagerness to protect her, but entirely without hope of favor either at her hand or her heart. He had no inclination to take part in the siege. Still ready to draw the sword, he yet began to think he had fought enough.

As he approached Raglan he missed something from the landscape, and only upon reflection realized that it was the church tower. Entering the village he found it all but deserted, for the inhabitants had mostly gone—and it was too near the gates and too much exposed to the sudden sallies of the besieged for the occupation of the enemy.

That afternoon, some officers from a large reinforcement had halted at the White Horse, where they were having a glass of ale when Richard rode up. He found them old acquaintances, and sat down with them. It was dusk when they rose and called for their horses.

The host, being a tenant of the Marquis, had decided Royalist predilections, but whether what followed was due to his contriving cannot be told—news reached the castle somehow that a few Parliamentary officers with their men were drinking at the White

Horse Inn.

Scudamore heard the sound of horses' hooves on the stones, and saw over fifty horsemen in the court, all but ready to start. He flew to his chamber, caught up his sword and pistols, and without waiting to put on any armor, hurried to the stables, laid hold of the first horse he came to, and followed the last man out of the court before the gate was closed.

The Parliamentary officers were just mounting when a sentinel carried the alarm of a considerable body of horses in the direction of the castle. Richard, whose mare stood unfastened at the door, was on her back in a moment. Unarmed save for a brace of pistols in his holsters, he thought he could best serve them by galloping to Captain Hooper and bringing help, for the castle party would doubtless outnumber them. Scarcely was he gone, however, and full half of the troopers not yet in their saddles, when the place was surrounded by three times their number. Those who were already mounted, escaped and rode after Heywood, and the rest barricaded the inn door and manned the windows. There they held out for some time, interchanging frequent pistol shots without much injury to either side. At length, however, the Marquis' men were attacked in the rear by Richard with some thirty horsemen from the trenches. A smart combat ensued, lasting half an hour, in which the Parliament men had the advantage. Those who had lost their horses recovered them, and a Royalist was taken prisoner. From him Richard took his sword, and rode after the retreating Cavaliers.

One of their number, a little in the rear, supposed Richard to be one of themselves, and allowed him to get ahead of him. Richard faced about and cut him off from his companions. It was the second time Richard had headed Scudamore, and again he did not know him, this time because it was dark. Rowland, however, recognized the voice calling him to surrender, and rushed fiercely at him. But scarcely had they met when the Cavalier, whose little strength was overcome by unwonted fatigue, dropped from his horse. Richard got down, lifted him, laid him across Lady, mounted, and led the other horse back to the inn. There Richard discovered that his prisoner was the one he feared he had killed at Naseby.

When Rowland came to himself, Richard asked, "Are you able to ride a few miles, Mr. Scudamore?"

Rowland was much chagrined, finding in whose power he was. "I am your prisoner," he said. "You are my evil genius, I think. I have no choice. Your star is in ascendance, and mine has been going down ever since I first met you, Richard Heywood."

Richard attempted no reply, but got Rowland's horse and assisted him to mount.

"I want to do you a good turn, Mr. Scudamore," he said, after they had ridden a mile in silence.

"I look for nothing good at your hand," said Scudamore.

"When you find what it is, I trust you will change your thought of me, Mr. Scudamore."

"Sir Rowland an' it please you," said the prisoner, his boyish vanity roused by his misfortune.

"Mere ignorance must be pardoned, Sir Rowland," returned Richard. "I was unaware of your dignity. But think you, Sir Rowland, that you do well to ride on such rough errands while not yet recovered from former wounds?"

"It seems not, Mr. Heywood, else I had not been your prize, I trust. The wound I caught at Naseby has cost the King a soldier, I fear."

"I hope it will cost no more than is already paid. Men must fight, it seems, but I for one would gladly repair, if I might, what injuries I had been compelled to cause."

"I cannot say the like on my part," returned Sir Rowland. "I would have slain you!"

"I would not have done so to you, in proof whereof do I now lead you to the best leech I know. She brought me back from death's door, when through you—if not by your hand—I was sore wounded. With her I shall leave you. Seek not to escape, lest, being a witch, as they say of her, she chain you up in alabaster. When you are restored, go your way wherever you please."

They reached the cottage, and Richard helped his prisoner to dismount, led him through the garden, and knocked at the door.

"Here, Mother!" he said, as Mrs. Rees opened it. "I have brought you a King's man to cure this time."

"Praise God!" returned Mistress Rees, not that a King's man was wounded, but that she had him to cure. Just as she had devoted herself to the Puritan, she now gave all her care and ministration to the Royalist. She got her bed ready for him, asked a few questions, looked at his shoulder, said it had not been well cared for, and prepared a little poultice, which smelt so vile that

Rowland turned from it with disgust. But the old woman had a singular power of persuasion; he yielded, and in a few moments was fast asleep.

Calling the next morning, Richard found Scudamore very weak, partly from the unwonted fatigue of the previous day, and partly from the old woman's remedies, which were causing the wound to drain. For a week or so, he did not seem to improve. Richard came often, sat by his bedside, and talked with him; but the moment Rowland grew angry, called him names, or abused his party, Richard would rise without a word, mount his mare and ride home, to return the next morning as if nothing unpleasant had occurred.

After a week, the patient began to feel the benefit of the wise woman's treatment. The suppuration of the wound carried much of an old haunting pain away with it, and he felt easier than he had since his return to Raglan. But his behavior to Richard grew very strange. At one time it was so friendly as to be almost affectionate; at another he seemed bent on doing and saying everything he could to provoke a duel. For another whole week, aware of the benefit he was deriving, and apparently also at times fascinated by the visits of his enemy, he showed no anxiety to be gone.

"Heywood," he said one morning suddenly, with quite a new familiarity, "do you consider I owe you an apology for carrying off your mare?"

"Put your case, Scudamore," returned Richard.

And Sir Rowland did put his case, starting from the rebel state of the owner, advancing to the natural outlawry that resulted, and going on with the necessity of the King.

"I know you regard neither King nor right. Therefore, I ask you only to tell me how it seems to you that I ought on these grounds to judge myself."

"All I will say is this, Sir Rowland," answered Richard, "that I should have scorned to carry off your horse or any man's."

"Ah, but you would have had no right, being but a rebel!"

"You must judge on my grounds when you judge me."

"True, and then am I driven to say you were made of the better earth—curse you! I am ashamed of having taken your mare—only because it was in a half-friendly passage with you it was I learned her worth. But, hang you, it was not through you I learned to know my cousin, Dorothy Vaughan."

Richard's heart stung as at the blow of a whip, but he answered with coolness.

"What then of her?" he said. "Have you been wooing her favor, Sir Rowland? You owe me nothing there, I admit, even had she not sent me from her. Besides, I am scarce to be content with a mistress whose favor fades with that which comes between us. This I say not in pride, but because in such case I were not the right man for her, neither she the right woman for me."

"Then you bear me no grudge in that I have sought the prize of my cousin's heart?"

"None," answered Richard, but could not bring himself to ask how he had fared.

"Then will I own to you that I have gained as little. I will madden myself telling you, whom I hate, and to your comfort, that she despises me."

"That I am sure she does not. She can despise nothing that is honorable."

"Do you then count me honorable, Heywood?" said Scudamore, in a voice of surprise. "Then honorable I will be."

"But honorable for honor's sake," said Richard. "When first we met, we were but boys. Now we are men, and must put away boyish things."

"Do you call it boyish to be madly in love with the fairest and noblest and bravest mistress that ever trod the earth, though she be half a Puritan, alas?"

"Half a Puritan!" exclaimed Heywood. "She hates the very wind of the word."

"She may hate the word, but she is the thing. She has read me such lessons as none but a Puritan could."

"Were they not then good lessons, that you join with them a name hateful to you?"

"Ay, truly, much too good for mortal like me—or you either, Heywood. They are but hypocrites that pretend otherwise."

"Call you your cousin a hypocrite?"

'No, by heaven, she is not! She is a woman, and it is easy for women to say prayers."

"I never rode into a fight but I said my prayers," returned Richard.

"Nonetheless you are a hypocrite. I should scorn to be forever begging favors. Do you think God hears such prayers as yours?"

"Not if He be such as you, Sir Rowland, and not if he who

prays be such as you think. Prithee, what sort of prayer think you I pray ere I ride into the battle?"

"It is a cowardly thing to go praying into the battles, and not take your fair chance as other men do."

"I have had my doubts, not whether my side were more in the right than yours, but whether it were worthwhile to raise the sword even in such cause. Moreover, I am no saint, and therefore cannot pray like a saint, but only like Richard Heywood, who hath his duty, and is something puzzled. Therefore, I pray to this effect:

" 'O God of battles! Who, Thyself dwelling in peace, beholdest the strife, and workest Thy will thereby, what that good and perfect will is, I know not clearly, but Thou hast sent us to be doing, and Thou hatest cowardice. Thou knowest I have sought to choose the best, and to this battle I am pledged.

" 'Give me grace to fight like Thy soldier, without wrath and without fear. Give me to do my duty, but give the victory where Thou pleasest. Let me live if so Thou wilt; let me die if so Thou wilt—only let me die in honor with Thee. Let the truth be victorious, if not now, yet when it shall please Thee; and let no deed of mine delay its coming. Let my work fail, if it be unto evil, but save my soul in truth.'

"Then I say to my mare, 'Come Lady, all is well now. Let us go. And good will come out of it to you also, for how should the Father think of His sparrows and forget His mares? Doubtless your kind are in heaven, else how should the apostle have seen them there? And if any, surely you, my Lady!' So ride we to the battle, merry and strong and calm, as if we were but riding to the rampart of the celestial city."

Rowland lay gazing at Richard for a few minutes, then said, "By heaven, but it were a pity you two should not come together! Surely the same spirit dwells in you both! For me, I should show but as the shadow cast from her brightness. But I tell you, Roundhead, I love her better than ever Roundhead could."

"I know not, Scudamore. Nor do I mean to judge you when I say that no man who loves not the truth can love a woman in the grand way a woman ought to be loved."

"Tell me not I do not love her, or I will rise and kill you. I love her even to doing what my soul hateth for her sake. Damned Roundhead, she loves *you!*" The words came from him in a shriek, and he fell back panting.

Richard sat silent for a few moments, his heart surging and sinking. Then he said quietly, "It may be so, Sir Rowland. We were boy and girl together—fed rabbits, flew kites, planted weeds to make flowers of them, played at marbles—she may love me a little, Roundhead as I am."

"By heaven, I will try her once more! Who knows the heart of a woman?" said Rowland through his teeth.

"If you should gain her, Scudamore, and afterward she should find you unworthy?"

"She would love me still."

"And she should learn to despise you, finding you had not only deceived her but deceived your better self, and she should turn from you with loathing, while you did love her still—as well as your nature could. What then, Sir Rowland?"

"Then I should kill her."

"And you love her better than any Roundhead could! I will find you man after man from amongst Ireton's or Cromwell's horse to love better than you, you poor atom of solitary selfishness!"

Rowland flung himself from the bed, seized Richard by the throat, and with all the strength he could summon did his best to strangle him. Richard allowed him to spend his rage, then removed his grasp as gently as he could, and holding both his wrists in his left hand, rose and stood over him.

"Sir Rowland," he said, "I am not angry with you that you are weak and passionate. You lie in God's hands a thousandfold more helpless than you now lie in mine, and like Saul of Tarsus you will find it hard to kick against the goads. For the maiden, do as you will. But I thank you for what you have told me, though I doubt it means little better for me than for you. You have a kind heart. I almost love you, and will when I can."

He let go his hands, and walked from the room.

"Canting hypocrite!" cried Sir Rowland in the wrath of impotence, but knew while he said the words that they were false.

And with the words, the bitterness of life seized his heart, and his despair shrouded the world in the blackness of darkness. There was nothing more to live for, and he turned his face to the wall.

51.
Under the Moat

Some time passed before Scudamore was discovered missing from the castle. However, there was the hope that he had been taken prisoner; things were growing so bad within the walls that there was little leisure for lamentation over individual misfortunes. Unless some change should occur—for there seemed no chance except the King should win over the Scots to take his part—it was evident that the enemy must speedily make the assault.

On the other hand, ever since the balls had been flying about his house, the loyalty of the Marquis had been rising, and he had thought of his King ever with growing tenderness, of his faults with more indulgence, and of the wrongs he had done his family with more magnanimity and forgiveness, so that, for his own part, he would have held out to the very last.

"And truly were it not better to be well buried under the ruins?" he would ask himself, looking down with a sigh at his great bulk, which added so much to the dismalness of the prospect of being, in his seventieth year, a prisoner or a wanderer—the latter a worse fate even than the former. To be no longer the master of his own great house and of many willing servants, while the weight of his clumsy person must still hang about him—such a prospect required something more than loyalty to meet it with equanimity.

But it was consolation enough to him to repeat to himself the text from his precious Vulgate: "For we know that if our earthly house of this tabernacle were dissolved, we have a building of God,

253

an house not made with hands, eternal in the heavens."

For the ladies, so long as their father-in-chief was with them, they were not too anxious. Whatever was done must be the right thing, and in the midst of tumult and threat they were content. If only Herbert had been with them too!

The Marquis found surrender hard indeed to contemplate, even when the iron shot was driving his stately house into showers of dirt. The eastern side of the stone court was now little better than a heap of rubbish, and the hour of assault could not be far off, although as yet there had been no summons. But he could not forget that, though the castle was his, it was not for himself but for his King he held it garrisoned, and how could he yield it without the approval of his Sovereign?

But that King was a prisoner in the hands of a hostile nation, and how was he to receive message or return answer? And Raglan itself was so beset no one could issue from its gates without risk of being stopped, searched, and detained until it should have fallen. For the besiegers knew well enough that Lord Glamorgan was still in Ireland on behalf of the King. And what more likely than that he should—with the men he was still raising in Ireland—make some desperate attempt to turn the scales of war, and strike first for the relief of his father's castle?

These things were all freely spoken of in the family, and Dorothy understood the position of affairs as well as anyone. And now at length it seemed to her that the hour had arrived for attempting some return for Raglan's hospitality. Thus far no service she had stumbled upon had any magnitude in her eyes. But now—to be the bearer of dispatches to the King! It would suffice, even if a failure, to prove her not ungrateful.

Fearful of the dangers, Caspar sought to dissuade Dorothy from her meditated proposal, but to no avail. He then told her one thing which served to clench her resolution—that there was a secret way out of the castle, provided by his master for communication during siege; more he was not at liberty to disclose. Dorothy went straight to the Marquis and laid her plan before him, which was that she should make her escape to Wyfern, and thence, attended by an old servant, set out to seek the King.

"There is no longer time, alas!" returned the Marquis. "I look for the final summons every hour."

"Could you not raise the report, My Lord, that you have undermined the castle, and laid a huge quantity of gunpowder, with the determination of blowing it up the moment they enter? That would make them fall back upon blockade, and leave us a little time. Our provisions are not nearly exhausted."

"Thou art a brave lady, Cousin Dorothy," said the Marquis. But if they caught and searched thee, and found papers on thee, it would go worse with us than before."

"Please your lordship, my Lord Glamorgan once showed me such a comb as a lady might carry in her pocket, but so contrived that the head thereof was hollow and could contain dispatches. Methinks Caspar could lay his hand on the comb."

"By George, thou speakest well, Cousin!" said the Marquis. "But who should attend thee?"

"Let me have Tom Fool, My Lord, for now have I thought of a betterment of my plan; he will guide me to his mother's house, and thence can I cross the fields to my own."

"Tom Fool is a mighty coward," objected the Marquis.

"So much the better, My Lord. He will not get me into trouble through displaying his manhood before me. He has a face long enough for three Roundheads, and a tongue that can utter glibly enough what sounds very like their jargon. Tom is the right fool to attend me, My Lord."

"Well, it is a brave offer, My Child, and I will think thereupon," said his lordship.

All the rest of the day the Marquis and Lord Charles, with two or three of the principal officers of house and garrison, were in conference, and letters were drafted to His Majesty and to Lord Glamorgan. Before they were finally written out in cipher, Caspar was sent for, the comb found, its contents gauged, and the paper cut to suit.

About an hour after midnight, Dorothy, Lord Charles, and Caspar stood together in the workshop, waiting for Tom Fool, who had gone to fetch Dick from the stables. Dorothy had the comb in her pocket. She looked pale, but her gray eyes shone with courage and determination. She carried no weapon but a whip; a keen little lamp borne by Caspar was all their light.

Presently they heard the sound of Dick's hooves on the bridge. A moment more and Tom led him in, both man and horse looking somewhat scared at the strangeness of the midnight proceeding. But Tom was glad of the office, and ready to risk a good deal in order to get out of the castle, where he expected nothing milder than a general massacre.

Lord Charles himself lifted foot after foot of the little horse to satisfy himself that his shoes were sound, then made a sign to Caspar, and gave his hand to Dorothy. Caspar led Dick by the bridle into the keep, and the others followed. They came to a chalked circle on the paving stones, and stood within the mark. Caspar operated a lever hidden behind a stone in the wall, and they slowly began to sink through a stone-faced shaft into the foundations of the keep. Dick was frightened, but a word and an occasional pat from his mistress sufficed to keep him quiet.

At the depth of about thirty feet they stopped, and found themselves facing a ponderous door, studded and barred with iron. Caspar took from his pocket a key about the size of a goose quill, felt about for a moment, and then with a slight movement of finger and thumb threw back a dozen ponderous bolts with a great echoing clang. The door slowly opened, and they entered a narrow vaulted passage of stone. Their lamp showed but a few feet of walls and roof, and revealed nothing in front until they had gone about a furlong, when it shone upon rock, ending their way. But again Caspar applied the little key somewhere, and immediately a great mass of rock slowly turned on a pivot, permitting them to pass.

When they were all on the other side of it, Lord Charles turned and held up the light. Dorothy turned also and looked—there was nothing to indicate whence they had come. Before her was the rough rock, seemingly solid, certainly slimy and green, and over its face was flowing a tiny rivulet.

"See there," said Lord Charles, pointing up. "That little stream comes the way your dog and the Roundhead Heywood came and went, where I now challenge anything larger than a rat to go."

Dorothy made no answer. They went on and soon arrived at the open quarry, whence Tom knew the way across the fields. Lord Charles lifted Dorothy to the saddle, said good-luck and good-bye, and stood with Caspar watching as she rode up the steep ascent. For an instant her form stood out dark against the sky, then vanished.

52.
The Untoothsome Plum

It was a starry night with a threatening of moonrise, and Dorothy was anxious to reach the cottage before it grew lighter. Over field after field they kept on, and at last reached the side of the bridge where Marquis had led Richard off the road, and there they scrambled up.

A sentry on the low parapet cried, "Who goes there?" and then caught at his carbine leaning against the wall.

"O Master!" began Tom, in a voice of terrified appeal, but Dorothy interrupted him.

"I am an honest woman of the neighborhood," she said. "An' thou will come home with me, I will afford thee a better breakfast, I warrant, than thou had a supper."

"That is, an' thou be one of the godly," supplemented Tom.

"I thank thee, Mistress," returned the sentinel, "but not for indulgence of appetite will I forsake my post. Who goeth with thee?"

"A fellow whose wit is greater than his courage, and yet he goes with many for a born fool."

"But knowest thou not that the country is full of soldiers, whereof some, though that they be all truehearted and rightminded men, would not mayhap carry themselves so civil to a woman as Corporal Bearbanner? And now thou comest from the direction of Raglan!"

Here he drew himself up, summoned a voice from his chest a story or two deeper, and asked in a magisterial tone, "Whence comest thou, Woman? On what business gaddest thou about so late?"

"I come from visiting at a friend's house, and am now almost on my own farm," answered Dorothy.

The man turned to Tom, and Dorothy began to regret that she had brought him: he was trembling visibly and his mouth was wide open with terror.

"See," she said, "how thy gruff voice terrifies him. He is but an innocent fool. If now he should fall into a fit thou wert to blame."

As she spoke she put her hand in her pocket, took from it her untoothsome plum, and popped it into Tom's mouth. Instantly he began to make such strange uncouth noises that the sentinel thought he had indeed terrified him into a fit.

"I must get him straightway home. Good night, Friend," said Dorothy, and giving Dick the rein, she was off like the wind, heedless of the shouts of the sentinel or the feeble cries of Tom, who, if he could not fight, could run. They were instantly lost in the darkness. The sentinel sat down again on the parapet of the bridge, and began to examine all that Dorothy had said, with a wondrous inclination to discover the strong points in it.

Having galloped a little way, Dorothy drew bridle and halted for Tom. As soon as he came up she released him from the plum, and told him to lay hold of Dick's mane and run alongside.

The moon had risen before they reached his mother's house, and Dorothy was glad when she dismounted at the gate to think she need ride no farther. While Tom went in to rouse his mother, Dorothy let Dick have a few bites of grass. But the next moment, Tom came out in terror, saying there was a man in his mother's closet, and he feared the Roundheads were in possession.

"Then take care of yourself, Tom," said Dorothy. She mounted and set off into the fields that lay between the cottage and her own house.

She had just popped into the second field, through a gap in the hedge, when she heard the click of a flintlock, and a voice she thought she knew, ordering her to stand; within a few yards of her was again a Roundhead soldier. Keeping a sharp eye on the man, she allowed him to come within a pace or two, but the moment he would have taken Dick by the bridle, she danced him three or four yards away.

"Fright not my horse, Friend," she said. "But how!" she added, suddenly remembering him. "Is it possible? Master Upstill! Gent-ly, gently, little Dick! Master Upstill is an old friend. What! Have you left your last and lapstone, and turned soldier?"

"I have left all and followed Him, Mistress," answered Castdown.

"Are you sure He called you, Master Upstill?"

"I heard Him with my own ears—called me to be a fisher of men, and thee I catch, Mistress—thus," returned the man, step-ping quickly forward and making another grasp at Dick's bridle.

Dorothy scarcely refrained from giving him a smart blow across the face with her whip. She gave Dick the cut instead, and sent him yards away.

"Say, what manner of woman art thou?" he demanded, with pompous anger. "Whence comest thou, and whither does thou go?

"Home," answered Dorothy.

"What place callest thou home? For no doubt thou art a consorter with malignants, harlots, and papists." Again he clutched at her bridle, and this time, with success. Dorothy dropped the bridle, struck Dick smartly with her whip, and as he reared drew the whip across Upstill's eyes. His mouth opened in pain, and she administered her plum.

It was thoroughly effective—he dropped hold of the bridle, and his efforts to remove the plum rapidly grew wilder and wilder, until at last his gestures were those of a maniac.

"There!" she cried, as she bounded from him. "Take your first lesson in good manners. That mouthful, is, as your evil words returned to choke you! You had better keep me in sight," she added, as she gave Dick his head, "for no one else can free you."

Upstill ceased his futile efforts, caught up his carbine, and fired. But Dorothy rode on unhurt, meditating how to secure Upstill when she got him to Wyfern, whither she doubted not he would follow her. Her difficulties were not yet past, however, for just as she reached her own ground, she was once again met by the order to stand.

This time the voice was almost as welcome as known, and yet made her tremble for the first time that night. It was Richard Heywood.

53.
Faithful Foes

Hearing Upstill's shot and then Dick's hooves, Richard had judged well and taken the right direction. But great was his astonishment when he saw Dorothy on Dick! What form but hers had been filling soul and brain, and there she was before him!

"Dorothy," he murmured tremblingly, and his voice sounded to him like that of someone speaking far away. He drew nearer, as one might approach a beloved ghost, anxious not to scare her. He laid his hand on Dick's neck, half fearful of finding him but a shadow—but he was flesh enough. Then suddenly a great wave from the ocean of duty broke thunderous on the shore of his consciousness.

"Dorothy, I am bound to question you," he said. "Whence come you, and whither are you bound?"

"If I should refuse to answer you, Richard?" returned Dorothy with a smile.

"Then I must take you to headquarters. And think, Dorothy, how that would cut me to the heart."

"Then will I answer you, Richard," she said, with a strange trembling in her voice. "I come from Raglan and go to Wyfern."

"On what business?"

"Were it so wonderful, Richard, if I should desire to be at home, seeing Wyfern is now safer than Raglan?"

"It might not be wonderful in another, Dorothy. But they of Raglan are your friends, and you are a brave woman and love

260

your friends. Confess—you bear about you what you would not willingly show me."

Dorothy, as if in embarrassment, drew from her pocket her handkerchief, and with it her comb, which fell on the ground.

"Prithee, Richard, pick me up my comb," she said, then continued, "No, I have nothing about me I would not show you, Richard. Will you take my word for it?" She held out her hand, received her comb, and replaced it in her pocket, while a keen pang of remorse went through her heart.

"I am a man under authority," said Richard, "and my orders will not allow me. And men say you are not bound to tell the truth to your enemy."

"If you are my enemy, Richard, then you must satisfy yourself."

"Will you swear to me, Dorothy, that you have no papers about you, neither bear news or request or sign to any of the King's party?"

"Richard, you yourself have taken from my words the credit. I say to you again, satisfy yourself."

"Dorothy, what *am* I to do?" he cried.

"Your duty, Richard," she answered.

"My duty is to search you."

"Do then your duty, Richard," she said, and slid from her saddle to stand before him. There was no defiance in her tone. She was but submitting, assured of deliverance.

Never man was more perplexed. He dared not let her pass, and dared not touch her, yet he must. She was silent, seemed to herself cruel, and began bitterly to accuse herself. She saw his hazel eyes slowly darken, then glitter—was it with gathering tears? The man was weeping! The tenderness of their common childhood rushed back upon her in a great swelling wave out of the past. She threw her arm around his neck and kissed him as he stood in dumb ecstasy.

"Richard, do your duty. Regard me not."

Richard answered with a strange laugh. "There was a time when I had doubted the sun in heaven as soon as your word, Dorothy. This is surely an evil time. Tell me, yea or nay, have you missives to the King or any of his people? Palter not with me."

But such an appeal was what Dorothy would least willingly encounter. A light appeared to her, and she burst into a merry laugh.

"What a pair of fools we are, Richard! Is there no honest woman of your persuasion near—one who would show me no favor? Let such a one search me, and tell you the truth."

"Doubtless," answered Richard, laughing very differently now at his stupidity. "Dame Upstill is even now at the farm there, where she watches over her husband while he watches over Raglan. Will she answer your turn?"

"She will," replied Dorothy. "And that she may show me no favor, here comes her husband, whose witness against me shall rouse in her all malice of vengeance for her injured spouse, For his evil language I have so silenced him that neither you nor any man can restore him to speech."

While she spoke, Upstill, following his enemy as the sole hope of deliverance, drew near in such plight as the dignity of narrative refuses to describe.

"Upstill," said Richard, "what meaneth this? Wherefore have you left your post? And above all, wherefore have you permitted this lady to pass unquestioned?"

Sounds of gurgle and strangulation were Upstill's only response.

"Indeed, Mr. Heywood," said Dorothy, "he was so far from neglecting his duty and allowing me to pass unquestioned, that he insulted me grievously, averting that I consorted with malignant rogues, and papists, and worse—which drove me to punish him as you see."

"Upstill, you have shamed your regiment, carrying yourself thus to a gentlewoman," said Richard. "Ask the lady to pardon you, Upstill. I can do nothing for you."

Upstill would have knelt for release, but Dorothy was content to see him punished and would not see him degraded.

"Master Heywood, here is the key of the toy, a sucket which will pass neither teeth nor throat." She took the ring from her finger, raised from it the key, and directed Richard how to find its hole in the plum.

"There! Follow us now to the farm, and find your wife, for we need her aid," said Richard, as he drew by the key the little steel instrument from Upstill's mouth, and restored him to the general body of the articulate.

Thereupon he took Dick by the bridle, and Dorothy and he walked side by side, as if they had still been boy and girl as of old. As they went, Richard washed both plum and ring in the dewy

262

grass, and restored them, putting the ring upon her finger.

"With better light I will one day show you how the thing works," she said, thanking him. "When these troubles are over and honest folk need no longer fight each other, I will give it to you, Richard."

"Would that day were here, Dorothy! But what can honest people do, while St. George and St. Michael themselves are at odds?"

As they reached the farmhouse, it was growing light. Upstill fetched his dame from her bed in the hayloft, and Richard told her what he required of her.

"I will search her!" answered the dame from between her closed teeth.

"Mistress Vaughan," said Richard, "if she offer you evil words, give her the same lesson you gave her husband. If all tales be true, she is not beyond the need of it. Search her well, Mistress Upstill, but show her no rudeness, for she has the power to avenge it in a parlous manner. Nonetheless, you must search her well, else I will look upon you as no better than one of the malignants."

The woman cast a glance of something very like hate, but mingled with fear, upon Dorothy.

"I like not the business, Captain Heywood," she said.

"Yet the business must be done, Mistress Upstill. And heark'ee, for every paper you findest on her, I will bring you its weight in gold."

"I warrant thee, Captain!" she returned. "Come with me, Mistress, and show what thou hast."

She led the way to the rickyard, and round toward the sunrise. Mistress Upstill began her search, which she made more thorough than agreeable. At last, as she was giving up the quest in despair, the eyes of her fingers discovered a little opening inside the prisoner's bodice, and there was a pocket, and in it a slip of paper! She drew it out in triumph.

"That is nothing," said Dorothy. "Give it to me." And with flushed face she made a snatch at it. "That paper has nothing to do with state affairs, I protest," expostulated Dorothy. "I will give you ten times its weight in gold for it."

But Mistress Upstill had other passions besides avarice, and was not greatly tempted by the offer. She took Dorothy by the arm and said, "An' thou come not quickly, I will cry that all the parish shall hear me."

"I tell you, on the oath of an honest woman, it is but a private letter of mine own, and beareth nothing upon affairs. Prithee, read a word or two, and satisfy yourself."

"Nay, Mistress, truly I will pry into no secrets that belong not to me," said her searcher, who could not read. "This paper is no longer thine, and mine it never was. It belongeth to the High Court of Parliament, and goeth straight to Captain Heywood—whom I will inform concerning the bribe wherewith thou didst seek to corrupt the conscience of a godly woman."

Dorothy saw there was no help, and yielded to the grasp of the dame, who led her like a culprit with burning cheek back to her judge.

When Richard saw them his heart sank within him. "What have you found?" he asked gruffly.

"I have found that which she would have had me cover with a bribe of ten times what your honor promised me for it," answered the woman. "She had it in her bosom, hid in a pocket inside her bodice."

"Ha, Mistress Dorothy! Is this true?" asked Richard, turning on her a face of distress.

"It is true," answered Dorothy, with downcast eyes—far more ashamed however of that which had not been discovered, and which might have justified Richard's look, than of that which he now held in his hand. "Prithee," she added, "do not read it till I am gone."

"That may hardly be," returned Richard almost sullenly. "Upon this paper depends whether you go at all."

"Believe me, Richard, it hath no importance," she said, and her blush deepened. "I would you would believe me." But as she said it her conscience smote her.

Richard, slowly, reluctantly, opened the paper, stood for an instant motionless, and looked at it. His face changed at once from midnight to morning, and the sunrise was red. He put the paper to his lips, and thrust it inside his doublet. It was his own letter to her by Marquis!

"And now, Master Heywood, I may go where I will?" said Dorothy, venturing a half-roguish, but wholly shamefaced glance at him.

But Dame Upstill was looking on, and Richard therefore brought as much of the midnight as would obey orders, back over his countenance.

"Nay, Mistress," he said. "If we had found aught upon you of greater consequence, it might have made a question. But this hardly accounts for your mission. Doubtless you bear your message in your mind."

"What! You will not let me go to Wyfern, to my own house, Master Heywood?" said Dorothy in a tone of disappointment, for her heart now at length began to fail her.

"Not until Raglan is ours," answered Richard. "Then shall you go where you will. And go where you will, there will I follow you, Dorothy."

From the last part of this speech he diverted Mrs. Upstill's attention by throwing her a gold noble—an indignity which the woman rightly resented, but she stooped for the money!

"Go tell your husband that I wait him here," he said.

"You shall follow me nowhere," said Dorothy angrily. "Wherefore should I not go to Wyfern and there abide? You can there watch her whom you trust not."

"Who can tell what manner of person might creep to Wyfern, to whom there might be messages given, or to whom you might send, credenced by secret word or sign?"

"Whither, then, am I to go?" asked Dorothy with dignity.

"Alas, Dorothy!" answered Richard. "I must take you to Raglan. But comfort yourself—soon you shall go where you will."

Dorothy marveled at her own resignation all the while she rode with Richard back to the castle. Her scheme was a failure, but through no fault of hers, and she could bear anything with composure except blame.

A word from Richard to Colonel Morgan was sufficient. A messenger with a flag of truce was sent to the castle, and the firing on both sides ceased. The messenger returned, the gate was opened, and Dorothy reentered—defeated, but bringing her secrets back with her.

"Thou and the Roundhead are well matched," said the Marquis when she had recounted her adventures. "There is no avoiding it, Cousin! It is thy fate. Mind thee, hearts are older than crowns, and love outlives all but lying."

"All but lying!" repeated Dorothy to herself, and the word *but* was bitter.

54.
The Crumbling House

At his mother's cottage, Tom Fool had just been boasting of his exploit in escaping from Raglan, and expressing his conviction that Dorothy, whom he had valiantly protected, was safe at Wyfern. Rowland was dressing as fast as he could to pay her a visit, when Tom caught sight of Richard riding toward the cottage, and jumping up, ran into the chimney corner. His mother looked from the window, and spied the cause of his terror.

"Silly Tom!" she said, for she still treated him like a child, notwithstanding her boastful belief in his high position and merits. "He will not harm thee. There never was hurt in a Heywood."

"Treason, flat treason, Witch!" cried Scudamore.

"Thou of all men, Sir Rowland, hast no cause to say so," returned Mrs. Rees. "But come and break thy fast while he talks to thee, and save the precious time which runneth so fast away."

"I might as well be in my grave for any value it hath to me!" said Rowland, who was for the moment in a bad mood. His hope and his faith were ever ready to fall out, and a twinge in his shoulder was enough to set them jarring.

"Here comes Master Heywood, anyhow," said the old woman, "and I pray thee, Sir Rowland, to let bygones be bygones, for my sake if not for thine own, lest thou bring the vengeance of General Fairfax upon my poor house."

"Fairfax!" cried Scudamore. "Is that villain come hither?"

"Sir Thomas Fairfax arrived two days agone," answered Mrs. Rees, "a sign that Raglan's end is near!"

266

"Good morrow, Mother Rees," said Richard, looking in at the door, radiant as an Apollo.

Pale as a dying moon, Scudamore deigned no preliminaries. "I want my horse, Heywood," he cried.

"Your horse is at Redware, Scudamore; I carry him not in my pocket. What would you with him?"

"What is it to you? Let me have him."

"Softly, Sir Rowland! It is true I promised you your liberty, but liberty doth not necessarily include a horse."

"You were never better than a shifting fanatic," cried Sir Rowland.

"If I served you as befitted, you should never see your horse again," returned Richard. "Yet I promise you that so soon as Raglan hath fallen, he shall again be yours. Tell me where you go, and—Ha! Are you there?" he cried, as he caught sight of Tom in the chimney corner. "Would you like to hear, you rascal, that Mistress Dorothy Vaughan got safe to Wyfern this morning?"

"God be praised!" said Tom Fool.

"But you shall not hear it. I come from conducting her back to Raglan in safety. You shall have your horse, Sir Rowland, but for your ride to Wyfern, that would not avail you. Your cousin rode by here this morning, it is true, but is now within Raglan walls, whence she will not issue again until the soldiers of the Parliament enter. It is no treason to tell you that General Fairfax is about to send his final summons ere he storms the rampart."

"Then you may keep the horse, for I will back to Raglan on foot," said Scudamore.

"Nay, that you will not, for naught greatly larger than a mouse can any more pass through the lines. Do you think because I sent back your Cousin Dorothy, lest she should work mischief outside the walls, I will therefore send you back to work mischief within them?"

"And you are the man who professeth to love Mistress Dorothy!" cried Scudamore with contempt.

"You are to blame in speaking what you do not believe, Sir Rowland. But will you have your horse or not?"

"No. I will remain where I am until I hear the worst."

"Or come home with me, where you will hear it yet sooner. You shall taste a Roundhead's hospitality."

"I scorn you and your false friendship," cried Rowland, and

turning into his room, he bolted the door.

That same morning at Raglan a great iron ball struck the marble horse on his proud head, and flung it in fragments over the court. From his neck the water bubbled up bright and clear, like the lifeblood of the wounded whiteness.

"Poor Molly!" said the Marquis, watching from his study—then smiled at his pity. Lord Charles entered; a messenger had come from General Fairfax, demanding a surrender in the name of Parliament.

"If they had but gone on a little longer, Charles, they might have saved us the trouble," said his lordship, "for there would have been nothing left to surrender. But I will consider the proposal," he added.

But there was no longer the shadow of a question as to submission. All that was left was but the arrangement of conditions. Captain Hooper's trenches were rapidly approaching the rampart, and six great mortars for throwing shells were now in position. Resistance would be the merest folly.

Various meetings settled the terms of submission, and on the fifteenth of August the surrender was fixed for the seventeenth.

The interval was a sad time. Tears flowed all day long—the ladies doing their best to conceal them and the servants to display them. Everyone was busy gathering together what personal effects might be carried away. It was an especially sad time for the children of the house, for they were old enough not merely to love the place, but to know that they loved it. The thought that the sacred things of their home were about to pass into other hands roused in them wrath and indignation as well as grief; for in the minds of children who have been born and brought up in the midst of family possessions, the sense of property is, perhaps stronger than in the minds of their elders.

As the sun was going down on the evening of the sixteenth, Dorothy came from the keep, and was crossing the fountain court to her old room on its western side. Everyone was busy indoors, and the place appeared deserted. There was a stillness in the air that sounded awful. For so many weeks it had been shattered with roar upon roar, and now the guns had ceased to bellow, leaving a sense of vacancy and doubt, an oppression of silence! But the sunlight lived on sweet and calm, as if all was well. It seemed to promise that wrath and ruin would pass, and leave no lasting desolation behind them. Yet she could not help heaving a great sigh, and the tears came streaming down her cheeks.

"Tut, tut, Cousin! Wipe thine eyes. The dreary old house is not worth such bright tears."

Dorothy turned and saw the Marquis seated on the edge of the marble basin under the headless horse, whose clear blood still welled from his truncated form. She saw also that, although his words were cheerful, his lip quivered. It was some little time before she could compose herself sufficiently to speak.

"I marvel your lordship is so calm," she said.

"Come hither, Dorothy," he returned kindly, "and sit thee down by my side. Thou wast right good to my little Molly. Thou hast been a ministering angel to Raglan and its people. I did thee wrong, and thou forgavest me with a whole heart. Thou hast returned me good for evil tenfold, and for all this I love thee, and therefore will I now tell thee what maketh me quiet at heart. I have lived my life, and have now but to die my death. I am thankful to have lived, and hope to live hereafter. Goodness and mercy went before my birth, and goodness and mercy will follow my death. What my Anne and my Molly hath passed through, shall I shun to meet? And wherefore should I not rejoice to depart? When I see my house lying in ruins about me, I look down upon this ugly overgrown body of mine, the very foundations whereof crumble from beneath me, and I thank God it is but a tent, and no enduring house—even like this house of Raglan, which ere long will be a dwelling of owls and foxes. Very soon will Death pull out the tent-pins and let me fly. I like to be old and ugly as little as thou wouldst, and yet my heart, I verily think, is little older than thine own. One day, please God, I shall be clothed upon with a house that is from heaven, nor shall I hobble with gouty feet over the golden pavement—if so be that my sins overpass not mercy. Pray for me, Dorothy, my daughter, for my end is nigh, that I find at length the bosom of Father Abraham."

Dorothy knelt and kissed the old man's hand, then rose and went weeping to her chamber, leaving him still seated by the broken fountain.

Of all who prepared to depart, Caspar Kaltoff was the busiest. What best things of his master's he could carry with him, he took, but a multitude he left to a more convenient opportunity. He sunk his precious cabinet, and a chest filled with curious inventions and favorite tools, into the secret shaft. But the most valued of all, the fire engine, he could not take and would not leave. He stopped the fountain of the white horse, once more set the water-commanding slave to work, and filled the cistern until he heard it roar in the wastepipe. Then he extinguished the fire and let the furnace cool. When Dorothy entered the workshop for the last time to take her mournful leave of the place, there lay the bones of the mighty creature scattered over the floor—here a pipe, there a valve, and here a piston. Nothing stood but the furnace and the great pipes that ran up the grooves in the wall outside.

"Mistress Dorothy," he said, "my master is the greatest man in Christendom, but the world is stupid and will forget him because it never knew him."

Among her treasures Lady Glamorgan carried with her the last dainty garments worn by her Molly.

Dr. Bayly carried a bag of papers and sermons, with his doctor's gown and hood, and his best suit of clothes.

The Marquis with his own hand put up his Vulgate.

The last night spent in the castle was troubled, and not many slept. But the lord of it had long understood that what could cease to be his never had been his, and so he slept like a child.

When breakfast was over, proclamation was made that at nine o'clock there would be prayers in the chapel for the last time, and that the Marquis desired all to be present. When the hour arrived, he entered leaning on the arm of Dr. Bayly. Dorothy followed with the ladies of the family. Young Delaware was in his place, and "with organ voice and voice of psalms," praise and prayer arose for the last time from the house of Raglan. All were in tears save the Marquis. A smile played about his lips, and he looked like a child giving away his toy. Sir Toby Matthews tried hard to speak to his flock, but broke down and had to yield the attempt. When the services were over, the Marquis rose and led everyone to the great hall.

On the dais he seated himself in his chair of state. On one side of him was a bag of gold, and on the other, a larger bag of silver. Then each servant was called before him by name, and with his own hand the Marquis gave to each a small present in view of coming necessities: they had the day before received their wages. To each he wished a kind farewell, to some adding a word of advice or comfort. He then handed the bags to the governor, and

270

told him to distribute their contents according to his judgment amongst the garrison. Last, he ordered everyone to be ready to follow him from the gates the moment the clock struck the hour of noon.

He went to his study, and when Lord Charles came to tell him that all were assembled, and everything ready for departure, he found his father kneeling. But he rose with more agility than he had for a long time been able to show, and followed his son.

With slow pace he crossed the courts and the hall, which were silent as the grave, bending his steps to the main entrance. The portcullises were up, the gates wide open, and the drawbridge down, all silent and deserted. In solemn silence the Marquis descended the white stair leaning on Lord Charles. At the foot of the stair stood four carriages, each with six officers in glittering harness, and behind them all the officers of the household and all the guests on horseback. Next came the garrison-music of drums and trumpets, the menservants on foot, and the women, some on foot and some in wagons with the children. After them came the wagons loaded with such things as they were permitted to carry with them. These were followed by the garrison, in all some five hundred, stretching far away round toward the citadel. Colors were flying and weapons glittering, and though all was silence except for the pawing of a horse here and there, and the ringing of chain-bridles, everything looked like an ordered march of triumph rather than a surrender and evacuation. Still there was something in the silence that told the true tale.

In the front carriage were Lady Glamorgan and the Ladies Elizabeth, Anne, and Mary. In the carriages behind came their gentlewomen, their lady visitors, and their immediate attendants. Dorothy, mounted on Dick, with Marquis' chain fastened to the pommel of her saddle, followed the last carriage. Beside her rode Caspar.

"Open the white gate," ordered the Marquis from the stair as he descended. The great clock of the castle struck twelve, and with the last stroke came the blast of a trumpet below.

"Answer, trumpets," cried the Marquis.

The governor repeated the order, and a tremendous blare followed, in which the drums unbidden joined. The warders at the brick gate flung its two leaves wide apart.

Another blast from below, and in marched on horseback General

Fairfax with his staff, followed by three hundred soldiers on foot. The latter drew up on each side of the brick gate, while the general and his staff went on to the marble gate.

The Marquis came down to meet them, and bowed to the general. "I would it were as a guest I received you, Sir Thomas, for then might I honestly bid you welcome. But that I cannot do when you so shake my poor nest that you shake the birds out of it. But though I cannot bid you welcome, I will notwithstanding heartily bid you farewell, Sir Thomas, and I thank you for your courtesy to me and mine. This nut of Raglan was, I believe, the last you had to crack. Amen. God's will be done."

The general returned civil answer, and the Marquis again bowed graciously and advanced to the foremost carriage. Lord Charles gave the word, the trumpets once more uttered a loud cry, and the Marquis' carriage led the slow procession through the gates, leaving forever the house of Raglan. In his heart the Marquis bade the world good-bye.

General Fairfax and his company ascended the great white stair, crossed the moat on the drawbridge, passed under the double portcullis and through the gates, and so entered the deserted court. All was frightfully still. The windows stared like dead eyes, and the very house seemed dead. They entered the great hall and admired its goodly proportions, regretting the destruction of such a magnificent house. Then as soldiers they proceeded to examine the ruins, and distinguish the results wrought by the different batteries.

"Gentlemen," said Sir Thomas, "had the walls been as strong as the towers, we should still have been sitting in yonder field."

Having satisfied his curiosity with a survey of the place, and posted a guard, Sir Thomas mounted again and rode to Chepstow, where there was a grand entertainment that evening to celebrate the fall of Raglan, the last castle to stand for the King.

55.
The Marquis' Prayers

As the Marquis' procession left the brick gate, a horseman joined them from outside. Pale and worn, with bent head and sad face, Sir Rowland Scudamore fell into the ranks amongst his friends of the garrison, and with them rode in silence.

Many a look did Dorothy cast around her as she rode, but only once, on the crest of a grassy hill that rose abrupt from the highway a few miles from Raglan, did she catch sight of Richard mounted on Lady. All her life after, as often as trouble came, that figure rose against the sky of her inner world, and was to her a type of the sleepless watch of the universe.

Soon, in this direction and that, each to some haven or home, the servants and soldiers began to drop away. Before they reached the Forest of Dean the parade had greatly dwindled, for many belonged to villages, small towns, and farms on the way, and their orders had been to go home and wait better times. When he reached London, after a week's long and weary journey, the Marquis had few attendants left beyond Caspar and Shafto, the chief officers of his household, one of his own pages, and some of his daughters' gentlewomen and menials.

In London, the Marquis was surprised to find himself in custody. As for some three years Worcester House in the Strand had been used for a state office, he was conducted to a house in Covent Garden, and lodged in tolerable comfort and mild imprisonment.

But his confinement was by no means so great a trial to him as his indignant friends supposed. Long willing to depart, he had

273

grown tired of life, feeling the oppression of growing years, of gout varied with asthma, and, worst of all to a once active man, of his still increasing corpulence. The journey had been too much for him, and he began to lead the life of an invalid.

There being no sufficient accommodation in the house for his family, they were forced to content themselves with lodging as near as they could. In these circumstances Dorothy, notwithstanding Lady Glamorgan's entreaties, would have returned home. But the Marquis was very unwilling she should leave him, and for his sake she conceded to remain.

"I am not long for this world, Dorothy," he said. "Stay with me and see the last of an old man. The wind of death has got inside my tent, and will soon blow it out of sight."

Lady Glamorgan's intention from the first had been to go to her husband in Ireland as soon as she could get leave. But it was October before this was obtained, five weeks after her arrival in London. She would gladly have carried Dorothy with her, but she would not leave the Marquis, who was now failing visibly. As her ladyship's pass included thirty of her servants, Dorothy felt at ease about her personal comforts, and her husband would soon supply all else.

The Ladies Elizabeth and Mary were in the same house with their father. Lady Anne and Lord Charles were in the house of a relative at no great distance, and visited every day. Sir Toby Matthews and Dr. Bayly had found shelter in the neighborhood, so that his lordship never lacked company. But he was going to have other company soon.

Gently he sank toward the grave, and as he sank his soul seemed to retire further within, vanishing on the way to the deeper life. They thought he lost interest in life; it was but that the brightness drew him from the glimmer. Every now and then, however, he would come forth from his inner chamber, and standing in his open door look out on his friends, and tell them what he had seen.

November brought with it November weather, and after it, December. Though the Marquis fought hard and kept the cold out of his mind, it got into his troubled body. The gout left his feet; he coughed distressingly and breathed with difficulty.

"I trust I have done my part," he said once to the two clergymen, as they sat by his bedside. "Yet I know not. There was a time in my life when I thought He was a hard Master. But now that I have learned a little more of what He meaneth with me, what He would have of me, and do for me, how He would make me pure of sin, clean from the very bottom of my heart to the crest of my soul, from spur to plume a stainless knight, verily, I am no more content to *submit* to His will. I cry in the nighttime, 'Thy will be done, Lord, let it be done, I entreat Thee!' and in the daytime I cry, 'Thy kingdom come, Lord, let it come, I pray Thee!' "

He lay silent. The clergymen left the room, and Lord Charles came in and sat down by his bedside. The Marquis looked at him and spoke in a kindly tone.

"Ah, Son Charles! Art thou there?"

"I came to tell you, My Lord, the rumor goeth that the King hath consented to establish the presbyterian heresy in the land," said Lord Charles.

"Believe it not, My Lord. A man ought not to believe ill of another so long as there is space enough for a doubt to perch. Yet, alas! What shall be hoped of him who will yield nothing to prayers, and everything to compulsion? Had His Majesty been a true prince, he had ere now set his foot on the neck of his enemies, or else ascended to heaven a blessed martyr. 'Protestant,' sayest thou? In good sooth, I hope not. What is he now but a ball to kick to and fro! God be with His Majesty. I can no more. There are other realms than England, and I go to another King."

He closed his eyes, and his face grew so still that he would have seemed asleep, but that his lips moved a little now and then, giving a flutter of shape to the eternal prayer within him.

Again he opened his eyes and saw Sir Toby, who had reentered silent as a ghost, and feebly held out his hand.

"I am dying, Sir Toby," he said. "Where will this swollen hulk of mine be hid?"

"That, My Lord," returned Sir Toby, "hath been already spoken of in Parliament, and it hath been wrung from them, heretics and fanatics as they are, that your lordship's mortal remains shall lie in Windsor Castle, by the side of Earl William, the first Earl of Worcester."

"God bless us all!" cried the Marquis almost merrily, for he was pleased, and with the pleasure the old humor came back for a moment. "They give me a better castle when I am dead than they took from me when I was alive!"

"Yet it is a small matter to him who inherits such a house as now awaiteth my lord," said Sir Toby.

"I thank thee, Sir Toby, for recalling me. Truly for a moment I was uplifted somewhat. That I should still play the fool, and the old fool, in the very face of Death! But, thank God, at thy word the world hath again dwindled, and my heavenly house drawn the nearer. Let me, so soon as thou judge fit, Sir Toby, have the consolations of the dying."

When the last rites had been administered, wherein the church yields all hold save that of prayer, his daughters with Dorothy and Lord Charles gathered around his bed, and the Marquis spoke.

"Now have I taken my staff to be gone," he said cheerfully, "like a peasant who hast visited his friends and will now return, and they will see him as far upon the road as they may. I tremble a little, but I bethink me of Him that made me and died for me, and now calleth me, and my heart revives within me."

Then he seemed to fall half asleep, and his soul went wandering dreams that were not all of sleep—just as it had been with little Molly when her end drew near.

"How sweet is the grass for me to lie in, and for thee to eat! Eat, eat, old Plowman." It was a favorite horse of which he dreamed—one which in the old days he had named Piers Plowman. After a little pause, he went on. "Alack, they have shot off his head! What shall I do without my Plowman—my body groweth so large and heavy! Hark, hear my Molly! 'Spout, horse,' she crieth. See, it is his lifeblood he spouteth! O Lord, what shall I do, for I am heavy, and my body keepeth down my soul. Hark! Who calleth me? It is Molly! No, no! It is the Master. Lord, I cannot rise and come to Thee. Here have I lain for ages, and my spirit groaneth. Reach forth Thy hand, Lord, and raise me."

Then he was neither old man nor Marquis anymore.

The Parliament, with wondrous liberality, voted five hundred pounds for his funeral, and Dr. Bayly laid him in his grave with his own hands. But let us trust rather that his wife and granddaughter received him into their arms, and soon made him forget all about castles and chapels and dukedoms and ungrateful princes, in the everlasting youth of the heavenly kingdom, whose life is the presence of the Father, whose air to breathe is love, and whose corn and wine are truth and graciousness. There surely, and nowhere else, can the prayer be fulfilled: Rest in peace.

56.
Richard and Caspar

The decree of the Parliament went forth that Raglan should be destroyed. The same hour in which the sad news reached Caspar, he set out to secure, if possible, the treasures he had concealed. He had little fear of their being discovered, but great fear of their being rendered inaccessible from the workshop.

Having reached the neighborhood in the dress of a countryman, he hired a horse and cart and drove to the castle. The huge oaken leaves of the brick gate, bound and riveted with iron, lay torn from their hinges, and he entered unquestioned. But instead of the solitude and desertion for which he had hoped, he saw men and women with baskets and sacks, and the space between the outer defenses and the moat of the castle filled with country vehicles of every description.

When the most valuable of the effects found in the place had been carried to London, a sale for the large remainder had been held on the spot, at which not a few of the neighboring families had been purchasers. But a great many things were not worth removing, and now the peasantry were, like jackals, admitted to pick the bones of the huge carcass, ere the skeleton itself should be torn asunder. Nor could the invading populace have been disappointed of their expectations—they found numberless things of immense value in their eyes. Pieces of furniture and panels of carved oak, bits of tapestry, antique sconces, and candlesticks of brass were found scattered in farmhouses and cottages all over Monmouth and the neighboring shires.

When Caspar saw what was going on, he judged it prudent to turn and drive his cart into the quarry. He secured it there, and walked back into the castle. There was a great divided torrent of humanity rushing and lingering through the various lines of rooms, searching for whatever might look valuable. Things that nowadays would fetch their weight in silver, some of them even in gold, were passed by as worthless, or popped into a bag to be carried home for the amusement of cottage children. The noise of hobnailed shoes on the oak floors, and of unrestrained clownish and churlish voices everywhere, was tremendous. Here a fat cottager might be seen standing on a lovely quilt of patchwork brocade, roughly pulling down curtains on which the newborn and dying eyes of generations of nobles had rested, henceforth to adorn a miserable cottage, while her husband was taking down a bed that was larger, than the room in which they would in vain try to set it up.

But there was a small group of men in whom a fanatical hatred of everything Catholic, coupled with a profound sense of personal injury, had prevailed over avarice, causing them to leave the acquisition to their wives, and aspire to pure destruction. It was the same company who had suffered misadventures in their search of Raglan for arms, under the misguidance of Tom Fool.

These men met in the midst of the surrounding tumult, and fell into conversation chiefly occupied with reminiscences of that awful experience, whose terrors now looked but like an evil dream, and as little likely to return as a vanished thundercloud. In the course of their conversation, therefore, they grew valiant, became conscious of a high calling, and resolved to take to themselves the honor of giving the first sweep of the broom of destruction to Raglan Castle. They satisfied themselves first that their wives were doing their duty for their households and Mistress Upstill was at least as good as two men at appropriation. Then they set out, armed with crowbars, for the top of the great tower, ambitious to commence the overthrow by attacking the very summit, the high place of wickedness, the crown of pride.

When Caspar entered the castle, he made straight for the keep, and to his delight found no one in the lower part. To make certain, however, that he was alone in the place ere he secured himself from intrusion, he ran up the stair, and reached the top just as Upstill in fierce discrowning pride was heaving the first capstone

278

from between two battlements. Caspar was close by the cocks; he quickly turned one, and as the dislodged stone struck the water of the moat, a sudden hollow roaring invaded their ears. While they stood aghast at the well-remembered sound, and ere yet the marrow had time to freeze in their stupid bones, the moat seemed to come rushing up for revenge upon them where they stood. Caspar shot halfway down the stair into a little chamber in the wall, and waited until their steps thundered down the stair. He sprang up again to save the water for another end, and to attach the drawbridge to the sluice. Then he hurried down to the water trap under the bridge and set it, and lurked in a convenient corner to watch the result.

He had not long to wait. The shrieks of the yokels as they ran quickly gathered round them a gaping crowd to hear their tale. The more foolhardy listeners, partly doubting their word, and partly ambitious of showing their superior courage, rushed to the Gothic bridge. Down came the drawbridge with a clang, and with it a torrent of water that shot along the stone bridge and dashed them from it bruised and bleeding, and half-drowned. Caspar withdrew satisfied, for he now felt sure of all the time he required to get some other things down into the shaft.

Having with much labor and difficulty gotten all into the quarry and then into the cart, Caspar did not resist the temptation to go again among the crowd, and listen to the various remarks and conjectures and terrors to which his trick had given rise. He had not been in the crowd many minutes, however, when he realized that he must have been seen on the tower. All this time Upstill and his party had been recounting with various embellishments their adventures, and when Caspar was recognized, the rumor presently arose and spread that he was either the devil himself, or his agent.

The faces and gestures of the younger men began to grow threatening; some of them, fired with the ambition of thrashing the devil, ventured to give him a rough shove or two from behind. Neither outbreak of sulphurous flashes nor even a kick of cloven hoof followed. They proceeded with the game, and rapidly advanced to such extremities that Caspar was compelled in self-defense to draw a dagger. This checked them a little, and then Richard Heywood came shoving through the crowd, pushing them all right and left until he stood by Caspar's side. The crowd drew back as Richard turned upon them with indignation.

"You Englishmen!" he cried. "You treat a foreigner thus?"

But there was nothing about him to show that he was a Round-head, and from behind rose the cry, "A malignant! A Royalist!" and the nearest fellows began to advance threateningly.

"Mr. Heywood," said Caspar hurriedly, for he recognized his helper from the time he had seen him prisoner, "let us make for the hall. I know a place, and can bring us both off safe. Follow me, Sir." And turning with brandished dagger, Caspar forced his way to the hall door. Richard followed with fists, his sole weapons, defending their rear.

There were but a few in the hall, and as they crossed it Caspar said, "Follow me over the bridge, but for God's sake, be sure you put your feet exactly where I put mine as we cross."

"I will," said Richard, and gained the other side just as the foremost of their pursuers rushed on the bridge, and with a clang and a roar were swept from it by the descending torrent.

Caspar hurried Richard to the workshop, down the shaft, through the passage, and into the quarry. And Richard was well rewarded for the kindness he had shown. The German, whose heart was full of Dorothy and understood her relation to Richard, told him all he knew about her life in the castle, and how she had been both before and during the siege a guardian angel to Raglan. Nor did he omit the story of her attempted visit to her old playfel-low in the turret chamber, or the sufferings she had to endure in consequence. When he and Caspar parted, Richard rode home with fresh strength and light and love in his heart. As much as ever he believed Dorothy mistaken, and yet he could have kneeled in reverence before her. He had himself tried to do the truth, and no one but he who tries to do the truth can perceive the grandeur of another who does the same. Alive to his own shortcomings, such a one the better understands the success of his brother or sister. We are bound to obey the truth, and that to the full extent of our knowledge thereof, however little that may be, for the way to know is to do the known.

Then why, thought Richard with himself, should he and Doro-thy be parted? All depended on their common magnanimity—not the magnanimity that pardons faults, but the magnanimity that recognizes virtues.

57.
The Skeleton

As the country was now a good deal quieter, and there was nothing to detain her in London, Dorothy resolved to go home. The thought of home was full of clear memories of her mother and vague memories of her father, not to mention memories of the childhood Richard and she had spent together—from which the mists had begun to rise and reveal them sparkling with dew and sunshine. As soon, as the Marquis had gone to his wife and granddaughter, Dorothy took her leave, attended by her old bailiff and some of the men of her small tenantry.

At Wyfern she found everything in rigid order, almost cataleptic repose. How was it ever to be home again? With only memories of what had rendered it lovely in her eyes, Dorothy soon began to feel the place lonely.

The very next morning she saddled Dick, called Marquis, and set out to see what they had done to dear old Raglan. Marquis had been chained up almost all the time they were in London, and freedom is blessed even to a dog. Dick was ever joyful under his mistress, and now was merry with the keen invigorating air of a frosty December morning. Between them the two animals soon raised Dorothy's spirits and hopes as well.

This mood made her the less prepared to encounter the change that awaited her. While she approached the towers, she had not an idea of the devastation within. But when she rode through one entrance after another with the gates torn from their hinges, crossed the moat by a mound of earth instead of the drawbridge, and rode through the open gateway, where the portcullises were wedged up in their grooves and their chains gone, into the paved court, she beheld a desolation which made her heart stand still. The rugged horror of the heaps of ruins was softly covered with snow, but what this took from the desolation in harshness, it added in coldness and desertion and hopelessness. She felt like one who looks for the body of his friend, and finds but his skeleton.

The broken bones of the house projected gaunt and ragged. Its eyes returned no shine, for not a pane of glass was left, and all the holes were black and blank with shadow. The roofs were gone—all but that of the great hall, which they had not dared to touch. She climbed the grand staircase, open to the wind and slippery with ice, and reached her own room. Snow lay on the floor, which had swollen and burst upwards with winter rains. Through room after room she wandered with a sense of loneliness and desolation and desertion such as she had never known, even in her worst dreams.

So severely had destruction altered the look of what it had spared, that it was with difficulty she recognized doors and ways of the house she had once known so well. Nearly a third of the walls had been leveled within a few feet of the ground. Here was a great hole to the shining snow, where once had been a dark corner, and there a heap of stones where once had been a carpeted corridor. All human look of indwelling had passed away. Where she had once gone about by instinct, she had now to rely on memory.

She found the door of the turret chamber, but the chamber was gone. Nothing was there but the blank gap in the wall, and beyond it, far down, the nearly empty moat of the tower. She turned, frightened and sick at heart, and made her way to the bridge. That still stood, but the drawbridge above was gone. She crossed the moat and entered the workshop. A single glance took in all that was left of the keep. Not a floor lay between her and the sky! The reservoir, great as a mountain tarn, had vanished utterly! All was cleared out, and white wintry clouds were sailing over her head.

It was like the change of centuries rather than months. The castle had half melted away, its idea blotted out, save from the human spirit. She turned from the workshop, in positive pain at the sight, and wandered till she found herself in Lady Glamorgan's parlor. There was left a single broken chair; she sat down on it, closed her eyes. But in a moment she opened them with a start—there stood Richard a yard or two away.

58.
Love Without Lying

Their eyes met in the flashes of a double sunrise. Then their hands met, but the hand of each grasped the heart of the other.

To Dorothy it was for a moment as if Raglan were rebuilt, and the ruin and the winter vanished. Then her eyes fell, beaten down by conscience, for the words of the Marquis shot like an arrow into her memory: "Love outlives all but lying."

But Richard imagined that something had displeased her, and was ashamed. He had heard of her return, and gone at once to Wyfern. There learning whither she had gone, he had followed, had tracked her footsteps through the snow, and found her. But in so doing, had he been presumptuous?

"Forgive me, Dorothy," he said.

"Nay, Richard," returned Dorothy, with her eyes fast on the ground, "I know no cause wherefore you should ask me to forgive you, but I do know good cause wherefore I should ask you to forgive me. Richard, I will tell you the truth, and you will tell me again how I might have shunned doing amiss, and how far my lie was an evil thing."

"Lie, Dorothy! You have never lied!"

"Hear me, Richard, first, and then judge. I did tell you that night as we talked in the field that I had about me no missives; the word was true, but its purport was false. As I spoke, you held in your hand my comb, wherein were concealed certain ciphered papers."

"O you cunning one!" cried Richard, half reproachfully, half humorously, but the amusement overtopped the seriousness.

"My heart did reproach me—but Richard, what *was* I to do?"

"Wherefore did your heart reproach you, Dorothy?"

"That I told a falsehood—that I told *you* a falsehood, Richard."

"Then had it been Upstill, you would not have minded?"

"Upstill! I would never have told Upstill a falsehood. I would have beaten him first."

"Then you thought it better to tell a falsehood to me than to Upstill?"

"I would rather sin against you, if it were a sin, Richard. I would rather be in your hands, sin and all, than in those of a mean-spirited knave whom I despised. Besides I might one day, somehow or other, make it up to you—but I could not to him. But was it sin, Richard? Tell me that. I have thought and thought over the matter until my mind is mazed. You see, it was my Lord Marquis' business, not mine, and you had no right in the matter."

"Prithee, Dorothy, ask not me to judge."

"Are you then so angry with me that you will not help me to judge myself aright?"

"Not so, Dorothy, but there is one command in the New Testament for which I am often more thankful than for any other."

"What is that, Richard?"

"*Judge not.* Prithee, between whom lieth the quarrel, Dorothy?"

"Between you and me, Richard."

"No, Dorothy. I accuse you not."

Dorothy was silent for a moment, thinking. "I see, Richard," she said. "It lieth between me and my own conscience."

"Then who am I, Dorothy, that I should dare step betwixt you and your conscience? God forbid."

"But if my conscience and I seek a daysman betwixt us?"

"Mortal man can never be that daysman, Dorothy. You must seek to Him who brought you and your conscience together and told you to agree. Let God, over all and in all, tell you whether or not you were wrong. If you cannot tell whether you did well or ill, you should not vex your soul. God is your refuge, even from the wrongs of your own judgment. Pray to Him to let you know the truth, that if needful you may repent. Be patient and not sorrowful until He shows you, nor fear that He will judge you harshly because He must judge you truly. That were to wrong God. Trust in Him even when you fear wrong in yourself, for He will deliver you therefrom."

"Ah! How good and kind you are, Richard!"

"How should I be other to you, beloved Dorothy?"

"Then you are not angry with me that I did deceive you?"

"If you did right, wherefore should I be angry? If you did wrong, I am well content to know that you will be sorry as soon as you see it. I am sure that what you know to be right, that you will do, and it seemeth as if God Himself were content with that for the time. What the very right thing is, concerning which we may now differ, we must come to see together one day. Let God judge us, Dorothy, for His judgment is light in the inward parts, showing the truth and enabling us to judge ourselves. For me to judge you would bear you no light. Why, Dorothy, that is the very matter for which we, my father and his party, contend—that each man, namely, in matters of conscience, shall be left to his God, and remain unjudged of his brother! And if I fight for this on my own part, unto whom should I accord it if not to you, Dorothy, who are the highest in soul and purest in mind and bravest in heart of all women I have known? Therefore I love you with all the power of a heart that loves that which is true before that which is beautiful, and that which is honest before that which is of good report."

Words failed them for a span, and they wandered all over the ruins together. Dorothy had a hundred places to take Richard to and tell him what they had been and how they had looked in their wholeness and use—among the rest her own chamber, whither Marquis had brought her Richard's letter.

Then Richard gave Dorothy a sadly vivid account of what he had seen of the destruction of the place; how, as if with whole republics of ants, it had swarmed all over with men paid to destroy it; how in every direction the walls were falling at once; and how they dug and drained at fishponds and moat in the wild hope of finding hidden treasure. He told her what a terrible shell the Tower had been to break—how after throwing its battlemented crown into the moat, they had in vain attacked the walls, might also as well have sought to tear asunder the living rock, and at last had undermined the wall, propped it up with timber, set the timber on fire, and so succeeded in bringing down a small portion of the tough, massive defense.

"What became of the wild beasts in the base of the kitchen tower, Richard?"

"I saw their cages," answered Richard, "but they were empty. I asked what had become of the animals but none could tell me. All Gwent is divided between two opinions as to their fate—one, that they are roaming the country; the other, that Lord Herbert, as they still call him, has by his magic conveyed them away to Ireland to assist him in a general massacre of the Protestants."

Mighty now in their renewed mutual faith, nothing was any more able to part those whose plain truth had begotten absolute confidence. They talked and wandered a long time, forgetting even their poor shivering horses.

At length an expostulatory whinny from Lady called Richard to his duty, and with compunctions of heart the pair hurried to mount. They rode home together in a bliss that would have been too deep almost for conscious delight but that their animals were eager after motion. So they turned into the soft surface of the fields, and at a tremendous gallop soon brought their gladness to the surface in great fountain throbs of joy.

Editor's Afterword

No war ever ends simply because the firing ceases, and the English Civil War was no exception. King Charles I was turned over to Parliament by the Scots in February 1647. He was eventually tried by a special Parliamentary Court, convicted of treason and other high crimes, and beheaded before Whitehall Palace on January 30, 1649. His political sacrifice of Strafford still weighed upon his mind, for he proclaimed to the crowd gathered around his scaffold, "An unjust sentence, that I suffered to take effect, is punished now by an unjust sentence on me." Witnesses of the execution wrote that he was brave and calm to the last, and showed all England how a King should die. He was buried in Saint George's Chapel, Windsor, in the midst of a blanketing February snowstorm.

In March 1649, the English monarchy was officially abolished by an Act of Parliament. Cromwell and his army ruled England until his death in 1658. In 1660, after Cromwell's son failed to hold the Commonwealth together, the son of Charles I was brought back from exile and crowned King Charles II to the cheers of noblemen and commoners alike. This Restoration established a constitutional monarchy in the land; England had her King once more, but never again would the man or woman on the throne rule England unchecked and alone. The true power remained in the hands of Parliament, and the ideas which defeated Charles I would forever check the power of the monarch.

Charles II rewarded the faithful Somerset family with the restoration of their lands and by officially elevating the Earl to a Marquis.

Therefore Lord Herbert, first Earl of Glamorgan, became the second Marquis of Worcester, and went on to distinguish himself as a man of genius, especially in the realm of hydraulic science. his written works include A *Century of Inventions*, and he is often credited with the invention of the practical steam engine.

* * *

The Last Castle is the fifth in the series of George MacDonald novels from Victor Books. As in the previous books, the aim has been to make MacDonald available, affordable, and readable. MacDonald has few equals as a storyteller, but his writing is overlong, often uneven, and does not always rise to the same level as his story. The book in its original version is lengthy and sometimes tedious; I have trimmed away the occasional outbreaks of irrelevancy, eliminated repetitive material, made consistent the choices of spelling and dialect, reshuffled out-of-sequence scenes, and tightened dragging narrative. However, I certainly do not represent my version as better than the original; it is only easier to read, and published now at a price within the grasp of many who cannot find or afford the unfortunately scarce originals. The original editions of any MacDonald novels (when and where they can be found) are well worth the reading.